Praise for

SIZZLE REEL

"*Sizzle Reel* by Carlyn Greenwald is a hilarious and tender romance featuring the most relatable journey through figuring out what love, sex, and friendship can mean. After I finished reading, all I wanted to do was explore L.A. with a camera, curate a playlist of my favorite angsty crush songs, and put this book in the hands of every friend I can think of who really, really needs this story." —Alicia Thompson, bestselling author of *Love in the Time of Serial Killers*

"*Sizzle Reel* is romance in Technicolor; every scene, emotion, and beat fully captivates the senses, leaving readers breathless. Carlyn Greenwald's writing is fresh, raw, and brilliant, whipping across each page in vivid, stunning strokes. The themes of sex positivity, deep self-care, and exploration of identity are beautiful, validating gifts to the queer community." —Courtney Kae, author of *In the Event of Love*

"Greenwald's coming-of-age romance is as charming and witty as it is tender, relatable, and poignant. L.A. and the high-stress world of the entertainment industry sizzle on the page. Greenwald affirms with gentleness and care the experience of grappling with sexuality and coming out later in life. This book is sexy, sweet, and full of love—for ourselves, for queerness, for found family, and for the one person your heart belongs to." —Ruby Barrett, author of *The Romance Recipe*

CARLYN GREENWALD

SIZZLE REEL

Carlyn Greenwald writes romantic and thrilling page-turners for teens and adults. A film school graduate and former Hollywood lackey, she now works in publishing. She resides in Los Angeles, mourning ArcLight Cinemas and soaking in the sun with her dogs. Find her online on Twitter @CarlynGreenwald and Instagram @carlyn_gee.

carlyngreenwald.com

SIZZLE REEL

SIZZLE REEL

Carlyn Greenwald

Vintage Books
A Division of Penguin Random House LLC
New York

Library of Congress Cataloging-in-Publication Data
Name: Greenwald, Carlyn, [date] author.
Title: Sizzle reel / Carlyn Greenwald.
Description: First edition. | New York : Vintage Books, 2023.
Identifiers: LCCN 2022026680 (print) | LCCN 2022026681 (ebook)
Subjects: GSAFD: Gay fiction. | Romance fiction. | Novels.
Classification: LCC PS3607.R46813 S59 2023 (print) |
LCC PS3607.R46813 (ebook) | DDC 813/.6—dc23
LC record available at https://lccn.loc.gov/2022026680
LC ebook record available at https://lccn.loc.gov/2022026681

Vintage Books Trade Paperback ISBN: 978-0-593-46819-7
eBook ISBN: 978-0-593-46818-0

Book design by Steven Walker

vintagebooks.com

Printed in the United States of America
10 9 8 7 6 5 4 3 2 1

*For Rachel and Will, for believing in
this book when I couldn't*

*For Mom and Dad, for believing in
me since the beginning*

SIZZLE REEL

chapter one

As I make my hour-long commute to work, I convince myself that the reason it was mildly difficult to come out to my therapist is because she looks like Rachel Brosnahan. Which, yeah, doesn't make much sense without context, and who's to say my brain's working at seven in the fucking morning as I inch along the slog of Vermont Avenue, longing for the respite of the equally-as-red stretch on Wilshire Boulevard? In fact, I can confirm it is not. I'm not even *really* listening to the *Bechdel Cast* podcast I clicked on an hour ago.

Facts: Beverly Hills is seven miles from my apartment. My therapist looks exactly like Rachel Brosnahan. I've been officially identifying as bisexual for four days.

Four days, and I'm already a bisexual disaster. Or, rather, I became a bisexual disaster the moment I came out to Julia. Imagine for a moment the bright lighting of a therapist's office a block from the beach, with sun spilling in from the east because some clown didn't put the windows in the office *facing* the beach. We're doing a P.O.V. shot; Julia's perfectly centered horizontally but shifted up a little vertically to suggest her slight authority over me, a slight authority we don't talk about.

I'm bisexual, I say. Camera tight on me, Julia off camera.

That's great! she replies. *When did you figure it out?*

I reply with: *While watching* The Marvelous Mrs. Maisel.

We quick cut to Julia's face and—

Even running the story through my head, my cheeks still go hot with the memory. I knock my air-conditioning up a notch. Everything's fine. Coming out has been fine. The Julia–Rachel Brosnahan story is the kind of shit my best friends, Romy and Wyatt, will lap up like, well, like stressed-out Hollywood assistants lap up hard liquor after work. And yes, I can tell them this specific story because they're the next people I'm going to come out to.

Just as I reach perfect homeostasis from the air-conditioning against the sizzling heat of Los Angeles in June, I'm tapping my employee card against the reader in the parking garage and locking away my freedom and sanity, along with an emergency change of clothing. I take my daily last longing look at my parked car, wishing I could crawl back to bed. But alas, I'm twenty-four, nearly two years out of college, and a Working Professional. A true old Gen Z with a *let death take me* aesthetic.

Slater Management is what Hollywood calls "boutique," which really just means we don't have enough clients to take up a whole building. We take up three levels: lobby/café/copy room, literary managers, talent managers. We're successful enough to have perks like a café but small enough that I know the name of everyone I pass as I walk through the floors.

I drop into my chair at eight fifty a.m., ten minutes before my boss, Alice, will be in. Or expects to be in. She's never on time. So, at the very least, I'm given a few minutes to reassess the scene. Slater has provided us with quickly declining Macs, headsets, and ancient office phones that don't even have caller I.D.—the Let's Push My Blood Pressure Up to 181/121 Trio. I start my deep breathing and do my standard morning routine: open up the digital Rolodex, click open Alice's call log, open email, headset on. Alice has a client coming in today. His name's John, and he's a director of midbudget films that people know of without knowing his actual name.

"Jesus, Luna, you gotta stop doing coke every Sunday," Wyatt Rosenthal, one of the two people I'm going to come out to next, says as he plops into his seat beside me.

While the six talent managers have their own offices separated from us by wall-to-wall glass, the assistants are all crunched on to one communal pod desk. Great for socializing, bad if you want to cry without five other people (and a straggling manager or two) having to force themselves to look away from you.

"Are you implying I look like shit?" I reply, softening the jab with my best attempt at a smile.

"Just tired."

I resist the urge to look at myself in my phone camera. I keep makeup minimal for work because like hell can I properly put on liquid eyeliner at six a.m. But apparently it's not covering up the bags under my eyes.

I give Wyatt a once-over. He's got a Sigma Alpha Mu, Jewish pretty-boy look. Wavy honey-brown hair, full eyebrows, ears that stick out *just* enough to be called cute, orthodontics-corrected teeth. The type of boy my Jewish parents are in *loooove* with. "I like to think I'd look worse if I were doing all that cocaine."

Wyatt chuckles. "I mean, around here, I'm sure there's someone who does."

Our brief conversation jolts to an end with the shrill ring of Wyatt's phone. He picks it up in a perfect swooping motion, like how basketball players are taught to make free throws. "Steven Wells's office."

Everyone in the pod has answered each other's phones at least once because of everything from sudden family emergencies to secret job interviews to having to pee. So it was inevitable that I'd have covered Wyatt's desk at least once. And Wyatt's boss . . . is fine, I guess. He makes Wyatt get him exactly eight chicken sausages from the café every morning and once called Wyatt at three a.m. saying he was lost in the Charles de Gaulle Airport and needed Wyatt to navigate him to his gate.

"Can we return?" Wyatt asks. Once the phone's hung up, he turns right back to me.

"How was your weekend?" I ask. My eyelids are already growing heavy, and Alice isn't even here yet. I'm gonna need coffee stat. To think I didn't even drink tea before this job.

Wyatt shrugs, readjusting a rolled-up sleeve on his pink button-down, the loudest piece of clothing he owns. "Eh, pretty boring. Went on another Hinge date."

It shouldn't—god, it *shouldn't*—but "Hinge" sends a snap of panic through my stomach. As it has in the six months since Wyatt and I broke up after dating for a whopping three weeks. My little brother, Noam, has joked that my parents mourned my and Wyatt's relationship more than I ever did, but the feeling in my gut isn't encouraging.

"How'd it go?" I ask, not a single negative emotion in my voice.

I'm the one who broke up with him. We agreed to be friends in order to keep our trio together. No drama has ensued since.

Wyatt shrugs. "I don't think I'll see her again. There's just never anything interesting about these random girls."

I've been mildly annoyed by Wyatt's casualness in regard to his dating life before, and yes, in my four days as a woman [who] loves women (w.l.w.) I've become more offended by it. But, again, he's my friend. He's just ignorant.

"Maybe if you went on more than two dates with these girls, you'd give them time to open up."

And in the perfect synchrony that is Alice Dadamo's ability to surprise me with her entrances when I'm about to initiate substantial conversation, my boss flies through the assistant pod in her Jimmy Choos. Her first words to me are "Go get John at ten!"

I diligently roll through our owed calls, which is usually this dozen-name-long list of executives/agents/clients who (1) called the day before and (2) Alice didn't want to talk to but (3) has to talk to in order to maintain her reputation. We manage to make it through three calls before Kiki from reception says John's here. I make sure my headset is still working and then dip down the stairs and into the lobby.

John manspreads as far as a human possibly can in a T-shirt and shorts that may or may not have a hole in the crotch, but I refuse to look back after one horrifying glimpse. He's definitely Alice's grubbiest client, and she'll be complaining about him to me once he leaves. He's flanked by two Chihuahua-like college kids in ill-fitting suits who are clutching résumés and mouthing answers to potential interview questions.

"Hi, John," I say in my peppiest voice.

At least I'm not interviewing for internships or bottom-of-the-barrel substitution-for-the-day assistant (coined "floater") gigs.

"Hi, Lacy," John replies.

I've lost the instinct to wince at this point.

"Would you like anything to drink?" I ask as we ascend our first flight of stairs.

Most clients ask for water, maybe the shitty coffee we keep on our floor.

"I'll get a latte from the café," John says.

Cool.

I exhale, lead John up to Alice, and jog back down to the café, otherwise known as the chillest part of this stress machine of a building. And bless, right now there isn't even a line. Just Romy Fonseca, the last but best part of the Luna-Wyatt-Romy trio.

Wyatt, Romy, and I all met freshman year at U.S.C. in Intro to Cinema, this blanket requirement for my film production major and Wyatt's business in cinematic arts minor, and an elective for Romy's "multimedia narrative studies" major. Some asshole was taunting her about how she dressed in section, saying she'd never attract men that way. I was emboldened from taking too much of an herbal antianxiety supplement, so I threw my arm around her and said she wasn't trying to attract guys. The asshole backed off within seconds and I lost my passionflower high within a few minutes, but our friendship remains unbreakable.

Romy has since become my roommate of five years, two of which have been spent in our own apartment that we had to have our credit scores checked to nail down. We're with each other all the time, but seeing her familiar face is still one of the best parts of working at this place. I slide up to the counter.

"John needs a latte," I say.

Romy looks up and smiles. The perfect eyeliner around her green eyes and her rose-covered cupid's lips just confirm what a different job could do for me. If Wyatt is a Jewish frat boy and I'm a quirky aspiring filmmaker lady, Romy is our slick and stylish nonbinary accomplice, all ripped jeans, patch-covered jackets, ring-lined fingers, and sleeve-peeking tattoos, with this hipster, volume-up-top, short-on-the-sides dark hair that makes men look like douchebags but just makes her look like she'll steal your girlfriend. She has one streak up top that's usually colored, but I guess she's left it at bleached out. The lack of color is usually a sign she had to go to a relative's birthday party over the weekend—both her Barcelona side of the family and her Waspy Boston-transplant side of the family have begged her to dye it back to a natural color.

"What're Caitlin and Jamie saying today?" she asks. We carpool to work only about half the time, because her shifts often start (and end) long after (and before) mine.

"I'd say *Shrek*, but you'd know I wasn't awake, so why bother," I reply as I lean against the counter.

"A valid response. What was on your mind instead?"

Part of me wants to come out to her before Wyatt, but the guilt won't be worth it.

"Do you think it's weird that I still feel weird about Wyatt dating other girls?" I ask instead.

"Is he being a shithead to girls again? These Calabasas real estate heiresses deserve at least some basic respect."

Romy lovingly calls Wyatt "our fuckboy." She stopped doing it only at one point in our six-year friendship: the three weeks I dated him.

"I don't know. Probably. Do you think I subconsciously still like him?"

Machines whir. I imagine Romy's processing. She's the thinker in the group.

"I'd rather lean into the idea that, as someone with generalized anxiety disorder, you're just stressed at the idea of someone not seeing you in a favorable light, even if you're not actually that interested in their attention itself."

It sounds like something Julia would say, but from Romy it packs more of a burn.

"Which family this weekend?" I ask.

She chuckles. "Damn, you're good. Mom's side. They refer to this"—she runs a couple of fingers through the natural dark hair—"as my dad's '*rich* color.' It's as if they *still* haven't realized my dad's side is white people who speak Spanish."

. I frown. "I'm sorry their learning curve still sucks."

Romy shrugs. "I'll just keep sending them articles and hope for the best."

As far as I know, Romy's Bay Area–based parents have been pretty chill with her gender identity and will listen to her talk about the woes of living in a world that's on fire, but she still sends her extended family a lot of articles. I'm not sure if they actually read them.

She slides me two lattes, close enough to me that I can clearly see the tattoo behind her ear: six dots arranged from red to purple in a line. It's possibly the only moment since I talked to Julia that I'm reminded of how excited I am to come out. At least to Romy. Thinking about that will be enough to get through the day.

"We're on for drinks after work today, right?" I ask.

She pushes one of the drinks closer to me. Our hands brush as the cup is exchanged, making my stomach flip. God, these coming-out nerves are killer. "Yes. I'm stoked for shitty Long Island Iced Tea Monday." She mimes lifting a cup. "Before you go. It's a new flavor."

Romy's only a barista because she tried to work as an assistant and quit in a week. Set screenwriting aside to pursue playwriting. But she embraces this barista job like it's her life passion. I leave every interaction with her at work with the energy to appreciate *my* job a little more.

I take a sip of the coffee. "It's really good. What is it?"

"Café bombón. If you think it's ready, I'll add it to the secret menu."

Romy has one of those fluid, honeyed, Angelina Jolie–type voices, and I'm almost tempted to ask her to explain how she made the new flavor just to hear it. But I'm at work. I'll suggest she start an audiobook-narrator career later.

I take another tug, the caffeine a welcome relief. "Do it."

I taste the words mixing with the sweetness and bite of espresso: *I'm bi.* But I swallow them along with the coffee. "See you later, Rom."

"Later."

Back to the wolves.

Work is fine. Which is to say Alice is short with me and her demands make zero sense, but I don't get yelled at or get fired or completely humiliate myself. Honestly, if Romy and Wyatt ask how my day was, I don't think I'll be able to recall it any better than I can recall the podcast from this morning. I guess the prospect of coming out for the second time in my life is more distracting than I'd anticipated.

But it's just about seven thirty, I've changed into a new shirt that doesn't smell of literal stress, and we're all sitting down to order drinks at our favorite terrible dive bar near work. Two Long Island Iced Teas and a glass of soda water for me. Romy or Wyatt will give me some of theirs, and I don't like tempting myself knowing I have to make the commute back to our place in Koreatown. That and, well, I'd like to be sober when I tell two of the most important people in my life that I'm bi.

"Any Alice stories, Film School?" Romy asks as she takes a sip of her drink.

Most executives, managers, and agents, once they reach a certain level of success, lose all ability to function as a basic human being. It's common. But Alice also has a certifiable personality disorder. You know how they say there's a certain gene common in serial killers, but that some percentage of people with that gene won't ever murder anyone? Alice is that percent. It's painfully obvious why her desk opened up so quickly and how I got the job with so little competition from other floaters.

"She was relatively tame today," I reply. "Still shit-talking one of our best client's agents, but that's standard." I sip my drink, the fizz stinging on the way down. "How's the play?"

After years of nose-to-the-grindstone writing and revising before and after shifts, Romy's undergrad playwriting thesis was accepted into this really cool diverse writers festival that tends to attract a handful of playwriting agents every year. Even though the festival is two months away and the writing's been done, the director still wants her around for rehearsals to tweak lines.

Romy's barely-subdued grin says it all. "I have to resist tearing the script apart, but it's surreal."

The urge to hug her overcomes me, even though we've hugged over this particular accomplishment countless times. I'm assuming it's the jitters from this coming-out thing. I settle for a smile back. "Look at you, achieving your dreams."

"Speaking of dreams, any word about Alice moving you?" Romy asks.

I shrug. "I'll ask soon."

"Do it with me!" Wyatt says. "I'm gonna make this my summer. Convince Steven to give me a promotion, upgrade apartments, get a summer fling . . ."

"No one says 'summer fling,' and bless whoever decides to fuck you," Romy replies as she runs a hand through her hair, pulling out a wisp that'd fallen into her eyes. She's got this really thick hair, and I zone out for just a moment wondering how it feels when she runs her hands through it. She uses, like, Pantene, but I imagine it's salon soft.

I take a swig of soda water, inevitably unsatisfied. Back in college, we all used to go out to drinks for fun. Now it just feels like we do it to relieve massive amounts of stress.

"Okay, English Degree, and what ladies have you fucked lately?" Wyatt asks.

"Any partner I have isn't a trophy for gossip."

Which is something Romy's maintained nearly the entire time I've known her. Things she's made clear about her identities over the years: *I reject society's ideas about gender, but I do find comfort in some things that would be considered feminine. I'm nonbinary, and I hate that people think being nonbinary means you have to be androgynous all the time. I use she/her pronouns, will only date non-men, and mostly identify as a lesbian.* But she never brings partners around. She mentions dates and occasionally drops names, but there are no faces to the names. I'm her roommate, and I've certainly never seen her bring anyone home.

While the idea of Romy's love life still mildly intrigues me, Wyatt drops the topic instantly and turns to me.

"What about you, Lune? Need me to set you up with any sensitive guys?" he asks.

A) I know he would never set me up with anyone.

B) No.

I rub my forearms. "It's cool."

A moment of silence passes. I can feel the words forming in my throat and I just have to let it happen. Ignore the possibility that when I open my mouth, instead of saying anything, I will have a heart attack. The lighting in here is bad. It casts shadows over Romy's and Wyatt's faces, and there are sparkles of light being picked up in glassware, reflections of orange off a weak electric candle on our table. I'd do a medium shot. Focusing on their expressions in the seconds before they know my secret is too painful, so no close-up. I'm too sober, my vision too clear, for *that*. I take my hand off my drink, force myself to stop fidgeting.

I force the words out. "I'm bi."

Much like what happened with Julia, there's a split second when Wyatt and Romy blankly process what's just happened. As if no one expected in a million years that I'd be the one who's secretly gay.

Then Romy breaks into a smile and pulls me into a side hug. "Hey, welcome to the club!" she says, her voice going higher.

My cheek rests against her shoulder, and I experience the same heat and lightness in my chest that I did when Julia reacted positively. It's an almost out-of-place feeling, like something ripped from a more innocent time in my life—the mind-numbing joy of making my first friend in kindergarten, of receiving exactly what I asked for for my birthday, of that night during fall semester of freshman year when Romy and I lay among a pile of take-home finals, never thinking we'd end up this connected to a friend from a general education course.

"Did you, like, kiss a girl and figure it out?" Wyatt asks.

Not to say the moment's *gone*, but the rush is really slowing.

"Uh, no," I reply, heat settling in my cheeks.

"Note for the straight: You don't have to have kissed girls to be sapphic," Romy says. "No one expects literal children to have fooled around with—"

"Okay, sorry," Wyatt says.

Both reactions are something I'll have to get used to. I take a deep breath.

"It's fine," I say. "No, I've just been thinking about it and it kinda hit me last week. And then I told Julia . . ." The embarrassment shoots its way back. "And . . . mentioned *The Marvelous Mrs. Maisel*."

Romy smirks. "You know, she probably doesn't *know* she looks like Rachel Brosnahan. When I saw her, she just . . . maybe had the vibe."

"You've met her therapist?" Wyatt asks.

"We briefly made awkward eye contact when I dropped Luna off a few months ago." Romy turns to me. "Did she say anything about me?"

"She asked why I brought my friend to therapy."

"You know what? *I* could seduce her. That's not illegal."

I put my hands over my face, even though this is a routine teasing. "Please don't."

"What's her last name? I wanna confirm or deny this Rachel Brosnahan thing," Wyatt says.

"We can't. Luna won't tell us her last name."

"There must be some way . . ."

I take Romy's drink and swig. It burns more than usual. "Thank you two for once again convincing me I'm *never* letting you get close to my therapist."

Romy throws her arm around me and rocks us back and forth. It could be tipsiness, but I think it might just be excitement. Either way, I melt into her embrace. I feel a massive weight lift off me. "Man, I can finally not feel bad dumping pictures of hot actresses in suits on you! Please send me every gay thought you ever have."

Romy removes her arm and scoots out of the booth. "Like, literally, text me your thoughts in the two minutes I'm gone."

It's not like I didn't think Romy would react positively to this, but it's a head rush watching her walk out. I've been lighting her in a glimmering halo filter for so long, and I feel lucky to be able to share my queerness with her. It makes me feel even more connected to her—a feeling I've experienced only to varying degrees with Jewish friends and partners. I can't even *imagine* what being with a Jewish queer partner would be like.

Once Romy is gone, Wyatt scoots in to take her place. He leans in, like we're going to discuss something secret. "So . . . what're you gonna do now?"

I shrug, running my finger along the condensation on my soda water. "Try to talk to Alice in the next few weeks about working under a D.P." The cinematographer, a.k.a. the director of photography (D.P.), is the top gig in my field. The master to my apprentice. "Maybe apply to grad school if it doesn't work out—"

"Luna, come on. I mean girls-wise. This is a huge opportunity! You can, like, make things official."

Somehow, I haven't anticipated this question. Julia just talked about how this is my process and *take all the time you want* and *have fun with it*. We were never very specific about getting with girls.

"I dunno, Wy. I have so many other things I need to be working on right now. I wanted you two to know because you're important to me, but I don't know if it's the right time to pursue anything."

I'm not in any particular hurry to come out to anyone beyond them anyway. In fact, combined with Romy's extra-strong drink, the idea of the words *I'm bi* escaping my lips in the presence of my family, in particular, is vaguely nauseating. If I already can't properly answer Wyatt's questions about being with girls, I don't want to even *think* about what it'd be like with my parents.

Wyatt pauses a moment, glancing beyond us. "I get that, but are you happy with the way things are right now?"

I'm still contemplating that when Romy slides back into the booth.

chapter two

Wyatt's words, I'm sure, are meant to instill a deep sense of existential dread. Which they do for exactly several hours before I use the coping skills Julia taught me and make a plan.

I've been identifying as bisexual for five days, I've been working for Alice for two years and one month, and I'm going to ask her for the next step today. Not in another six months. Today. I'm going to be a straight white man. I'm going to make my life better than it is right now in the only way I fully understand.

I just need to bring my Emergency Xanax to do it.

Yeah, it's kind of fucked up to have to take supplemental drugs to talk to my boss, but here's the thing about Hollywood:

Yes, we all know it's corrupt. But what outsiders never seem to really get is just how nonlinear the process of becoming a creative is. It's something Romy and I have been trying to explain to Wyatt since we met him. Wyatt wants to be a manager. Nothing creative about it. And thus, his path is similar to a lawyer's or accountant's. He starts off at an entry-level position in a mailroom, where he and another dozen or so college grads deliver mail to managers/agents in hopes of actually getting a job on a manager/agent's desk, then he gets a spot on a manager/agent's desk, impresses his boss, becomes a junior manager, and *voilà*, career.

Then you have Romy and me. Creatives. She's a writer, and I'm a cinematographer. Two jobs that, while, sure, are lacking in *women*, let alone *queer* women—heck, even *queer people*—are oversaturated with eager applicants. Jobs that don't have a linear path. Instead, they have a few routes. They tell you this in your $60K-per-year film school: *There's no one set way.*

The most common route, the one most creatives will throw their hands up in crisis mode to embrace, is the Agency/Managerial Route. The idea is an aspiring writer, director, cinematographer, etc., will sit down with a company's H.R. rep and lie the shit out of an interview, claiming to want to be an agent/manager. The company hires. And you then proceed to spend years having to rewire your likely introverted artist personality to be able to schmooze and backstab and answer scary fucking phones in hopes of hopping on to the desk of an agent/manager who represents the same type of creative as you aspire to be. You dedicate your every waking second to them for a year (says film school; the reality is most assistants have to stick it out for around two nowadays), and instead of asking for a promotion, you give a sudden reveal: *Oh golly, boss, whoopsie, turns out I don't want to be an agent, I wanna be a cinematographer.*

And your boss has two options: either get you a gig legitimately working toward that creative goal or fire you. All that work and all that stress, and the toll they take on your body, could be for nothing. I've developed at least three different physical ailments since I started this job.

I specifically pick Tuesday to drop my reveal on Alice, figuring she won't have the stress of Monday to use as an excuse to ignore the question. She's an hour later than she usually is. She's wearing designer clothing and has full makeup on, but her hair isn't brushed for some reason. Though maybe it's a new style, I never really know with her. No demands when she walks in, just "Morning, darling."

I stand up from my seat before her hand touches the handle on her glass office door. "Can we talk today?"

Alice stops, lightly pursing lips that have definitely gotten fuller in the past six months. "Yeah. Let's talk right now."

My heart sinks into my stomach. Not even the Xanax could work that fast. Shit, I was expecting her to push me off until at least the end of her workday. "Yeah, great!"

There is no proper amount of *fucks* typed across the page of my mind to convey just how much I'm freaking out. Like the expression that the walls are caving in, *I feel faint*–type thing people did in the 1800s? Ringing starts going off in my ears, and I legitimately might faint taking the three steps to her office. In the back of my mind, I'm looking for a good place to fold myself to the floor so I don't hit my head and die in this hell building.

Alice keeps her office pretty sparse decoration-wise. Just one abstract painting that probably cost a lot of money. A desk and chairs that aren't from IKEA (unlike the assistant pod). But beyond that, she's got papers scattered everywhere, *despite the fact that I made her a filing system THREE FUCKING TIMES.*

I take a seat in one of her guest/client chairs. And she just sits in her seat, crosses her legs, and makes eye contact with me. Her eyes are a cerulean blue, like what big-budget movies do to Chris Hemsworth's eyes in post. "What's on your mind, Ms. Luna?"

I take a deep breath, even though it won't prevent my fainting spell. "So we hit the two-year mark four weeks ago."

Her eyes light up. It looks genuine, but I think she can just manipulate her face like that. "Did we? Well, happy anniversary!"

I unroll my blouse sleeve out of her view. "Yeah, and, uh, if you think I've done a good job with you—"

"You have."

A single muscle in my chest loosens. It doesn't really help. "I was hoping to discuss my future."

"Yes, I think you'd make a wonderful junior manager."

Okay. SO.

1) Blatant lie. I'd make a horrible manager. I can't convince anyone to do anything unless it's over email. And this business is ruled by phones. Also, I'm not skeevy enough. I have, like, 1 percent skeev when you need at least 78 percent skeev.

2) This is already going badly, and all the time I spent rehearsing last night has been for naught.

"I was actually . . . I don't want to be a manager, although I really appreciate your confidence." I pause, looking at a spot just past Alice's face. I can't watch her expression change in real time. "I really want to be a cinematographer."

"Oh." She's frowning—a tight-jawed frown that implies it all. "Yeah . . ."

I need to get out of here.

"I appreciate your honesty, but connecting you to any D.P. clients of mine to mentor you or even just to get you a specific camera P.A. job is a much larger burden on me than just pushing you up this company. Of course, someone of my caliber *can* get you a job on a buzzing indie or even a blockbuster, but . . . well, you understand, right?"

I feel like a fish that's having a hook violently yanked out of its mouth. She's *killing me* here, but "buzzing indie" and "blockbuster" send my heart fluttering. She never has to remove that hook. It'll be fine. Let it get infected and kill me that way.

"So, you . . ." I don't want to suggest *are going to fire me*.

"I'd need you to work with me longer," she says. "Prove you're really dedicated enough for me to call in a huge favor like that. A year should suffice." She pauses. "Let me know by the end of the day. If you're not interested, I'll have to let you go. Shouldn't hold you back from your dreams."

My whole body goes numb, nerve by nerve, until I exit her office and return to my position. I can't even feel my fingertips hitting the keyboard. We owe a lot of phone calls. Phone calls, I realize as the dejection builds up, on behalf of her director and D.P. clients.

The standard in agencies is two years. Three years are for people like Wyatt, who actually need the extra year training for a promotion to a manager position. Not as a stepping-stone to something else entirely.

Alice wants *three years*.

Wyatt's listening in on one of Steven's calls, so only Rain, my other next-door neighbor, notices me sit back down. Rain wants to be a screenwriter and has been in the process of transferring to the literary department for months now. Nice girl but visibly bitter she can't get into literary. She leans toward me.

"Referral meeting?" she asks. She smells like watermelon, and

I'm suddenly unsure if I'm just noticing the scent of her shampoo by accident or if this is the first sign that I like her.

"Yeah," I reply.

"I'm so sorry you're with Alice," she says. "She's really flighty, right?"

Yeah. No one told me this when I jumped on her desk, but after two years, I believe it. "She said another year and she'd get me a big-name starter gig."

Just the way Rain stares at me, her brow slightly wrinkling before she averts her gaze, says it all. She doesn't believe Alice, and she's never even worked with her. As I sink lower in my seat, I don't really either. Another year with Alice for the *chance* she'll push me toward my dreams, or I'm out of a job. I have enough savings to last only through July without income, and I refuse to return to my parents' house, especially now that there's a little looming bisexual secret between us.

It feels like this couldn't get worse.

Wyatt sets his phone down. Looks at me. Frowns. "You okay?" he asks.

My throat is suddenly very tight. "Alice won't give me a referral."

"Ever?"

"She said in a year. Maybe."

"Oh, shit. I'm so sorry."

And suddenly Wyatt's on his feet. Grabbing his phone and keys.

"Is everything okay with *you*?" I ask.

Wyatt's eyes widen into a look of fear and panic I almost never see on him. "Lune . . . I have a doctor's appointment. We talked about this yesterday. You're covering my desk until lunch."

Oh. Yeah, that conversation did happen. We're low on floaters because of some summer flu. Steven wasn't happy about the arrangement, but since there was so little time—fuck.

Okay, well, I guess I was wrong before—it could get worse. Everything has now officially gotten worse.

But I just smile. "Of course. Hope your appointment goes well."

He smiles back, teeth and dimple and all. "Thanks! Steven's client's in the lobby right now. She's meeting with A.D.s all day, but she's easygoing. Good luck."

And with that, Wyatt's gone.

Covering two desks. An assistant's worst nightmare. Well, I don't really have a choice. So c'est la vie, guess it's time to die. I take a deep breath, set Alice's phone calls to forward to my cell phone, and put on Steven's headset.

I adjust my hair, make sure I didn't somehow ruin my makeup, and head down the stairs.

Let's do this.

According to the schedule, Steven's next client meeting is with Valeria Sullivan. She's an overnight Oscar darling from three years back, and all the blockbusters she booked off her award hype are now coming out. I've been told to see her debut a million times, but given this job has been fourteen-hour days five days a week, I'm lucky if I don't spend the entire weekend passed out from exhaustion. The idea that I could watch hundreds of movies in my free time seems laughable.

So, Valeria's on my *oh, cool* list and easy enough to stay professional around. Of course I have teenage crushes, and who wouldn't freak the fuck out if Meryl Streep showed up? But I've gotten pretty good at treating acting clients I'm not a superfan of normally. They all tend to be quirky at best or dysfunctional ego trips who can't open a pack of yogurt alone otherwise, and you get used to dealing with the latter pretty quickly in this industry. Nothing particularly godlike about these people when you listen to their managers console them over their IBS or cheating spouses day in and day out.

This'll be fine.

Valeria Sullivan sits with her legs crossed in the middle of one of the couches. Her phone is turned sideways and has—and I'm not kidding—a picture of a very disturbed wet cat on the phone case. That's what catches my attention first, but then it's like the bisexual part of my brain just decides to turn on. Information floods in. She's wearing a long-sleeve-blouse-and-black-high-waisted-shorts getup, and the curves of her legs spill out like brushstrokes on a painting. She's at an angle to me, and her jawline is sharp enough to cut glass. Well, I guess I've at least learned that it's not just Rachel Brosnahan.

"Valeria, right?" I say as I approach her.

She looks up from her phone and frowns. I don't even know the context, but my heart's already hammering. Please no one call right now.

"Did Steven fire Wyatt?" she asks, sounding genuinely upset.

Oh. Yeah, not related to me. "No, no, Wyatt's just at a doctor's appointment. I work with Alice Dadamo, and I'm covering for a few hours."

She gets to her feet and shakes my hand. "Okay, good." She puts a hand on her chest, then slowly lowers it back down. "He writes these weird email sign-offs, and sometimes they're the only good thing that happens to me all day."

I genuinely chuckle. Never would've thought a dramatic actor would be self-deprecating. "Well, let's get you up to Steven."

We make the walk up the stairs. Her brown eyes travel along the modern paintings that hang on the walls. My eyes are the same color, but hers have a soft beauty I've never seen in my own. "This place is so sterile, but it has the coolest paintings."

Not gonna lie, it *does* have the coolest paintings. "Yeah, Laura Owens is incredible. The physicality of the texture can keep me staring forever. Slater picked one of the more muted pieces, though."

I haven't talked about art, composition—anything in that realm—for so long. It's the first moment all day I feel myself starting to relax. And, unlike most of Alice's clients, Valeria is making eye contact with me.

"Do you have a favorite of hers?" she asks.

"*Pavement Karaoke.* It was part of an exhibition on display at the Geffen a couple years ago. It's just got these incredible bold colors and overlapping texture. It's, like, visually arresting, but if you look deeper, it's covered in these sixties and seventies counterculture magazine articles. It's just like she's trying to say a million things and becomes this gestalt . . ."

When I look over at Valeria, she's got this half smile on her face, eyes lit up. Not the way Alice smiles, but genuine happiness. "I have not heard someone wax poetic about contemporary female-created art in a while."

I don't know why, but I mirror her half smile and tease her: "Treat, or are you ready to run?"

"Treat. Have you seen Julie Mehretu's work at the Broad? She does a similar mixed-media thing."

"I'll have to check it out." It's just hard to find people who'll go to the Broad with me. Romy prefers pop culture and kitschy museums where everything on display is fake but treated as real.

We reach the top of the stairs. We're almost at Steven's office. I get this weird mushy urge to thank this random actress for having a pleasant conversation with me.

"I like your phone case," I say instead.

Valeria pulls out her phone, as if she's forgotten what's on it. She chuckles a little and returns it to her purse. "Thanks. I try to keep funny, irreverent images on there. You gotta have something to consistently cheer you up, you know?"

I take the extra few steps to Steven's office. He's apparently taken the initiative to answer his own cell phone. Maybe his wife? He gives me a firm *one minute* sign.

I return to Valeria. "He needs a few minutes." I pull out my own phone and pull up my lock screen. "I get you on the funny images."

My lock screen for years now has been this one random frame I took from *Toy Story 2* in which Buster the dachshund is midjump in a chaotic dog blur with Mr. and Mrs. Potato Head really awkwardly kissing in a pile of wrecked Lincoln Logs in the background.

Valeria cranes her neck over and laughs, the corners of her eyes crinkling. It brings a warmth to my chest. "I love it."

I rub the back of my neck. It is so suspicious that no one's called Steven or Alice. "I feel like an underrated part of great cinematography is making a film where you can stop every frame in a comedic scene and it'd be funny."

And *then* Alice bursts out of her office. "Luna, where the fuck is—?"

And she stops the moment she looks at Valeria. Valeria, who

at the moment is frozen in a *I don't spend all day in a management environment what is this hell* shock.

"Valeria, it's been too long!" Alice says, switching to a sing-song tone and approaching us. She and Valeria do that air cheek-kissing thing.

Alice turns to me, faux sweetness still dripping off her. "Luna, darling, we need to roll calls stat. Another assistant can get Valeria coffee if she needs it."

A knot forms in my stomach and lingers even after Alice returns to her office. I feel like an old-timey prisoner about to be pulled apart by oxcarts.

I turn to Valeria.

"I have never met that woman in my life," Valeria says.

I give a wry smile. "That's Alice. Always schmoozing."

"Jesus Christ," Valeria mutters.

Oh, what I'd give to rant about Hollywood agents/managers to this woman who clearly has no clue, but I have to go. My actual life is calling, and it's probably going to involve getting my head bitten off by Alice for the hundredth time this year.

"I have to go, but it was nice talking to you," I say.

She smiles again. "Nice talking to you too, Luna." She grabs my hand to shake. Then she leans in. Just a little bit. "Good luck with Alice."

And with her breath warming the air between us, she slides her hand out of our handshake, her fingers slowly running across mine as she pulls away.

But before I can even mentally capture the frame, she's walking away. My thoughts flutter as I approach Alice's door. That was— She did that on purpose, right? That wasn't just accidentally brushing my palm. I blink a few times, gaze heavy on my hand. Even the lingering tingling is gone. It's as if it never happened. The whole exchange happened in the blink of an eye, one frame in a film that viewers could miss if they glanced down at their popcorn. Yet the memory has latched on to me.

"Can I have until the end of the week?" I ask Alice once I'm in her office.

Alice agrees.

chapter three

I slog through the rest of Tuesday and through Wednesday. The workload is surprisingly heavy for June. Projects are filling up the docket like mosquitos at my grandma's place in Florida. We had so many clients in on Wednesday that I went from six a.m. to eleven p.m. on a single smoothie. Then I dragged my husk of a body to a Jack in the Box, and I don't even like Jack in the Box.

Needless to say, I've managed to ratchet my tension back up to an eleven out of ten with one stupid decision: asking Alice for more time.

"I think I need better stress-relief options," I say to Romy as I wait for a coffee and a breakfast sandwich before Thursday's shift.

"Well, there's always quitting this job and joining me in relying on tips to make our ridiculous-even-for-K-Town rent," she replies, sliding my egg-and-Swiss into the microwave.

I give a wry smile. "I think Julia bought a fire station blanket on the off chance I do that and have a just-under-5150 mental breakdown."

Romy gives me a look. "Fine. Go get a stronger vibrator."

My cheeks go hot as I scan the area for pricked ears. No one's looked up. Too early; everyone's still in zombie mode. "You are the objective worst." I take a sip of my coffee. "But also, Pleasure Chest date?" I wink, my literal only skill.

"Hell yeah," Romy responds, leaning against the cabinets by the microwave as it hums. "Any updates with ole Alice?"

"Not yet. Still in limbo." I look up, spotting the edge of Romy's laptop case, which peeks out of the black Herschel she left on the floor. "Are you writing anything new?"

Romy wipes her brow in a flourish, and the bleached streak in her hair lifts with her hand. "I wish. We got a different budget for the show and I need to adjust a scene or two."

Romy's thesis is about a claustrophobic novelist on deadline who gets stuck on the L.A. subway. All her characters from previous books manifest as real people to help her escape. It's about intersectionality and is surreal and super cool, but the festival directors feared that they wouldn't be able to pull off any scene changes in their venue, so she's been trying to write out the scenes that take place off the train for a week now.

"Did I already ask if you had projectors?" I ask.

She pushes the heels of her hands into her eyes. "We do, but there's no way I could capture the surrealism without the sets."

I point to myself. "Am I real to you? Use the projectors as the background and I can capture the surrealism on film easy."

She furrows her brow a moment and then leans back, shaking her head. "Luna, I can't ask you to do all that work."

The microwave beeps and Romy turns to it.

"It's nothing. I need to get back behind a camera anyway. Just readjust the play as you had it and send me the script again. I'll get them to you A.S.A.P."

She noticeably relaxes, and it warms my chest. "You're the best."

She hands me my sandwich. The smell has my stomach aching, a reminder that I need to work on that whole actually-eating-three-balanced-meals-a-day thing.

"How about a movie tonight?" I ask.

She smiles. "Just get your ass out of this place before eight p.m."

"I'll be sure to ask Alice." I squeeze her hand. "Thanks, as always."

She shrugs. "Make me your slutty brownies and I'll forgive you."

I make my way to the office, already halfway through the sandwich when I reach my desk. Wyatt's munching on a protein bar, the same kind that he said last week was mankind's worst invention. He smiles when I approach.

"Hey, neighbor. I never asked—how was meeting Valeria?" he asks.

"She was cool. Very into contemporary female art." *And touched my hand,* I think, and my stomach flutters.

"Yeah, she's awesome, isn't she? She's all over that intellectual stuff. Did you see *Stroke*? Her Oscar movie?" I shake my head, earning myself a wide-eyed stare from Wyatt. "Well, she plays a woman who uses art therapy to piece together this night she disappeared as a kid at a traveling carnival. It's the most harrowing film I've seen in years."

"I'll have to check it out."

"You know, she—"

Alice pops her head out of her office. "Luna! I want you working in my office today."

Wyatt and I exchange a glance. Having an assistant work in a manager's office is . . . not really something anyone does. As long as we do our work, we're fine to be in our pod. Steven even told

Wyatt once he didn't want to see his face for more than an hour total a day.

"I'll have to use my iPhone," I say.

"That's fine. I have a spare laptop."

I forward Alice's incoming calls to my cell, give Wyatt a shrug, and head into Alice's office. When the door shuts behind us, my heart's hammering like the walls are closing in, even though we're surrounded by glass. It'd be bad enough to be in such close quarters with a normal person, but Alice's personality takes up the space of five people.

"Just so you know, I'm not pressuring you either way, but you've been a great assistant," Alice says.

I look to the laptop screen. We have plenty of emails to answer, thank god.

"Thanks."

Alice looks at her own screen, her sudden frown barely visible from the corner of my eye but taking up the whole room. "Can you believe those emails from John's fucking lawyer?"

I haven't read the emails, but I would guess they involve normal work stuff. That seems to be what pisses her off most. "Ridiculous."

Just smile and nod. Those penguins in *Madagascar* knew their shit.

"I just—look at me, Luna." I look up, my chest constricting around my ribs. "Men have it so easy, especially in this fucking business. Women eat each other alive like it isn't the men with their cocks hanging out at holiday parties ruining our lives and careers. Women have to have each other's backs. And I have yours."

My hands slide off my keyboard. Did Romy put something in my sandwich?

And right as I think Alice is making a breakthrough into a compassionate person, my phone rings.

"Alice Dadamo's office," I say. "One moment." I put the phone on hold. "Devon."

He's one of her few acting clients, a filmmaker who stars in his own YouTube Shorts. Cool style, but not my thing. Still, I'll put his videos on if I have to turn my brain off during work but can't go on Twitter.

Alice frowns. "I'll call him back."

I take the line off hold. "She's unavailable right now. Can we return?"

I hang up.

"Say 'we'll return.' Your phrasing is weak."

My ears go hot. Real Human Alice was nice while she lasted. "Of course. Sorry."

"And don't say 'sorry.' Goddamn it, you millennials are so *weak*."

I could mention she's a cusp millennial and I'm Gen Z, but I won't. I look back to my emails. Less than twelve hours until the movie with Romy tonight.

"I can't get over those emails from John's lawyer." I'm not given time to reply. "What business does he think he's in? Sorry, you don't get time off for your kids. This whole hustle is for your kids. You know what I did for my kids? When my daughter was four and I was driving her and her little friend to my house and my star client called, I pulled over and had them join some kiddie birthday party on the first lawn I saw."

A look of abject horror crosses my features. Of course it does. But it lasts only a split second. One of the many skills I've had to learn for this job.

"Yeah, I mean, you gotta make sacrifices. Be innovative."

That and the lying. I have heavy Yom Kippurs lately.

She slaps the desk. "Exactly!"

A moment of silence. Just the sound of me writing out an email for a client who's got a meeting on the Disney lot this week, explaining *exactly* how to drive into the lot and find a producer's office.

"Call Devon back."

I drop the typing, call Devon. Return to my typing. "Devon, you're on with Alice."

I press the MUTE button, but the conversation still filters through my headset. It's not a big deal when I'm outside—I'm expected to take notes on most client calls—but watching Alice's body language go completely relaxed just feels awkward here. It's as if I'm not supposed to listen if I can hear Alice without the filter of the phone line. They didn't talk about this in the mailroom.

Devon's voice filters through the call, deep and smooth. "I mean, look, the damage control is done, but it's just wild, y'know? You say your dumbest thoughts on Twitter and it just blows up."

My heart leaps a little. Twitter? Devon has a publicist, but I should be on top of whatever he said. I type his Twitter handle into my browser as the phone call goes on.

"Look, Devon, what you said wasn't that bad," Alice says, her faux nice voice back on.

I find the tweet instantly. It's been ratio'd. Hard. Thousands of replies to a hundred likes.

> Sorry, but if you don't identify as straight,
> don't drop into the DMs, ladies. I'm not
> here for indecisive chicks.

My heart sinks so hard and fast I'd swear it turned into a rock.

"No, Alice, I get it," Devon says. "I . . . It's complicated, y'know?

I just think I should be able to say what's on my mind if it's honest and not get attacked."

I'm not here for indecisive chicks.

"And you shouldn't," Alice says. "Between you and me, I get that we have to appease leftist Hollywood, but come on. It gets so hard to follow sometimes."

I stare so hard at the space between my keys the image starts to blur.

Hollywood's liberal. That's the rule, right?

Hollywood's liberal, yet Alice is really saying this. Just being in this room feels like inhaling garbage. Inhaling it into my lungs and spreading it through the arteries into every inch of my body. I'd give anything to crawl out of here.

"No, but, like, I listened to what people had to say. I learned. I just hope they know that."

Alice waves dismissively. "You're fine. People are just so sensitive nowadays."

I sink into my chair, my throat tightening.

Indecisive chicks.

People from one of the most liberal industries in America don't think this is real. And so what? If I were in a Lifetime movie or whatever, I'd turn to Alice, tell her off, and quit. Give justice to my identity and a community that I've never even really interacted with. Send the message of the week.

But I've never felt smaller. My voice has never been so quiet.

Alice hangs up. "Can you believe that? Devon tweets once about not wanting to date bisexual girls and everyone loses it."

I take a deep breath. My grip on the phone has turned my knuckles white. I can sort of imagine saying the right thing. Telling her off. Being the right person.

"People are weird on the internet. Better safe than sorry."

And even after Alice has long forgotten her conversation with Devon, I can't help but feel like I did something horribly wrong.

Alice and the phone call sit heavy with me long after Romy and I make our way over to the movies. I don't even know how to begin to approach it as the two of us stand in front of a sparse AMC movie showing list. It's displayed on one of those robot screens, because who interacts with people anymore? It felt terrible to hear Alice say that, and I know I should've said something, but that doesn't even feel like the real issue here. Something else is eating at me.

"Do you still hate new kid movies?" Romy asks me, her purple-painted nail hovering over a poster of a yeti, a chupacabra, and a Mothman hugging.

"I only hate when they use fart jokes as a crutch."

I'm not here for indecisive chicks.

Things like that don't just come out of a vacuum. I've been so disconnected from queerness—even living with Romy—that I don't even know *stereotypes* of bisexual girls. And it's not like I haven't thought it these past seven days: How do I *know* I'm really bisexual if I've never even been with a woman? If someone were to say, *Bi girls are just indecisive*, to my face, could I really stand there and say, *No, it's not like that*?

Romy makes a face and toggles over to a different movie. "Action?" We click to the description. Romy clicks right out. "Too many male feelings."

I laugh as she hovers over the one remaining movie that we

haven't seen—some modern western-type shoot-'em-up called *Goodbye, Richard!* with a very Las Vegas aesthetic poster. It's headed by none other than Valeria Sullivan.

"I could do this," I say.

Curiosity had gotten the better of me after I met her. One sweep through IMDb, and I learned she's a Pasadena-raised daughter of dentists. She came out of nowhere, her Oscar film her first acting credit anywhere, and she's since costarred in three ensemble studio films, one other indie that has 92 percent on Rotten Tomatoes, and this film. This movie's been out for a couple of weeks, but her IMDb STARmeter has only just dropped into the top five hundred (as in, she was high to begin with). She's got a smattering of late-night interviews and magazine covers and a dedicated fanbase, but her only appearances in tabloid magazines are things like "Valeria Sullivan Spotted Leaving Whole Foods in Hollywood Hills," and they occur exclusively around when her films are released. She's one of those celebrities who disappears from the public eye only to reappear when their movies come out. From what I've observed on the manager end, those celebrities tend to be shy and their appearances are the team's idea. Keanu Reeves–like.

Romy nods. "Valeria Sullivan looks super queer coded and that's enough for me." Her eyes light up. "I should make you a list of essential sapphic films. We could watch together."

I smile. "That'd be fun."

One credit card swipe, one Venmo request, and two tickets later, we head over to the food counter. I haven't eaten an actual meal all day, and the subpar dine-in options suddenly look luxurious.

"Hey," I say as we wait in line while the workers let someone in the premiere line cut ahead of us. I mildly regret not being in the special AMC club. I really should go to the movies more than I do. "Do you . . . You're willing to date bi people, right?"

Romy scrunches her brows together. "Yeah, of course. Why wouldn't I be?"

"Just . . . you know, curious about my prospects."

She looks me up and down. "Lune, your prospects are fine."

Romy goes silent, chewing on her lip. I finally make it to the front of the line and get called to order. I pick a bacon ranch burger. Romy orders popcorn and a Sprite before we circle back to my question.

"Do you have a girl in mind?" She chews on her inner lip after she says it.

Bi girls are just indecisive.

"I dunno. I don't even think I'd know an attractive girl, like one I'd want to have sex with, if she were right in front of me."

Romy bites back a laugh. "Do you know with guys when you're attracted to them?"

"I think so."

"Same concept. You have a type; people come along who break that type. For instance, I'm *really* into that artificial red hint on brunettes. It's just an automatic reaction."

I run a hand through my hair instinctually, my heart beating much harder than it needs to be. With her encouragement, I've been getting a red tint put into the usually nondescript light brown. She hasn't complimented it out of the blue like this. "You're fucking around, aren't you?"

Romy squirts butter onto her popcorn. "You make it too easy."

We walk into the theater. The movie is still playing in big theaters, but the crowd is sparse considering it's eight something on a Thursday night.

"I just—what if I'm doing this attraction thing wrong?" I blurt.

Romy sets the popcorn down between us. "Dude, you can't do this wrong. You're a baby gay. Non-assholes will give you a break while you're figuring everything out."

I give her a look. "Aren't baby gays like actual children?"

Romy slides her horn-rimmed glasses on. I think she's supposed to wear them all the time for distance, but I've only ever seen them when we watch movies or plays or while she's driving. It's not her usual look, but she could make even an outdated hipster style look great. "Baby gays are people who've just come out. Can be any age."

An attendant comes by with my burger. I adjust the bacon that's threatening to fall out. My Jewish ancestors frown down on me. "But I just—how do I know if I'm actually attracted to women or just think I am?"

Romy stops the jokes and looks me in the eye, a line between her brows. "Did someone say something to you?"

I exhale. "Alice . . . She had this conversation with a client . . ."

Romy stiffens as I tell her what Alice said, as if my words were a physical blow. She puts a hand on mine. "Luna, I . . ." She exhales, her body slowly relaxing. "With attraction, you know how you just kinda knew with Wyatt?"

A knot starts forming in my stomach. "I guess." Ranch is sliding from the burger onto my hands, and I don't know if this is the universe telling me how far I've fallen or risen since Wyatt.

Full disclosure: Wyatt and I waited three weeks before fumbling our clothing off. Wyatt was a mediocre kisser, and I'd been out of my mind nervous that I was falling out of love/lust/whatever with him with each passing kiss. When we'd gotten past second base, Wyatt, despite describing numerous successful sexual encounters to me, couldn't even get himself in the right region. I'd guided his fingers right to my clit, and he still couldn't find it. And maybe this wasn't the *right* choice, but I'd broken up with him over text an hour later. We just didn't work as lovers, and if we couldn't have that, why be more than friends?

"It's not something you have to think about. Clearly you've had situations where you were attracted to women or you wouldn't be questioning this. The Rachel Brosnahan thing was real. All the stuff you've been describing to me is real. All that other shit is just white noise." She squeezes my hand. "Please. Slow down, enjoy the movie." She pulls away, looks at her hand, and makes a face. "What did you put on my hand?"

I smile. "Ranch and bacon grease, probably."

"Glamorous."

I look away as she licks the ranch off her hands.

"Thanks, by the way," I say.

"Anytime," she replies as she steals a few fries.

I study the movie ticket. "You know, Valeria Sullivan is Wyatt's boss's client. I talked to her for a second earlier this week."

"She seems cool."

"Very cool. Nicest client I've had to escort around."

And I guess now I'll get to see one of her movies, finally.

The lights go down. I can't say Romy has made me feel any more secure in whatever I'm doing with this queer thing, but there's at least the assurance that I have someone to talk to to figure it out. *Are you happy with the way things are right now?* Sitting in that movie theater, I'd kill for some stability in this identity. An anchor. Something that tells me this isn't all in my head. That I *can* fight back against the people like Alice in my life. That I'll eventually be confident enough to answer the barrage of questions I'll get when I tell people like my extremely heteronormative parents I'm bi, even if I haven't been with a girl.

I find it exactly twenty-two minutes later.

chapter four

Based on what I've just said, one might suspect that my life, if divided into a before and an after, would be bisected by my sexuality. But no, it isn't. It's bisected by Before I Fell in Love with Valeria Sullivan and After I Fell in Love with Valeria Sullivan.

Before I.F.I.L.W.V.S. Luna had limited movie taste. Before I.F.I.L.W.V.S. Luna was very, very concerned that discovering the wonders of the female aesthetic because of Rachel Brosnahan might have meant she was in love with her therapist. Before I.F.I.L.W.V.S. Luna, if I'm being honest, had never truly had an all-consuming crush. Definitely not with Wyatt. Not with the handful of Hinge dates in college or the boys from across the classroom in high school or that one female physics teacher in college.

Now, After I.F.I.L.W.V.S. Luna is a baller. No, I get it now. I get what it feels like to sit in a move theater and see an attractive woman I met once be transformed into someone larger than life, on a screen where I could see the flecks of green in her eyes, see her silhouette framed against sunsets and grimy streets. To crave the sound of someone's voice, to want to know what every tone and word sounds like from her mouth. To feel like an archivist of my own mind, desperate to restore the not-so-present memories of my time physically in Valeria's presence. *I get it now.* When I told Julia all this the next day in therapy, she smiled and called it my "first girl crush."

First girl crush,

I kind of love it.

"Text me before midnight tonight," Alice had said to me after I left work.

But it's five p.m., work and therapy are over, and I'm in a dress that stops midthigh and enhances my decidedly average-to-small chest as best it can. Red lipstick and eyeliner and everything. It doesn't even matter that I'm going out with the other talent assistants to fucking Dave & Buster's in Hollywood & Highland. Ordinarily, this particular location's proximity to the Walk of Fame, a.k.a. the worst place in L.A., would have me ruffled. But this girl-crush thing is getting me high, and my brain is working in overdrive. Even just sitting at an overcrowded booth, Romy's hand on my shoulder to keep herself from falling out of said overcrowded booth, I feel creatively turned on for the first time in years.

"Here's to another week of survival," Wyatt says as everyone raises their drinks.

Most of my other coworkers are two drinks in by the time we get appetizers and everything, but my first drink's still half-done. There's something about larger social gatherings where I'm just less inclined to go hard.

"Except you, Romy," Trevor, the assistant who sits across from me, says.

Romy laughs. "Yeah, well, you know I *am* paid at the same hourly rate as you guys for half the workplace abuse." She sips her drink. "Plus tips."

"You're the literal worst," Wyatt says. Cassidy, one of the other future-manager-type assistants, nods along.

"Hey, you guys can abandon your shitty paths too. Especially the creatives in the house."

Rain, Trevor, this guy Jared, and I exchange looks.

"Okay, so," I say. "While everyone's sufficiently drunk, poll: Do I stay with Alice or bounce?"

Romy gives me a look. The kind of look that somehow perfectly says, *This is something you should ask Julia, not your drunk coworkers.*

"There's a floater out there who just woke up from a badly timed sleep in a cold sweat saying, 'Is a desk opening up?'" Trevor says.

Everyone laughs.

Rain crosses her arms. "I heard the dirt on Alice from Benjamin once. He says she only places about half her assistants if they don't quit first."

"Can you even get really good gigs for cinematography from a manager?" Trevor asks. "If Alice isn't offering up some big fish, like *naming* a client she'd hook you up with, it sounds like a bad fit."

I'm buzzed, but, man, is that buzz being swallowed by everyone's words. I can't even bear to look at Romy right now. As usual, she was right. As usual, my best bet in outings of more than three people is to shut up.

"All right, people, let's not scare her," Wyatt says. "We're all stressed enough as is."

Rain leans back in her seat. "Speaking of which, did anyone find a nondrug catchall stress reliever?"

"Come on, Rain, everyone knows it's sex," Trevor says. "The only way I survive is having my girlfriend sleep over every night."

My heart twinges. The direction of this conversation is so obvious. The feeling is old, familiar, but much like stubbing a toe, no amount of experience makes the pain less surprising.

Rain exhales. "It's hardly been a cure for me."

"People can also be on the ace spectrum," Cassidy mumbles into her drink. Romy rolls her eyes in solidarity.

"Maybe your boyfriend isn't good in the sack?" Wyatt chides.

Rain smiles. "Yeah, sure." Rain turns to me. "Luna, was *Wyatt* here good in bed?"

I'm not drunk enough for the truth. In any sense. "He got the job done."

Wyatt relaxes as Romy flicks me in the back. I ignore her. She can burn Wyatt's lack of skills in bed another time.

"They have the right idea," Jared says. "I started hooking up with Andrew in literary, and it's the best decision I ever made."

"Jesus, when are you doing it?" Romy asks. "You're all at that fucking office until midnight."

Jared grins. "Any break I have. Lunch. That weird sort of dinner break. Before, right after. It's like a miracle cure."

Yeah, hah, who cares, right? I might be losing my job and livelihood tonight, and I'm yet again the only virgin at the table, but life's good, right? I sink back to the position I've been in since I was a teenager. Friends grin and shriek and pile on story after story of sexual escapades—good, bad, and everything in between. Everyone nods in easy recognition, creating a laser barrier I can never cross. They use words like *everyone knows*, and I bite my tongue, knowing I don't know. Knowing if I say anything, I'll get pity at best—furrowed brows and *it'll happen someday*, when they can't guarantee anything—straight-up mockery at worst. So, I stay quiet, waiting for the conversation to veer away like I'm waiting for a cavity filling to end. Try not to think about the technically possible scenario where I'm in this position for the rest of my life.

Even today, it's only the sickly sweet drink in my hand that's allowed my brain to move into thoughts of sex without the spiraling feeling.

I glance at Wyatt, my brain shifting over to Valeria. I've gone back through her filmography since seeing the western, and watching her act in the Oscar film is what truly hooked me. Her work is so visceral. When I got to her second indie and discovered that she had a (straight) sex scene . . . I can't get the tilt of her head into the kiss, the curves of her silhouette against the other actor, the sound of her character coming, out of my mind.

That little spark of excitement is back, but it fades as quickly as it came.

It's a crush. On a person I'll never see again. I'm twenty-four, and the closest I've gotten to someone inside me is imagining it.

"What about you, Romy?" Rain asks. "They *do* say sapphic sex is the best sex."

Romy smirks. "You're on the wrong team, Rain. Anything a man can do, *I* can do ten times better while improving your self-esteem."

I find myself longing for Romy's confidence as she speaks. Romy could have not had sex in months and she can still blow these straight people out of the water. Nearly every sapphic person I've ever met has said the same thing she's saying. Queer sex is killer. And even when Romy is casually talking about sex in a roomful of almost all allocishet people, she's royalty.

"Um, Romy, I think you're forgetting a big piece of missing equipment," Trevor says.

Romy just keeps smiling. "Strap-on. You pick the size and the shape, and no pregnancy in sight." Her voice lowers as she speaks, making me shiver. "And non-cis men can actually find the G-spot. I've been intimately familiar with the clit since I was twelve. And get this—both parties are primed for multiple orgasms. And I know that tongue is much more of an accent flavor in kissing than the main event."

I watch Romy as she speaks, the curve of her lips, the way her index finger is drawing little circles on the table surface. We've cuddled over the years. I know the feeling of a body pinning me down from Wyatt. But I also know what a non-man's body heat feels like. And right then, I'd give anything for her to keep talking. For a non-man to move their hand off the table and slip it onto my leg. Draw circles on my thigh, our lips doing their own dance. For them to pin me to the ground with their hips.

I think about Valeria's lips. The weight of her, the firmness of her arms that, at least according to that movie, have power behind them. Her fingers doing the same circle motion Romy's are doing. Hearing her moan like in that movie. On my thigh then inward . . .

"Honestly, if I were bi, I'd date only women," Rain says. "Men suck."

Romy shrugs. "You don't have to identify as bi to hook up with a non-man."

Rain suddenly reaches over and slaps me on the back. "Take your chance while you have it, Lunes. You're the tensest among us, and Romy's available twenty-four seven for you."

I imagine playing along with Rain, joining in on Romy's little pro–queer sex bit. Agreeing with Romy's points, pretending to flirt with Romy, say exactly what we're gonna do to each other when we get back to K-Town. Get a taste of that ruler-of-the-table feeling. Pretend I have that secret key to love, sex, and happiness everyone else here has.

But it'd be a lie. Just like my lies about sleeping with Wyatt.

"Rain, come on," I say. "Rom's my roommate. Just because we're not a guy and a girl doesn't mean hooking up couldn't fuck up our platonic relationship."

Romy laughs, glancing at me. A muscle in her throat twitches as she speaks. "Yeah, shit, Rain, respect *the inherent value of friendship*. Anyone can eat me out; only Luna knows how to convince our landlord to keep fixing our toilet for free."

Even something as small as the way Romy twitched settles uncomfortably inside me, that she's *that* awkward even at the prospect of us together. Not that I *want* it, but . . . I'm clearly not drunk enough to be having this double crisis in an adult Chuck E. Cheese. I pick up my drink and knock it back, peering over the rim to see Romy slam her drained glass down too. I turn to her as the burn sizzles inside me. "Wanna go play games?"

Romy breaks from the others as if she'd been waiting for me to say those exact words. "Yeah, let's go."

Highlights, in the form of potential shots I would've used, to describe the next two hours of my life:

- Low lighting, color saturated. *Dance Dance Revolution*. High angle, watching Romy's and my feet swipe across the squares. Blur effect to show that, yes, I'm pretty drunk. The swipes will be beautiful, though, to show my inner peace amid the chaos.

Romy says, "I. Can't. Believe. You. Didn't. Tell. Me. ABOUT. VALERIA. TOUCHING. YOU!" perfectly to the beat.

- Low, dark lighting. *Ghostbusters* game. Over-the-shoulder shot focused on the silhouettes of Romy and me as we sit in the machine. There's a GAME OVER sign adding reds and greens and blacks to accent the frame, but it's blurry. The theme music is still playing softly in the background. Intimate, shut off, peaceful. I'm close enough to smell that she's radiating the soft lavender scent of her shampoo.

Romy says, "You know, there've been rumors ever since she stepped on the scene that she plays for our team."

I say, "Really?"

Romy says, "She only brings this one other actor dude to premiere events and is never seen with him otherwise, vehemently supports L.G.B.T.Q.+ causes, and if you looked at a photo lineup of her style and the way she carries herself . . ."

- Bright lighting, back into the hustle and bustle of the D&B's floor. Romy, Wyatt, and me on *Mario Kart*. In my movie I clearly hate our faces, because now I'm doing an angle shooting inward, just slightly, to capture profiles of all three of us. Low angle this time. Really oversaturate the color because I'm *wasted* and feel like I'm in Candy Land or some shit. So wasted that I definitely can't even map out the shots anymore.

"I want to cry, Romy," I say as I slump in the plastic *Mario Kart* seat. I lost, badly. "I don't even remember what she was wearing."

The space between Wyatt's eyebrows creases. "What are you guys talking about?"

Romy sits up straight, maybe a little less wasted than me but not much. "Your boss's client. Valeria Sullivan." Romy pulls out her phone, shows Wyatt a photo of Valeria looking goddess-like in a white suit and Converse, making manspreading the hottest thing ever. "It's, like, the gayest thing on the planet."

Wyatt squints. "The suit?"

Romy throws her hands up in a faux *praise Jesus* gesture. "Wyatt! The suit! The sneakers! It's *gay*."

"Is it, though? Can't she just be wearing a suit?"

Romy swings her legs out of the machine just to face Wyatt head-on. "Look, Het Boy, she *exudes* woman-who-loves-women energy. It's not something I can explain. It just *is*."

"Steven's never said anything about her personal life, but we'd have heard . . ."

I've slid so far down into the machine, I might slip into the pedal area. My throat is genuinely clogging up, and I have no idea what emotion is happening. "Ugh, Wyatt, you don't get it! Can Valeria just *top* me already?" I think I'm even using that term correctly this time.

When our game ends, Romy helps me to my feet. "Such a gentlethem," I whisper to Romy. She smiles.

The actual transition to getting back into a booth at the Dave & Buster's restaurant area is beyond me. I just know that, well, we're back there. Wyatt has placed a glass of water in front of me as well as a plate of bread. Romy nurses a water too, but she's with it enough to be on her phone. Yet another moment in my life to curse being five feet three inches: no alcohol tolerance in sight.

"Wyatt," I say as I rip a piece of bread into more aesthetically pleasing pieces, "virginity sucks. Like first I just have to, like, get with a guy, and I'm twenty-four and haven't done that, but now I have to have a whole new kind of sex I haven't had. I'm, like, a double virgin!"

"Virginity is a social construct," Romy drawls. "You can't have a new one for every type of person or you'd have, like, fifty virginities."

I try to give a dismissive flick of my wrist, but it comes across as more random hand-waving. She can rant to me about social constructs when we're both sober.

"So you don't want to get with guys right now?" Wyatt asks.

"No. But who's there to be with? Romy's too cool for me, Rachel Brosnahan isn't Jewish, what are Tinder, and I'll never see Valeria again!"

I lay my head on the table. It's sticky and smells like grease. I'm not sure if I'm craving mozzarella sticks right now or if I want to throw up. Romy looks about as uncomfortable as I feel. She opens her mouth to speak, but Wyatt cuts her off.

"But this, like—you wanna do it?" he continues. "Like really? Committed?"

Romy sighs and grabs a piece of bread, some of her discomfort sloughing off.

"I don't even know what attraction is," I say.

"You are very clearly attracted to Valeria, bub," Romy says through a mouthful of bread.

Where did our other coworkers go? Should I ask about that? Even if I lied to them about sleeping with Wyatt, and that I'm bi, and that I too would like to date only girls since they look better in suits than men and can be pretty and know where the clit is. And circles. Circles are so much hotter with girls. So many erotic circles.

"I'm so late to the game," I say.

"Dude, you're twenty-four. Chill," Romy says. "The longer you wait, the closer you get to that perfect twenty-five to thirty-five age bracket for maximum hotness and maturity."

Wyatt turns to Romy. "Is that a thing?"

"For literally everybody."

"So I'm not at my peak yet?" he asks.

"I have to do something different," I say, mostly to myself. I'm not even sure if Romy and Wyatt are still here. "I'm done being like, *Oh, whatever you say, universe, even if this sucks.*"

Wyatt looks to me, smiles. "You wanna see something cool?"

"Is there a new Jenny Nicholson video?"

"No."

He shows me an email instead.

From Valeria Sullivan.

Hi Wyatt!
Hope your appointment went well, and yeah, the meetings went great yesterday. The girl covering your desk—Luna?—was fantastic. Not that I have any power, but if you have to step out again, put her on Steven's desk, okay? Or tell her to say hi or something.

See you next week!
~ Valeria

I squint, not sure if I'm reading an actual email or an email I'd have in a dream.

"She remembers me?" I mutter.

"She *likes* you. Like she apparently bought a Laura Owens because of you."

Even Romy is sitting up at full attention now, stock-still. When I look to her, she gives a brief smile.

I look up. "You can buy *Pavement Karaoke*?"

Wyatt glances at Romy, then back to me. He's got his scheming face on. "Luna, look at me. I know Valeria is single. Steven checks in on that for press reasons. But if you two are right and she really is gay, why not do something bold like ask her out? You've got nothing to lose and she really is cool. She's, like, twenty-eight. She'd be a realistic dating prospect anyway. Just test the waters getting to know her, see what happens."

Romy blows a raspberry. "One issue, Cupid. Sure, she'll be in next week, but like Luna said, when would she ever see her again?"

"One step at a time. But if we do find some way for them to connect regularly, it could actually happen."

I shake my head. Drink more water. I need to focus. "This is completely insane."

Except, here's the weird thing: it isn't. In my years at the management company, I've seen clients, even pretty big acting clients, befriend the assistants. Especially if they're young actors. They're often lonely, and they have to interact with us by default anyway. The office will *never* forget the time a talent assistant started dating an up-and-coming client. The client took her to the premiere of his movie, and I think she's doing her own creative work now.

Could Valeria and I have the same trajectory?

"But if it works . . ."

Wyatt shrugs, smiling.

It would be incredible.

"Wyatt Rosenthal saying gay rights. Never thought I'd see the day," Romy says.

I turn to Romy. She still looks a little wound up.

"You're on board too?" I ask.

She sips more water, eyes on her glass. "It's worth a shot while she's around the office." She sways a little. "And let's be friends with her."

A tiny shot of soberness falls over me. I pull out my phone. "Guess I'm telling Alice I'm still committed."

"You cool with that?" Romy asks, a line forming between her brows.

I think about seeing Valeria again. Making her smile again. Talking about art with her and maybe even working with her. She liked my phone background. What would she think if I could show her my actual cinematography? What if I got to the point where I could film *her*?

"Worth the risk."

So I type the message to Alice. She lets me know she received it and adds: only if ur on ur best behavior xx

chapter five

Somehow, sitting in bed for two days straight didn't quite get my energy back up after the hangover of a lifetime Saturday morning. Yet it takes maybe five minutes at work Monday morning to get me totally wired. I'm reading Romy's play to get a sense of the "outdoor" scenes that I'll have to film. Alice is yakking to one of her big clients, her conversation such a familiar buzz in my ear that I figure why take off the headset. After all, I'm a committed assistant now, and committed assistants wear headsets and iron their blouses.

It's while Alice waxes poetic about some producer and I read a soliloquy from a gay detective prodigy that I first spot Valeria.

She's wearing a suit.

Which, okay, doesn't quite describe it enough. It's one of those stylized suits where the pants stop midcalf, with those designer slipper shoes and a cream blouse that has a loose tie accent in the front that flows a bit past her waistline.

She's wearing a suit and she's leaning against the wall behind Wyatt's desk, a half smile on her face.

"Hey, floater," she says, her voice a few notches lower than her usual higher-pitched SoCal accent. She's from Pasadena. My reading is syncing with the person in front of me. Either way, it makes me shiver.

I slip the headset off. Minimize Romy's play. Turn to her. My heart's already hammering after one second of exposure.

I force down a sip of my iced coffee, the best means to cool myself off. "Your suit's really cute."

The crooked smile shifts to a purer joy. She tucks a blond lock behind her ear. A silver ring shines from her index finger. I wonder what the weight of her hair is, how it'd feel to move that piece myself. "Thank you."

I glance at Steven's office. He's on the phone. "Is he keeping you waiting again?"

"*I* think the meeting today is important, but who knows how the fairer sex lives?"

I laugh, but the real jolt of dopamine comes as her eyes light up *watching* me laugh. But I shouldn't be watching her microexpressions like this.

When I quickly glance over at Wyatt's desk, I realize that's empty too. Apparently I've been too preoccupied to notice. "Wyatt's getting you coffee, right?"

"There's"—she narrows her eyes—"a decent chance." She looks at me, and I swear it's like she's burning a hole right into my chest. "Could you spare a Post-it?"

I rip off a Post-it, my hand quivering as much as my heart.

As she grips the other end of the Post-it, there's a moment when the balance is perfect, this quasi-touch connection blinking in a sea of Things That Don't Actually Mean Anything. Then I lift my finger, and Valeria retreats back to her wall, snagging a pen of Wyatt's as she goes. His U.S.C. pen. I become a prouder alumna, seeing the U.S.C. logo between Valeria's knuckles.

"Thanks, Luna," she says, eyes on her paper.

My name slides out from between her lips, casually, as common as the word that came before it. It's not a declaration of love or hate or anything. She's just saying my name like it's the most normal thing in the world. Suddenly I'm craving that sound— Valeria Sullivan just *saying my name*. I can't believe I live in a time line in which Valeria Sullivan says my name out loud and is talking to me. Holy shit.

"Don't let anyone tell you success takes away your ability to be a glorious dumbass," Valeria says.

"You could get an assistant," I say.

Valeria exhales. "Yep."

I can't help but watch her fingers flow as she writes.

And she writes an *A-S*.

Wyatt comes running up right then, handing Valeria her coffee. He smooths out his hair the moment the coffee lands securely into Valeria's grip. "Sorry about that," he says.

Steven invites Valeria into his office. She gives a wave in the general direction of Wyatt and me, but I have no idea whom it's for. Once the door's shut, I scoot over to Wyatt.

"Does Valeria need an assistant?" I ask.

"I don't think—" Wyatt's eyes light up. "Did she mention it to you?"

"Yeah."

"I'll do some recon."

I return to Alice's work with a fluttery feeling in my chest. It's the same feeling I used to get when professors said they loved my work in undergrad or when Romy gets major praise on her plays. It feels like lightness and joy, even if it doesn't have a path to sustainability just yet.

"Hey, guess what?" Wyatt says after I've spent ten minutes trying to distract myself.

I've been focusing on emails, the only magnet strong enough to hold my racing thoughts down. "What?"

"She wants to work with a marginalized woman. Queer was among the examples."

I look up to find Wyatt grinning. Deep down, I know exactly what he's going to do. I do. But it still doesn't keep my stomach from tightening, my brain from firing off in ten different *what the hell is he doing?* directions.

The moment stops pretty quickly.

Because Wyatt gets up and bursts into Steven's office, leaving the door open so their voices carry through the assistant pod.

"What, Wyatt? Did you get all that?" Steven asks.

Through the glass, there're perfect views of everyone's profiles. Valeria and Steven are looking at Wyatt. If I were to use this angle in a film, it'd feel voyeuristic. Yes, it feels voyeuristic right now, but this angle would also look perfect framing Valeria if it were pitch-black and the only illumination was coming from a light source in the room.

"You know Alice's assistant, Luna?" Wyatt says.

And in that moment, Valeria turns around, looking right at me. I look away so fast I might've injured my neck.

"Yeah," Valeria says.

"She's got two years working with Alice, super reliable, remote or in person. She's bi."

No.

No, no way. No—there's no way he just—

She's bi.

No one at work knows I'm bi.

Wyatt just told Steven Wells and Valeria Sullivan I'm bi.

My own parents and brother don't know. I haven't even told my friends besides Romy and Wyatt. I haven't even told my other *queer friends*.

And now Steven Wells and Valeria Sullivan know.

"And Jewish, if that counts," Wyatt continues.

My face goes hot. My heart hammers so hard it's causing chest pain. I squeeze my eyes shut, begging the universe that, when I open them, this won't have happened.

"In Hollywood, it doesn't," Steven says. He pauses. "Bisexual, huh?" Steven turns his body to Valeria. "Sound interesting to you?"

Valeria nods; I should be acknowledging this, but the blood's left my head. I force the watered-down coffee still on my desk into my mouth. Anything to tip me back to full consciousness. This is not good. My body, as usual, is betraying me.

Wyatt's out of the office again, his head cocked at me.

"What did you *do*?" I squeak out.

"You're *gay*?!"

If I thought I was going to pass out a second ago, looking over to see Alice in front of me just proves that I have already passed out, died, and officially landed in the purgatory that Jews don't believe in. She must have come out of her office just in time to hear Steven say "bisexual."

The office has also gone dead silent. One slow pan across this room and everyone, like every assistant, along with Alice, is staring at me. The assistants hold their gazes on me for seconds before their attention falls elsewhere. Alice is downright *giddy*, like she won the lottery. Steven and Wyatt seem blissfully unaware of anything going on. And Valeria—Valeria's not even looking at the scene. She's frowning, a line between her brows, wringing her wrists, staring at a far-off wall. She's the only one seemingly reacting to how oversaturated the white light is in here. The only one not an unsettling smidgen out of focus.

That's the image that gets my throat to constrict.

I turn to Alice in all her glee. "I'm . . . actually bisexual."

I've never said this out loud to any adult-adult besides Julia.

"Look at that. I made a diversity hire without even knowing it!" Alice says.

The line is so absurd I'm launched out of the emotion of the moment. Or, at least, the emotion isn't mortification anymore. It's anger. Everyone's crystal clear again.

Alice? The woman who said bisexual girls were just seeking attention less than a week ago? She's not even hiding it. I went from good assistant to diversity hire with one unwilling reveal.

"Um . . ." I rub my forearm. "I guess."

"What a perfect day," Alice says.

Alice pulls out her phone, *pulls me into her*, and takes a selfie.

A photo. She takes a photo of us together. Just like that.

She's got Twitter up. I can only watch in shock as she posts our selfie with the caption: *WITH MY ~PANSEXUAL~ ASSISTANT. THESE BRAVE KIDS ARE THE FUTURE. #WENEEDDIVERSITY #PRIDE.*

This can't be real. Wyatt didn't just out me to my boss. My boss didn't just reply by instantly using me as fodder for more viral tweets.

"Are my parents gonna see that?" I ask.

I don't even follow Alice. I know what the answer to that question is. But I can't even fathom asking anything else. Because what if they *do*? I'm not ready to explain bisexuality to them, for them to call it a phase—

"No, but people in the industry will, love. They'll see it after our extra year. Jobs will be flooding your house."

I automatically move to glance at Valeria, to ground this. Remind myself that *good* things are happening right now, even if I can't breathe.

But Valeria's gone.

I get an email from Wyatt confirming the meeting/interview with Valeria for Wednesday evening, but it's the only communication we have. I'm not talking to him because of a combination of the usual monster Monday workload and a constant pressure behind my eyes that seems to be anger and betrayal.

And it's not like Wyatt doesn't try throughout the day. I store up six texts and three emails—variations on *are you okay?* and *what did I do wrong?*—throughout our shift. The answer is so obvious, I could type it up in a split-second email, but it's like my fingertips have lost the muscle memory to spell it out. A defense mechanism, maybe? Because it feels *obvious* to me.

But I know I'm not straight now. For one of the first times since coming out, I feel that in my bones. Wyatt can like girls all he wants, but he'll never know what goes into liking girls as a girl. We can never again relate to the same banal privilege of being straight white Jews. Understanding that new barrier between us makes my chest tighten.

Today there has been an irreversible change in this environment.

Alice is making sure that's drilled into my brain; she made me order rainbow pride decals for her office door. She is genuinely being nicer to me because she found out I'm gay, but I don't think she even knows what pansexual is. I always knew Alice was scheming and that she used every tool in her arsenal to advance her career and reputation. I knew Alice saw diversity in the industry as a trend to capitalize on. But this change is making my skin crawl. It's like I've stopped being human for her.

Needless to say, when I walk to the parking lot that evening, I'm not happy.

"Luna!" Wyatt says, his clobbering footsteps sounding behind me. "Wait up!"

I slow down—a little bit. "What?"

He reaches my stride. "Please, will you talk to me? Are you mad at me? I got you the interview! This is going amazingly."

Heat simmers my insides, from my face to my stomach. "You outed me."

"I what?"

Now I stop. Turn to look him in the eye. "You *outed* me. I hadn't come out to anyone in the office. You don't get to do it for me!"

Wyatt frowns, darting his gaze around the parking lot. Like he's not sure how he got here. "But you—when you told us—"

"No one but you and Romy and my therapist knew before this. That hasn't just changed."

"But I thought you tell everyone at once. You haven't told your *parents*?"

A lump forms in my throat. "It's not that simple. No, I haven't. But we're talking about you. You have to *ask* me about that, even if it was for my benefit."

Wyatt digs his hands into his pants pockets. "But you would've had to tell Valeria sooner or later. How would you ever get with her if she doesn't know you're into girls?"

"It didn't need to be right then. It didn't need to be *so loud that Alice heard!*"

"And again! Look, Luna, I'm sorry I outed you, but this is *good*. Alice is treating you better! Valeria knows you're gay and wants to interview you. Could you just chill for a minute? It's not the end of the world."

It's like talking to a wall or an unfortunate YouTube comment section. One of my best friends, my only ex-boyfriend, and what the hell is he *saying*? "It's not the end of the world"? Fuck that. I don't need this right now.

But he's also my only connection to Valeria right now. And my *friend*, I think as my anger dissolves from a solid heat to a gelatinous uncertainty.

"I have to go," I say. "Long commute, y'know. Thanks for setting up the interview."

The minute I'm in the car, tears burning in my eyes, I get a text from my mom just saying to call her later to chat. Is it weird that I haven't come out to my parents? Julia said it wasn't, but Julia's also trying to prevent me from having a mental breakdown twice a week. What if what Wyatt's saying is right—

No. I squeeze the steering wheel. I'm not having a crisis about my decisions surrounding coming out. I know exactly why I haven't told them yet. Why I will continue to not tell them.

It's not like they're blatantly homophobic. It's not like they have an actual problem with queer people. They just don't get it. They literally don't understand what bisexual is. They don't understand why queer rep is important. They occasionally make comments about how hard it must be to be in a gay relationship. At one point my mom said I was "lucky" to be straight, that my life would be easier for it.

They are just part of a generation where queerness couldn't be open, where it was seen as a deviation from the norm and not ideal. When they grew up, it was something that existed in pockets, nothing they'd go out of their way to prevent but something they were comfortable not having to deal with. They've always just lived their lives a certain way. Until a roadblock comes up that makes them challenge their views, they simply won't challenge them. I don't doubt that Mom and Dad have the capacity to change and become more aware people; they just don't seek out personal evolution.

The problem with that is the roadblock here, the teacher for them, is a person. Is me. And I don't *want* to be a lesson for them. I just want them to have already had the epiphany, because that's what you have to do to be a compassionate person in this world.

But those aren't the parents I was blessed with. So they're not being blessed with being among the first five people I come out to. Maybe not even the first ten. Maybe not the first fifty.

Although now Valeria is among my first five.

It wasn't my choice, but I'm going to make it worthwhile.

chapter six

"Are you doing okay after all that?" Romy asks Tuesday night. The first stop on my Make Romy Backgrounds for Her Play trip involves developing the psyche of her thirteen-year-old detective prodigy character, and the vision I developed on the way home from work was to take something with overwhelming bright colors, try-hard artificiality, and an underlying grittiness. So we're at a 7-Eleven. "I'm always here if you want to talk about it," she adds.

Wyatt hasn't really apologized since the incident on Monday. My instincts are to just forgive him, move on, brush it under the rug, but I'm trying to hold strong. Not to mention I've just . . . not had the emotional energy to even deal with him. Julia would tell me to use the list of coping mechanisms we've made and gone back over five times in my years as her client, so I'm trying.

"I don't even know what to talk about," I admit. "I know he's a deeply flawed human being, and I know it wasn't personal or malicious, but it just—I dunno, it stings like it was."

Romy flashes a tiny, playful smile. "So just to be clear, I can shit-talk Wyatt now? Like no holding back, can analyze his failings like Edith made us analyze Flannery O'Connor in Intro to Fiction?"

"We're just in a spat right now," I say. "It'll blow over. So, you know, don't go too hard."

"'Too hard'? Lune, he outed you to your freak boss. We don't have sympathy for Martins. Rule one of being queer."

Martins is what Romy and I call people who out other people, after the dude from *Love, Simon*. And it isn't a word we throw around lightly. The last time we called someone a Martin was when one of the middle schoolers Romy was tutoring told all her little brother's friends that he was gay at a theater rehearsal.

"Do we really think he's full Martin, though? Like Wyatt's exceptionally stupid. We know this."

Romy sighs and runs a hand through her hair, the bleached strand shining in the weird lighting.

"Look," she says. She slides over to me and rubs my back. Not an unfamiliar move, but I stiffen upon first contact this time. But her hand is warm, and the strokes of her fingertips make my muscles soften like melted butter. "If he doesn't come to his senses, just—fuck him." She slides her hand off me, which leaves me feeling oddly hollow. "Okay, how's Valeria? Are you still feeling okay about this after the outing?"

I grab an energy drink out of the refrigerated section, and Romy disappears behind an aisle as we continue to speak. The place is empty, so I guess we can just speak at an obnoxious volume until the guy working the register kicks us out. I pull out my camera and start getting shots of the inside. It's too bright in here. Perfect for the ebb and flow of the scene.

"Honestly, she seemed more agitated about it than me. She left the room while it was happening," I reply as I click RECORD.

Romy pokes her head out from the aisle, Hostess CupCakes in

hand. "Damn, she did? What excuse did Wyatt give for her just bouncing?"

I shrug as I adjust my angles. "Bathroom."

"Yeah, 'cause people just *suddenly have to piss* after watching someone be outed."

I kill the recording and join Romy in one of the many room temperature aisles. Grab a bag of Flamin' Hot Cheetos off the rack. "Do you think it means anything?"

"Not sure, but I'll give her major props for knowing it's a bad thing. You know, unlike everyone else in your office." She raises her eyebrows. "Or . . . Well, it's most common to know that feeling through experience."

I hate how the thought curls a little ball of warmth in my stomach. "You think that means she's gay?"

"I'm saying it's a win-win. Either she's a solid ally or queer herself. Game's still on, basically." Romy smiles. "Did you two get to talk before?"

Inside, that warmth is spreading all the way to my fingertips, but I offer a blasé shrug. "A little bit. She still remembers my name, bantered a little, got a sticky note." And Wyatt. "And Wyatt got me that interview with her."

Romy frowns. "Oh, right. He's actually very efficient as a wingman." She looks down at the camera bag on my shoulder. "Are you done with the inside?"

I look around. 7-Elevens always have harsh light, and the effect is cool, but Romy doesn't need much of it for the story. The gritty outside parking lot is honestly more the vibe. "Yeah. Let's go outside."

We pay for our junk and head into the parking lot. I pull open my trunk, and we sit in the open back like a couple of vagrants. It's a familiar scene for us. Out of the three of us, I was the only one with a car in our first three years of college, so when Wyatt was away with family, we'd go on little adventures like this. Park at Griffith, park on the cliff shoulders of Palos Verdes and Malibu Roads, park in Old Pasadena. We'd bring food and cheap alcohol, gossip until we ran out of names, lament or celebrate the state of storytelling, and I'd film and she'd write. When the night grew too old, we'd curl up under blankets together and watch the few stars we could see from L.A.

As I set up my camera again, Romy stares intently at her phone.

"Did you finish the dialogue revision to go with the changes the director mentioned?" I ask.

Romy is a genius with dialogue, at least in my opinion. She used to use her free time to record conversations in the food court or the film school or the engineering quad at U.S.C., and she would read every line of her dialogue out loud in as many ways as possible for each assignment in any writing class she took. Whether it was prose, screenwriting, or playwriting, the dialogue shone. But the festival involves revision as part of the experience, and as a creative, I know how much that can hurt, especially with a project as personal as this one.

"Yeah," she says.

I leave my camera, sliding a hand on her shoulder. "Want me to send them to your actors? You have the emails ready, right?"

She exhales. "Yeah." Looks to me. "Will you?"

I smile. "It's the only skill I gained from Alice."

I take her phone, scan each email for typos, and hit SEND. When I look back at her, everything from her face to her shoulders has relaxed. She puts a hand to her chest.

"I kinda love you," she says as she leans her head on my shoulder. Her voice lowers as she says the words, but they still have that playful edge.

I smile as I lean my head against hers. "I kinda love you too."

I eat a couple of Cheetos from the bag using shitty 7-Eleven chopsticks and return to my camera. Wyatt and Romy have been making fun of me for eating chips like that for years, but guess who doesn't have to clean her fingers before touching her equipment?

I pull focus to go between putting the 7-Eleven sign completely in frame and using just enough of a piece of the color pop to get the contrast. I'm a huge fan of kitsch, but sometimes you gotta wonder if you're playing into spotlighting brands when you're just trying to use the image itself.

"This is gonna be so badass," I say.

Romy leans back in the bed of the car. "Man, remember when we used to collab in your filmmaking class because you couldn't write?"

I whip my gaze over to give her the stink eye. She giggles. She would "script doctor" my shorts for production classes. I still did all the visual storytelling. And the writing. I did *write*.

But it was really fun.

I wonder if we could write something really gay and personal, now that we're kind of in the same boat. I've had this image stuck in my head for months of roommates in college kissing while trying to study for an exam together. I'd utilize the shitty lighting in dorm rooms—ours didn't have an overhead light, so we had only Bed Bath & Beyond lamps. I'd use a shot from the other lofted dorm bed, a straight shot to their bodies connecting. Then one from the bottom, watching as the cheap bed shifts under their moving bodies.

A lot of people in my production classes would have these graphic sex scenes in their works. Romance in some capacity. I'd never done it because I always made Romy act in my films opposite me. (Were there other actors at U.S.C.? Yes. But I hated the theater kids.) Anyway, I never wrote kissing scenes because I'd feel bad making Romy ever kiss a man, and if it came to Romy kissing a girl, it'd have to be me because of lack of resources and—

And we were friends. And I thought I was straight and it'd been weird.

Thinking about that theoretical short, though, I think about it being the two of us. What image our entangled bodies would make. How my theoretical lighting and shots would look with us.

Which means I need to *stop* thinking.

"Are there legit ways to tell if someone's gay?" I ask.

Romy presses her lips into a thin line. "I mean, this isn't everyone, but short nails are a good indication. Do you remember Valeria's nails?"

I lean closer to her. "What does fingernail length have to do with being into girls?"

Romy gives a wry smile. Looks down at her Hostess cupcake package. Her green eyes light up. "All right, my Padawan, imagine this cupcake is a pussy."

Which . . . is not a phrase I ever expected to hear in my life.

Romy then proceeds to *dig a hole in the bottom of the cupcake*. Like just casual vaginal construction. But of course she chose a Hostess cupcake, so then the filling falls onto her hand. Romy looks down at it with a sort of *whoopsie* expression, like she truly didn't see this coming.

"I shouldn't have used a filled cupcake for—anyway, it's a vagina. Here's a hole."

She shows me the hollowed-out cupcake. I'm imagining a vagina and it's horrifying.

"So a good queer girl such as yourself, knowing what activities she'll likely participate in, takes the time to make sure her fingers are as smooth as possible."

Romy slides her finger into the cupcake hole, dipping it in and out and running it along the edges. It's like a parody of eroticism, but there's always a droplet of sincerity in it, and I hate that she's showing me how she fingers her partners. Fuck. This was not what I meant when I was telling myself to cool down.

"But long fingernails, well . . ."

She reaches over, grabs my chopstick, and the visual has gone ten steps past too far, and I suddenly have opened Pandora's box and know everything and it's horrible and makes a shit ton of sense, wow, I need to trim my nails and—

"Okay, I get it!"

Romy pats me on the back with her clean hand as she licks the cream off the other.

"But yeah, when you interview with Valeria, look for short fingernails."

I look at Romy. I've known her for six years, yet I swear we've never gotten this intimate before. And this was a joke. She's always been pretty open about sexual stuff, but the willingness with which she just schooled me is . . . is the word *kind*? It feels kind. Anyone else would've just said, *You don't wanna scratch the vagina during fingering*, but she made me this wacky demonstration.

I get up and turn my camera to her. "Can you repeat that whole thing with the other cupcake while I frame you in moody lighting?"

Romy bursts out laughing. "I'm not even drunk, and yes, I can." She flashes a *V* by her mouth. "Eat your heart out, my lady."

She makes the phrase sound like it was never a cliché.

When Valeria and I meet for our interview, it's after we both have been in the Slater Management building for several hours straight. She's got another incredible suit on, this periwinkle linen blazer and shorts, and a necklace chain dips into her shirt. I know she's trying to impress people, and I come to work here every day and sweat through everything anyway, but god, she makes me want to try harder.

It's just us in the café, because we're here past the time most assistants go home. There's one barista behind the counter, who doesn't make a fuss when she hands Valeria two coffees. I offered to get the coffees, but Valeria insisted she wanted to move around. So here I am, looking but not really looking at my printed résumé as Valeria glides around in these incredible cream Gucci loafers and a shade of rose lipstick I watched her coat her lips in while she waited for the coffees. There's so little about her vibe that makes her seem famous, but the designer clothing is a subtle marker—*I'm rich; I made this money leading successful movies.*

"Do you take your coffee with anything?" Valeria asks.

I just can't quite reconcile it right now. It's dangerous, in a way. Like I should go through her Twitter indirects to remember exactly how famous she is, how different we are.

"Cinnamon," I reply.

She tips cinnamon into both our coffees and returns to the table. And finally, I'm face-to-face with her. The details are just flooding in, and I don't know what to store in my memory. The sharpness of her nose and the light dusting of freckles across it, the piercings along her helixes and the earlobes that don't have earrings in them.

"So," she says, her voice airy and high, like how she sounds in interviews where she looks relaxed, "I took a look at your résumé, and I gotta say—very impressive, but I don't quite get it." She flips the résumé around, pushing it toward me. Her nails are short, and just *that* forms a weird knot in my stomach. "What's the story? Why do you want to be a personal assistant when all your experience is in production?"

If I could lie my way into this place, surely I can butter Valeria up. "I mean, I know how the industry works. It's about building connections and being as helpful to people as possible in a collaborative environment until someone wants to help you back. Cultivate talent in the meantime. You seem really cool, and I appreciate your advocacy for underrepresented voices."

Valeria's smile shifts to a sort of smirk. "Beautifully crafted response." She raises a brow. "Let's cut the BS. I know it's Hollywood, but let's give it a shot. What's your bigger goal? And don't say 'personal assistant.' No one actually wants to be a personal assistant."

I sip my coffee. Slowly. There's no way this could go worse than when I told Alice. This isn't even a real interview. "Cinematographer."

Her features light up. The sight is somehow so beautiful that a lump is forming in my throat. I take another sip of coffee.

"Trailblazer, huh?" she says. "That's fantastic." She glances at a piece of art on the wall. "And explains the art knowledge."

I shrug. "Fine art is more a hobby, but yeah, there are so few female visual storytellers, especially as parts of features, and I think it's the kind of position we need that eye in. Plus"—I rub my wrist—"I just . . . I've only been able to tell stories through images."

"Right, your *Toy Story* thing." She shakes her head. "I should've guessed."

"Do you have any formal background with fine art?"

She makes a face. "Not quite. I wish. My mom loved taking us to art museums when my sister and I were younger, though. Parents made me volunteer at the Huntington all through high school to 'stay out of trouble.'" She smiles to herself, as if remembering an old joke. "And then I became an actress and embarrassed their Pasadena sensibilities with my politically radical soft porn and premiere dresses with 'too much damn cleavage.'"

I chuckle. "Oh, come on. They must be thrilled for you."

Valeria laughs. "Nah. They're still pissed I spent so much money at Hot Topic as a teen. God knows what they think of what I do now." She looks to me. "Did you cause your parents trouble?"

I shake my head. "I hardly left the house. Just made a lot of short films."

"As someone who never leaves her house but doesn't produce art, I respect that."

In fact, my parents did and still do brag to their friends about what an easygoing kid I was and what a delightful and hardworking adult I became. Even in this environment, my heart twinges thinking about how they're probably saying that shit to this day, and it's all about someone they don't even fully know. They might *stop* saying that stuff if they did know me.

But no time for that. I'm with Valeria Sullivan right now, talking work, dreams, my future.

If I'd gotten advice for this meeting/interview, I would've been advised against this more than anything else. But it's not enough that Valeria remembers my name and my lock screen and that I'm bi. Yes, I've neglected my art, but my art was once my whole life. I want it to be my whole life again. It's my hook.

"I would never make you watch a reel, but I'd be honored if you looked at some of my work. Your directorial debut sounds so exciting, and I'm sure you have a great eye too."

And I swear Valeria Sullivan blushes because of what I just said. "Yeah, I'd love to."

I open my cinematography folder on my phone and hand it over. Our hands don't touch, but for a moment I just watch as her slender fingers wrap around my phone case, as bits of her fingerprints plant onto my screen. My photos reflect off her dark eyes as little blots of color. It's a beautiful shot in and of itself. My heart hammers in my chest.

"Do you have any favorite female cinematographers?" Valeria asks, her voice airy again, almost far away. Like she's barely aware she's speaking.

I take a deep breath. "Rachel Morrison, Charlotte Bruus Christensen, Ellen Kuras, Iris Ng."

She looks up from the photos. There's a smile on her open mouth, like she's somewhere between beaming and perplexed by what she's seeing. Ready to say something but it keeps slipping away. It's an expression I've never seen her use in film. It's almost . . . giddy, childlike.

"Are these all L.A.?" she asks.

"Yep. With film school, you don't go much past L.A."

She zooms in on one image, but I can't see what it is from my angle. "This doesn't even look like L.A. It's got this mood that feels almost otherworldly. You're, what, early twenties and already have this point of view? I could hardly operate a new iPhone at your age."

I laugh. "I'm twenty-four, and I hope you've figured it out since."

Valeria just shakes her head. Takes the résumé back with a flourish. The air from the movement puts the fine hairs on my arm on end. "U.S.C. Okay, so good education."

"I have some of my shorts on Vimeo. They were all supposed to be like three minutes, so . . ."

Valeria takes out a pen and hands me back my résumé. "If it's password protected."

I raise my brows as I write down the name and the password. "Right. You guys do the locked thing for audition tapes."

I slide the résumé back to Valeria. She smiles. I smile back, my insides positively on fire. I must be dreaming. There's no way that shitty white male move actually worked. There's no way Valeria just saw some of my photography and asked to see a video. This is too—

And for a moment, I think we both forget what we were here for.

Valeria looks up first, her mouth forming an *O*. "Shit, we were supposed to talk about a personal assistant gig, weren't we?"

She chuckles, and I follow suit. "I think so."

"I really don't want to subject you to it. *I'd* hate being my personal assistant."

A bolt of cold goes through me. This meeting wasn't about showing my art. It was showing my art to get Valeria to remember me, so she'll hire me as a personal assistant, so we can get close and hook up and maybe fall in love or whatever.

"Really, I'm sure your life is super interesting. Even just watching you on set when your movie starts filming would be incredible."

"Your talent is so wasted . . ." She takes a long sip of her drink. "I'll get back to you."

Suddenly even more clarity falls upon me, the part when I said I'd stay with Alice for another year, when I'm pissed at Wyatt. "Could you contact me directly? I just—I don't want Alice to get the news before I can tell her, you know? And the office is so gossipy."

Valeria's eyebrows raise and she pushes the résumé back to me. "Yeah, go ahead."

I write down my personal email and draw a smiley face for no reason.

When I look back up at Valeria, she's frowning. "Are you doing okay, by the way? I got the impression you hadn't told Alice about your sexuality."

My whole face goes hot. It's as though Valeria has stumbled upon a picture I'd saved of her in that first frenzy of obsession. "Yeah, I'm doing okay. Thanks for asking."

She runs a hand through her hair. "Sorry I disappeared. I just—" She licks her lips, and the image sears itself into my memory. "It was messed up and I'm sorry it happened. If it is still a secret, it's safe with me."

Her words are like being lowered into a warm bath on a cold night—safe, secure, at a distance from the chaos around us. Like the walls in this café have fallen away and the only things that exist are Valeria, me, this table, the résumé, and the two steaming coffee cups.

But I can't express that kind of gratitude. All I can do is smile.

"I don't know who you'd tell anyway," I say.

She gives me a look. "Accept my attempt to apologize for my manager, please."

I take a faux deep breath. "Okay, fine."

We say good night with nothing but smiles and handshakes.

Her hand is soft, her grip tight and strong. She has a vein that's raised on the back of her hand, like the kind my brother, Noam, gets when he goes on his gym sprees.

Driving home, I wonder if she has any other veins like that.

It leaves me confident, in an almost spiritual *I believe in signs* way, that I got the gig. That we really connected.

Which only makes it harder when, that Half-Day Friday morning, Wyatt emails me:

You didn't get the job. :(I'm so sorry!!! Hope you're feeling better pls tell me when we can talk :(:(

chapter seven

In the wake of Wyatt's lack of apology and the failure on the job front, Romy and I end up spending the remainder of our Half-Day Friday in WeHo over at the Pleasure Chest, which, yes, is an adult entertainment/sex shop, and yes, we regularly do this for cheap fun, but when you both hate clubs there's only so much to do.

Despite its unassuming facade—nothing but palm trees and a neon sign—the place is a frickin' L.A. landmark. You just won't get it on the TMZ tour.

"You know, with the ebb and flow of traffic, we're going to have to stay here for hours," I say as we open the double doors.

Romy shrugs. "We can just go to Barney's Beanery after and look for some ghosts."

She has a serious thing for ghosts, like she studies hauntings and reads books and everything. She claims it's gay culture, and I don't know if she's joking or not. Either way, she loves urban legends, and I love the patty melts that kitschy burger joint serves, so it works.

"A very incongruent set of activities."

"*Incongruent* was incongruent in your sentence."

"Hey, y'all," Quinn, one of the very cool and very queer employees of this fine establishment, says as we enter the doors. She taps her hand on the counter, indicating that yes, even if she knows we're over eighteen, we have to pull out some I.D.

"Hey, Quinn," Romy says. "Anything new on the horizon?"

"We're doing some B.D.S.M. classes this month if you're interested."

Heat prickles around my ears as they talk about sex even for the briefest moment. It's so overdramatic, I know, but it feels like every time sex is brought up, I'm outside a home and forced to look in the windows. I've been trying to get in the door for what feels like years, and it's like it just keeps getting heavier the older I get.

"Nah, but thanks for letting me know," Romy says.

Romy grabs my hand, jolting me out of my misery bubble with a shock. Yeah, we've held hands before, but in the context of this queer platonic friendship we have, it's still like my body thinks it's a new sign to interpret.

There's a curtain separating the front room from the back, and once it's pulled back, it's like entering another world. The showroom itself is huge, with displays lined up like a museum. On the back wall is every kind of vibrator, and the right wall has a glass case of the really expensive shit. There are dildos displayed for tactile demonstrations, harnesses behind that, and B.D.S.M. masks and whips in the left corner. There's even a display bed where you can try out one of the hammocks. It's like Sex Toys "R" Us (R.I.P.).

"You need a new vibrator, right?" Romy says.

I flush. "I don't need a new one, I just said my Lelo broke."

Romy's eyes widen. "How did your designer vibrator break?"

Hot tip: Don't buy fucking expensive vibrators because they all break, and why spend $130 of well-earned cash when you can spend $30?

"It said it was waterproof and it lied."

"Sue them."

"Obviously."

I follow Romy to the novelty section, where she immediately plucks out a box that advertises vibrating panties. Just the sight sends a pang to my heart. When we dragged Wyatt here, this was the only item he said he'd ever consider buying after Romy and I foisted anal beads and Fleshlights on him for nearly an hour. Needless to say, if Wyatt and I had had sex, I know it probably would've been a lot of missionary. Maybe I'd get to go on top once a week to spice things up. It should make me feel better, but it never does.

Breaking up with him led me back here, standing in a sex store where there's only ever one section I need to go to, even when I want to be here with someone else, buying everything else. Sometimes I miss the possibilities I had in those three weeks Wyatt and I were together.

But mostly I miss Wyatt himself. Wyatt and his alarming straight-boy ways.

"I feel like this is the kind of thing two friends would jokingly buy for each other, and then it would lead to them having sex in their car," Romy says.

I dig my hands into my pockets. "Yeah, I can see that."

Although I don't need to think about that.

Even if there is something exciting about it.

Maybe not in a super-public place where you could hear mechanical whirring. Maybe a movie theater or a bar—

"Should we get it?" Romy asks, waving the package.

It's a little like what I imagine being tased is like, that shock. Is she—no, she has to be—

She starts laughing. "Roth, I'm joking!"

I turn bright red as Romy puts the panties back. Bright red because I feel so gullible. Bright red as I fail to send away the little burning pit in my stomach her comment ignited.

I turn to the dildo display, the smoothest pivot I can think of in a store filled with nonplatonic items. "Hey, Rom?"

She turns away from another novelty vibrator. "Yeah?"

"How do sapphics have sex? Like with men and women and men and men it's kinda obvious. Is there a home run?"

Romy makes a face and walks over to the dildo section. I scurry behind her. "So . . . sort of. Sex is seen less as events in a sequence and more as an overall collection of activities. Like yeah, kissing and boob touching all come first, but beyond that, dry humping can be sex, fingering can be sex, oral can be sex. It's just the pursuit of orgasms and connection." Her gaze falls on a harness. "But there are also activities that mimic penetration, which isn't, like, the top of the line or anything—some couples never pull on a strap—but if you want to be penetrated by a not-cis dude for your little 'virginity' quest . . ."

"But that wouldn't be having sex with a guy."

Romy shrugs. "You could say you've been penetrated, which appears to be your idea of sex." She shakes her head. "I'm not giving you good advice. Seriously, if your partner gives you an orgasm, you've had sex in the sapphic world."

I chew on my lip as Romy pulls a harness off the display. "But if that's the definition of sex, then have I already lost my virginity to a guy?"

In my handful of dating experiences, I've been fingered, been eaten out, given one or two blow jobs. No one's made me come, but that's another story.

Romy feeds a rainbow dildo into the harness. "If you wanna follow queer-girl logic, then you haven't, because you've never had an orgasm. Honestly, the emphasis on penetration is ridiculous, and why should one set of lovers have to do more or less to achieve the same idea of experience? Like I said, virginity is a ridiculous concept."

Romy tosses me the strap-on.

"But penetration can be a part of sapphic sex," I say.

"Yeah, but you'd never want to instill an idea that a penis-shaped thing has to enter a partner's vagina for sex to have occurred. Like how straight men don't lose some new virginity if they get pegged. Also, the pursuit of orgasm should be enough, so you know what? Yes, you're not a virgin, even though you haven't come. There are *so many layers.*"

Already I have no idea what Romy is talking about. Am I supposed to be thinking about *philosophy* when talking about sex?

I know I'm at square one with Valeria and that it's not gonna happen, but I can't help but hold this thing and wonder what I even want out of any potential encounter we have. Do I just want to kiss her? Touch her? Exchange orgasms? And then there's this thing.

"Is there any advantage to a strap?"

"Don't get me wrong, dude. I own one and love it, and a lot of my partners have loved it too."

My stomach flips at her words. Guess I *do* know how Romy has sex after all.

"There's also, uh, a lot of blatant power play that goes into it." Romy eyes me, a smile forming on her face. "Which—not gonna psychoanalyze you—but I bet is a *little* of the appeal with Valeria." She shrugs. "Like, *I'd* want to be topped like that by someone like her."

I frown. "Not that that's even a remote possibility."

Now or ever. Although I do like the idea of a strap; it kind of combines the experience of a home run with queerness. It feels tangible, comforting to think about doing one day. Like if I had *that* experience under my belt, I'd know what Rain and Jared and even Romy and Wyatt are talking about when they talk sex, no follow-up questions needed.

Romy's off the subject, though.

"I don't think you would've liked being a personal assistant," she says. "The dynamic would've been way off anyway."

My phone goes off. A text from Wyatt. A long text.

> Hi so I was emailing back and forth with Valeria to set up her last set of meetings next week and she got me thinking. I get it. I'm so, so sorry about outing you to try to get you that job. I know you know I had good intentions but it doesn't dismiss the harm I did to you. I'm so sorry. I hope that you can forgive me and we can be friends again. For real, Valeria LIKES you. I don't think losing this job is the end, although I'll admit I don't have any other ideas.

After reading, I hand my phone to Romy.

"So the boy wants out of the doghouse," she says.

I sigh. "An apology is all I wanted." I'm relieved, and then I think about the rest of the text. "Do you think he's right about Valeria?"

"So she only needed a new personal assistant because of the shoot, right?" As Romy speaks, she's running her hands along the dildo. I don't know if it's worth commenting on. "But it's a film shoot. There are so many stupid jobs on even an indie film. It just doesn't seem like . . ."

Valeria's the director on an indie film. There are menial jobs on an indie film. I'd been unwilling to seek out entry-level jobs before because you have to establish your clout with someone who may never make it in the industry anyway and I wasn't mentally prepared to take that leap. But this is an indie film with an A-lister as the director. A director who has seen my work and likes it. Maybe I did gain a little sleaze from Alice.

"Why am I not just asking to be a P.A.?" I say to Romy.

A smile forms on Romy's face. "I dunno, Luna. Why aren't you?"

Now that I'm talking to Wyatt and he's officially on Team Getting Valeria to Like Me, I learn that Valeria's last meeting at the office is set up for Tuesday morning. So despite the fact that it'll make no difference, I wake up at god knows what hour, do my makeup and hair, put on my best business-smart attire, and caffeinate with herbal tea instead of coffee in the hopes of no jitters. I didn't even try this hard on dates with guys I *really* liked, so go figure.

Alice isn't in when I arrive, but thank god Wyatt is. There's a softness in his posture when he turns to me, like he's relieved our issues are resolved. I can't say I'm completely healed. It feels more like one of those forgive-but-trust-differently situations than anything else. And yeah, I need him.

"I just need a minute to ask her about P.A. gigs," I tell him. "And *I* need to ask, not you."

"Got it. Let me know if you don't catch her. She usually debriefs before heading out. Noon at the latest."

Noon. Got it.

"Sounds good." I force a deep breath. "Thank you."

"Of course. Good luck."

I speed through emails for Alice, sending them into the ether with such swiftness I know I've achieved a level of nirvana where email anxiety ceases to exist. Clients email me back with phrases like *OMG thank you for answering so quickly!!!!* Alice and I roll calls remotely while she drives her Tesla, the one I had to get serviced once, probably emailing clients as she drives, like usual. I'm on fire, basically. Best I've performed in months.

Still, it's Valeria who arrives first. She's in a muted outfit, physical notes in hand. Once again she's leaning against the wall waiting for Steven. My palms sweat just seeing her.

"Good luck today," I murmur, instead of, say, any standard greeting in American English.

Valeria looks up from her notes and smiles. "Thanks." Her gaze travels up and down my body, sending shivers through me. "The tweed is really cute. Is there color on the inside?"

I pull out the side of my blazer; it's lavender. "Guess there is."

"It's a great piece."

I blush. "Thank you." Steven could call her in at any moment. She's here, not for long enough to hear me out, but long enough for me to set the intention. Act like a white guy would. "Hey, Valeria?"

"Yeah?"

"Do you have a minute after your meetings to talk? I just wanted to ask you something."

She shifts her notes. "Yeah, for sure. I just—"

Alice comes in before Steven opens his office door. "Luna, you know we have John coming in today, right?"

I glance at Alice's calendar. "Yes."

"Take care of him. He just booked a franchise directing spot and I need to keep him happy." She disappears into her office.

I can only watch as Steven opens his door and Valeria slips in. No matter. John won't be a problem. I need to give him, like, five minutes' worth of attention.

Wyatt turns to me once our bosses' doors are shut. "Why does Alice want you to be so nice to her client when he's actually happy?"

I shrug. "She thinks clients will leave her for one of the big-name companies once they get good gigs."

He frowns. "That's . . . paranoid. Usually Steven butters up his clients only when he forgets to update them for like a month."

"Go figure."

Back to emailing.

"Dare I sense confidence with Alice?"

I smile, barely. "Just have other stuff on my mind today."

"It's gonna be fine." His fingers twitch, like he considered grabbing my hand but decided against it. "Great. It's gonna be great."

Wyatt brings another guest into Steven's office five minutes later, presumedly some investor or higher-level creative for Valeria's movie. Most meetings last an hour. John's due here in two hours. It should work out perfectly.

The hour passes. Valeria and the investor (Wyatt was happy to inform me) remain in Steven's office. I keep doing my work for Alice. She doesn't yell about anything.

The investor walks out a half hour later.

I do my work for Alice. Ten minutes with Valeria still inside Steven's office turns to twenty. Twenty to twenty-five.

My phone goes off. It sounds shriller than normal. My heart beats in my ears as I answer it.

"John Harrington is downstairs," Kiki says.

"Thanks, Kiki," I reply.

I glance at Steven's door.

And Steven's office door opens, Valeria's hand wrapped around the side.

My heart rises to my throat. "Wyatt . . ."

Wyatt turns to me. "I can get John. Tell Valeria I went to the bathroom."

"Tell John ditto."

Relief washes over me, but it doesn't quite dissipate as Wyatt disappears downstairs and Valeria emerges from Steven's office.

"Wyatt went to the bathroom," I say once the door shuts behind her.

Valeria nods. "Cool. Steven just sent something to the printer, and I should be good . . ."

I jump up from my seat. "I can get it."

She glances at the leather-strapped watch on her wrist. "Let me come with you. You wanted to talk, right?"

"Yeah." I want to rub the back of my neck or fidget with my jacket, but I resist. Barely. "Let's go."

I swallow and take another deep breath. My stomach's starting to just plain hurt. Maybe this is how ulcers start. I'm certainly old enough for them now.

"So what's up?" Valeria says.

This close to her, a whiff of her perfume hits me. It's floral, sort of regal, with these notes of rose and orange and expensive, which, yes, you can smell. I'd guess Chanel. The scent is bracing and pleasant, but it makes me wonder what she smells like when she's not impressing people.

"So I was just wondering . . . I know you said I'd be wasted as a personal assistant"—she winces—"and honestly I get why I was passed up. I didn't even have qualifications. But . . ." I swallow again. "I was just thinking that if you happen to need an extra production assistant, I'd be honored to be considered."

I'm sure my face is bright red right now, and honestly, I'd love to grab her paper from the printer and run so far from this building that I end up in the ocean and swim to Japan. Or go back in time and tell the version of myself from ten seconds ago to shut up.

But I'm here in my shoes. I did a white-boy confidence move. Now it's time to fake the white-boy confidence.

There's one piece of paper sitting alone in the industrial printer. I'm guessing it's Valeria's. Valeria, who still hasn't spoken, who is driving me to pull my hair out with this—this fucking ability of hers to just not emote while thinking. How does *that* help her act?

"I think my producer said we filled the P.A. positions, but I'll check," Valeria finally says.

Usually anything that isn't *yes* isn't good. But she hasn't run out of the room yet.

I hand her the piece of paper, unable to hold back a smile. "Thank you so much. You have no idea what this means."

She finally smiles. "Don't thank me yet. I made a huge deal about paying all the P.A.s above minimum wage, and everyone's a stickler for a tight budget, but one of my best friends is an E.P., so . . ." She winks; I force myself to stay upright. She glances at the paper. "And thank you for this."

"Yeah, of course."

The world almost seems stable as Valeria and I walk back to the assistant pod.

That is, until I see Alice standing outside her office, arms crossed. Wyatt's back at his desk, typing. His eyes are heavy on the screen.

"I'm sorry, Luna, is something more pressing?" Alice asks me. "I forgot I share you with Steven."

Valeria, looking more like a deer caught in headlights than I think I even do, turns to Wyatt. Wyatt mouths, *Talk later*, and shoos her out. She mouths something to me before she steps down the stairs, but I can't make it out. The room has seemingly tilted.

I glance at Alice's closed office door as the heat falls over my face. "Wyatt's printer connection was down so I was just—"

"And John's latte? Have you gotten that?"

I glance at Wyatt's desk, where a coffee is sitting, still steaming. I pick it up and am halfway to handing it to her when she gives me the deadliest death glare. My muscles freeze.

"He gets a latte from the café. You know this," Alice says, her voice wavering.

"I'm sorry," I say as I scurry back to my desk. "I asked Wyatt to get the coffee while I worked on the printing thing. I can get—"

"And why did Steven's assistant get this? What're you off doing, huh? Bothering someone else's clients?" Alice strides across the space between us, stopping two feet from my face. She's so close, I can see the way her lipstick doesn't quite follow the curve of her lips, the red in the whites of her eyes. "Steven's assistant works for Steven. You work for me, and I needed a simple latte for a major client. And you couldn't even do that."

My chest is collapsing on me; the room is going fuzzy at the edges. I know I deserve this. (Even though Alice has told me to give John regular coffee before and he didn't care. He literally doesn't care about any of this.) But I can't have Alice this close. Her anger is palpable, turning the air to steam. It's choking me. This whole fucking place is choking me.

I move to get up.

"I'll get him his latte right now," I say.

"*No, sit down!*" she yells.

My heart stops. Every pair of eyes in the assistant pod looks to me. Not in confusion; not like what happened when Wyatt outed me. They look at me with pity, with self-satisfaction. The Hollywood look of *Glad I'm not stupid like her.*

I drop into my seat.

"I've given you so many chances," she says, gesturing wildly. "You have no idea. I can't run with an assistant who can't keep up. And look, you're not built for this. But I can't be your fucking babysitter."

The tears burn in my eyes before I realize they're even welling up. It's like holding water about to spill out of a cup. I'm not sure if I can keep it together. This makeup isn't waterproof either.

"Alice, I can—"

"I should fire you."

The moment flows like molasses. A log stuck in a roaring river, stopping everything in its path.

She wants to fire me? After months of catering to her, fulfilling her unreasonable requests, and being the most easygoing assistant on the planet? All because Wyatt got John the wrong coffee? We were on fire this morning. Alice said I was a great assistant last week. Alice said women have to look out for each other in

Hollywood. She has a *fucking pride decal on her office window because of me*. And she still looks indignant. Like I've said something that's shattering *her* world.

"I'm not the bad guy here," Alice continues. "I tried to help you. All I want is for gay kids to make it in Hollywood. But some—"

She pinches her nose. Her too-thin, Beverly Hills–made nose. Her cerulean-blue eyes that are still hugged by stress-induced crow's-feet that even the best plastic surgery can't get rid of. There would be no blurriness if I were framing this. No tricks. A simple 4K close-up reaction shot with our too-bright light to show off every fucking fake detail on Alice Dadamo's fucking face.

I'm done.

Tears have already fallen down my cheeks, and I'm so done.

I get up out of my seat. Grab my purse. "I'm bi, and I quit."

And that's that.

Alice might have eventually regretted what she said and rehired me, but I've killed that opportunity. I've killed every opportunity, and I have to pay rent.

The only place I have left to go in this hell building is the bathroom.

It's empty when I slam the door open. The sound echoes off the hollow walls, the hard floor, and the mirrored wall. I force breaths, dropping onto the sink as the room spins. For a moment, I just clutch the edges of the porcelain. The tears have fallen, but I can't start sobbing here. I have to make it to my car, at least. Preserve a shred of my dignity.

The hinge on the door whines as someone enters.

Valeria's image plays against the mirror, her figure behind me. I turn around, all raccoon makeup and tear-streaked cheeks.

"Please tell me you didn't see that," I say, choking out a sort of strangled laugh.

She smiles softly. "This business is hell, but your boss seems like an asshole."

The whole moment feels like something out of a dream, down to the oversaturated lighting and the distinct lack of witnesses.

I sigh and work to wipe my eyes with a paper towel. It doesn't fix much. "You really don't—"

"Do you want a job?" She runs her hand through her hair in the mirror.

I must be dreaming right now. It's the only explanation. I wouldn't quit. Valeria Sullivan wouldn't offer me a job.

"What?"

She turns to me head-on before she speaks again. "A job. A P.A. job. Like you asked me. I called my line producer, and he said if I moved a set P.A. to the office, then I could hire another set P.A. You wanted the job, didn't you?" She smiles. "Besides, I don't want to waste your talent."

"I'm not that—"

"We're calling it a P.A. gig, but the production is small. My D.P. especially needs an assistant. He's pretty fresh himself, and I'm sure he'd love a P.A. dedicated to his unit."

I blink a few times. This sounds like Valeria, looks like Valeria. The Chanel smell, the trimmed nails, the Grace Kelly blond hair, the dark eyes. It's all her. I'm pinching myself, and I feel the pain. I'm here. Unless this is a huge hallucination, I'm here.

Valeria just offered me a job helping a real D.P. "You're serious, aren't you?" Even my voice sounds like me, but it's like I'm watching this happen. Like I'm on a set.

Valeria laughs. "Yes, I'm really serious. Do you want the job?"

Even if this is a dream, I know what the right answer is. And the beaming smile spreading across my lips feels real.

"Absolutely," I say.

chapter eight

When I wake up on Saturday, I think I have to return to Alice on Monday for only five seconds before I remember what happened. Valeria's shoot starts in a few weeks, which leaves me with actual significant time to do nothing. The possibilities are both endless and very simple. With Wyatt mostly at work, I can hang out with Romy more during the day since her shifts aren't as long as mine used to be. I can attempt to reach out to other film school grads I was friends with who're also unemployed. I can read this script Valeria sent me and work through potential visuals. Not that I'm really gonna get the chance—I'll likely just be fetching lenses for Brendan, the actual D.P.—but it might be worth doing a little homework. And finding some way to thank Romy for putting up with me the past couple of weeks seems in order too.

The script is read by nine a.m., and slutty brownie ingredients are spread across my parents' kitchen by ten a.m. (They have a better oven, and their kitchen is best for surprise effectiveness for Romy.) The script, currently titled *Oakley in Flames*, is really cool. It's an L.A.-noir-type piece in which the protagonist is a queer bartender in a WeHo male strip club where one of the strippers goes missing. Super moody and atmospheric, but ultimately a very found family story with a happy ending. Lots of big names involved, including the now box office hit *Goodbye, Richard!*'s director Mason Wu as an E.P. and buzzy genre staple Charlie Durst as the male stripper who disappears. Based on interviews Valeria has done with each of them, they're *actually* her friends. Every detail I learn gets my heart racing in excitement. This movie might be a big deal. I *have a job* on a movie that might be a big deal.

There's also a particularly interesting pursuit/fight scene that takes place in a moderately wealthy L.A. home during the day. It's obviously easy to accomplish chaos and surprise with a night setting, so the timing feels like a very deliberate decision the screenwriter made.

Noam walks into my parents' living room, wearing pajama pants but no shirt to show off his six-pack. Never mind that it's currently being devoured by beer every weekend. "You're making those for us, right?"

He doesn't mean to, but Noam brings me back down to earth. I might be a part of this huge movie, but right now I'm in my parents' home wincing every time I see someone.

I came home a fair amount during college, but lately, every visit back is just a reminder of how much more functional the whole family is when I'm here as a guest. My parents can keep the house cleaner without my shoes accidentally left in the living room, they turned my bedroom into the neutral-tone guest room they always wanted, and even Noam seems more relaxed without us bickering from the moment we wake up every morning.

I glance at my made-from-scratch fudge brownie batter. "No."

Noam frowns, stuffing his hands into his pajama pockets. His pants sag under the weight, and I make a mental note to keep my eyes elevated because I'm sure his ass crack is currently out. "Good. Because Mom banned carbs from the house."

"I know. I can see the lack of carbs."

"She's gonna be mad." He says it with such a lack of enthusiasm that it's almost comical. Neither of us is winning any child-of-the-year awards. "I'm gonna put on a mov—"

"Can you fall down the stairs while I film you?" I ask.

Noam stops everything he's doing to blank-face stare at me. "Why would I agree to that?"

I glance at my mix. "I'll give you a tray of these."

He pauses, considering. "Why?"

"I want to play with too-bright lighting to show discombobulation."

"I don't know what that means." He pauses again. "Why?"

He wants to be an engineer, so neither of us understands half of what the other is saying. And that's on a good day.

Butterflies float through my stomach as I spoon the cookie dough into tray number one. "I got a job on the movie Valeria Sullivan is directing."

Noam blinks slowly. "She's the chick in that western movie that just came out, right?"

"Yeah."

He sniffs. "Cool. She's pretty hot."

"Yeah."

Cookie dough ceases to be scooped in the pan. The A/C flowing through the house stops. I think my heart stops too. I can't believe I just said that Valeria is hot.

Noam blinks a few times. "What?"

I put the cookie dough aside and lay down the Oreos. "So will you do the stairs thing?"

Noam reaches over and steals an Oreo. Easy to do when you

have giant hands. "Will anyone see it? Will Valeria Sullivan see it? I don't need people seeing me in that state."

Slowly, slowly, the gay panic subsides.

I sigh. "I'm testing out a lighting technique. No one will ever see it."

Except, yeah, if prompted I'd 100 percent show Valeria and Brendan the D.P. And Romy and Wyatt if it's funny enough.

"I want the first tray out," Noam says. "And you're gonna end up a weird perfectionist endangering your actors like Tarantino."

I give a wry smile. "Thanks, Noh." I pour the brownie batter over the layer of Oreos.

"Did you get fired from your job with the crazy lady, or are we just not gonna talk about that?"

My stomach pinches at the mention. "I quit for this P.A. job."

"Isn't that only temporary?"

Can't he shut the fuck up? "Valeria's mentoring me."

"That sounds fake."

First tray in the oven, and now I can focus on my camera and the script open on my laptop. "Go get on the stairs, ya little asshole."

Noam sighs. "If I die, don't come to my funeral."

I set the camera up on a tripod facing the stairs and open every window in the house. Grab every lamp I can carry and set them up facing the stairs. Noam clambers up and waits at the top, out of frame.

"Rolling," I say as I press RECORD. "Action!"

Noam does the slowest fucking roll down our stairs I've ever seen, landing in a heap at the bottom. I kill the video. Play it back.

Noam's roll looks stupid, and the light is just light—kind of oversaturated. It's hard to look at, but it doesn't quite *say* anything. Maybe a different angle?

"Thanks. Don't leave."

He huffs like the whiny little shit he is, plopping onto the living room couch and turning on the Apple TV. The brownies are still cooking.

We have a window that's at eye level with the top of the stairs. The light coming through it is painfully bright, so much so that I actively avoid looking at it while going down the stairs. But what if someone was fighting and running through a house and accidentally looked at the sun through a window like this? Use those dots you get to heighten the panic and the discombobulation.

I climb up the stairs and get a shot of the sun peeking through the window. I pull back from the shot once STOP is pressed, blinking away the colored splotches from my eyes. It'd obviously be too much to put the color splotches in prominently and do a bunch of P.O.V. shots, but maybe just one shot, when the main character is lying at the bottom of the stairs and the pursuer approaches. That could be good.

I step down the stairs, get on the floor with the camera.

"What are you doing?" Noam asks.

"Come climb toward me and reach for me."

He huffs again, and I'm getting close to hitting him with the brownie tray instead of giving it to him.

I press RECORD, and Noam does his little menacing walk. I reverse the focus as he gets closer, the background in focus but Noam more of a shadowy figure. When I press STOP, Noam's nearly grabbing my arm.

"Great, thanks," I say.

I can add the color in post, and shit, it might be cool.

"Yeah, please just tell me when the brownies are done." He walks back to the couch, pausing before he reaches it. "Are you even allowed to touch the camera during this shoot?"

Heat goes to my ears, but I ignore it. "I'm just playing around right now. It's exciting."

"No offense, but you sound delusional."

"And you're gonna live a boring life and die alone when your wife leaves you on the off chance her female assistant will go for her. The kids will all prefer their stepmom to you."

"That is a *low blow.*"

Noam's high school girlfriend dumped him and has been dating women ever since. As if I need another reason to not tell my family. I'd be more inclined to come out to her than I would to my own brother. It's a weird feeling.

I remove the brownie tray, and Noam descends on it like a vulture. To the tune of him yelling, "Hot-hot-hot!" I upload the video clips to start editing.

I know I won't be touching the camera on this job, but I can't help but feel grateful Valeria's breathed some creative life back into me. I'd almost forgotten how happy filming makes me.

All that's left to do is see what else Valeria and I can do for each other.

chapter nine

It's a scorching day in Century City when we start filming. The kind of morning when you look at the weather app and the first thing out of your mouth is *Fuck*. I spend a half hour accepting the dire reality that I cannot impress Valeria with my looks without dying. Then again, maybe my sensible outfit will indicate my other positive traits, like diligence and not being a complete dumbass. Good Darwinian traits, which play into attraction.

Our first location is on the Fox backlot, which is cooler than I care to admit, because given the Disney acquisition, it's likely going to be sold and torn down to make way for condominiums like everything else even slightly cool in L.A. Productions shot at the lot include oldies like the '60s *Batman* show (although the Bat Cave was actually filmed on location at Bronson Cave in Griffith Park), the original *The Fly* (so not the hot Jeff Goldblum one), the 1967 Academy Award–nominated *Doctor Dolittle* (that I had to read about in a terrible film class I got a B– in), *Die Hard* (although the destruction scenes were done at the Fox Plaza on the unfinished thirty-third and thirty-fourth floors), and, of course, *Ted 2* (which I have no plans to ever see). The whole lot is a little like my maternal grandpa, who has amazing stories if I ever sit down to talk to him but mostly watches golf when I'm over.

Still, there's no beating the *thrill* of being handed passes and getting the thumbs-up to enter the labyrinth of the studio. Even the physical relief of going from wiping the sweat forming between a Freddy Krueger sweater–patterned baseball cap and my hairline to a building so cold the fine hairs on my arms are up is a thrill.

A pit grows in my stomach the moment I'm inside the air-conditioned location, though. The production isn't huge, but there are still several dozen people running around, laser focused and clearly not interested in stopping to tell me where I'm supposed to be. It's like I'm standing here in my underwear.

One seemingly fellow P.A. holding a clipboard approaches me. She doesn't even look me in the eye. Just looks right to the badge hanging off my neck.

"Luna Roth." She glances elsewhere, I'm not sure at what. "Check in with Frank every morning, but otherwise just go directly to Brendan."

I gotta say, I don't know who Frank is or how I'd locate him in the future, but hearing Brendan's name again gives me a prickle of warmth.

She pulls out her phone, gives it one glance, then looks back at me. "You're going right to Brendan today. He should be over by the blue marker over there."

I spot the blue marker. I thank the P.A., who didn't even introduce herself to me, but cool, it's the first day, I'm sure everyone's balls to the wall. I head over to the blue marker and nearly walk right into Valeria.

For the first time, I get a glimpse of out-of-the-office Valeria.

Or, well, costume Valeria. Dark makeup, a form-fitting dress, heels three inches taller than I've seen on her hanging out of her hands as she walks around barefoot. There's still an immediate smile on her face when she sees me, though. A smile that grounds me, takes the chaos out of focus until there's nothing but her and a blurred background behind her.

"Just the person I wanted to see," Valeria says. "Brendan, get over here!"

I shake out of my laser focus just in time for an Asian man in his thirties to jog up to Valeria. He's got a decidedly modern haircut, some fade pompadour style with lots of waves and volume up top. A single silver ring hangs out of his left ear.

"Hey," Brendan says, holding out his hand. We shake. His hands are calloused, more than a normal D.P.'s. I wonder what sport he does to get those. "I'm Brendan."

"Luna," I say back. "Thank you for the opportunity."

"Course." His voice is deep, almost gravelly. "So, as I'm sure our mad leader"—he motions to Valeria with his chin—"has explained, with her starring and directing, the hierarchy is a little wacky. This production is obviously small, so I'm D.P., operator, and first A.C., which is fine and all, but when this one has to be particularly focused on acting, the A.D. will be stepping up to director work to call shots and I may have to be away from A.C. duties. You went to U.S.C., right?"

I nod. "Production."

Brendan runs a hand through his hair. "Great. Work well as a camera P.A. and I may let you do some A.C. work. Cool?"

First camera assistant. I could prove enough to this young, fresh D.P. to get to do *camera assistant* work on a film that has a better chance than not of getting distributed. "Absolutely."

"Awesome. Today's mostly gonna be slating. Show me you're

useful and, well . . ." He smiles. "I'm trying to stick with A.C.s and P.A.s who I can bring with me to my next indie, so this could become a more permanent relationship. Hear me?"

I've operated a slate before. Obviously when I was in film school, I'd been the first A.C., the camera operator, the D.P., the A.D., the director. But shit, this is a real film set. This is a legit fucking camera, and if I play my cards right, Brendan might let me operate it. Hell, if I play my cards right, *I could go work on another indie after this*. I have to get to pull focus on this set. Brendan's the mentor I wanted Alice to hook me up with in the flesh. It's so wild. I have no idea why I wasn't on the Production Route to begin with.

I catch Valeria's gaze as she talks to someone else. She throws me a smile. My stomach flips, and the butterflies soar inside me.

"I hear you."

The first scene we're shooting is on a bar set, the lighting dim.

"I want the darkness of the bar to reflect a certain amount of relief," Valeria says to Brendan. "Like how being in a Forever 21 is migraine inducing from the lights, so it's this huge relief to go back outside and be somewhere less abrasive."

It gets my heart beating hard. Maybe she'd even *want* to hear my ideas for that staircase scene. And if Brendan likes them, I'd have to stand out to him.

Brendan chews his inner cheek. "But not *specifically* the artifice?"

"No, just the relief. I want there to be an . . . unexpected contrast. Like how"—Valeria looks to me—"cars usually feel safe, and unfiltered darkness once you get out of a car is perceived as dangerous. But if you were, like, in an Uber with a creepy driver, the outside darkness of arriving at the club is good. Opposite than expected."

Brendan snaps his fingers. "Yeah, I get what you mean. Got it." He turns to me. "Can you grab the twenty-four millimeter?"

I fetch it out of Brendan's equipment, and he clicks it into place and sets up the scene, then hands me a slate and the script. We're starting with scene twenty, where Valeria's character rushes into the strip club after hours.

The first A.D., a middle-aged woman, steps up to the scene. "Quiet on set! Roll sound."

The sound recordist sets up. "Speeding."

My heart soars in my chest. This is real. Jesus, this is real.

"Roll camera."

Brendan stands next to the camera. "Rolling."

My heart's soaring, but now it's speeding up. I seek out Valeria automatically, but she's in acting mode. "Scene twenty, take one."

"Action!" the first A.D. says.

And Valeria does her take. Bursts into the bar set and acts a full repressed panic moment. Panic moment shifting into a sense of calm.

"Cut!" the first A.D. calls.

Valeria jumps up on the fake bar. "How's it looking? I feel like we need another take."

The A.D. exchanges a glance with Brendan. "Yeah, let's go again."

I pick up the slate and write *TAKE TWO*, only for someone to tap me on the back.

It's the girl I met before. I can now see her name is Ivy. "Hey, can you do a coffee run? I'll take over."

Right. That was why I didn't do the Production Route before.

But who said this would be easy?

By the end of the shoot, it's past eleven, and I've spent a majority of my hours doing general menial tasks. Which is fine. I'm not saying that it's not fine, but it's like someone opened Pandora's box for me, showed me what I *could* be doing, then yanked me back ten feet away to where I could only look at it longingly. The sole impression I made on Brendan was that I can give him the correct coffee order.

I don't even see Valeria until the very end of the day as she emerges from a makeup trailer, now decked out in a black hoodie, cutoff shorts, and sneakers. Hood up. The yellow-orange-red-blue rainbow design on the hoodie sleeves pops out immediately. Half my brain says it's just some designer loungewear riffing off '70s peace motifs, and the other half is like, *Rainbow?? Gay??*

Valeria jogs up to me and throws the hood down. "Hey, is there any leftover food from craft services?"

I glance in the general direction of catering. "Uh . . ."

"It's all good."

She digs her hands into her hoodie pockets. She's got this soft beauty about her. She has no makeup on, so I can see the previously covered shadows around her eyes, her moles, and the fade of her eyebrows as they thin out near the edges. It all adds texture to her whole look. She looks younger too. With the hoodie, she looks like someone my age, someone set to blend into the background as much as possible.

"So there's a Burger King right off the lot, and I'm guessing it's the only thing open. Wanna walk with me so we don't get murdered?"

Did Hoodie Valeria just ask me to go somewhere outside of work one-on-one? On day one? Shit, I don't think even Wyatt thought it'd go this fast.

"Really?" is my response.

"Yes." She pauses. "Granted, if you had a car, we could reduce the murder likelihood. And yes, I can drive. My car's just in the shop."

"I . . . wasn't going to assume." I exhale. "I actually Ubered, but there's no one else I'd rather be murdered with."

She throws me a cheesing smile, the seconds passing, me not getting it. The smile shifts into a smirk, an eyebrow raise.

And I get it. My face goes hot.

"I said that wrong . . ."

"Come on. Before they close too."

Valeria grabs my hand.

Valeria's bare skin touches my bare skin, and she's wrapping her fingers around my knuckles and her finger pads are smooth and her grip is loose yet clinging, like she thinks my hand is fragile but doesn't want to leave me. I don't even know how to describe it. An avalanche of good feelings, probably something scientifically akin to thousands of my dopamine receptors being rendered useless. It's dark outside, but as Valeria leads me into the night, it's as if she's a radiating light source. Or like with her by my side, the dark is no longer scary.

It feels like anything is possible.

She lets go after less than five seconds, but my hand's left tingling our whole walk to Burger King.

It's a moody Burger King. The kind of Burger King that you're certain has been open since the '70s and where there was a high-profile murder in the '80s that no one talks about. Peeling paint, lopsided decorations, a poster for an item that I saw advertised on a billboard along the 405 six months ago. But Hoodie Valeria strides in like this is her favorite place on Earth.

"I meant to say before, by the way, the contrast with the outside being a relief?" I say once I settle into the idea that I have Valeria one-on-one, no chance for interruptions. "I get that. It's like . . . when you go outside while having a panic attack and can cool down."

Valeria smiles. "Exactly!" She grimaces. "I hope Brendan got that."

"I'm sure he did."

Valeria eyes me a moment. The full up-and-down scan makes me feel both stripped down to my skin, vulnerable, and coiled up in my stomach, readying for a release I won't get right now. "You look like you came off a movie set and I look like your garbage sidekick and I love it."

The cashier is a teenager. It feels like he's not supposed to be working this late for legal reasons, and he's conspicuously on his phone. Valeria steps aside, letting me order first.

"Um . . . chicken fries. Spicy."

"Meal?"

I glance back at Valeria, as if begging for her approval on more or less food even though I'm starving. Valeria nods.

"Yeah. Um, Sprite."

I shuffle aside for Valeria.

"Whopper meal and . . ." She cranes her neck beyond the cashier, and her eyes light up like a spotlight. Like I'm talking this may be the greatest moment of her life light up. "Is that a Detective Pikachu crown?"

Yes, this is *definitely* a Burger King that is stuck in the past.

The cashier glances behind him. "I guess."

"What do I have to pay you to get it?"

I can't help but smile; Valeria's, what, one of the best working actors today, and she's going this apeshit over a Pokémon crown?

I love it.

"Um, I don't think we charge for those things . . . It's just, like . . . an extra someone found."

Valeria slaps her credit card on the counter.

"She needs a crown too."

The cashier grabs two crowns and takes the credit card, eyes glazing over the name before he goes into shock. Bug-eyed, *oh fuck what have I done?* shock.

"Oh my god, Ms.—"

Valeria shoots him a finger gun, grabs the crowns, and walks away. I follow, making awkward eye contact with the cashier, a little sympathetic. I'd also be the person who'd completely not realize that I'm talking to a celebrity.

Once we get our food, we retreat to a table in the back of the restaurant, where it's quiet enough that the chatting between the two staff members is hardly louder than a whisper.

"Do you have to be worried about being photographed when you're just out?" I ask.

Valeria makes a face. "*Steven* always wants me to be more done up on the chance, but people tend to ignore me when I look this sloppy-casual. Plus, remove all the makeup I have to wear for press and films and a lot of people can't tell."

"That's . . . kinda nice."

She shrugs. "Honestly, I just don't give a shit if someone gets a bad picture of me. I post terrible pictures of myself on Instagram every week." She sips her drink. "How was the first day?"

My leg taps from under the table. "Good. I can't believe Brendan was just down to potentially let me touch a camera."

Valeria smiles. "Small production goes pretty far. He watched your horror short and thought you had spark. Keep going the way you are, and I'm sure he'll pull you into his next picture. He's rising fast, and I'd love to see you work under him."

My leg is still tapping, but now the room seems sharper. The Whopper wrapper and the little chicken drawing on my chicken fries box are a brighter color, Valeria's voice is coming in clearer, even the smells of the greasy food are stronger. Is this what excitement feels like? "I'm—I feel like I can't say thank you enough."

"All good." She takes a sip of her drink. "Like I said, if you're happy to put in the work, I'm happy to help."

As I take a bite of chicken, I'm shaken into an out-of-body moment. We're sitting in a lull, like the day's over twelve hours of work have finally hit us. I can see it in her face, and I'm sure the same weariness is reflected back at her in my own features. We're just two people sitting in a crappy fast-food restaurant eating exceptionally crappy fast food (sorry, B.K.) because sets provide only lunch. Neither of us is wearing makeup, Valeria's got us both wearing these Burger King crowns, and it's just . . . it feels normal. It feels like I could be sitting across from Romy or Wyatt and there'd be this same lack of pressure. How can it be this easy?

What can I get her to talk about in this environment? Who is Valeria if it took only five minutes to uncover that she dresses like a teenage boy on the regular and is into Pokémon? It's almost comforting how *weird* she is. I find it endearing, but I can easily see how Steven would be at odds trying to keep Valeria's otherwise classy, intelligent, sexy persona in the forefront. I'm almost tempted to scroll through her Instagram and find a ratio for how many weird/quirky pictures she has versus model shots.

"Did you go to college or just go straight into acting?" I ask.

Valeria gives a weak chuckle. "I . . ." She shakes her head. "I was one dissertation approval away from a Ph.D. in culture, media, and creative industries at King's College."

Now okay, I could see her having gotten a bachelor's degree. Plenty of actors went to college. Hell, Natalie Portman went to Harvard.

But Valeria just said she almost got a *Ph.D.*

You have to be fucking *smart* to get a Ph.D. in anything.

"That's amazing."

She shrugs. "It was *almost* amazing."

Valeria was one step from getting a Ph.D. I can't even properly process that. I'm sitting across from someone who might as well be called "Doctor," who's intellectually on par with the various professors I encountered in undergrad. Was that what she really wanted to do? Work in academia?

"What did you study?"

"I had a focus on music and culture, and the dissertation was on the Beatles."

Now I'm the one shaking my head. "You were a legitimate Beatles scholar before acting?"

She nods. "I'm sure the twelve other Beatles scholars in the world were very angry I didn't become the thirteenth. But life happens."

I'm suddenly flashing back to freshman year. I was enrolled in this honors G.E. track, and one of the classes I took was all about the intellectual analysis of popular culture. The T.A. in that class, it'd been this guy who looked exactly like a short Warren Beatty, and I used to poke into his office hours every week so he'd explain the theorists to me. It hadn't even just been that he was cute; I could just absorb his words about theory for hours, entranced by the idea that he had so much in his head—that he *knew* all this.

That probably 99.9 percent of the population would never be able to say what he was saying.

Now I'm sitting across from someone who's in that 0.01 percent. And she's wearing a Detective Pikachu crown. "Do you have a favorite theorist?"

She shrugs. "Judith Butler is a superhero, but if we're talking specifically pop culture–type stuff, Baudrillard is my favorite. Sontag and 'camp' are also great."

These names all genuinely sound familiar, coming back to me in soft waves. "Camp is kitsch, right?"

She holds up a fry as a pointer. "Technically *camp* is the consumption or performance of culture, and *kitsch* is the work itself. But, like, no one gets kitsch. That Met Gala? Like ninety percent wrong. Kitsch isn't about bright colors; it's about being so unappealing and in such low art taste that high art is able to accept it. It's a . . ." She shakes her head. "It's like a co-opting of pretentious people who want to enjoy low art, and the only means to do it is to act like you know it sucks. But everyone at that gala, for instance, still made their looks, like, *good*. Kitsch is . . ." She looks around. "Kitsch is literally the image of us sitting in this Burger King actually eating while wearing the crowns. It's the greatest."

She's *smart*. Smart in that way where she could teach a class on this shit. And now I'm imagining her in a tweed blazer with glasses and it's getting hot in here. Tweed jacket, glasses— actually, she doesn't even need the glasses. A T.A. office with four empty chairs, us facing each other. A paper as thick as a novella between us, her long fingers flipping through the pages. Meeting each other's gazes and—

Valeria's looking at me right now. Chewing on a half-eaten fry, but still looking. "Am I boring you? Most people would've told me to shut up by now."

I dig one nail into my thigh. "No, you're fine. This is all really interesting to me."

She exhales. "Can we talk about your horror short, though? I can analyze it through a pretentious lens if it'll get you going."

It sure feels like I go bright red at the suggestion, but maybe I don't, because Valeria is carrying on like nothing happened.

And my level of flirting back, if this is flirting, is to say: "Oh my god, I need to pay you back for the food."

Valeria goes from confused to neutral in a second flat. "Oh, right. It was five dollars."

I can't believe I just let her pay for my food. She must think I'm some ungrateful brat. Not brat. Shit. Romy says that's a B.D.S.M. term, and for all I know Valeria is into that. And by some miracle, there's five dollars in my wallet.

I slap it on the table. Valeria gives a brief smile. "Thanks."

"Yeah, no—"

Valeria snaps up the five, reaches over the table, and puts one hand on the side of my forehead. Heat gushes from the spot through my every nerve, igniting me. My breath is caught in a metal box and I can't get it out. Her other hand lifts part of my crown, scorching my nerves like a Malibu forest fire.

She slips the five into the space.

As fast as she was there, she's back to her friendly distance now.

"Please," she says. "Don't give me something else to feel guilty about."

Does she know? Does she have *any idea* what she's doing to me? And why did she even do that?

Valeria then pushes my phone . . . back to me. When did she take my phone? She must've been doing that sleight-of-hand thing: distract me with the crown and take my phone to . . . be cute? Does this woman flirt with up-close magic? I'm in *love*. I focus on her hand, taking in all the details I've noticed before: the short nails, the raised veins, the way her index fingers are double-jointed and flatten as she pushes down.

I take my phone back.

"If you changed the language to non-Latin characters like Romy always does . . ." I say.

Valeria chuckles as I swipe through.

I go to texts first. It's a good-enough instinct because now there's a text conversation I never started being held with *VAL(ERIA) SULLIVAN*. There's a single blue text from her:

> IF YOU VENMO ME I WILL MURDER
> YOU.

So Valeria just paid for my meal. Valeria just . . . Did she just give me her number?

I sit with that fact long after Valeria and I leave each other.

But when my driver merges onto the 10, I open Venmo, select my new contact Valeria, put in five dollars as the amount, and leave it with the caption: *Is it wrong to say my favorite Beatle is Yoko?*

She replies a minute later in our text chain.

> Well shit she's MY favorite so idk

There's just no way all this doesn't mean something. For once in my life, I actually feel like I know how to communicate over text.

Now I just have to not fuck it up.

chapter ten

The moment I applied to U.S.C., I knew my life would be about critique—my classes were focused on critique, every wannabe agent in Slater I showed my work to had something to say about it, and even my unqualified parents had opinions on my work.

Yet sitting across from Romy at Philz Coffee on the border of Manhattan Beach and El Segundo about to get my texts with Valeria critiqued, I feel like I've never been evaluated in my life. I absolutely should not be this nervous, especially given Romy's been in a pretty great mood ever since I surprised her with the slutty brownies. But here we are.

Romy swishes her iced coffee as she reads; I'm focused on the pink of her eyeshadow as she looks down at my phone. The cars passing by on Rosecrans Avenue are a distant whir. There's a Philz in Downtown L.A., but we're willing to brave a 110–105–405 journey for the fifteen-degrees-cooler temperatures closer to the beach. My brain suddenly bombards me with the most useless Gen Z information, like how the definitive coolest things that have been filmed in Manhattan Beach are 100 percent the *Hannah Montana* intro/outros (the pier and Miley's high school are not in Malibu) and the train sequence in *Captain Marvel*, which was filmed about two blocks from where I'm at. When Cinema-Sins made a comment about how the metro station was "super conveniently" located right next to a functioning road, all I could think was *Yeah, of course it's well designed, it's along one of the most affluent stops on the Green Line.* So I'm thinking that, and I'm also thinking about how I already feel guilty using Romy as an excuse to make my usual *I'm in the area* pop-in to see my parents as brief as possible. They'll want to hear about the P.A. gig, which will inevitably lead to Valeria, which will lead to *I'm bi* thoughts, which I do not want right now. So, brief.

"You guys are incurring so many Venmo fees," Romy finally says. "But I have to admit, it's also fucking hilarious."

I snort. "You haven't laughed once."

"If I'd read these in my room, I'd have laughed." She slides my phone back to me. A cloud moves, casting a ray of sunlight down onto Romy's bracelet-covered arm. She retreats like the vampire she is. "So how are you feeling about all this?"

I grimace. "What do you mean? Things are going super well with Valeria, and I got back on camera P.A. on Friday. It's great."

Romy chews on her inner cheek. "I'm just . . . I can't figure out Valeria's intentions. The way you guys talk and hang out outside of work seems to imply she wants to be closer to you in a friendship way. Or, hell, romantic, though that'd all kinda depend on if she's queer or not for real. And if she is interested in you, that's fine, like she's, what, twenty-nine?"

"Twenty-eight."

"Yeah, so the age difference is whatever. But given how sensitive she is to #MeToo and paying P.A.s fair wages and creating environments where the lower folks on the ladder don't feel taken advantage of, it's like, she must know she's your boss."

I'll admit it—Romy's tone surprises me, puts a pit in my stomach that the coffee isn't helping. She didn't have all this criticism
about what I was doing before. Is it revision stress? Something
with her grandma and the rent help she's giving? I can't think of
any other stresses in her life.

But I speak as if I haven't noticed anything. "I don't report to
her."

"But she's *there*, Lune. And again, I'm not saying she's being
predatory or anything. It just makes me think that *she's* thinking
of all this in a very professional sense. Like you're a project for
her." Romy throws her hands up. "And I think that's a *good* thing!
Why are we analyzing Valeria's texts where you gush about art
and culture back and forth for *flirting* when she's clearly begging
you to ask to collab?"

I hold my phone closer to my chest, as if defending the digital words inside. "She's never said anything like that, and aren't I
only doing all this because I'm pursuing a romantic relationship
with Valeria? Besides, I have the professional angle covered with
Brendan. Everything's compartmentalized and it's good."

Romy exhales. "Have you even changed your dating app preferences? I want you to have these milestone queer experiences,
and it'd be a dream to be with someone as awesome as Valeria,
but you need to have some perspective on this. You've been out
for a month. What happens if Valeria *is* gay and *does* want to have
sex with you and you realize you're not ready? It could get messy
so fast. And you've worked your ass off for years and now this
Hollywood angel is ready to swoop down and push your career,
and I'd just hate for you to ruin it by pursuing the romantic relationship too fast."

Tears burn in my eyes, hidden behind my sunglasses. Could
that really happen? Could I ruin all this because I'm not ready for

a girl-on-girl encounter? I can't screw this up *that* badly, can I? I firmly believe that Valeria is a good person, so she wouldn't stop having an interest in my art because of a sexual encounter gone wrong, right? And she wouldn't just be pursuing my art to get in my pants, would she? There's no way someone like her would like plain old me that much.

No way. It isn't that complicated. She likes talking to me, and maybe there's a spark growing between us. Her love of my art is just a piece of that. Plus she's someone who goes out of her way to boost underrepresented voices. I watch her do the same thing for the other P.A.s on set, all from marginalized backgrounds. Romy's giving me her best advice as an outsider, but she's clearly stressed about something else. It doesn't matter. I can read another human's intentions just fine.

But I do see Romy's argument about going slower. Starting with the glaring fact that I don't even know if she's gay.

"I think it's just something she likes about me," I say. "I know her being the director is weird, but what if I treat it like that time I was in love with my history T.A.?"

"You were too scared to talk to your history T.A."

The pit still isn't going away. It's like I've avoided some out-of-nowhere fender bender–type tension with Romy, but we still scratched doors. Even though I don't think this is ultimately detrimental to our friendship, I can't stand not having it fixed and soothed *right now*.

"Okay, I'll make you a promise. I'll only spend time with Valeria outside of work in professional circumstances. Like normal mentor-mentee situations. Once the shoot ends, as long as there's nothing weird—which there won't be—if something happens, it happens. Whatever she decides to do with my career is what it is."

There's a moment of silence. I sip my coffee, desperate for the seconds to fall away.

"That sounds like a good idea," Romy says.

I fold and unfold a napkin I swiped from the sugar station. "Can I still try to figure out if she's gay? In, like, a professional identity-politics way?"

Romy sighs long and hard. "You're an adult, dude. Do what you want."

"You literally just gave me, like, ten minutes' worth of advice. I'm asking as a baby gay to the wise older gay. Is that a faux pas?"

"Not when you're queer and don't force the answer."

This isn't working. I know she said *when* you're queer, but the bite in her answer feels more like *if*.

"Has your perspective changed on the queer thing?" I ask, trying to keep my voice steady.

Before Romy can answer, my phone goes off. A Venmo payment from Valeria. Five dollars and the caption: *How dare you question the validity of the circle jerks the Beatles did together when Paul CONFIRMED it in 2018.*

I let Romy read the message. She smiles. "Lemme test something."

Finally, the pit releases. I take a deep breath as Romy responds.

When she hands me back my phone, though, I can only stare in horror as I read the caption Romy's added to the five-dollar payment: *COME TOGETHER, RIGHT NOW, OVER ME.* 🖕

"How is *this* professional?" I squeak.

"It's Beatles song lyrics and us responding to the queerness of the band."

Valeria responds right away. Five dollars and: 😂 🖕 👀

Romy looks on and nods. "That's an exceptionally gay response."

I think Romy and I are okay. Good.

My heartbeat picks up. "Is it for sure?"

Romy shrugs. "We can ask Wyatt tonight."

Well, *fuck*. "We're seeing Wyatt tonight?"

Which, honestly, thank god. Perfect excuse to shorten my visit to my parents'; they *love* when I see Wyatt.

Romy bursts out laughing. "Check the group chat, dumbass. You responded yes."

Now she's back to normal. Was I imagining the tension earlier? Man, I need to get a grip.

I know Romy picked the location we end up at for our little reunion (as if it's been more than a *week*), because the next thing I know, Romy and I are carpooling up to the L.A. Zoo.

Excuse me, the *old* L.A. Zoo.

The one that opened in 1912, using the then-standard cages-inside-caves style of animal enclosures, only to go through the usual early- to midcentury maltreatment-of-animals backlash and close unceremoniously in 1965, when the city moved the zoo to its current location. The old zoo itself was, obviously, abandoned, leaving cages open to hikers, who would slip into the labyrinthian halls and enter the enclosures. Graffiti, most of it satanic, covers the walls like a coat. During the day, it smells like piss and is an incredible urban exploring spot.

At night, it still smells like piss, but it also feels like you're being descended upon by the restless souls of dozens of dead animals, like in *Pet Sematary*'s straight-to-D.V.D. sequel.

Oh, and this is where they filmed *Anchorman*.

"What are we doing here, exactly?" I ask as I turn on my phone's flashlight.

The midcentury carousel, still operational, is tented down for the night. The hiking trail curls upward and into the mountainside where the cages reside. You look north and you can see the city of Glendale; look to the immediate south and you're staring at the cages.

"Wyatt said we eat and drink too much," Romy says, glancing at Wyatt as he fans air into his Lakers T-shirt. "So exercise!"

It's one of those nights when it'll only go from the eighties to the high seventies even in the pitch-black. I trudge up the hill first, just to make sure I can do it. Straggling in the back is the easiest way to get murdered by either the animal ghosts or the satanic cult members. By the time I reach the flat part of the trail, I'm already hands on chest, trying to get my heart to stop hammering. At least the remaining 1.5-mile hike is flat. Bless the zoogoers of the 1910s for that.

I reach for my camera, which is in its case hanging off my shoulder. Might as well see what images I can capture in this light—

Someone grabs my shoulders.

No, *Romy* grabs my shoulders and yells, "BOO!"

I know exactly what's going on, but I still scream like a little girl. Wyatt doubles over in laughter from just behind us. Romy is giggling into my shoulder as she holds me from behind, rocking us both. The adrenaline rush from the scare shifts into a rush of calm as I feel her arms around me, hold a fraction of her weight on me.

And when she doesn't pull away, instead shifting us both toward Wyatt, there's a twinge of excitement that shoots through me.

"So how's the talent section without us?" Romy asks.

Wyatt puffs his cheeks, slowly blowing the air out. "Steven's been on my ass since Luna left. Apparently being pissed at your assistant for literally nothing is contagious."

I loosen Romy's grip on me and feel her slink off.

"What are you talking about?" I say. "Why would Steven—?"

Wyatt shakes his head. "It's no big deal."

One of the first cages on the trail, a rectangular one built on a sloping hill, stands rusting in the dirt, door open. It was made for a smaller large animal, and it's completely covered in paintings and graffiti. Wyatt scurries inside, ducking his head under the low roof.

"Wyatt!" I call into the cave.

"Can you take a picture of me?" Wyatt calls back.

I roll my eyes. I'm a cinematographer, but I guess I take decent pictures. At least I can play with angles.

"Thirst trap or just cool?" I ask.

"Please just cool?" Wyatt pleads.

I exchange a glance with Romy. She's smirking. I think I catch her drift, but I can only guess what she's implying.

"I think this was meant for monkeys, so can you hook your feet into the top of the cage closest to the concrete enclosure?" I ask. "Then reach the upper half of your body into the inner enclosure."

Wyatt follows my every request, and the picture makes his ass look incredible. Romy's barely not on the floor laughing in the background. He better post this. The composition is incredible, and more straight guys need to show off their butts.

"How're things going with Valeria?" Wyatt asks once the photo is done (he doesn't ask to see it, so I expect a shocked reply later tonight) and we're off to the next cage.

I can't help but smile. "Pretty good. We've been texting for several days now."

Wyatt breaks out a grin. "Jesus, that's amazing! What do you guys talk about?"

I pull my phone/flashlight to my face. "I could show you some of the messages—"

Romy grabs my arm. "C'mon, you gotta see the view in here!"

The next cage was home to a much larger animal than the first one. The door opens with a little push into another concrete structure sheltered from the heat. Farther into the space, a staircase descends deep into the dirt. The only light down there is whatever manages to filter through the cage bars. Everything is rough, graffiti-covered stone. Rough enough that if you fell or rubbed against it wrong, you'd come out with a bloody elbow or knee.

I hesitate at the top of the stairs. The way down is too dark for my phone's flashlight to illuminate.

"Do you need me to hold your hand, champ?" Romy asks.

I shoot her the finger and climb down the stairs. And from down here, looking up into the strips of moonlight highlighting the uneven, color-washed stairs, the spot is gorgeous.

"Rom, this is amazing," I say.

"Got you," she says.

I take a photo with Romy's shadow just within frame. Do a full pan up. Try different focuses. At some point I make Romy jump deeper into the frame. I've always loved her silhouette, the way the shape of her hair gives uneven lines to an otherwise fluid set of curves. It almost makes me miss my outrageously stressful production classes. At least, I ache a little for the intimacy the two of us gained making movies together under ridiculous deadlines, cursing my pretentious classmates and professors at three a.m. while trying to get our lines right. She was always better at it than me. There's a softness to the nostalgia, though, knowing that we share that same closeness in different settings now: around new work hours, responsibilities, and views on life. Somehow, though, I think any art we make, even the little backdrops I made for Romy's play, is better just because we have more years of knowing each other behind us. Still, I'd love to see that intimacy in action, to make more art together.

By the time we're outside again, Wyatt's hanging off a cage door, completely oblivious to the rust he might be getting embedded into his skin.

"Are you feeling good about Valeria?" Wyatt asks.

I glance at Romy. Rehashing the entire conversation with him seems fruitless. "We're just trying to figure out if she's gay."

Wyatt wrinkles his brow. "Don't you two know?"

"She hasn't come out to us yet," Romy says, deadpan.

I hand him my phone. "We've just got the texts as evidence."

Wyatt scans the texts.

"Seriously, what the hell is up with Steven?" I ask.

Wyatt hands me the phone. "I just assume anyone who uses the gay pride flag casually is gay."

Romy shrugs. "There's your straight opinion."

"And really, Luna, it's fine," Wyatt says. "I'm way more into this gay mystery."

Romy runs her hands over her face. "Wyatt. Please never call trying to figure out if someone's queer a 'gay mystery.'"

"I can give you my filing system," I say. "Alice loved it, and I know Steven's also a mess."

"Do not give 'gay mystery' boy your organizational secrets," Romy says.

I cross my arms. "And how could Valeria's *manager* not know whether or not she's gay?"

Wyatt shrugs. "I barely know she's single. She used to date

Charlie Durst, but Valeria mentioned he was her buddy last time he came up." Even though I trust that Wyatt's information is pretty reliable, I cringe hearing about Charlie Durst. He hasn't filmed his part yet, and I mentally note to pay attention to the vibe between him and Valeria when he does. "Beyond that, Steven doesn't tell me much. I think he and Valeria text, but I can't see his personal phone. And yeah, can I see that system?"

Shit. That actually checks out.

I rub my forearms. It's not getting much colder, but I'm still shivering. "Yeah, sure."

"So what next?" Wyatt asks.

I look to Romy. She shrugs. "Luna here will have to do some observing. See if Valeria likes rainbows, how she reacts to men, stuff like that."

I exhale. "Is it really this hard to date women?"

"When they're A-list actors, yes." Romy pats my hand and goes off to the next cage. "Change your dating app preferences."

I sigh, open up Hinge, change my preferences, and return my phone to a flashlight. I'm still focused on Valeria, but nothing that'll make me feel more accomplished in my bi self will hurt, right?

Unfamous girls/enbies/non-men are people too. The goal is to make Valeria feel like a unfamous person.

I catch Romy illuminated in the moonlight, mid-climb up a cage wall. Her arms are spread out as if she owns the open air and the blinking blanket of city lights below us.

Yeah, unfamous people are pretty great too.

chapter eleven

When I came out to myself, I gotta say, I thought I'd just develop an inherent gaydar. I mean, isn't it some kind of survival skill for queer people? *Apparently not*, because my observations over four days on set as I bust my ass being the best clapper in history are:

- Brendan and Valeria are standing in front of a display of ice cream at a local parlor. The flavor choices encompass a full range of color, including a rainbow sherbet. They're trying to decide if having a quick pan P.O.V. shot with the rainbow sherbet in frame would work. Brendan asks Valeria if it'd be too obtuse. Her exact response: "Ugh, you're right. I have a photo like that on my defunct MySpace."

- Some male crew member is suggesting an edit to a piece of dialogue for an off-color joke some nothing character says. The joke is something along the lines of "I knew a girl so ugly that she fell asleep at a frat party and she woke up with more clothes on." Valeria literally gives a fake smile and walks away.

- Valeria is equally as touchy-feely with Charlie Durst as she is with Mason Wu (an open lesbian). With that said, her affection for Charlie Durst seems limited to constantly flipping him off, whereas Mason Wu sits in Valeria's lap (God, I wish that were me) whenever they watch dailies together.

- Valeria is deciding how to sit in a chair for a scene at a house, ends up doing the one leg thrown over the armrest look, and Brendan, who has now mentioned his boyfriend twice, yells, "That's so *gay*, Valeria!" She laughs.

- She says she's allergic to North Carolina.

- Between shooting nights she's sent me, like, five photos of her without makeup posing with her Chihuahua at, like, three a.m., and that just feels gay to me.

Which, *okay*, this is a lot of signs. But fuck if I know. It's been like four days this week of hard-core investigation, and the only real accomplishment I've made is Brendan regularly makes eye contact with me as I hand him lenses.

Today we're filming the chase scene in the house, which means we're paying off some rich person in Studio City to borrow their home. I promised myself that if there was a good moment, I'd casually mention my ideas for this scene to Brendan. He picks me first among all the P.A.s for work. It has to mean something.

"Hey, Luna, get over here!" Brendan says.

We aren't filming anything at this exact moment and I haven't been assigned to grab a lens. My stomach clenches as I jog up to him.

"So Valeria's gonna fall down some stairs today and I'll be working A.D. stuff too. You down to be my first A.C.?"

I've been preparing for this moment for weeks: killing it at my menial gigs, practicing the technique if called upon at home, rehearsing my thank-you response. Yet somehow I still never thought today would be the day. My hands tremble, whether from nerves or excitement I don't even know. I stuff them into my pockets.

It's around then that the nerves are the dominant dog in this fight. Because focus pulling, the technical term for what a first A.C. does, is one of those things you don't have a margin of error for. The job itself is adjusting the lens to capture exact sharpness of the image from whatever distance the focus is. So if the actor moves a millimeter, the first A.C. adjusts. If the subject of the image moves from one person to another, you have to move too. It's considered one of the, if not *the*, hardest jobs on set.

It's also around then that Valeria runs up, still in her hoodie outfit. She's sweating, but not gross sweating. Like that sweating that shouldn't even be legal, where it's just making her skin glow. "Can someone feed me the line?"

Brendan laughs. "You don't *have* any lines. This is when you fall down the stairs, remember?"

Valeria grins. "You expect *me* to know this script?"

Then, in the most casual move I've ever seen, she just *lifts up the bottom of her hoodie* and wipes the sweat off her face. I know it's not really in slow motion, but goddamn it, it might as well be. I've seen preteen boys and teenage boys and college boys do the exact same move over the years, but nothing has ever been like this heart-stopping moment. She's not wearing a shirt under the hoodie, and it's nowhere near showing her chest or anything, but her abs are—her abs are straight-up deep enough to eat cereal out of.

She shakes her head a little, letting the hoodie creep back down to cover her midriff. Absolutely no awareness.

"Jesus, Val, you wanna stop body-shaming me?" Brendan jokes. "Do you *know* what kind of pressure gay men are under to look perfect?"

Please no one talk to me. I have literally nothing productive to say right now.

"Look, *Bren*, I'm on a team-mandated prepress slim down and am legally obligated to eat only plain chicken and vegetables while doing full-body strength training at one a.m. because of this. Get back to Yosemite with me and I'll stop unconsciously shaming you."

Oh. I guess that explains the pictures with her dog at three a.m.

"Do you rock climb?" I ask.

I watched *Free Solo* once. Alex Honnold has ridiculously chiseled abs too. Maybe it's a rock-climbing thing.

"I did," Valeria says, running a hand through her hair. She needs to stop. "I broke my ankle bouldering, and my partner didn't stop laughing until I said I needed to go to the hospital."

Okay, ignore the abs—

Partner?

Yeah, it's getting cooler for straight people to call their girlfriend or boyfriend "partner," but it's still mostly a queer thing.

Fuck. This should add up to a very clear *yeah, she's gay*, but I can't decide.

The scene around me loses its sharpness as I get lost in my head. It's like looking up at the surface of a pool from below, this growing sensation of *I'm not where I'm supposed to be*. I need to be at the surface. I'm about to focus pull. The hardest job on set.

I'm about to do the hardest job on set and I'm thinking about Valeria and her partner.

I don't even realize I'm hyperventilating until Brendan says, "Deep breaths. It's just one scene."

And literally all I'm doing is putting the camera in focus. Brendan does the rest. I've done this job hundreds of times in school. I can do this even while distracted by Valeria.

The camera notes are already planned. They're doing a wide shot for the fall. The camera is new enough that there's a monitor for me to look at to put the shot in focus without putting my eye to the viewfinder. I adjust the aperture, the white balance, etc. By the time I've got that done, I'm working twice as hard to suck breath in, so focused I stop feeling my fingertips.

Brendan takes my place, nods, and shit, that's it.

But then Brendan frowns after the take.

"It's"—he squints—"not quite there. Luna, come here and give it another shot."

My heart bangs against my rib cage as I redo my work. It looks perfect to me, so I'm adjusting for the sake of adjusting. The crew's eyes are on me as I tinker. *Stupid knew-someone hire,* they must be thinking.

I pull away, hoping well enough is good.

We do another take.

"Hey, I want to try something different," Valeria says. "One more take."

I move to adjust the camera, but Brendan stops me.

"Hey, all good," he says. "I got it for this one."

By the time I'm placed back on camera P.A. duties, I can't even feel the rubber of my shoes hitting the wood and tile that's all over this house. Brendan's glances at me go from friendly to furtive, pitying. My insides melt and slosh, fingers shaking with every tiny task.

And when he delegates the first A.C. duties to another camera P.A., my guts have pooled into my shoes and my body is nothing but an aching shell.

I lost Brendan's interest.

By the time the shoot ends, I'm officially back on coffee duty. We end so late that there's no traffic on my drive back to K-Town. I'm physically spent, but my mind is racing. If I can't get back into Brendan's good graces, I officially don't have a job in less than a week. I have to pay rent, I have to follow my dreams, and everything ends in a week. There's no more room to mess around with Valeria on set.

Yet this may be my only time with Valeria too.

"So you still want your bedroom, right?" Romy says as I drop into the chair in her room. For some reason we always end up hanging out in each other's bedrooms when it gets late, despite having a tiny but perfectly fine common space. Old dorm habits die hard, I suppose.

I smile wryly. "We're not turning my bedroom into an arcade, no matter how good of a stress reliever it would be."

After having shared a bedroom dorm style for years, it'd more been our parents who thought it was time for us to have separate rooms. And don't get me wrong, I appreciate my own space, but sometimes I miss the days when we didn't even have walls to separate us. It just felt like we knew everything about each other in those times. And okay, an arcade would be fun.

I glance at her bedroom door, wondering if I should kill this conversation to go change into pajamas or leave the door open to continue it. Prior to my coming out, we had no shame, going full locker room. And, of course, if Straight Me was fine with changing in front of Romy no matter her sexual orientation, why should I act differently now that I'm aware of the fact that Romy's body is attractive? It feels like such a ridiculous conundrum that I don't even want to voice it out loud.

The moment, naturally, is stolen from me when Romy throws off her barista T-shirt, crumples it into a ball, yells, "Kobe!" and throws it into her laundry basket. It makes it in. She whoops, cheesing. I smile, but then my stomach turns into knots when she unhooks her bra. She wrinkles her brow at me and turns around, grabbing a shirt out of her drawer. I wipe my palms on my sweat-stained shirt. At this point I'm just waiting for an opportune moment to go quickly change.

"These ended up in my stuff," Romy says, tossing me a shirt and pajama shorts of mine.

I glance at her door and exhale. Turn around. Shirt off, bra off, nightshirt on. I step into my pajama shorts. Finally, I look at Romy. She's got little fried eggs on her shorts and a matching shirt with fried eggs right over her nipples. A present I got her.

"How do you keep coordinated pajamas together?" I ask.

She flops onto her bed stomach-first, curling up to look me in the eye. The shirt isn't revealing at all, but I still paint the lines of her body as she sinks into the mattress pad. "Any cool girls on the apps?"

I want nothing more than to spill what happened at work to Romy, but I can't process that right now. I need a distraction. I don't even know where to start with Brendan, and I don't want to make Romy shoulder it all anyway. She's doing enough with the Valeria thing.

I open the one dating app I've decided I don't hate this month. I've gotten three girl matches, one who's chatted me up. "Why don't the girls talk to me?"

"Girls are less likely to be aggressive than guys."

"Even though I'm a bottom?"

"*Luna*, look at me: a sapphic who has the confidence and the top energy to pull you along the way an alpha dude will is rare. No one will stop liking you because you pursue a little. Promise."

Trauma clarification: I have lost at least three guys I liked because I came across as "too eager," which basically meant I asked them out on second dates. Men suck.

I exhale, opening up my chat with this girl named Jo. We talked about *Pose* last night when we matched. Part of me feels like I'm doing the dating app thing more for Romy than me. These girls' photos are stunning, sure, but my chest tightens thinking about stripping naked for anyone I don't, well, know. Taking off my top for guys on promising second or third dates felt strange enough, and I've been told by friends, cousins, and cool aunts to expect to be doing that my whole single life. The idea of getting naked with a *girl* I don't know, trying to be vulnerable and hot and not show how clueless I am—it's a lot. But I guess I should at least *try*. Be ready in case the Valeria thing ends up being all in my head.

"What does your profile look like?" I ask.

Romy hands me her phone. I'm flattered to see that most of her photos are ones I've taken of her on our adventures. Her profile is pretty simple: states her pronouns and gender, that she's a writer and a big-game veterinarian for the Mob. And that she's not here to be anyone's unicorn. I'd swipe right.

I shake away the heat traveling to my cheeks as I hand her phone back to her.

"Jo responded," Romy says, glancing at my phone. "And how's figuring out if Valeria is gay?"

Jo's response: It's SO GOOD. Btw, if you don't mind me asking, what are you on this site for?

I tug at the collar of my shirt. "It is so obvious that I don't think she is."

"What does *that* mean?"

I drop into her reading chair. "She said she used to post rainbow photos on her MySpace, very obviously dislikes men who aren't our gay D.P., lets our lesbian E.P. sit in her lap to watch dailies, won't go to North Carolina, knows how to sit gayly in a chair, *and* referred to an ex as her partner."

Romy breaks into a wide grin. "I like the idea that she's just a straight unicorn enthusiast who knows what's comfortable and really fucking hates men and North Carolina."

I drop my face into my hands and huff.

"Dude, that's very gay. Your observations are astute," Romy says.

"Really?"

I reply to Jo. The coming-out thing is so much easier with strangers. Well, I've been out for about a month and a half and just want to start making connections to other sapphics. Friends or more.

Jo responds almost immediately. Oh, that's so great!! And shit, kudos to you for being on here so early. Very brave.

My chest lightens as I read the message.

"What're you smiling at?" Romy asks. "Did Valeria send another pic of her dog?"

I shake my head. "No, just Jo. She's being really cool about the fact that I just came out."

Romy smiles. "See! Valeria's not the only person outside our friend group who will treat you nicely."

I glance at the time: eleven thirty. "Besides, it's too early for Valeria to send me pictures of her dog." I glance at her. She's typing too. "Are you talking to anyone?"

She shrugs. "I talk to a couple people at once. If one sticks, the apps disappear."

I furrow my brow. "But you never bring them around for us to meet."

Romy frowns. "Yeah. I dunno, things just usually end quickly. A couple of them weren't out yet and I didn't want to introduce them to my non-queer friends. But now that you're out, I think it'd be a nice idea."

Her explanation feels weird to me for some reason. It seems like she's not telling me the whole truth, but why would she lie to me?

I exhale. Another message from Jo. Hey, can I do something kinda bold?

"Shit! Romy, shit, I think Jo's gonna ask me on a date!" I say.

Which feels weird with the Valeria thing, but still.

I reply, Yes.

"Hell yeah!" she says.

And we both watch the screen as . . .

. . . she sends me a picture of her tits.

I practically throw the phone into Romy's lap. My face burns like it's on fire. Romy picks up my phone, eyes wide.

"Is that normal?" I ask.

Why am I so freaked out about seeing a stranger's tits? Is this a bad sign?

Romy shakes her head. "How long have you been talking to her? Didn't I *just* tell you to change your preferences?"

I take a deep breath. I'm so tired I'm overreacting. "We've been talking for, like, a few hours total."

Romy scowls. "Yeah, that's a weirdo. Delete her."

I do. Including the app.

"Why didn't I like that?" I ask, raking my hands through my hair.

"Because it was an unsolicited tit picture? It's like a dick pic. If you don't want it, it doesn't mean you don't like that gender."

"Rom, I don't even know if I *like* tits. What's appealing about them?"

Romy squints. "Oh god, they're like . . . soft, nice . . . circles? I don't know, it's just a thing."

"I don't get it."

"You don't have to fetishize boobs to be gay. You don't look at Valeria's chest?"

I blush again. "It feels objectifying."

"Okay. But I doubt you're capable of seeing someone as a piece of meat, so even if you *did* like her tits, it'd be fine."

I turn to Romy. "But I saw her abs today. They were amazing."

Romy throws up her hands. "That's a woman's body, dude! That you're attracted to! I know it's hard for you, but *please*, don't let these thoughts crowd your mind. You're doing *fine*."

It's getting late. I set my phone on Romy's bedside table and crawl onto the bed with her. We're next to each other, face-to-face. We're not quite touching, but it'd barely take a movement to do it. I'm close enough to hear and see her chest rise and fall as she breathes. Distraction time is over. The Brendan situation is back to an ache I can't ignore. And Romy and I have already transitioned into talking about Valeria on set. I should tell her.

"Valeria's abs are the only good thing that happened today, though," I say. "Brendan gave me the opportunity to focus the camera and I did it wrong. We have less than a week left of shoot-ing and I'm all but fucked."

Romy frowns. "I'm so sorry, Lune. But you aren't completely dead in the water yet. You're an incredible D.P. and you know cameras like no one else. You got this."

I put the pillow over my face. "But he already put another camera P.A. on focus pull. There's nothing above that to impress him with."

"Come on. There has to be some way for you not to have to do barely-paying P.A. gigs forever. Valeria fucking Sullivan thinks you're talented."

My phone goes off.

A text from Valeria.

> Hi Gen Z Steven booked me on Hot Ones
> without meaningful consult and Wyatt's
> laughing over the phone am I going to die

I laugh too.

"What?" Romy asks.

"Steven booked Valeria on *Hot Ones* for her next press set."

Romy raises her eyebrows. "Guess actor consent isn't needed after all."

And an idea hits me.

Valeria thinks I'm good. *Valeria* wants to foster my talent. And Valeria is Brendan's boss.

Here's the thing. I don't want to ask Valeria to have Brendan recommend me for a job. But Valeria is also the one telling Bren-dan what shots to do. And we're still shooting in the house, doing the exact scene I blocked out ideas for with Noam.

What if I pitch it to Valeria and she uses it? She'd tell Brendan

I came up with it, and he'd have to let me come back into an A.C. position, right? And *then* I'd focus pull the shit out of the scene and he'd take me on. I just have to show I'm a great D.P., not just a good camera P.A. That I could be *someone*.

I just need Valeria's help to transition. I need to convince her of my talent first.

"Do you remember my high school friend Will?" I ask.

"Who?"

Me: If you want to practice, I know someone who works at Howlin' Ray's. I could film and you could see how you perform on camera.

"He works at Howlin' Ray's now," I say.

"The death chicken place?"

"Yeah."

Valeria replies almost instantly.

> You're amazing. Does tomorrow at noon
> work?

"Well," I say, "Valeria still likes me."

I just have to show Valeria what I can do and slip my idea for the scene in. She's said nothing but yes before. It's not a guarantee, but it's the best chance I have.

Well, the only chance I have.

Romy just shakes her head, smiling. Clearly she knows what I'm up to. "You're ridiculous," she says.

chapter twelve

People stare at Valeria and me as we bypass the Howlin' Ray's line at noon. And for probably the first time in Valeria's life, they're not staring because of her. They're staring because we're cutting the Howlin' Ray's line. Despite the fact that Howlin' Ray's itself is just a tiny chicken restaurant in Chinatown, it has a line that rivals Space Mountain at Disneyland. It boasts a hefty forty-five-minute to an hour wait time—from a spot halfway through the queue. Even though the place only opened in 2015, it's a Los Angeles institution.

Valeria's brown eyes have gone wide looking at the sea of people.

"Are you sure they aren't selling immortality here?" she asks me as we continue to walk.

In all honesty, Will told me to meet him out back, but I wanted to show Valeria all this first.

"Nope. Just good chicken."

Right before we reach the door, I take a hard right and lead Valeria around to the back door.

"This feels strangely like the time my grandpa paid the host a hundred bucks to get us into Ellen's Stardust Diner in New York when I was a kid," Valeria says.

"Well, basically it is. Just with a little less obvious bribing."

Will Garcia was one of my closest friends in high school. He wanted to be a screenwriter, and we were the only committed students in our film class. I had a major crush on him, but he preferred my friend. I set him up with her, and they're still together. She supports him as he does the Artist Route like Romy—working side gigs to directly support making the art now. While I could have taken the fact that he wasn't into me as a major L, I decided long ago that Will just owed me for setting him up with his life partner. With just the right amount of subconscious guilt, Will seemed rather happy to get me an order of chicken. Is this fucked up from both sides? Yeah, I guess. But my interest in Will has faded.

All six feet four inches of Will smiles as I approach. He already has a take-out bag in hand. "Hey, you!"

We exchange a quick hug. "It's great to see you."

He seems so happy, and I guess even this gig at Howlin' Ray's has its glamor.

And yeah, it's a little fun to watch his brows come together as he stares at Valeria.

"This is my friend Valeria," I say.

Valeria doesn't flinch at the word *friend*. But saying it sends a bolt of nerves digging into my stomach, even after the moment ends.

They shake hands.

"You look so familiar," he says.

Valeria exchanges a knowing glance with me and shrugs at Will. "I get that a lot."

He slides several sheets of paper toward us. "So legally I gotta have you guys sign some release forms."

Valeria scans them, losing just a touch of color in her face. "Cool . . ."

Once everything is signed, he swipes the waivers away and hands us a case of drinks.

"Wear the gloves," he says.

Right. They make you wear surgical gloves to hold the howlin' wings since the rub is made with Carolina Reaper extract.

I reach for my credit card, but Valeria's already got hers slapped down before I have the chance. I can't read lips, but I would bet she's saying *Don't Venmo me*.

We end up driving to nearby Grand Park, where we spread the wings across a picnic table. I can't think of anything that's been filmed here. It's mostly just a low-key spot of green amid the concrete of D.T.L.A. Calm, cooler than anywhere else in the surrounding area, and not crowded enough for us to draw attention with my camera and Valeria's exposed face. She inspects the to-go container full of surgical gloves with a mix of confusion and fear.

"We're not starting at the gloves," I say as I set up two little plates with the various wings. I leave the handle-with-gloves wings in their container for when the time comes.

We got medium, medium plus, hot, and howlin', with one "country"/nonspiced sandwich to pick off for carbo-loading. Call it a combination of watching YouTubers do hot pepper challenges and a general interest of my own, but I feel pretty at ease doing this. I have a higher spice tolerance than most (mountains above most white people, anyway) from a couple of *eat this ghost chili and I'll give you $300* challenges in college. Still, this'll be painful. But it's fine.

"So no one's gonna see this. Just do what you gotta do—take

breaks, cry, eat carbs, whatever. I've got questions written and everything," I say. "Should be fun."

Valeria glances from the wings back to me. "You're doing this too, right?"

I nod. I've got my phone hooked up to my tripod, so I should be able to move the camera and zoom in as needed while sitting across from her. With my first A.C. experience still fresh, I pretty much know my adjustments based on distance and one or two checks. I mic her up and we're good to go.

"Rolling," I say, and we start. "So there's water and an ice-cream cart"—I motion to a tiny cart boasting highly-processed ice-cream-truck ice cream a few yards from us—"if it hurts too much. And you're free to tap out, but remember that on *Hot Ones* you'll be judged for it harshly."

"Okay," Valeria says. She takes a deep breath. "Let's do this."

We each pick up a medium wing. "So this one's got mostly cay-enne pepper." Will explained all this when I asked for the favor. "With a hint of ghost pepper."

She sniffs the wing. "What is a ghost pepper exactly?" she asks.

"It's just a famous hot pepper." I figure we can get into that when we get to the hot wing. "Cayenne, though, is something like forty thousand average on the Scoville scale."

She blinks at me. She's clearly not much of a spice aficionado.

"Five times as hot as a jalapeño but less hot than a habanero," I clarify.

She gives a little shrug and bites into the wing. I do the same. It's definitely hot and gives a slight kick to the back of the throat, but it's nothing outrageous. In fact, I'll hold off on the water. It's actually rather enjoyable. Valeria reaches for the water but doesn't seem too disturbed.

"You seem to have a vast knowledge of hot peppers," Valeria comments. "I learn something new about you every day."

I smile. "I'm supposed to be the one asking the questions."

I have four of them, sort of modeled off what the show would do. Needless to say, I did a lot of research last night. "I know you said in the press tour for *Stroke* that you were originally made aware of the project because of your background in pop culture academia. Did they actually use you as a consultant when you were cast?"

Valeria puts her hands behind her head, leaning back to look just past me. "I was, I think. They asked me questions throughout the process and would switch lines if something seemed off or if I mentioned it. But"—she smiles—"not to call anyone out, but Dustin said he'd change this one thing: my character mentions this one well-known Beatles myth, and I told him to change it to the true story, and he never did it." She looks right into the camera. I adjust the position. "So I apologize on behalf of academics everywhere for that mistake."

"Would you say that on the show?" I ask.

She raises her eyebrows. "No way. That's just for me, you, and this camera."

Warmth rolls over me. Yes, of course there's intimacy in the fact that we're out here in public together, but I never would've thought she'd really *trust* me with something.

We each go for the medium-plus wing.

"So what's in this one?" Valeria asks after she's already taken a bite.

"Cayenne, but this one also has a solid mix of ghost pepper and habanero."

Tears are welling in her eyes now. She fishes for the water, shaking her head. "Jesus Christ."

Yeah, these are definitely a lot hotter. I can't even imagine what the last two wings will be like. I finally take a sip of water.

"How did you like Pasadena growing up?"

She stops gulping water and starts fanning herself. She's still crying. "Oh god, when did this become some twisted therapy session?" She wipes away more tears with a napkin. "It was boring and everyone there was content with a midline plateau sort of life and they gentrified everything. It was physically safe, which I appreciate, but very stifling. Fair Oaks Soda Fountain in South Pasadena *is* worth a visit, though, if you're forced into the area." She pauses. "You?"

I slide the paper aside. "Hermosa Beach."

"Wanna switch? Why aren't you reacting to this?"

I shrug. "It's no Trinidad scorpion. Like, it's hot, don't get me wrong, but—"

She picks up a hot sauce bottle I brought. "What's this?"

I smirk. "It's for the end."

She takes more water. She's already eyeing the ice-cream cart. "Can you ask the question really slowly? This goes away, right?"

I look back to my questions. "So what prompted you to pay P.A.s living wages?"

She coughs a little, wipes her eyes again, and answers. The people around us must think we're filming some tragic documentary. "Bringing actual diverse talent into the business involves more groundwork than these diversity programs do. At least—" She's back to blinking furiously. "Most people can't afford to take these minimum-wage jobs if they come from historically marginalized communities, so I was like, 'Why don't I just pay them the right amount of money?' Sure, it's, like, denying benefits to straight white men, but who cares about them anyway? Do you have any more napkins not covered in death?"

I hand her a wad of napkins and she blows her nose. I'm into this anti–straight white men thing.

"And take someone like you. I see you, and you're an under-represented voice, and just by existing, you're changing things. But then you have *talent*, and it's like I can't let that go? I want you to, like"—she's crying again, and I genuinely don't know how much of this is emotion—"make movies and shorts and music videos or whatever."

I have to ask her today. Just maybe when she's less freaked out about the spice.

"Next wing?" I ask. I pour half of my water into hers. "You're doing great, by the way. These are really hot."

"Again, you are not having the same reaction."

I shrug. "If you really want me to taste the extra sauce, I'll do it."

I reach for the bottle, but Valeria grabs it first. "You keep your hands clean for the camera."

I watch her dab hot sauce onto her fingertip with a growing tightness in my gut.

Then suddenly Valeria's fingertip brushes against my lip. Nerves light up in sensitive parts of my skin I didn't even know existed. I feel every swirl and loop of her finger as it runs against the microridges of my mouth. It's as if there's an invisible string that attaches her to my every organ, yanking them all sideways as she swoops her wrist. And when our skin is no longer touching, my lips are tingling. I suck my bottom lip into my mouth, tasting her touch, wondering what it would've been like if she'd left her finger there and I did the same thing.

In fact, there's a solid second when I'm completely unaware that Valeria just swiped the equivalent of Satan's jizz across my lips.

Then the burning hits.

And god, *okay*, now this hurts. Whether Valeria realizes it, she poured Trinidad scorpion pepper onto my lips. I'm frantically trying to preserve the memory of that tingling touch as my physical lips genuinely *burn*.

"I"—I hiccup—"probably should've told you what's in that."

The ice cream is looking really good right now.

Her little smile fades into a frown. "Are you okay?"

I nod, blinking away my own tears. "Yeah. The next wing is just more of that."

I take my minute or so to recover, and we go for the hot.

"This one is all the spices I mentioned before and the Trinidad scorpion. It's in the, y'know, millions in terms of Scoville units."

And yeah, okay, this thing is *hot*, even after what I just went through. My eyes are watering harder. The pain is definitely scorching and it's there to stay. My muscles twitch, ready to sprint for that ice-cream cart.

Meanwhile, Valeria is straight up leaking bodily fluids too quickly for any napkin to wipe up.

"So what's your—"

She reaches into her purse, grabs a wad of random bills, and shoves them into my face. "Get like five."

I return with an ice-cream sandwich, an ice-cream cookie sandwich, and three SpongeBob pops. She rips the paper off a SpongeBob pop, digs the gum out, and bites off a chunk. It's like watching someone attempt to claw herself out of a sinkhole.

I unwrap another one of the SpongeBobs and start eating it. Whatever amount of dairy is in this is helping, a little.

"Are you good?" I ask.

She wipes her face again. "Who needs internal organs, right?" She sniffles. "Keep going."

I look to my page. I have either a joke question where I ask her to describe Baudrillard's concept of the simulacrum or . . .

"What's your opinion on straight actors taking queer roles in major motion pictures?" I ask. My throat hurts at this point.

She exhales. Takes the ice-cream sandwich, removes the chocolate part on top, and laps up the ice cream. She exhales again. "Sorry, this isn't helping as much as I thought."

"Do you want—?"

She holds up a hand. "It's okay." Another pause. "Jesus, I feel high right now." She rubs her exposed arm. "It's like, of course it's a shitty thing, but there are two sides to it, you know? Because when closeted actors take on these roles that they can play authentically, they are making audiences privy to information in a way, and it can mentally wreck them. So it's like, we shouldn't expect an actor to present their sexuality in order to make the role valid. But then you will have people who are straight and will always be straight just wanting to do queer roles because it's trendy."

How do you personally interpret that?

Can I ask? Jesus, can I *ask*? Would someone less considerate and less in the middle of coming out *ask that*? I mean, she's playing a queer character in a movie that's got heavy content around the theme of coming out.

I look from my notes to Valeria. She really isn't coming down from having her internal organs blasted. Like she's noticeably pale right now.

"Why the—?" she says before swallowing. "Why the fuck did Steven book this without asking me? Like climbing rocks and eating this shit aren't the same kind of adventurous. I don't have the skill set for this. I swear to fucking god, Luna, sometimes I just—"

The rest of her sentence falls out somewhere in the park trash can she heaves into. My muscles seize. Like I want to jump up and help her, but I'm stuck to this bench. She spits into the garbage can, clutching the edges of the bin.

"Luna?" she calls.

"Yeah?"

"Am I dying?"

I glance at her water cup. It's empty, but there's a water fountain nearby.

"No, you're just white," I say as I scurry to the fountain.

"You're white too!"

When I get back, she's slumped face-first onto the table.

I let her just sit like that for a bit. When she glances up at me, she genuinely looks like she went to war. "So . . . I'm gonna go no on that last wing."

I force a smile. "Smart."

It takes her about twenty minutes of nursing water and melted ice cream to get back to normal. That's enough time for the guilt to settle like a rock inside me, scarred and rough. It slices into the fine skin of my guts. Once Valeria's no longer actively accelerating her death, she starts peering at the footage I got.

"So," she says, "do you think I should make Steven go in my place?"

I smile. "Steven definitely wouldn't make it halfway down the line."

"But really. I get that people probably puke on that show and whatever, but I wouldn't be able to keep going past that third wing. Steven's such a fucking idiot sometimes."

I open up Safari on my phone. "The last wing you had would've had Scoville units into the millions, and only the last sauce on the show goes that high. I think you'd be okay. You know, if there's a lot of pressure on you to do it."

An ache manifests in my chest thinking about that. Valeria's in a giant place of privilege and who am I to feel bad, but I can't imagine having your life dictated the way hers must be. The diet comment she made the other day pops back into my head. It only adds to the ache.

She sighs, settling her cheek against her fist. "Steven would get pissed if I didn't do it, and he thinks it's great for my image. That I need to expand my audience as much as possible for *Oakley in Flames* to have the best chance."

"I think you'll do fine," I say.

And I put my hand over hers.

My heart jumps into my throat and the seconds slow to minutes as I process what I did. The top of her hand is still sticky, but it's also soft. God, it's so soft, which exaggerates every vein and tendon under the surface. It's like a topographical map, with her heartbeat pulsing under the surface.

Then she puts her other hand over mine, and I'm struck by the weight of her and the difference between the rougher back of her hand and the swirls and arches of her fingertips. It's like being wrapped in a security blanket; it's cutting out all the sounds and sights and smells around us. Touch is the only sense left.

We make eye contact.

And we both retract our hands.

"Either way," she says, "could I get a frame of this?" She points to the image of her post–dry heaving with her hair flopping into her face as she lies on the picnic table, surrounded by the wings. It's the clear winner. "And then do I have your permission to tag you on my public Instagram?"

It takes everything in me to not gasp.

"For what?" I ask.

She gives a slight head shake. "It's your footage," she says.

"Oh." I shake my head. "Yeah, totally. Go ahead."

She beams. "Great! What's your handle?"

"Not Eli Roth, all lowercase."

Valeria chuckles. "Useful."

A notification pops up on my phone: **valeriasullivan** *started following you*

She smiles as she checks her phone. "Already following me?"

I shrug, but there's no way the move is hiding my blush. "Work purposes. Figured we all had to."

Two means of communication.

Strike that. One public means of communication.

"Do you want me to do this now?" I ask.

"Can you?"

I pull out my laptop and the camera cord. "Yeah. Just give me a second."

I upload it via iMovie, the quickest means to extract the still. I capture the frame and AirDrop it to Valeria. I do it all within five minutes as she watches in admiration.

"Come to my side for a sec," she says.

I do as I'm told.

Valeria scoots in close to me, so our bare thighs and shoulders are touching. I think Valeria's done everything she can possibly do to me, but then some new part of our bodies brush against each other. This time it's outer thigh to outer thigh. The skin's not as sensitive, but the sensation still goes right to my inner thigh. It curls itself up like a cat and stays there.

"Which filter would you use?" she asks.

All my energy is focused on the way her leg feels, so I can

barely concentrate on her voice. It sounds like it's coming from underwater. Somehow I manage to say, "Juno makes the color pop."

She puts on the Juno filter and starts typing a caption: *Practice is going well. (Heave)n on Earth.* 📷 **@noteliroth**

I can't believe this is real.

"So I'm gonna queue it up once the announcement goes out. Don't be alarmed if a couple hundred of my stans follow you."

I want you to make movies and shorts and music videos or whatever.

I shouldn't.

But it just comes out. "Hey, do you know how you're going to shoot the scene where you pass out in the house in act two?"

"Do you have an idea?"

Heat rises to my face. "So you know how the house we rented has that prominent window and the scene is set during the day?" She nods. "I was thinking Dahlia looks right into the sun while she's going down the stairs, so we do a P.O.V. shot of her where the background and the sunny interior are the focus, but we add color splotches in post. Like the dots you see when you look into the sun. Then when the attacker approaches, the point of view shifts—it's low and he's out of focus, showing her discombobulation and compromised vision as she passes out."

For a moment, as the words flap their wings outside of my mouth, relief falls over me. I can't believe I just *did* that. Without any prep. I've made more progress on the being assertive thing in a month than I have in a year. I can't believe it.

But then I actually look at Valeria's face.

She's not smiling. Her expression is just . . . neutral. "Huh. I kinda like that. I'll drop it by Brendan."

chapter thirteen

That night, I find myself in a state of self-inflicted torture. My phone sits dormant next to me as I hunch over Final Cut Pro, stitching together a reel to send to Valeria. Even though all I can think about is her lukewarm reaction to my suggestion for *Oakley in Flames*, how she hasn't texted me since we separated in the park, how she probably won't even use this reel and she'll think I'm pathetic for trying so hard. How of course this thing with Valeria isn't going perfectly, because there was no way it was going to be any different from my experience with the dozens of guys who've fallen short or had different intentions from mine over the years.

But then my phone lights up from my bedroom desk. Not even a text; a call. I nearly fumble it out of my hands as I check the screen.

My heart, soaring, sinks down to earth. It's just my mom. She's been calling me several times a week since I left Alice. I'm going to have to answer her at some point, and I guess I'd rather do a few minutes now than potentially hours tomorrow.

"Hi," I say, keeping Mom to my AirPods as I focus my eyes and fingers on Final Cut.

"Hi, sweetie," Mom says. I hear the TV droning in the background; she and my dad are probably watching— "Are you watching *Saturday Night Live*?"

Bingo. She always calls to discuss media with me—also not something I'm going out of my way to do tonight. I click and drag a few seconds of footage to delete. "No. Rom and I only use streaming."

"Well, your girl is on it."

First of all, I don't know what girl she means. This is Mom's comphet way to say literally any girl I've ever mentioned more than three times to her. Sometimes she *almost* gets it and it's celebrity crushes I didn't acknowledge as gay. But most of the time it's people like my high school English teacher who did my college rec letters; at one point it meant Senator Elizabeth Warren. Don't get me wrong, it's nice that she remembers specific details about my life. But her still seeing me as *so straight* digs under my skin as I strain to focus.

"Which one?" I say, although I have no intention of playing twenty questions to find out who.

"The one in that flower horror film you love."

Oh. Florence. God, maybe I do have a type. "I'm sure *Florence Pugh* is doing great, but I—" I suck air in between my teeth. I usually kinda like catching up with my mom, but tonight her voice feels like a mosquito buzzing. "I'm working right now."

But instead of grumbling to my dad about me always working, she keeps going. "Oh, what're you working on?"

I stare at Valeria's adorably scrunched-up face as she inspects one of the wings mid-lineup. "Video editing."

"Of what?"

Of a one-on-one outing with a woman within my dating age range. Of an outing that, despite how spectacularly bad it got, still resulted in another woman pressing her leg to my leg and touching my lip and it—it making me horny enough to *do something about it* while Romy ran out to the grocery store hours later. *Because I'm bisexual, Mother.*

"Stuff." It comes out curt. Unexpectedly curt.

But I can't even give her the G-rated version. She calls random blond actresses "my girl," but the idea even right now of her calling Valeria my girl and it being romantic—it makes me nauseated. Talking about my crush shouldn't do that. If it were Wyatt, it wouldn't be like this. I told her about Wyatt the second he asked me out. The muscles in my arm quiver as I try to navigate the editing program.

"How's work?" She continues trying to make conversation.

"Fine."

I can't talk to Mom about Valeria touching me and saying nothing about my scene. I can't talk to her about Wyatt outing me, about Alice tokenizing me, about Julia and the Rachel Brosnahan thing, about whether she *really* supports marriage equality, about whether she'd cry if I said I might not marry a Nice Jewish Boy. I **can't** even *really* talk to her about Florence fucking Pugh on fucking *SNL*. And it's her fucking fault for being such an opaque—

"Fine? Is that Valeria—?"

My heartbeat slamming in my ears, I snap. "*Fine*, Mom! It's fine and I'm *working*! Can you just—?"

But Mom, a stone-cold New York bitch, doesn't just cower and hang up. She never will, and I'm the idiot for thinking she would. "Jesus *Christ*, Luna. Call me back when you're feeling less bitchy."

Then she hangs up, leaving me to scream into a pillow, my

whole body flushed. She didn't even say anything homophobic; why am I so *mad* at her? Will this feeling really only go away if I come out and get my answer once and for all?

As the guilt pricks cold along my arms, I do my best to focus on editing. Like the hardworking daughter she loves so much.

When I drag myself out into our living room hours later, for once I think I'm less seeking out Romy for comfort and more being drawn to her effortless queerness. I hear the comforting lilt of her speaking Spanish.

Romy's from a San Francisco suburb, and because I'm Jewish and my family doesn't have Christmas plans, I get to revel in Romy's family drama one day a year. Romy's dad gets tired of traveling, demands his Spanish relatives fly out to California, and ends up angrily making fancy entremeses, roast lamb, and turrón for me, Wyatt, and Romy's older cousin who's doing a Ph.D. at Stanford. Romy constantly apologizes for it, but it's like music, listening to her, her dad, and her cousin argue and tease one another in Spanish. Even now, hearing Romy speak the language brings me back to specific memories of curling up with her ancient family cats next to a roaring fire, leaving a spot for her in the La-Z-Boy her mom hates so we can watch *Home Alone* in peace.

Still, there's nothing particularly peaceful or friendly about the way Romy's speaking on the phone now as she sits in front of the television, the Netflix menu open and static. I retained only high school–level Spanish, and Spain-Spanish accents are impossible to understand, but I can usually tell whom she's talking to through little phrases, her body language, her expression. In this case, it's her grandma, and Romy is muttering, "*Lo sé lo sé lo sé*," in her customer service voice.

She watches me as I join her on the couch. We've bitched to each other about family so much by now that we don't really care if the other listens in on phone calls. Still, I give her thigh a couple of pats as I pull up my phone and check my messages. Valeria confirmed she got my reel, but nothing more.

"Nieto, Abue, por favor," Romy says. She winces as she says it.

The plea hits me, piques cold in my chest, but it's the soft, almost defeated way she says it that keeps the feeling there. *Sorry* and *hopefully she'll get it next time* hover in my head, but I don't want to intrude where I'm not welcome. With Romy, it's a toss-up if she wants to acknowledge gender stuff. So when she wraps up the conversation and lets out a long sigh as she leans into the couch, I let her lead.

"You look upset," Romy says, leaning on her fist, clearly setting the tone.

I chuckle. "You always say that about me." Still, I'll give her one chance to talk. "Are you?"

Romy takes a deep breath, eyes on the TV, but she doesn't do anything. "Doesn't matter. She's paying my rent because she thinks I'm a wonderful writer; how mad can I get about a conjugation she doesn't even realize she's doing?"

I think back to my conversation with my mom, shame settling in the back of my throat. If Romy's this forgiving with her grandma, what am I doing? "Pretty mad, I've found. And mine haven't even done anything yet."

Romy gives this sad smile. "They're centrist and aggressively heterosexual; that's enough."

God, it feels so good to be surrounded by queerness, to be seen for who I am. But since Romy is the one making me feel seen, let me focus on her.

The conversation pauses.

"You can be mad at your family too, you know."

Romy stretches, bones in her shoulders popping. "I don't wanna be mad right now." Her eyes light up. "In fact, pick a movie off this list that took me a million years to do."

Romy hands me her phone, the screen boasting a Note titled *ESSENTIAL SAPPHIC MOVIE/TV LIST FOR BABY LUNA*. A very welcome warmth pricks as I see the first ten films. But as I scroll down to at least twenty-five more, my heart drags down my body. By the time I realize there are more than a hundred films on this list and individual items include shit like *THE ENTIRE FILMOGRAPHY OF SARAH PAULSON*, I feel like I've been handed a very potent psychedelic and am having a terrible trip.

"Um, why is this list so long?" I ask.

"Look, this is for your benefit." Romy seems to have gotten her bounce back. "It's the only way for the sapphic meme accounts to make sense. So you can build a community."

I scrutinize it. Surely there cannot be this many films that depict sapphic feelings and/or star a sapphic actress. In the larger scheme of cinema history, it stopped being illegal to *be* gay, like, a very short time ago.

"Do you wanna start with a single icon and work through their filmography or start with the gay classics?" Romy asks. "I can adjust the first film based off that."

I flip to her *ICONS* section—*Cara Delevingne, Cate Blanchett, Kristen Stewart, Gillian Anderson, Aubrey Plaza, Kate McKinnon, Tessa Thompson*, the aforementioned *Sarah Paulson, Princess Diana* (insert: Since when?), *Winona Ryder, Jodie Foster*, etc.

"Uh, is this every film they've ever done?"

Romy huffs. "Yes! Every film!"

I hand her back the phone. "Okay, but if I'm going to commit to a yearlong 'Watch All of Romy's Nineties Idols' disguised as a sapphic movie marathon, I can't do *Panic Room*—"

"What? Why can't you?" Romy scowls.

I look her in the eye, trying my damnedest not to smile. "Because you masturbate to it."

A beat passes. Two. More, as Romy sits there, utterly caught. Her mouth opens a few times, sounds come out, but nothing forms into words until: "I see no reason I can't respectfully admire a beautiful woman—" She speaks through gritted teeth.

"She is fully clothed in that movie."

"—in a cami—"

I happen to be wearing a cami and pajama bottoms right now, and it's too hard to resist. I lean over *right* in her eyeline to grab her phone again. "Where, if I recall correctly, she *puts on more clothes*."

I pull Romy into a side hug and laugh a little while she blushes as hard as I've ever seen her. I let this rare moment of vulnerability soak in for as long as I can. This moment of Romy loving me, trusting me enough to be her raw, depraved, hysterical self.

"Luna." She's trying so hard to be as authoritative as she usually is, but she's still bright red. "If you understand anything about the sapphic gaze, know the fundamental principle of *sometimes more clothes is sexy*."

"It's fucking weird, and you're my favorite person." I look back at the list for whatever is—a small mercy for Romy—not a 1990s-slash-2000s thriller with a female protagonist. "Was Princess Diana gay?"

Romy literally shakes the embarrassment away. "*The Crown* it is."

For a while, the two of us exist in our little bubble as we put on season four, Romy's hand on my thigh and my cheek on her shoulder, only breaking away to sip whatever cheap wine we had in the fridge, watching young Princess Diana have a really bad time. I send my mom an apology text between episodes one and two, saying I'm just on my period. Easy out, even though the anger still purrs inside me.

Romy usually gives color commentary when we watch stuff alone, but she's quiet when the third episode starts.

"Do you think I could be like Emma Corrin?" she says suddenly. I look down at my sapphic cheat sheet; that's the actor playing young Diana.

I smile. "I think you have to be five-eight or taller to play Diana."

But Romy doesn't even reply to my joke. She just keeps staring at the TV. "I mean, hot, talented, adds *they* to social media bios."

She doesn't pause the show, but I look at her like she's what we're supposed to be watching. The hand not on my thigh is clenched into a fist at her side. She stares hard at the screen, but it's the tiniest things in her face that really give it away: the flexed muscle in her jaw, the glassy quality in her eyes. It hits me suddenly, the shame and the anger shifting into a full-on lump in my throat at Romy's cracking facade.

She doesn't need to say it again after saying it in so many ways throughout our friendship. How even now she dreads asking her relatives to call her their child/nibling/grandchild instead of daughter/niece/granddaughter. How she didn't originally go with dual pronouns because of how much she can't stand the idea of the seconds before her parents pick which pronoun, which side of her they'll honor while being overheard on the phone.

Up until now, Romy hadn't done any explaining of the sapphic nature of this show. It's sitting here, looking at her, processing what little she's said, that I get it. This isn't sapphic, and Princess Diana wasn't gay. Emma Corrin's presence comforts Romy. I wonder if they make Romy feel as solid, as real and important, in her gender identity as watching bi actresses in movies does for me.

I put my hand over hers, squeeze. "You can be those three things. Already got two." I wink.

"Maybe someday. Ask me later." She smiles at me, inhaling slowly and taking the glassiness in her eyes with it. "That's the trick with all this, Lunes. You never really stop coming out."

But as we sink back into watching TV, Romy starts making comments. I join in, stowing away my phone and all my lingering worries about Valeria. Everything is okay for a few hours as we lie there, fully seen and known by each other.

chapter fourteen

The next day, Romy and I reject Wyatt's invite to a party near his family's home in Malibu to, of all things, write in the minicourt-yard in our apartment complex in the early sunshine. It's certainly not a bougie SoCal day rager, but the courtyard's got nice chairs and grass that's not completely dead and a little firepit that'd work if we bought logs. It's also one of Romy's and my places. I've always appreciated the way we accumulate these locations. Each one is like a little locked diary with our memories snug inside.

"Okay, so, one more time," Romy says, "what was so upsetting about your chicken date with Valeria?"

Even a full day later, my attention is torn between watching my texts in case Valeria comments on the footage I took and watching my Instagram go bananas now that her post is up. And how the hell am I going to cinch Valeria's and my connection, professional or otherwise, if I'm so stuck on this? I don't *want* to bug Romy with Valeria stuff, but it's still come out somehow over the course of our morning together. "I—I just don't think she was happy in the end."

Romy glances up from her computer, her hair blowing in the

soft wind. One of Romy's playwriting friends just got representation without having gone through an MFA program and told her last night that she should send personalized invitations to the festival to anyone she knows with even a vague agent connection. With Romy out of her funk from the night before, we've come up with twenty names so far. "She touched your lips, and you and Steven nearly killed her, but she blames Steven and not you. What would Julia tell you to be doing right now?"

I recognize the tightness in my chest, the racing thoughts. I *know* I'm especially anxious right now, that nothing I say is coming out entirely rationally, but it's like I have to spit out these thoughts. I wish I could tell Romy to just ignore me.

"I don't know. She'd be fact-checking me or something."

Romy's still not looking up from her laptop. "What bad thing happened? We can disregard the guilt from destroying her digestive system with chilis, because Valeria's an adult who consented to your practice round."

I exhale. "She said she'd run the concept by Brendan."

Romy doesn't speak for a few seconds. "And what about that says 'my career and love life have died'?"

"She didn't say yes."

"Luna, she's probably contacting Brendan right now. Please, chill. This is a *good thing*."

I know. I *know*, but I can't dismiss the subconscious thing I picked up. The look on her face when she said she'd tell Brendan . . . it just wasn't the same enthusiasm she's given everything else about my work. Before *she* was buttering *me* up the whole time. And now something has changed. So how do I know all her resentment about the press booking was about Steven and not me? *I'm* the one who gave her the hell wings. And I should've brought milk.

"I just—I don't feel good about this. Valeria's been my rock in this weird production world, and it seemed like . . . I just got a bad vibe."

Romy closes her laptop. Moves from her position across the table and comes to sit next to me. She pulls me into a side hug. It's a strange feeling, the way her heat loosens my muscles yet tightens them right back up. I rest my head on her shoulder. I'd never have the nerve to do this with Valeria. But man, do I love the way my cheek molds against the curve of her shoulder.

"Lune, I know this is getting intense for you. But none of this extra work with her is going to change the course of your life."

"But didn't you say to focus on my career with her? The personal stuff went so well, but the career bit just feels like I ruined everything. Like I asked for too much." I thought I could separate my professional and potentially romantic relationships with Valeria, but the whole thing is becoming murkier and murkier.

Romy sighs, heavy and long. "Maybe I was wrong about the career focus. When you think about the day you spent with her, what made you the most excited? And don't tell me it's her putting death sauce on your lips, because that's already the most sado-masochistic thing I've ever heard and I don't need the image of how hard-core your sex life would be if left to your own devices."

I eye the hot sauce bottle that's sitting between us. She'd been reading and googling the ingredients earlier. "I was trying to comfort her when she was talking about Steven, and I put my hand over hers. She put her other hand over mine, and it was . . . I don't know." I lace my fingers with Romy's, testing the feeling. Romy's fingers are a little shorter, and, unlike Valeria's, her nails are polished. The cold of her rings presses against my skin. She rubs my knuckles right away, though. I like that. "It's not like holding guys' hands. They're big and usually harder and just—sometimes it feels like a puzzle that doesn't fit. But I feel like there's a weird primal comfort and familiarity in a woman's hands."

Romy pulls her hand away. "Not to mention the most sexual part of a sapphic." She blushes and stares out at the firepit before turning back to me. "She seems to be flirting with you."

My heart flutters. "Yeah?"

Romy motions to the hot sauce. "I wouldn't brush that on your brother's lips no matter how funny it would be to see him in pain."

"Yeah . . ."

"Something isn't clicking, though. What would you do if *she's* closeted? Like even more than you? Maybe she's just better at flirting in general."

I'm sure this is meant to discourage, but my heart picks up. "If she's closeted, though, then she's gay? And we have a chance?"

Romy pauses. "Not . . . quite. Like, in college would you have kissed a non-man?"

I refuse to make eye contact with Romy. Yeah, of course I would've. She was actually at the top of my list back then. "Yeah."

"But would you have been like, 'Cool, I'm gay,' and started a relationship?"

I rub my arms. "No."

"Exactly. Closeted girls tend to be very unsure. They're trying to test the waters and they're easily scared. And there's nothing wrong with experimenting with them and helping them figure it out, but it can also be a *whole* lot of pain. And I'd hate for you to be with someone who's still doubting their sexuality. You don't need any external doubt. You should be with"—she inhales sharply—"someone like me, you know?"

Someone *like* her? Or—

"Look, dude," she says, "I have to work on these invitations." Her tone sounds alarmingly similar to mine with my mom last night. "Sit with it for a bit."

I still have more questions bubbling around my head, but signal received. I need to be a better friend to her. She's been so supportive of my art, and I need to do the same thing for her. Getting her those backgrounds is barely the equivalent of all the writing help she gave me in undergrad. So no more Valeria talk today.

"You know," I say as I inch my hand closer to hers, "it's pretty fucking amazing that you're about to be showcased. With the script you said was niche and weird and uninteresting. I'm so glad that soon everyone's going to see what I already know—that you're completely brilliant." A tiny smile forms on her face. "Also, do you want to talk about last night? About the pronouns?"

Red creeps up Romy's face. "Yes, that." She kicks her feet. "I'm still figuring everything out. Right now, she/her still feels right. Thanks for asking, though."

I smile. "Of course."

But Romy returns to her work almost immediately. The window she opened about gender is now firmly shut.

Once I realize she's really not going to continue the conversation, I turn back to my phone. My Instagram notifications are still going wild. I've gained about two hundred new followers, and now all my recent posts are suddenly populated with comments like *how do you know Valeria?* and *do you have more of Valeria?* My DMs are from film school acquaintances suddenly hitting me up, but obviously all they want to do is ask about her.

My phone goes off.

My heart leaps. It's a picture from Valeria. I glance over at

Romy, who hasn't noticed. Guilt nibbles at me; did I really need to take up Romy's time making her talk me down when all it took for the anxiety to disappear was a text?

I sigh and open it.

It's a meme with the caption, *Boss: This position is actually being an assistant to 2 people but it's the same pay since we split you. Me:* [the picture of Valeria dying on the table].

Her text reads: The true milestone of fame.

So she isn't mad at me after all. I didn't mess everything up.

I text back: I can make you look better than that.

Fuck. Why the fuck did I text that?

I add: On a camera.

Can you?

I just need another chance. I need a spot where we can be fully alone, where it's just the camera and us. I can give her footage that won't be shared with anyone. I'll show her how well I can execute my ideas. Do her a favor, show her how well I can frame her. She'll be fully on my team again.

> I know it's last minute, but would you want to do a legit photoshoot? There's this incredible cliffside spot in San Pedro called Sunken City. The aesthetic is 🔥

> Can we do later today? My sister's devil's advocate Calabasas trust fund baby husband is back in town and I'll call this "mandatory work." 😛

This is the first time Valeria's mentioned her family in the weeks I've known her.

> What time specifically do I have to save you?

What time do you need for lighting? It's an outdoor location, right?

> I'd want an hour before golden hour. So could you be at the spot at like 7?

ORRR I show up at your apartment and we carpool so I can kill an extra hour of avoidance? 😏

> You'd really drive like an hour out of the way and make the drive to Sunken City longer than it'd be from your house? 😆

Absolutely. What am I wearing?

My chest is getting warm already as I send her some inspiration ideas.

I glance at Romy, hard at work. Something tells me this isn't a rash decision she'd approve of. I've yet to fully figure out what I'm doing that's bothering Romy with the Valeria thing (Wyatt's been on board so far), but at this point, I don't need her constant advice. It's probably better this way anyway. I can focus my attention on *her* art and whatever our personal problems are and deal with Valeria on my own time. Maybe I'm graduating from baby gay to, like . . . regular stupid twentysomething gay? An independent gay.

I make my plan with Valeria. I don't say anything to Romy. When she finishes her list, I read it over and give notes. Everything is calm.

I can juggle this, easy.

Sunday evening, the world's a miraculous seventy-five degrees, sun out, and I can't find a second backpack to stuff my lighting and camera equipment into. My phone goes off by the front door, and Romy glances over at it.

"Honey, you've got a text," Romy says, completely deadpan as she types at her laptop on the kitchen table.

My chest tightens as I look her way. Romy never reads my texts unless I ask her to while I'm driving, but I still run through the scenario of what would happen if she knew I was sort of seeing Valeria behind her back. It shouldn't feel so wrong, but I can't shake my unease.

I still don't have my backpack, but I slide over and look at my phone.

Valeria says she's pulling up.

"Hey, Rom, do you have an extra backpack?" I ask.

"Yeah, hold on."

Romy lumbers into her bedroom, rustles around a little, and emerges with a novelty backpack I bought her for her twenty-first. It has this absolutely ridiculous design: a tree with a face and branches that look like a human hand with the words *Palm Tree*.

I peer through the front windows, watching as a red Porsche pulls onto our street and my phone goes off again.

"Where are you off to in such a hurry anyway?" Romy asks.

I stuff my equipment into the palm tree backpack. "Just hanging with someone from S.C.A."

Romy chuckles. "Sounds more like you're getting kidnapped, but okay. Should I remember this Porsche?"

"No, it's not Pete Welsh, don't worry," I say as I step out the door. "Thank you for the backpack."

I shut the door behind me, and my muscles tense as I jog to Valeria's car. I refuse to look up at the fucking window of our apartment.

Valeria's car is all leather and lacquered wood. There's a Madonna song playing through the speaker system, and an amused grin is already smacked onto her face. "Ready?"

I force a glance at the window. I can't believe I lied to Romy about this. "Absolutely."

And we head out.

There's no one in the parking lot closest to Sunken City, which is a sort of dilapidated piece of the San Pedro ocean cliffside. The city built a fence that's meant to be unclimbable around the walkable path that leads down to the cliff, but I've been using an even more dangerous entrance for years now.

"So Sunken City used to be a land development—like houses and roads and everything. But in 1929, the land eroded so quickly that the whole thing just slipped into the ocean," I say as we jump the maybe three-foot concrete wall that leads to the back entrance.

Valeria's eyes widen as she sees what we've still got to go around.

"At this point, the only things left are broken foundations for houses, abandoned streetcar tracks, buckled sidewalks, and empty streets."

We're on a slab, maybe two feet maximum, that skirts an uneven drop down the cliffside. A sort of *V* leads down to a fence with a giant hole in the middle, and then the land becomes uneven ground that you can follow back into the Sunken City remains. There's also a several-hundred-foot drop into the glimmering ocean, and certain death, below. No rails, no guarantee that this little "trail" won't erode under our feet.

"This is the worst spot," I say.

"As long as it's not more death wings," she says.

I take the downward trail first and wait near the bottom, one hand on the hole in the rusting fence as she steps down. Her steps are confident enough, even with half my equipment on her back. And when she lands, her hand lands in mine. I'm not scared— I've never been scared of this area—but her touch gets my heart going. We duck through the hole in the fence one at a time, separating again to climb back up to the solid hiking path. When everything is said and done, we're back on the other side of the fence—and we have several dozen yards of solid cliff to cross before reaching Sunken City itself. Chunks of glistening teal beer bottles are scattered throughout the dirt, and the edges of graffiti start to pop up as we get closer.

"So this area is mostly just a local hiking spot and party area now," I say. "It's technically illegal and dangerous—there's usually an old lady warning everyone that they could fall off the cliffs— but most people consider it a hidden gem. Also a really cool guerrilla art spot."

"Has anyone ever died on the cliffs?"

I shrug. "Someone running from the cops died in the eighties, and there are a couple stories about people falling and injuring themselves, but it's not that common."

I stop just short of the hiking trails down into Sunken City. There's an absolutely gorgeous view of the remains and the ocean even from here.

"Oh my god," Valeria mumbles as she pushes a stray hair out of her face. "Who does the art?"

I beam. It really is one of the coolest places in L.A.

Nearly every chunk of what was once a road or a building is now covered in neon splashes of graffiti and paint. It feels like a modern addition to the inherent art of the wrecked buildings and something that just appeared naturally, an eerie juxtaposition of mankind's failures in architecture with its triumphs in visual arts. It's like having an urban art exhibit drawn into the natural beauty of the sea cliffs.

"It started off as gang graffiti in the eighties, but it's evolved. Now anyone can come and spray-paint. People even use acrylic now.

"C'mon," I say. "There's a rock here that I adore."

I lead her down a hiking trail, over to a rock shaped like a lopsided *T* that used to be a chunk of road. It looks ready to slide off its base and into the ocean below, but it's been reliable and steady since before my parents were born. It's covered in a gorgeous coat of paint.

"You know, if this film thing doesn't work out, you'd make a great tour guide," Valeria says. "Do a guerrilla tour of L.A."

I chuckle. "Thanks. Good to know I have options."

The rock itself is maybe four and a half feet off the ground, and the only way up for short people like me is from a small rock that juts out next to it. It's not close enough for the climb to be comfortable. I grab the top of the *T*, step up as far as I can using the helper rock, and scramble onto the road chunk's surface belly-down like a worm. Valeria, who's taller, climbs up with a bit less squirming.

But after a couple of seconds on the road piece, which is noticeably tilted away from the cliff, she's gripping the surface. I giggle. "I swear, it's not going anywhere."

She takes off the backpack and hands it to me. Her hesitation melts away, and she crawls to the edge that overlooks the ocean. The palm trees in the area sway in the gentle breeze, and god, the sky around us is crystal clear. You can even see a little bit of Long Beach harbor to the south, the Queen's Necklace to the north.

"Did I pick the right look, by the way?" she asks.

It's an ultimately very casual look: a black cotton cropped T-shirt boasting the words *BITE ME*, high-waisted jean shorts, combat boots. She's also brought a yellow-white-blue-purple flannel. Her makeup is a standard street look; her hair is teased to look artfully messy. Beach waves, or whatever it's called. But yeah, even dressed this casually, she looks incredible. The bit of graphic in the shirt is already picking up the art around her.

God, I can't believe I'm the one capturing her on camera.

When I was a child, my anxiety used to manifest as these out-of-the-blue sucker punch thoughts I couldn't escape. The one I still remember, even all these years later, was about how irreversibly flawed human vision is. Eyes are just these highly vulnerable organs that are ruled by biological mechanics that are flawed when we're born and only decline over time. So few people have perfect vision, and no two humans can truly know if they're seeing the same thing when they're looking at a palm tree–lined boulevard in L.A. Even with glasses and contacts and laser surgery, humans can never all be perfect in the same way.

But then there's film. Cameras are, in fact, the perfect eyes.

Every human with vision can look through footage captured by a camera and objectively see the same image. And the photographer knows that. Maybe that's what I love about cinematography. When I capture something on film, I'm capturing the perfect version of a slice of my memory. Everyone can see what I see. Exactly what I see. They can see something more beautiful than they could with their naked eye.

When I see a movie done by a master cinematographer, I always get the same feeling: the breathless thrill of seeing beauty in our world. When I sat in an overpriced movie theater with Romy and Wyatt watching Holdo light speed–ram into that First Order ship, it was like time stopped. I want to be the one giving people new images, new conceptions of beauty. Looking at Valeria, I feel my heart flutter. I'm already imagining the pictures.

"Do you use a different skill set for photography?" she asks as I finish setting up my camera to capture some stills, maybe some moving images if the moments are right.

"A bit. Ultimately as a cinematographer, you need all the skills of a great photographer, but then you have to take it to the next level. You start integrating the image with motion—how will an actor look walking across a landscape, what scale do you want to use to emphasize the importance of a moment. But I can do both." I smile. "I just have a preference."

Valeria's pretty much gone rogue in the minutes it's taken me to set up the camera, and she's now arching her back halfway over the edge, hanging upside down so she can see the ocean. I smile, walk over, get the stray hairs out of her face, and start shooting.

Once I've gotten all the shots I can from this rock, I set my camera somewhat close to the edge, jump off, grab the camera from the ground, and survey the angles.

"Did you happen to get a chance to talk to Brendan?" I ask.

She nods. "He wants to talk to you about it. Was this just an idea you had, or do you have concept art or footage or anything?"

My heart leaps. I thank god I have a brother. "I do."

"Let's watch it tomorrow before we shoot."

My heart flutters. "Thank you."

For a few moments, I just snap photos. I can't believe that just . . . worked?

It did just work, right?

"So you're not super close with your family, I gather?" I ask, pushing down the anxiety that's already burrowing inside me.

She shrugs. "I don't *hate* my brother-in-law or anything, but it's a lot of comments like, 'Oh, Hollywood turned you so radical,' as if I wasn't an *academic* starting arguments for fun before I started acting. With Dave, a lot of the time it just ends up being one of those things where you're like, *I know this is going to go badly.*"

My heart twinges. "I get that. My parents have been commenting about how liberal I've become since leaving college. Like, they dismiss the idea that any of it could be positive growth."

She flips over, making real eye contact with me. "Are you out to your parents?"

The feeling in my chest graduates to a plain ache. Mom was so quick to forgive me after our phone call Saturday night, but it's not like I felt any less tense talking to her this morning as she went on her daily walk. I was stressed out, waiting to have to fumble through a lie if she asked about dating, tasting the bitter flavor of *I'm bi* on my tongue knowing I'd never say it out loud.

"No. It's . . . not the right time."

She reaches over the rock and takes my hand. "I'm sorry about that."

My throat closes. This is not something I want to deal with

right now. This is a conversation I only want to have with Julia. "Can you relax your face?"

She breaks into a quick smile before obeying. "Call this one *I Can't Believe the Photographer Just Skirted That.*"

I smile and snap my pictures. Get back on the rock and take some more pictures. But when I want to capture motion again, we return to conversation. I let her move around within a composed frame.

"You've got a support system, though, right?" Valeria says.

"Yeah," I say. "My friends are great about it. And it's . . . I try to just ignore that part of it—my parents. The thing I'm really focused on is . . ." I change the shot, keep my hands occupied. "Is just this sense of being a late bloomer. I was a late bloomer with guys, and I hate going through that stress again."

"If it's any consolation, late bloomers aren't any better or worse than people who've been at it for years. Sometimes it's a safety thing to disclose, but otherwise it really only matters if you *want* people to know. No one will ask or care otherwise. I was a late bloomer too."

I can't hide a prickle of surprise. "Really?"

"Yeah. And I bet you weren't as late as you think. How old were you when you had your first kiss?"

My stomach tightens.

"Nineteen," I say, just as she says, "Nineteen."

A moment of silence passes. She breaks out in a grin. I make sure it's on camera.

"See? You don't think I'm some undesirable loser, right?"

She flips over on the rock, pressing her cheek into the warm surface. Her body rises and falls softly as she breathes. Bathed in the golden light, her curves hidden, she looks *sublime*.

"No, I don't."

Her eyes flutter open, and her gaze is suddenly heavy on me. She's drilling into me, pinning me to this spot. No one's looked at me this way before. "I see you the same way."

For a moment, I feel the tilt of this slab of concrete, and my upper body starts swaying down the slope. I catch my body, but my mind can't focus, not even on this shot I spent hours pre-composing this morning. Valeria? Didn't have her first kiss until nineteen? Valeria? Sees me as someone desirable?

"You do?" I ask, turning the camera off. I don't want to share this moment with anyone. Not even future me, a few hours from now, a few hours outside of this feeling.

I leave the camera on the little tripod and crawl over to her. She rolls over onto her side, skin still pressed into the concrete. I do the same, leaving a foot of space between us. I think it's a foot. My muscles, from my core to my legs to my face, are quivering. Getting closer makes everything worse, but somehow it's also all I want to do.

"Obviously I don't know what shit you went through before this, and that's all valid, but yes, right now, all I see is this clever, talented woman who should maybe flip the camera on herself once in a while."

She scoots closer to me. There are inches between us. My heart is beating so hard I swear it's reverberating off the dense rock; the butterflies are packed so tightly it hurts. We're so close. God, we're so close. I can see the pores on her face, the individual hairs in her eyebrows, the creases in her lips. The different shades of brown in her eyes.

She moves a hair out of my eyes. Just like I did to her earlier. "Trust me," she says, her voice lower now. My stomach flips.

"Assuming you want it, if someone right comes along, it'll be no time before you're so deep in it that you don't even remember what it felt like before."

She looks to my lips.

"Hey!"

Getting this close took as long as it does to wade into the ocean when it's cold. Pulling away is like being launched out of a cannon. Valeria and I roll over onto our knees, those few inches magnifying to feet. We look toward the source of the voice, pushing pebbles off our legs and arms and out of our hair.

It's just a young couple, all jean shorts and T-shirts, one holding a spray can.

"Do you two have any more spray paint?" the boy asks. "We're out!"

I look around our rock space, as if I forgot I brought spray paint. "I, uh, we don't!"

"Okay, thanks! Sorry!"

They walk over to another part of Sunken City, but they remain in view. Valeria looks at me. There's a little bit of red staining her cheeks. "Do you want to take any more photos?"

"I have a couple ideas for after sunset."

The sky's bleeding into an orange-and-pink watercolor painting. Valeria runs a hand through her hair. "Can we look around until then?" She smiles. "Maybe I can even take pictures of you."

As we climb off the rock, I still can't decide if anything was going to happen.

chapter fifteen

At the shoot on Monday, Valeria's acting as if the entire weekend didn't mean anything. Which, okay, might be dramatic, but
I can't believe she goes around set actually doing her directing/
acting job, and she acknowledges me only at previously established
appropriate moments, like requesting nearby props or asking my
opinion when she and Brendan can't fully commit to a minute
detail in a shot. There's absolutely no attempt by either of us to
dissect what the fresh hell happened the day before.

Maybe nothing *did* happen. Maybe the only things that really
happened were that she tagged me on Instagram, I have footage of her to edit, and she forced us to take a picture together at
Sunken City. (*Forced* in this sentence means *I acted camera shy
but was internally screaming and the photo is now my lock screen*.)
But as I hand Brendan a wide lens on our last day on location at
the house in Studio City, I can't help but wonder if there's something else that *should* be happening.

We almost kissed. I've had very few situations where I was
almost kissed, but that has to be what happened. We were inches

from each other and she looked at my lips. I don't know what else that could mean.

Brendan starts talking to me. "Hey, so I saw your test footage."

My heart all but stops. "You did?"

He crosses his arms.

Smiles.

"I did. I love the concept. And we'd credit you in the film. Not *as* D.P., but I can for sure put your name first under the camera assistants. You did technically do some shots . . ."

He still doesn't trust me with the camera. No one would hire me as D.P. with just this scene under my belt, but I have his attention again. "I fucked up before," I say. "But I promise I'm a great focus puller. Give me one more chance?"

Brendan takes the longest pause of my life, long enough for my lungs to seemingly collapse as I hold my breath.

Then he says, "Sure."

The assistant who'd replaced me the other day gets unceremoniously sent off for coffee. A P.A. holds the slate. And Brendan steps aside for me to stick the lens I envisioned into the camera. Lets me adjust.

Valeria gets into her position at the bottom of the stairs, crumpled, with makeup-painted bruises on her body. She sells exhausted and battered better than I could've imagined. And I get right down there with her, adjusting the camera to a low-angle P.O.V. shot.

"This is really cool," she whispers to me.

Her voice, speaking to me with the casualness of our time on the cliffs, sounds unfamiliar. Unfamiliar, at least, in this setting. It's like I've lost the ability to process us having a one-on-one conversation when other people we know are around.

But still, I know kind words when I hear them.

Yes, with this image, *my* image, I know exactly how to focus it. It's unconventional, and it might turn out terrible in post, but Brendan's trusting me.

Brendan takes over my spot.

Gives me a thumbs-up.

And we do a couple of takes.

The A.D. yells cut, and Valeria comes walking up to me.

"Hey, can I get your opinion on something?" she asks.

I'm still basking in the joy of that successful scene. Her voice sounds like it's coming from far away, especially as Brendan smiles at me from his spot at the camera.

"Yeah, for sure," I reply.

She leads me through the crew setup to a random bedroom on the first floor where costumes have been stored. There's a mannequin head with a blond wig sitting on top of a vanity. She removes the head from the table.

"Does this look queer to you? It just—the longer I look at it, the more it looks like a Karen haircut," Valeria says.

Queer. All the joy from my success with Brendan disappears and I'm left with a sinking anxious feeling. I'm on my game focus pulling, but romance has me back in the clueless baby gutters.

I examine the wig. It just looks like a pixie cut. Fuck, I don't even know if this is gay.

"Why?" I ask. "I mean, I know why, but . . . it seems like a basic pixie cut."

Valeria sighs. "Shit. Yeah." She runs her hand down her face. "I was gonna actually *get* this haircut to finish filming, but I refuse to get this if it's not even getting the point across."

Jesus, she's so committed to this queer role she'd get a queer-coded haircut like her character when she could just wear a wig? Her press is in less than two months. Does this mean she's willing to drastically change her look to make sure *Oakley in Flames* is authentically queer?

That . . . sounds very gay.

Is today possibly the greatest day ever?

"So I clearly have a, y'know, femme aesthetic." I run a hand through my hair. "But my roommate, Romy, is a queer style icon and can definitely recommend a great barber."

Romy should be off work right now and able to answer her phone.

Valeria's eyes light up. "That's amazing. Seriously, I need this done A.S.A.P."

Romy's a fan of Valeria. And I've been forcing Romy to interpret everything happening between Valeria and me, yeah, but it's all been filtered through my own biases. There's no reason Valeria would bring up Sunken City, which I'm starting to think I didn't even need to lie to Romy about. And I'm growing more and more curious: What would happen if I got Romy and Valeria in the same room? Would Romy stop being weird about how much I talk about Valeria if they had more of a friendship connection?

Romy picks up. "Hey, don't use your phone in class, Roth," she says.

I glance at Valeria. "We're on a break. Hey, what barber do you go to?"

"Are you getting the Bisexual Bob, or is this for someone else?"

I glance at Valeria. "Valeria needs an edgy short cut for *Oakley in Flames*."

"Oh. I go to this place on Fairfax in WeHo. My favorite barber's named Sid."

I sneak another glance at Valeria. I twist a piece of hair in my fingertips. "Do you wanna come?" I ask Romy. I turn to Valeria. "Is that okay?"

"Are you literally asking Valeria if you can invite me *after* you invited me?"

Valeria's lips curl upward; clearly this phone call is not quiet enough.

"It's cool. I'm happy to meet your style-icon friends," she says.

I pull the phone closer to my now flushed face. "You're invited."

Romy laughs, one of the sweetest sounds in the world. "When should I meet you?"

Valeria flashes me a *ten minutes to leaving*. "We'll be leaving Studio City in around ten."

"Cool. Text me when you're heading out and I'll send you the address."

I hang up with my heart fluttering. This is definitely the most ambitious crossover I've ever attempted, but here we go. I know I just told myself I wouldn't involve Romy with this Valeria stuff, but just this once. One last thing I need from her. I'll make it up to her. And she agreed without hesitation. This can't be complete torture for her, right?

Romy's a genius with this stuff; if she can't determine whether Valeria gives off gay vibes, no one can. I'll email Brendan at the barber, ask if he'll recommend me, and everything will be perfect.

The barbershop has a *perfectly* curated Romy aesthetic: brick wall facade outside leading into a converted warehouse housing an industrial design shop, complete with brightly covered geometric furniture in the waiting area, floating shelves that display the shop's organic products, and maroon old-fashioned barber chairs that serve as the main attraction in the salon section. Silver vents line the ceiling and the exposed brick walls, and for the life of me, I have no idea if those are the actual guts to this place or if they've been put in for aesthetic purposes.

As we walk in, we see Romy waiting on a lime-green chair. There's only one person working in the shop. Sid, I imagine. Somehow, even though it's my friend and my idea, I walk half a pace slower than Valeria. Romy's up to meet us, pulling me into a hug.

"I'm sorry if I freak out for the first five minutes," she whispers in my ear, her breath prickling the fine hairs along my neck.

She wheels around, wiping her palms on her shorts before holding out a hand to Valeria. "Romy, she/her, Luna's sanity line. I'm very excited to meet you."

Valeria smiles, the same honest grin she gives everyone. "Val, she/her. It's great meeting you too, and thank you for the honest recommendation."

Romy's eyebrow twitches at Valeria's intro. I wonder if we're both registering how fluidly Valeria did the pronoun thing. Not that straight cis people can't do it without hesitation, but it's rare. Hell, it took me a few months to respond smoothly when Romy started introducing herself to new people with her pronouns.

And *Val*?

"You go by Val?" I ask her.

"Yeah, everyone I know in normal life calls me that. Either is good." Her eyes widen a moment. "If I haven't given you permission to start calling me that, please feel free."

Romy slides from *Val's* handshake right back to me, putting an arm over my shoulder. She leads us over to Sid's counter.

"So this is Sid, and I'll leave it to them," Romy says. "They're a genius."

Sid, who has the perfect flannel-and-light-wash-jeans-with-chains aesthetic for this place, nods at Valeria. Either they're too cool to freak out over her or they don't recognize her. "So what're we thinking today?"

Sid leads Valeria back into the middle barber chair. Romy releases me to take one of the empty seats next to her. I take the other seat, brushing my hand on the spot on my arm that Romy just touched. Was she just acting . . . shy? Romy's never not bubbly with fellow artsy queer people. In fact, the last time I remember her being like this was before she came out as nonbinary to me.

Valeria runs a hand through her hair. "So I need something short and stylish, but it's been a long time since I chopped it that short."

Sid runs their hands through Valeria's hair, showing off chipped rainbow nails. I glance at Romy's hands on instinct. She's changed her nails to dark pink.

"Undercuts are always a winner, but we can do something less dramatic with the fade. Keep the base about crew cut length but give lots of volume up top." Sid smiles. "Give your partner a little something to run their fingers through."

I've run my hands through short hair before. I can still recall the different textures, the boys whose short hair I liked the most. I bet women's hair will be softer. The strands of Valeria's hair that I got to touch on Sunday were certainly like silk. The idea of being that partner, running my hands through her hair as we make out, has my stomach tightening.

"Let's do that," Valeria says.

Once Sid does Valeria's shampoo and conditioner, the conversation really starts.

"Did you write the movie you're working on now?" Romy asks as Sid works silently with the scissors and comb.

Valeria makes a face. "I wish, but I'm a terrible writer. No, the script's by this really cool queer woman and L.G.B.T. activist named Zoe Davidson. She worked at an Italian restaurant my producer friend goes to all the time. My friend asked for a sample and brought it to me."

Romy's eyes light up. "That's so cool the writer's queer too."

Valeria smiles, and I'm not sure what emotion she's feeling by not replying.

"Romy writes," I add.

Valeria's eyes light up, breaking the tension in my chest. "Oh, that's great. Novels? Screenplays?"

Romy holds eye contact with me. "Plays and a little screen-writing and prose."

"Do you write from your experience like that?"

Cold stabs me in the back. Romy stiffens for a moment too, but then she relaxes. "Yeah, I do. I have a couple identities thrown in the mix, and I've yet to do anything that fully represents the entire me, but different aspects of me have definitely shown up." Romy folds her fingertips together behind her head. "It's been really empowering for me."

"Absolutely."

I take out my phone as Valeria's hair falls in wispy little chunks to the floor.

Me: Are you getting gay vibes?

Romy's phone dings. She pulls it out of her pocket, and I'm forced to watch her read in real time. She raises her brows.

Romy: Omfg am I here to do intel?

My stomach sinks. Shit, is she mad? How was that not implied by—shit. Shit, shit, shit.

Me: I should've told you earlier I'm sorry!!!

Romy: Yeah, you should've 😝

Okay. She used an emoji. She's not mad.

"How much longer do you guys have on your shoot?" Romy asks.

"We wrap on Friday," Valeria answers. "I should be proud of keeping to a schedule, but I'll miss it."

Romy glances at me. Smirks. "Is Luna the worst P.A. you've ever had or what?"

Valeria looks to me—only eye movement, though. "The absolute worst."

"She *absolutely* doesn't want you to scoop her into the next gig," Romy says.

Jesus. No. I haven't even discussed what happens after this week with Valeria.

"I'm going to email Brendan right now and ask him to recommend me," I say. I turn to Valeria. "You're not doing anything other than acting for the next few months, right?"

Like I said to Romy, Valeria's all a romantic relationship now. I've got Brendan.

I start typing up an email.

"No. I've got post for the next couple months, some charity appearances, some press for another indie I did last year." She makes a face. "I actually don't think I'm filming again until next year."

"She'll be your personal slave," Romy jokes. The joke lands, but I swear there's a tiny crack in her voice.

"Does Steven think you'll direct more?" I ask.

Valeria takes a deep breath. "I don't know. Steven's so fixated on this film getting distributed before we discuss anything else." She exhales. "He's very . . . uninspired."

"If it helps, Steven used to ask for Americanos with milk when he ordered coffee himself," Romy says.

Valeria laughs.

"What?" I say. "Why call it an Americano?"

I press SEND on my email. It was good, but I'm suddenly wishing I'd asked Romy to read it. I'm one for one on recommendations actually working out, so I suppose all I can do now is take a deep breath and cross my fingers.

Still, I can't help but feel like I'm staring down six months of unemployment. Hearing Valeria doesn't have any projects in the works doesn't help, even though that wasn't ever an option.

I practically jump out of my seat when Romy texts me again.

> I have an idea to give you some
> confirmation. Are you willing to talk about
> Matías?

Heat bursts up my neck even thinking about Matías, but I nod at Romy. Nervously.

Romy glances at her phone, then leans back and groans. "Jesus Christ, do y'all ever get those random fucking DMs from your comphet boys in high school?"

My throat tightens, but Valeria's lips curl into a smile. "I didn't date in high school, so can't say."

Romy clicks her tongue. "You were spared. I wasted at *least* ten continuous minutes of my life on five-pump chumps."

Valeria full on laughs. The sound is like music, but my ears have started to ring. Another text from Romy: Lead in with college guys not being better. Trust me.

I look to Valeria and Romy, wishing for nothing more than to disappear into this chair and see what chaos Romy can unleash on her own. But here we go. I guess. Matías.

"You say that like college is any better," I say.

Romy gives me the tiniest nod as Valeria's eyes fall on me. "Oh god, wait—tell her about *Matías*." Said in her perfect accent.

I run a hand through my hair. This better be worth it, whatever it is. "It was junior year I think? We met in some film studies class. Turned out we all lived in the same apartment complex, so he literally asked me to get coffee in the shop below our apartment when there are a billion other places around U.S.C. But things go well enough, and we . . ." I glance at Romy, who nods, urging me forward. *Please don't be actively blushing.* "We go to my apartment. He gets dramatic, starts saying that he'll make me his girlfriend when he's back. He's going home to Spain that summer."

"*Noo*, he's European?" Valeria interjects, her body shaking as she seemingly holds back a laugh.

Romy leans toward Valeria. "He was fucking Spanish, Val. I feel like you get what I mean."

But I sure as hell don't. But they nod. I keep going, wringing my wrists. Eyes on my wrists, in fact. "So, uh, we start making out, and that's going well and all"—I raise my brows—"and then he kind of just transfers into dry humping, only our shirts are off."

The next words, the *really* dirty words, catch in my throat. Is Romy really having me tell Oscar-winning actress Valeria Sullivan about this? In a barbershop in WeHo past eight p.m.?

"And *of course*," Romy says.

"And of course he stops before I can come." *Come* comes out like a dry cough. Valeria still has her gaze on me. Even *Sid* is paying attention. "And so he kinda tries to reach his hand down my pants but gives up after, like, two minutes. Asks"—God, the humiliation of this night is starting to slide back in—"no, *insists*, really, that he wants to see how I do it. I think he just wants, like, a demonstration. But he literally just *watches* me as I, uh, touch myself. Finish, whatever, and I ask him if he wants a hand job or something because I'm a huge pushover." Romy nods emphatically to Valeria; I rub my nose with my middle finger. "And he just looks me in the eye, lids half-closed, smiling, and says, 'Don't worry, *bella*, I came already.' He creamed himself when we were dry humping and that's why he stopped."

And for a moment, Valeria and Sid just stare at me, wide-eyed. Then they burst out laughing.

Sid shakes their head and goes, "Girl, please tell me your sex is better now."

The words catch at my throat. *That* wasn't sex—

"Jesus fucking Christ," Valeria says with a laugh. "That's— mmm, look, that happens with sex sometimes. But with sapphics, someone's on an S.S.R.I. because we live in America." She makes eye contact with me, smiling before swiping her tongue across her lips. "And then your partner brings out a vibrator. Resourcefulness over raw talent."

Ho-ly shit.

I look to Romy. Okay, I get why she did that. Did Valeria just—? Romy, cheeky bastard, shrugs with a flash of a smirk on her face.

Okay. Valeria likes girls.

I sit through the rest of Valeria's haircut in silence. With Valeria, a sapphic.

Before I know it, Sid's done. They do the full rip-the-cloak-off reveal. Technically I'm here, watching the cloak come off and Valeria hold the mirror to inspect the back of her head and Sid explain how to best maintain the style, but god, I can't stay focused.

Valeria just said she's gay.

But Valeria's also busy until next year. I'm in Brendan's hands, and while I killed it today, I don't know what pull he has or even if he really likes me. Valeria's not happy with Steven, so I can't use Wyatt. She lives in L.A. and I have her number, but it still feels like seconds with Valeria are like seeds on a dandelion—they disappear faster than I can comprehend.

But she is gay. I just don't know the most important part.

If she likes me.

All I know is that she's *beaming* at the sight of her new hair. It's exactly what Sid described, complete with wisps that fall into her eyes. She looks like an edgier Jack from *Titanic*. It looks perfect on her; an entire short erotic video could be made just from her running a hand through the volume up top, but I can't focus.

"Jesus, I should've done this years ago, you have no idea," Valeria says. "Steven thought short hair would kill my leading lady appeal."

We exchange eye rolls.

My gaze flickers across the room, lands on Romy and Valeria. Man, I really do love non-men with short hair. And that's not a feeling I can be sitting with in this empty barbershop.

I slip out of my seat, grabbing Romy's arm. "We're gonna run to the bathroom," I say.

Valeria gives a noncommittal word of acknowledgment, and I speed the escape until I hear the bathroom door shut behind us. Romy shakes off my tight grip.

"If you're here to cool your lady boner, just think about your dad in that orange Hawaiian shirt he always refuses to button when he goes to the beach," Romy says, snickering.

I dampen a paper towel and pat it along the back of my neck. "How did you know that would work?"

She waves a hand. "Oh, people are just more likely to talk shit at the barber." Romy joins me at the adjacent sink. Adjusts her hair. "I can't believe she really is the gayest blond femme actress I've ever seen, *and* she just ripped 'femme' off her blinking gay sign."

"Yeah," I say. I really thought my chest wouldn't be this tight after learning such a crucial piece of information.

Romy looks me up and down. "What's up?"

"I still don't know if she likes me."

Romy huffs. "Oh my god. Come on." She grabs my hand.

My heart's beating faster and faster. The cool towel isn't working.

Romy grabbing my hand isn't either.

The world seems to slow as Romy and I return to the salon. Valeria's at the counter with Sid, paying.

My career with Valeria is likely ending this week and I may never see her again. Everything could just end without any of my questions answered. Now I know she's gay, but that doesn't explain our almost kiss, what she said to me, why she's taken me along with her so much over the past several weeks. I can't stop thinking about it. She's officially not my boss starting on Saturday.

The only thing left for me to do is to just go for it. Whatever "it" is.

"Hey, Val, do you want to go karaoke-ing on Saturday?" I blurt out.

Silence. Romy looks at me like I've just pulled a live chicken out of my pocket.

Valeria turns to me. "Yeah, sure."

Fuck. I just asked Valeria on a date. There's no filming shit I can use as an excuse to say that this is anything but. I'm a baby gay. I'm not ready to ask people on dates. I don't know how to flirt. I don't know how to make her kiss me or how to kiss her or how to even *look* at another woman on a date.

I look at Romy. She's still confused. But she was so at ease with Valeria today.

"It's my birthday," I add.

Romy's expression shifts into one of even deeper confusion, like I changed the chicken into a dinosaur.

"Oh, yeah, for sure," Valeria says.

"It's gonna be small. Just Romy and Wyatt." I rub my forearm. "I'll text you the address."

Valeria smiles. "Awesome! I'll see you then." She turns to Romy. "Great to meet you."

It's only when Valeria leaves the salon that Romy breaks the silence to turn to me.

"Did you just lie about your birthday to get two cockblockers?" Romy asks.

I swallow. "I was hoping you'd be wingpeople."

Romy shakes her head. "You are such a disaster." She pats me on the shoulder. "Happy super-late birthday, you chaos Gemini."

chapter sixteen

By Friday afternoon, I've slept for twelve hours total all week and have no clear memory of what happened during the last few days of the shoot. I definitely got to do one more scene as first A.C., I think Valeria promised I'd get credit for that, and I think Brendan said he got my email and that he will have a response for me by the wrap party. But the only clear memories I have are of the hours upon hours I've spent trying to *confirm* that Valeria is out and wants to be with me.

Julia opens the door and invites me in. Her blue eyes travel across the room with me as I drag my feet to my usual spot, the black couch. I grab the bowl of brightly colored connector toys she has out for children. I momentarily consider flopping onto the sofa, but I don't need her to be concerned. That, and I'll probably fall asleep and waste the $150 for this session.

"How're you feeling?" she asks as she settles into her chair.

I start constructing a fancy cube out of the toys. "I've been driving Romy so insane that she told me to emergency schedule you, but she said that yesterday, so . . ."

She frowns. A soft frown. I've never really seen her display big negative emotions in here. I can get her to laugh or smile fairly regularly, but she never really expresses sadness or anger. Maybe it's a therapist thing. "Is something going on with you and Romy?"

"Oh, no, no. I think she was just annoyed I stayed up all night the past few nights combing through Valeria's and my messages to decide if she likes me."

Her eyes light up. "Oh, right, your actress friend." She pauses, shaking her head. "I still can't wrap my head around how you went from that session where you were crushing on her to this."

"It's gotten worse."

"The crush?"

"She told me she's gay. Which means there's a chance she *actually* wants to sleep with me. But that doesn't mean she likes me." I wedge the toy pieces together faster and resist rubbing my arms. "I think I told you about that. I'm trying to catch up on the sex front."

She's taking notes. I can't imagine what she's got on that pad about me. "Let's remember coming out doesn't have a deadline. But okay. Remind me, weren't you going on dating apps to try out flirtation with women?"

"I did, but they were weird. Valeria and I have an established thing; it's a lot more comfortable."

She nods. "Okay. So you're romantically pursuing Valeria, and it's stressed you out to the point of losing sleep and irking your friend. Why are you so interested in knowing if she likes you *right now*?"

I take a deep breath. "Because I asked her on a date and then invited my friends, so I guess it's not a date anymore, but . . . I don't know, I just got so nervous and it seemed like they'd make it better, but now I want to kiss her, which is why I'm poring over these texts, but then why'd I invite Romy and Wyatt too?"

"Oh, wow. So she said yes to a date?"

"A kind-of date."

"So it sounds like you have two concerns with this. One: 'Does Valeria like me romantically?' Two: 'Is the environment I created even ideal for the romance to happen?'"

"Yeah."

"I'm curious about what compelled you to create this safety blanket with Romy and Wyatt. If you want to date Valeria, what about her intimidated you away from asking her on a traditional date? Is it that she's famous and seems unattainable?"

Faster with the toys. "No. I've done one-on-one stuff with her before. I don't know what's different about this." I set the toys on the free space on the couch.

"Keep trying to articulate it. We have time."

"I don't know. I mean, I pretty much am. It's just—I try to think out scenarios where this happens, and what if I lean in to kiss her and she doesn't like me back?"

"And what would be so catastrophic about that?"

I return to my toys. "I just . . . This is all so new, and I don't feel ready for that kind of rejection."

There's a long pause. "I'm struck by what you're saying about not feeling ready. I was going to bring that up. It seems very telling that you'd invite Romy and Wyatt on a date with you. Are you sure you *really* want to go on this date? Does it feel like you're not ready for that? Perhaps the reason you were at ease before with Valeria is that you didn't have any romantic intentions. *Has* Valeria given you any unquestionable indication she's interested besides saying yes to the date?"

I think back to Sunken City. "Well, when we were doing a photo shoot alone, she almost kissed me."

Julia's eyes widen for just a moment. "So this isn't actually that unclear to you. The real issue is whether you feel ready to put that romantic interest between the two of you to the test. When is the date?"

"Tomorrow."

"Okay. So I think I get it. This is huge for you. You could get your first kiss with a non-man tomorrow. For argument's sake, let's ignore the extra baggage with the fame. This is your first date with an older woman whose intelligence and artistic talent you really admire. She likely has more experience than you. It's a huge leap. I'm so excited for you to explore, but do you think this is the pace you want?"

My stomach clenches, and tears well in my eyes. "I don't know. The fantasy of the kiss feels so amazing, but I just think about the date itself and I want to throw up. It's . . . I don't want to screw a date up, and if this goes wrong, what if it affects my entire gay experience? I already feel like I'm jaded with guys, and I don't want to get jaded with girls too."

There's a long pause. "Do you want my advice?"

"Yes."

"If you don't feel comfortable telling Romy and Wyatt not to come on your date, I don't think you're ready for this step yet. Which is *fine*. It's been two months. But I want you to always be aware of the toll what you do has on your mental health. Nothing you orchestrate is worth falling into a mental breakdown. And truly, when you have confidence in your choices, it *will* make the experiences positive. Confidence in yourself isn't a guarantee you'll get the outcome you want, but it does mean you'll be ready to accept the consequences."

Okay.

I send a message to the group chat with Romy and Wyatt immediately after therapy:

> Folks I think I need to cancel the date
> tomorrow. I'm not ready to do this without
> you. It's not time.

Romy responds first.

> Bummer bc karaoke is bomb, but I
> understand. I'm glad you're doing what's
> best for you.

Then Wyatt right after.

> WTF WTF WTF NO. I'M CALLING YOU.

Right on cue, my phone rings. I answer.

"Hey, Luna, where are you?" he asks. His reception is a little
scratchy, like he's running.

"At my therapist's office?"

"I'm coming now."

"What? Why are you even in the Beach Cities?"

Wyatt lives in Santa Monica, an hour's drive from my therapist's office with Friday traffic.

"I was doing an afternoon date with this girl from there, but
yeah, I'm here. Can I meet you at North End Caffe because I
really want to see you."

I guess that's like a question. "Okay."

Within ten minutes, Wyatt and I are at one of the local Manhattan Beach cafés. Wyatt's hair is a little ruffled, but his button-

down is still unwrinkled. I ignore the sting in my chest when I think about what he's been doing. He orders a coffee, and we find a table with a gorgeous view of the ocean out the window. Sometimes I wonder if I could convince Julia to have therapy outside. It would make my decision to not switch therapists for someone closer to my apartment than my parents' place make actual sense.

"All right, what evil force has compelled you to drop this?" Wyatt asks, nudging me like this is a joke. Or like he doesn't know how to process it if it's not.

"Just . . . talking to Julia," I reply.

Wyatt's expression softens. "What's got you hung up?"

"I shouldn't be calling this a date if I can't even do it without you guys."

He frowns. "Why would that make it weird? This is a huge deal with a girl you really like. I think the support makes sense."

I hate to say how much his words loosen the knot in my stomach.

"But who brings their nondating friends on a date?"

"I think it's not a big deal, and we can take some of the pressure off of you at the start. You seem super nervous even now, and having us there will make things easier. We'll bring drinks, joke around. Romy and I know Valeria, so it's not awkward. We'll have fun, and if you want us to leave, I'll say I forgot I have an early appointment or something and drag Romy out."

A spark of anticipation is lighting inside me, but something is still just . . . off.

"But what about Romy? She didn't agree to this."

Wyatt waves his hand. "Romy's . . . Don't worry about Romy. I'll deal with her. She just wants you to be happy, you know? Sometimes she just has a weird way of showing it."

I don't know to what extent I'd say Romy's *weird* about our friendship, but okay. I'm tempted to prod Wyatt further but end up dropping it. Gotta focus on the here and now.

"And you guys would stay the whole time if I chicken out?"

That way, if I truly am *not ready*, we never have to broach the dating thing.

"But you're not gonna chicken out," he says. "What's bugging you about this?"

I rub my arm. "You know I've never been with a girl before. Or flirted with one."

Wyatt grins. "Well, hey, I can show you how to do that."

My eyes light up. "Really?"

"Yeah. Come on, that was the one thing I was good at with you, right?"

It was.

"You were good at other stuff . . ." He *was* always good at flirting. So much so that I was spared months of *does he like me?* stress that I was not appreciative of enough back then.

He waves me away. "It's all about accidental touching. When she reaches for a drink or the karaoke book . . ."

He reaches over and brushes his hand over mine, immediately pulling away.

"Or when she's looking at the songbook you say you want to see, you . . ."

He scoots in, bridging the space between our legs.

"Then, when the night starts getting long and everyone's had something to drink and it's just getting lazy, you just keep closing the gap until you've got as much skin touching as possible."

Wyatt puts an arm around me, his leg between my legs, head on my shoulder. It's a blast from the past. I've been thinking about girls so much lately it's like I forgot that guys are nice to be this physically close to too. It used to be my favorite part of being with Wyatt, having all our skin touching, sharing each other's heat and heartbeats and breath.

"Then you just lean in," he says.

It makes sense on paper, but we'll see if I can pull it off. "Thanks. That helps."

I push his limbs off me. It *was* nice, but it's not what I want right now.

He smiles. "This is gonna be so great." He fidgets with his shirt. "By the way, thank you for that organizational system. Steven says he's talking to the higher-ups about promoting me."

I pull Wyatt into a hug. "Wy, that's amazing! Congratulations!"

But as I'm hugging him, that excitement fades into anxiety about my own career path. There's nothing more I can do with Brendan. I feel good about my prospects there, but should I be applying for more jobs? And Jesus, what happens when Wyatt has no connection to Steven? Will I have *any* means to check in on Valeria if this date doesn't work out? I'm obviously sad about a very fun P.A. job ending, but in addition to looming unemployment, this separation from Valeria is barreling toward me. I'm far from ready for the hit.

Maybe Julia and I had the "not ready" thing wrong. It's not that I'm "not ready" to be with Valeria. It's that I'm not ready to lose her.

With God, Wyatt, and Romy as my witnesses, if Valeria likes me as much as I suspect she might, there's no way in hell I'm not getting with her tomorrow night.

Everything has to be perfect.

chapter seventeen

I told Valeria to meet me at Pharaoh Karaoke Lounge at eight, and it's seven thirty and I'm in my bathroom. I've completely lost the ability to apply makeup.

"Luna? You almost out?" Romy asks, knocking softly on the door.

I take a deep breath. In all honesty, I'm not even sure what set me off. Romy came on board with Wyatt's new idea without any protest. Valeria seemed excited when she texted me earlier today. Sure, I didn't sleep well last night, and I haven't been able to eat much today, but it isn't like anything *happened*. I picked out my outfit without any issue—black overall shorts with a crop top, which leaves a whole lot of side waist and cleavage on display. Hell, I was excited picking out an outfit.

"Yeah, just give me a minute."

I slowly rise from my knees-to-chest position on my bathroom floor. I turn on the sink, splash a little water on my face. Tonight has to go well. It will go well. Wyatt and I are gonna make sure things go well. Then he and Romy will leave once I'm comfortable, and I'll get my first girl kiss. No more ruminating thoughts. This is all my stupid fucking body. If I can just get myself to physically relax, I can get my makeup on. We can get started.

I open my medicine cabinet. Pull out the Emergency Xanax. Consider it.

I set the newest antianxiety supplement my mom recommended beside the prescription bottle. I've never used it before, but Mom says it's effective.

But if it's not . . .

I've taken Xanax before. It's killed my panic attacks before they started. This isn't a *full* panic attack, but the Xanax will definitely help. I need calm right now. Karaoke is a calm activity anyway.

I twist open the Xanax bottle, take a pill, and wash it down with sink water.

More knocking. "I can help you with your makeup if you want."

I push the Xanax and the herbal supplement back into my cabinet. "Sure! Come in!"

Romy helps me pick out a makeup palette. It gets put on my face. The two of us Uber over to the lounge, where Wyatt is already waiting with a huge grin on his face.

The hallways are lined in tile, and neon lights flash across the walls and the ceiling. We've already rented a private room.

A nice private room, in fact. The couch wraps around a lacquered wooden table that has songbooks neatly placed in the middle. The TV is new and clear, and there's a Warholian painting of a chimpanzee on a green background on the wall. The dim room is already illuminated by a moving neon display. Even watching the colored dots fall on and off Romy's face is mesmerizing.

Valeria comes in exactly on time in a formfitting black dress.

She hugs Romy and Wyatt. Everything is going smoothly. When she gets to me, she pulls me into a particularly snug hug.

"Happy birthday," she says, and kisses me on the cheek.

The Xanax is working. I'm so chill, but god, that kiss goes through me like a rocket. Face hot, hands numb, *holy shit she just put her lips to my face* stokedness.

Maybe this will just work. I can't believe I almost canceled.

"So for a present, I was gonna get you alcohol anyway, but you probably have a minimum, so I'm buying whatever," Valeria says.

"You're my favorite client," Wyatt says as he scans the drink menu.

We arrange ourselves very specifically, with Valeria on the far left facing the door, me next to her, Romy next to me, and Wyatt on the other end.

"Are you two allowed to hang outside of work?" Romy asks. "Genuinely curious."

"I dare you to rat us out," Wyatt says, nudging Romy.

"I've become friends with a couple assistants. It's fine," Valeria says.

Wyatt grins. "Besides, I'm not gonna be an assistant for long."

"Awesome," Valeria says. "Talent?"

"Hopefully."

Romy throws an arm around Wyatt. "Don't lose the ability to answer phones too quickly."

We get a first round of drinks and everyone cheers to my non-existent birthday. I take barely a sip in order to keep the Xanax working at optimum level.

I pull over one of the songbooks once everyone's had a bit to drink. Scoot just a bit closer to Valeria. Close enough that I can just about feel her body heat on the couch. "Do you have any preferences?" I ask her.

She leans over to read the songs, running her finger along the lines to follow. "I can make whatever you pick work." Valeria looks over to Romy. "By the way, no one told me how important product is for this cut."

Romy laughs. "Guessing you forgot what Sid told you?" Valeria nods. "Yeah, product's king. Do you have any in right now?"

"Barely," Valeria answers. "Hence the desperate cry for help."

I look at Valeria, about to say, *Your hair looks great*, when Romy climbs over me to get to Valeria's other side. "Luckily, I'm the gayest and most prepared bitch in this room."

So someone's getting a little tipsy already. Noted.

But to Romy's credit, she does pull out a bottle of mousse. She winks at me. I don't know why.

"You have *mousse* in your purse?" Wyatt asks.

"Judging by your flat hair, you don't," Romy replies.

I chuckle and look back at the songs as Romy does her quick hair fix. I can't help but notice she's getting more intimate with my date than I am, and she's not even flirting. Cool.

I turn to Wyatt. "Wanna do a song while they do salon?"

Wyatt grins. "Billy Joel?"

Inside joke between us. Another nice memory from our time together.

"If you two do 'Uptown Girl' I'll murder you both and pin it on Valeria," Romy says.

"Rude," Valeria retorts. "I've known you for like a week."

"Think of it as an opportunity. You could be Hollywood famous, or you could be that-bitch-might've-murdered-someone-but-got-away-with-it Hollywood famous."

Valeria takes the Romy Humor™ in stride. "True."

I'm still not sure what Romy's doing.

But Wyatt and I pick our song. I'm not too embarrassed to

sing. When we're through with it, Valeria's right back next to me, and Romy returns to her spot on my other side.

"Do you wanna see the book?" I ask Valeria. "I was thinking some Britney."

She was playing it on the car ride to Sunken City. "Yeah, sure."

I scoot in close enough for our thighs to touch, dropping the book over our knees. Valeria doesn't react, just starts flipping.

Which I think is good. She didn't flinch or pull away or anything.

Like this position has become natural.

"I feel like I know 'Circus' better than 'Baby One More Time.'"

Valeria smiles. "Yeah, because you didn't come of age in the peak Britney era."

I give her a look. "You didn't either. Since when does anyone exaggerate how old they are?"

"Fine. The best years of my life were during the peak Britney era. We peaked together. You, on the other hand, were in kindergarten, so it better not have been the best years of your life."

"Were we in elementary school at the same time?"

"One year, probably."

I don't know why that's reassuring.

"How about 'Gimme More'?" I ask, hovering my hand over the song on the right edge of the book before letting it rest, my pinkie just barely touching her thigh. *Just* enough to feel the fine hairs prickling up.

She turns to me head-on, full eye contact. Her eyes seem to glisten. Her lips, those perfect lips, pull up into a smirk. "Sounds great."

The song passes. Another goes, and another. Wyatt and Romy match each other shot for shot in their own little frat corner.

Romy is now lying across the entire right side of the couch, and Wyatt is tucked into the left. Valeria and I have been moved to the middle.

"Is anyone down for Post Malone?" Wyatt asks, eyes intent on the songbook.

Valeria's and my legs are still touching. There's no songbook between us now. My stomach's so tight I swear I'm getting a workout. What even is personal space? I mean, if our thighs are touching and that's, like, less than a foot to our crotches touching, then what's holding me back?

I lean over to Valeria, my breath in her ear. "How many Venmo processing fees do you think we've gotten?"

She chuckles. "Enough to buy many, many B.K. meals."

I drop my head to her shoulder. My cheek is against her neck, which is hot and exposed because of the short haircut. "I really like your new hair."

Romy has somehow gotten it to look even hotter than Sid did, before she decided to get wasted and do a solo rendition of "Hellfire," which she's shredding right now.

"I really like how you know every word to that Natalie Portman *SNL* rap," she replies.

And as she speaks, her fingers run along the seam of my shorts, leaving a trail of goose bumps. She settles her hand on the exposed skin of my side, just above my hip. I can already imagine what it would feel like if she'd just move her feather touch down. It's sending heat through my legs, thinking about everywhere I want her to go.

This is real. I can't even pretend this is something platonic. She's running her fingers along my *side*, for god's sake. Fuck.

Romy's song ends.

"What about Spice Girls?" Valeria asks the room like a true millennial.

Romy all but jumps up from her spot on the couch. "Fuck yeah, I do!" she slurs.

She then proceeds to crawl through the minefield of drinks on the table just to squeeze in between Wyatt and Valeria. We scoot over to accommodate Tweedle Dumb and Dumber, who, for all that they've been useless wingpeople, have been helping calm my nerves. I think. Or maybe that's just the drugs.

We pick "Wannabe" like basic bitches.

More songs pass. The clock on our allotted time slides by. Bodies move across the room again. Wyatt's stopped, but Romy's still drinking. I shift from waves of concern to pinches of annoyance. Valeria might just think this is what Romy's like, but doesn't Romy know I know better? Of *all* the nights to get wasted, she chose this one? Maybe she didn't mean to get this drunk, but I can't shake the bad feeling.

"I think we're out of here soon," Wyatt says. "One more song."

At this point, Romy's all but gone. Her head is in Wyatt's lap as she attempts to throw popcorn into her mouth, which is cool and all, but it's nothing like having *Valeria's* head in *my* lap right now, our hands lazily interlaced as she flips through the book one more time.

"Any suggestions, birthday girl?" Valeria asks me, smiling.

"It's your birth—?" Romy says before Wyatt covers her mouth.

"Do you want some water, Rom?" he asks.

"How about a Beatles number, scholar?" I say.

"Which one?" Valeria says. " 'Happiness Is a Warm Gun'? 'She Came in through the Bathroom Window'?"

I select "Come Together" and make sure Valeria doesn't see my choice. She sits up, slides next to me so we're back to side-body contact, her hand in my lap. One look at the screen and she starts laughing.

When the song starts, it's like the world truly does fall away—Romy's mysterious decision to get drunk, Wyatt's random outbursts of Hollywood networking sleaze, everything else that's ever been on my mind. All that's left is the reflection of the colored lights off Valeria's eyes and the buzzed air between us. The buzzed air and my buzzed heart, all sending buzz to every bone in my body. It's never been like this before. Part of me thought it never would.

And when Valeria sings, "*Got to be good-looking 'cause she's so hard to see*," I want to write poetry about it.

I take her hand. Not as a tease, not as an uncertainty, not as a question. As an answer. *I like you, and you like me back.* She wraps her fingers around mine. We finish the last lines of the song, and my body sways, like my sense of balance has gone out the window. I lean back against the sofa, and Valeria leans back with me. Her arm snakes around my shoulders.

I catch only a glimpse of Romy looking at me, but there's a certain stiffness in her posture, a set to her lips that makes her seem more sober than I know she is.

She turns to Wyatt. "Hey, I think we should go. I have an early day tomorrow."

My stomach flips. Our code. I take a deep breath. This is *really* happening.

Wyatt helps Romy up. Turns to me. "You're good to Uber?"

"Yeah," I reply.

"Good to see you, Valeria," Wyatt says.

"Bye, Val!" Romy says, cheery again.

"Bye!" Valeria says back.

Once the door shuts, the air becomes static. Heavy. It settles into my insides. The lights even seem to have slowed down, slicking their color across the black room like a master painter. The karaoke home screen plays a preview song softly.

We're alone.

We're alone in this room, and there are no more secrets. We like each other.

I scoot away, just enough so we're at a conversational distance.

"Did you have fun?" Valeria asks.

"Tons."

I look toward the door. The curtain on one of the windows is just slightly open.

I get up to move it, my stomach already tightening in anticipation.

Once it's shut, I turn to her. "Sorry. Just realized. You know, paparazzi."

I scurry back to my spot on the couch.

Valeria's smiling. "I appreciate the effort, but I promise you that paparazzi aren't as big a deal as you think. Not for me in my off-season."

She leans in, bringing us back to within a foot of each other. And I just see everything. The way she taps her fingers on her thigh, the way her chest rises and falls, the slight tilt of her head as she watches me. She's ethereal, otherworldly, yet for the first time since being near her, I see how *human* she is too. How solid. Valeria's a living, breathing being like me. She is, when you get down to it, no different from any other person I've sat alone in a room with.

Except she's better. The best person.

And her lips shimmer under the weak light.

I kiss her.

The action jolts me forward before I can even think. The space between us is gone, the air blazing hot. And I thought it was just a cliché, but her lips really do feel different. Fuller, softer, gentler, smoother. It's such a soft kiss, a melting kiss. There's a second of surprise before she molds against me—

I pull away, face burning hot.

"I didn't ask if you wanted to do that," I blurt out.

Valeria, her own cheeks flushed red, twitches her mouth for a moment. Half a moment. Then it cracks into a smile in the corner of her mouth. "Yes."

She slams her face into mine, pulling me into a wholly different kiss. It's a cacophony I've never experienced before. There's the tenderness and restraint of the dance our lips are doing, but there's something in the pressure of her mouth, in the way her hands slide up my neck and into my hair, that feels desperate and indulgent.

First off, I don't know where my hands go on a girl. I settle for her waist. It's overwhelming and beautiful and everything I could ever want, but if I could just . . .

She pulls her mouth from mine. Kisses the skin just under my lips. I shiver.

"How long were you planning on doing that?" she asks, her voice low.

This is real. This is Valeria. And we're kissing.

"I mean . . . since I shut the curtain," I say.

She chuckles into my skin, kisses my chin. "Never pegged you as spontaneous."

When she kisses the skin under my chin, brushing kisses along my jawline, it's like she's setting my skin on fire. I rag doll into the couch, losing sense of everything but her touch. Gladly melting into the sensation.

She moves her hands from my hair and grabs my hands. She

slides them up the curve of her chest, up her collarbone, before settling my fingertips on the fine hairs on the back of her neck.

"I can be spontaneous," I reply.

I dig one hand into her hair, settling the other onto her hip. My mouth back on hers. The kissing only gets more aggressive, with heavier pressure. Our lips are prying open, but there's still no tongue. I don't even like tongue and this is an agonizing game. She tightens her grip on me, pressing our chests together. She's so hot, and I can't even remember if this is how it usually is or if girls store heat differently. And there's a rhythm. A slow, sensual, starving rhythm. Kisses deeper, grips tighter, Valeria's body sliding forward until she's straddling me.

Jesus, until she's *straddling* me, our crotches sliding against each other in one confident buck. I sigh into her mouth, quiver under the sensation. I know this. It's familiar in a physical sense, but wholly unfamiliar in every other way. Yet it's not as scary as I thought it'd be. I trust Valeria; I've never trusted myself to unravel with anyone more than her.

She pulls away, pressing her mouth to my ear. "Is it getting a little tight here?" She speaks with ragged breaths. "We could stretch out."

"Yeah," I mutter.

She grabs the backs of my shoulders, slowly lowering me until I'm on my back. She drops her upper body between my knees. The image of her head and chest between my legs, that crooked smile on her lips and that short rebel-boy hair framing her face—I've never wanted to burn an image into my head more. She kisses my thigh, her grip tight on my leg. It's not even a place I like, but I sink into the cushion. But when she kisses my inner knee, Jesus, *that's* something else. The kiss goes zero to sixty and hits me right between my legs.

I can't believe I thought for a second that Valeria had less experience than me. This is someone who's been gay for a while and knows exactly what drives girls insane. This is someone with tricks and moves. Someone who is *oozing* confidence.

"You like that, darling?" she asks.

I can only nod as my heart swells. No one's ever made *darling* sound so good.

She peppers kisses up my inner thigh, and just when I think she's going to kiss the shorts on my overalls, she skips right to the exposed spot on my side. I jump at the sensation, making Valeria giggle.

"Ticklish?" she asks.

I flush. "Yeah."

Guys don't usually talk this much.

She kisses the bib of my overalls, my collarbone, my neck, and then she's back at my lips. She's draining every ounce of sanity out of me, until I'm squeezing my legs against hers, hands on her lower back. Her mouth isn't enough. It isn't enough and she knows it.

As I grind into her, pushing her hips deeper into mine, she half pulls her lips off mine, moaning into my skin. The sound explodes in my heart, the joy spreading like water.

"You like that?" I ask, a hint of teasing in my tone.

"Yes."

I press our bodies as close together as I can, dragging the pleasure out with each movement. And as our hips slide past, as the pleasure grows with each second, I can't help but think—for just a second—that she's not snorting or half-assing it like guys did when we were grinding while kissing. That she *wants* this as much as I do.

It feels so fucking good.

Valeria unhooks a buckle on my overalls.

Then the door opens.

It isn't like at Sunken City. It's more like trying to jump out of a hot bath when wine drunk. Valeria turns toward the door as I prop myself up. I can only imagine what we look like right now. Valeria's hair is tousled to douchebag-jock-who-just-had-car-sex-in-an-'80s-movie level.

It's a guy who works at the lounge. He's fidgeting like mad. "So if you guys don't leave in three minutes, I'll have to charge for another hour."

He exits upon delivering the message, and Valeria climbs off me. Runs her hands through her hair.

"Can I tell you a secret?" I say.

"Yes."

"It's not my birthday."

There's a moment of silence.

Then Valeria laughs.

"Why did you lie about that?" she asks.

"I thought you wouldn't want to hang out with me otherwise."

"Have I said no to anything you've suggested?"

I dart my gaze to the table. "I can pay you back for the booze."

"Please."

She gives me a firm kiss on the lips. Just when I thought there weren't any more fireworks to go off.

"This was worth the booze," she says, pushing a hair out of my face.

She holds my hand until we reach the street.

chapter eighteen

I could've stayed in that karaoke room all night, but I still bask in the relief of the world opening up to Valeria and me as we slip out the lounge's front door. The summer air charges and sparks around us, and a biting breeze rustles my hair. It's as if Mother Nature herself knows how much I'm aching for Valeria to put her hands back on me.

"Here, I'll get you an Uber," she says.

As she glances down at her phone, the heat flows out of my chest. It feels like someone took my hat off in the snow. "Oh. Thank you."

Valeria glances at me. The corner of her mouth, lipstick kissed off, tips up. "Something else you want, birthday girl?"

My stomach tugs tighter and tighter, winding me up head to toe. All I feel is the tingle on my lips, the words slipping out numb. "This to not end." My hand twitches to grab hers, but I hold it back. We're in public. Too many eyes, even if those walking down the street are late-night drifters and people stumbling from bar to bar. "To go somewhere more private."

Valeria clicks her tongue. "Well, good thing I have this private dwelling not too far from here."

I inch closer to Valeria, eyes glued to her phone.

I watch her fingers glide across the screen, changing the destination from my apartment to an address in Hollywood Hills . . . It's an image that I'll tuck away in a memento box just to recall the fire it ignites inside me. She's inviting me back to her house.

We kissed, and she's inviting me back to her house.

When the Uber arrives, I manage to stay on task for one minute. Just long enough to text Romy that I'm gonna be at Valeria's. Romy texts a confirmation and a bunch of unintelligible emojis. The Uber driver doesn't say much beyond confirming Valeria's name and destination, then he quickly fades into the background. We got an UberX with leather seats, and the material under my thighs is already wet. It's not even hot in here yet.

Then the seat belt clicks. Valeria slides from the left seat into the middle. Her thigh presses against mine, bare skin to bare skin. More skin touches mine as her dress rides up. She grips my left knee. My heart leaps, sparks and crackles in my stomach as she slides her hand up my thigh. My eyes sting as I hold them open, capturing the image of her hand as clearly as I possibly can.

"This okay?" she whispers.

"Please," I whisper back. Hopefully we're being quiet enough that the driver doesn't hear. Everything's white-hot. I'm the biggest stickler for rules, and the idea of doing this right now has me dying.

She slides her hand through the section of my overalls between the shorts and the bib. And Jesus, Jesus, fuck, when her fingertips roll over the crotch of my panties, I can't take it. One touch and I already buck against her.

Valeria presses her whole upper half against me, her mouth in my ear as she strokes. "Eager, aren't we?" She giggles a little, warm breath against my skin. "Don't alert the driver."

We both glance forward; the guy has headphones in. Illegal perhaps, but neither of us cares.

She strokes in wide, light circles. A predator stalking prey. I press my thighs together, constrict around her.

"You know what's funny?" I say, my voice still low. "I . . ." I twitch against her touch as she rolls over my clit. "I've never come with a partner."

Valeria's lips curl into a smile. "Is it unfair to guess they were all boys?"

Boys feel so far away. With Valeria pressing her fingers into my clit, I can't even remember a world where I liked boys. She's all I see. Valeria's soft hair against mine, Valeria's lips against my ear, Valeria's slender fingers down my shorts. Soft. Everything is so fucking soft, and I never want anything but soft again.

"They were," I reply.

Her circles grow narrow, harder. Like she's digging a moat around that sweet spot.

"Well." Her voice lowers into a growl. "I promise that'll end tonight."

I swallow down a squeak as she presses hard on the next roll. One more stroke before her fingers slip under my damp panties, gliding along the soaked skin. I grab her thigh, her shoulder. The seat belt whines against me as I twist in it. Fuck, what I'd give for her weight on me. Something to pin me down, ground me. The colored lights blur outside the window.

"You close?" she asks me.

It couldn't be more obvious. I'm stifling ragged breaths against her. All I can manage is a nod as my muscles tighten. I know this. God, I know this feeling, so why does it feel so much larger than before?

"Val . . ." I say.

"Yes?" she says, flashing that smirk again.

I'm so close. Fuck, I'm so close, and—

"I don't know if I can—" *Be quiet enough for this ruse.*

Somehow, she . . . gets it. Her fingers soar, so fast I can't even trace the circles, and she pulls me into her chest. And as the orgasm rips through me, blazing hot and earth-shattering, I cling to her, burrow into her skin, her Chanel smell, her solid body.

I stumble out of the car when we arrive. It's pitch-black. I know Valeria's house is amazing, but I can't focus on any of it. All I notice is the transition from dark to light, from the silence of carpet to the patter of wood, as we kiss our way up to her bedroom. The whine of a hinge as she shuts her door. The spring of a mattress as we drop onto her bed.

I just came in front of someone else. Someone else made me come. A girl made me come. This isn't even sex. I don't know why I feel like this. Like I'm a puppet and someone's cut my strings. My bones are so light, I feel as though I could fly instead of walk. I feel *older*. Wiser. Like now I can sit with my old work friends and talk about exactly why dry spells suck. Like I'd give almost anything for Valeria to keep touching me day after day for the rest of our lives. Like I'm shaky and my mind is racing and I'm so grateful that I've made it to her bed.

I know what I have to do. What, despite all the freaking out I've done for months, I want to do.

I run my hand from Valeria's inner thigh up to the crotch of her panties. "Is this okay?"

"Absolutely," Valeria replies.

I don't fully understand the anatomy from this angle, but the panties are an added source of friction. They can give her the same pleasure that my actually knowing the exact location of the clit would give. I take a deep breath. I can do this.

"Tell me if you want me to adjust," I say as I mimic what she did, drawing long, wide strokes on the crotch of her panties. My stomach clenches as I speak. The words playing back in my head make it sound like I'm an inexperienced teenager.

But Valeria just mumbles, "Course, baby," like this may even be a normal thing for her.

Even with the barrier of the fabric, my finger still glides across her skin. Already wet, which, thank god. I try copying Valeria, sliding over sideways to keep my wrist angled the way I do when I touch myself, but somehow my fingers are already starting to cramp up.

So as I shake my hand out, I pull her closer to me. I shift over to my side, twine a leg over hers, kiss the soft skin on her neck. Hand, slightly rejuvenated, back in.

"Use your pointer and middle," Valeria says as I litter kisses up her throat. The buzz of her words reverberates off my lips, and wow, it's really cool. "It's less tiring."

I add my middle finger, speeding up the circles. This angle is right, familiar. The strokes come harder, faster. But somehow that's not even the fun part. The fun part is the way Valeria's face grows warmer, the way her breathing—now that we don't need to be quiet—audibly grows quicker, the way the abdominal muscles under my arm clench up. The way she grips on to me.

My fingers draw her panties aside. I don't even know if she's hotter than I was, wetter, but there's something about this that's got my heart racing, a dumb smile stuck on my lips. I did this to another human being and—oh, Jesus, when I know exactly where her clit is to finish the job, I'm sorry, I'm pretty fucking pleased with myself.

My strokes are frantic, almost taking on a life of their own as my wrist cramps again. Faster and harder, and Valeria's sighing and twisting, and god, when she comes, it's like the world explodes. She comes with a desperate grip on me, with a muted sigh.

As I pull my hand out from under her dress, I think of that sex scene in that movie she did. I'd been imagining that was what she sounded like during sex. I'd wanted to hear that version for so long, but lying here with that sigh against my skin, her grip on me, this version feels intimate, like a secret. I can't believe I'd wanted what was in that movie.

Thinking about it makes me laugh beside her.

"What?" she asks, her voice back to its normal pitch.

The heat of embarrassment washes over me. "I . . . I thought you'd sound like you did in *Needlepoint* when you orgasmed."

She chuckles. "Oh my god, as if I'd share that information with the world." She takes my hand, plants a firm kiss on it. "There are some things I only want a special few to know."

A special few. I'm part of a special few in this woman's life, a life surrounded by adoring thousands, millions. Our experience truly is a locked-box secret.

And I made a girl come for the first time.

Valeria sighs and turns to me. Pushes a hair out of my face. "Wanna do anything else?" She glances down, smirks at me. "You still wet?"

I take a second to think about it, and yeah, doing that to her means I'm still very wet. "Can we come together?"

That cocky smile remains on her lips as she clambers to her

knees, pushes me into the plush bedding, straddles me. Her weight on me sinks to my core, heavy, pulsing, and it brings me back to life. And when she kisses and bites my neck, starts grinding against me, for once in my life, my brain shuts off.

I just let the magic happen.

I have a monthly family brunch the next morning, so as much as it kills me, after my hair's been teased into a nest, my makeup has been kissed and sweated off, my fingers are aching, and I'm barely able to walk, I get an Uber back to my apartment. Romy's asleep when I return. Valeria texts me when I'm in my bedroom and invites me to see her Monday evening, if I'm down. I text that I am and fall asleep like a rock.

In the morning, Romy brews coffee, reading a paperback at the kitchen table. For all that I expected to be as hungover as she is, this dress feels light against my skin and I'm ready to run around skipping.

"Where are you off to?" Romy asks.

"Brunch with Noam and my parents."

She nods slowly. "How'd last night go?"

I break into a grin. "Amazing. I came for the first time. We came. Like I figured out fingering and everything."

Romy smiles. There's a light in her eyes, but her mouth is wobbly, unsure. It's the hangover, I figure. "That's great, Lune! Look at you, having gay sex."

The lightness drops. A little. "What do you mean? That was just fooling around."

Because as amazing as that was, that wasn't sex, right? I'd know if I'd done something as huge as lose my virginity. As much as I want it to happen, that was just *really* good foreplay. I suddenly wish Wyatt were here to back me up.

Romy shrugs wearily. "Okay, buddy. One day you'll listen to me." She says the last line with a smile. Even after her face relaxes, she studies me. "Valeria doing a vampire movie?"

I crease my brow. "No? We saw her in a western."

Romy raises her brows. "Well, you might wanna look at your neck, lover girl."

I rush to my bathroom, heart hammering.

And goddamn fucking shit, there is a hickey just chilling there, taunting me, right on the side of my neck. I don't even remember when that happened. I'm having brunch with my family. I'm about to have brunch with my family, and the evidence that I fucked around with a woman is just displayed on my skin. With a whole lot of grief, I manage to reduce the hickey down to a spot of discoloration that can really only be seen if you're staring hard enough and know what to look for.

Which, as I drive down to the Beach Cities, is exactly what I'm paranoid that they'll be doing.

We picked Nick's in Downtown Manhattan Beach for this brunch. More than likely, Mom will jostle all three of us to walk the couple of blocks down to the ocean, probably snap some pictures. The idea already has my stomach aching as I walk up to the restaurant. Still, as much as I don't miss the Beach Cities where I grew up, this consistent ocean breeze is heavenly compared with what I left in K-Town. In fact, for about two minutes, I'm happy to be home.

Then Noam and my parents arrive. Mom is in her all-day workout attire; Dad is in one of his many Hawaiian shirts. He collects them on the trips he takes every year or so to the islands.

Noam has barely shrugged into sweatpants and a T-shirt. He's probably already heard an earful from Mom about his sloppy appearance and how that frat is taking up too much of his damn time.

Mom pulls me into a hug, kissing my cheek, and her pink lipstick sticks on my skin. No, I don't understand the logic in wearing makeup while in workout clothing, but Mom, who met my dad when they attended Claremont McKenna College together, became a Southern California housewife stereotype long ago. New York toughness in California skin.

Still, I picture the smudge of lipstick as I rub it off my skin. Soft pink. Not quite the red stains Valeria and I left on each other's necks last night.

"You look tired, sweetie," Mom says. "Out late?"

"Out late with a boy?" Dad suggests.

I know it's a joke. Usually when they call me at night I'm watching a movie with Romy. During the past few conversations we've had since I snapped at Mom, I was, in fact, doing exactly that, as Rom and I work through the sapphic movie list. But the insinuation is so perfectly aligned with what I did that my chest tightens. "If Wyatt and Romy count as 'out,' then yeah."

Mom's eyes widen a bit as Dad gets a table. Outside. It's too nice of a day not to. "Oh, excellent! What did you guys do?"

"We went to a karaoke lounge. Wyatt says he's going on a third date with a new girl."

Wyatt said nothing of the sort, but I need to kill that weed before it grows. They never say it, but Mom and Dad definitely want me to get back with Wyatt. He's the only man I've brought home, he's Jewish, and I think they're convinced that I can catch, like, only one in a million humans. Gotta hold on to the one I did catch, amirite? Still, somehow, even though it'd be a less devastating blow to the idea that I exclusively like men, I can't stand the thought that Mom and Dad might think this hickey came from Wyatt. Wyatt couldn't even get close to making me feel as safe and satisfied as Valeria had the night before.

The host leads us to our table, and Mom takes the one sunny spot. She's like a lizard in that way—always cold, even in Southern California. It's like she has to steal every ray of sunlight to keep herself alive. I have no idea how she lived on the East Coast before.

Dad looks between Noam and me, a grin spreading across his face. For some reason, Noam's growing facial hair. If a razor materialized at this table, I'd have no problem shaving his face right now. "I can't tell which of you looks more tired right now. Youth is great, isn't it?"

Dad is from Bakersfield—the son of the owners of the only Jewish deli in town. He's self-made and is now a mathematician prominent enough to afford a house in this affluent area. He apparently joked his way through college and always claims humor is what leads to success in life. It should be so easy to think if I came out he'd just make a joke, be chill, but I can't even imagine *that* with certainty.

Noam looks at me. Tilts his head a little. "Do you have a job yet, Lunes?"

Okay. That's cool. Noam is definitely hiding something, and when I find out I'll destroy him.

Mom and Dad turn my way, Mom with her steely-eyed warden glare and Dad with his puppy dog eyes.

"Yeah, what happened with that cinematographer you were working with on Valeria Sullivan's film?" Mom asks.

I wince as Mom says Valeria's name. The hickey, I swear to

god, feels hotter at the mention. Hot enough to melt the makeup hiding it.

"I emailed him about taking me to his next gig, and he still hasn't gotten back to me."

"You should follow up with him," Mom says. "Squeaky wheel gets the grease."

I stare at the menu. My stomach is churning, and I feel queasy thinking about the grease and the salt that are on nearly every item on this menu. I pre-pick a waffle.

"I dunno," I say. "I don't want to be pushy." I take a swig of water. The condensation on the glass feels heavenly against my fevered skin.

"Are you exploring other avenues too? Valeria Sullivan herself, for example?" Dad asks.

It's not even funny, the way I choke on my water. I give several hearty coughs, and my mom springs forward as Noam giggles in the background. Yeah, there's been plenty of exploring with Valeria Sullivan. The heat travels past my neck to my face.

"I, uh—" My voice cracks. I clear my throat. "She's kinda busy, but she's always a resource. She's not doing any producing in the next year, but she'll hit me up otherwise."

"Jesus, she *talks* to you?" Noam says in shock.

I shoot Noam a glare. "Yeah, she *talks* to me. She's my friend!" *I made her come, like, three times last night, fucker.*

"That sounds . . . precarious," Mom says.

My heart twinges. "What do you mean?"

"Well, when will you know with this Brendan guy?" Dad asks. "I'd love it if he came through, but shouldn't you be applying for other jobs if you don't have a recommendation yet? Or ask Valeria for one too?"

I rub the back of my neck. "That's a lot to ask of her."

"Bullshit, hon," Mom says. "You're in an industry where you demand until you can't. They're definitely comfortable doing the same thing. Writing a recommendation is nothing for her."

I pull my hand back, and my stomach drops. Makeup's on my fingertips. When did I even touch the hickey?

"You're not being strategic with this, Lune," Mom continues. "You're only in Valeria Sullivan's scope for so long, and you need to make as many connections with these people as possible. You can't rely on this Brendan guy."

Her words dig into my chest. Is Mom right? Did I gamble too much on a prospect that will never come through? Asking for a recommendation would have been totally within my power before. But now that Valeria and I are involved romantically, there are all these other factors at play. Factors I can't entirely control.

"I'll—" I move to touch my neck and then quickly rub my arm instead. "I'll ask Val about it today."

The waitress comes by. Noam cocks his head at me as our parents order. I mouth, *What?*

He shakes his head and waits until the waitress is gone to say, "You call her Val?"

"Yeah," I say, heat rising to my neck. *Don't touch it. Can't touch it.* "We're friends."

Noam covers his mouth with his coffee mug and takes a sip. "*Really* good friends."

Bitterness rises in my throat. Did he say "really good friends"? I touch—

Fuck, I touch my neck again. Right on the hickey.

"Look, honey," Dad says. "I love that you're following your dreams, but I'm not helping pay for you to live out of the house if you don't need to. If all you have on your plate are independent projects, you're not going to have enough to pay rent. You're welcome to come move back in with your mom and me, but if you like living with Romy, you need a job."

Sweat slicks my palms. I wipe them on my napkin, splotching it with makeup. Makeup that's supposed to be covering my hickey. "It'll be fine, Dad. Brendan will come through. And from now on it'll be none of that barely-paying P.A. work. I'll be—"

"This is what you said about working with that psycho manager," Mom says. "You said it was a shortcut past all the bullshit. Lune, have you ever considered that maybe you'd enjoy doing menial camera work for a few years and rising naturally? You can apply to work in television instead of movies. Yearlong gigs at a time, and then you'd have time to submit to festivals and galivant around stroking some actress's ego outside of work."

I cringe at the word *stroking*. Then I cringe again at the whole insinuation.

I'm not hinging my career on creative projects with Valeria, but Valeria isn't just some actress. The anger burns in my gut. Anger at them, anger at myself. I want to say it. I want to tell them what Valeria is to me, what she means. What status she should have at this table. That yes, this . . . this thing with her is a wild gamble, but it's worth it.

"It's not like that," I say. "She believes in me. And, either way, I have Brendan working on getting me a job."

"Try to be ambitious and practical," my dad insists.

"Honestly, love," Mom says. "Treat this cinematography thing the way you treat dating. You're so damn practical with that. Wyatt was a gem—"

"I'm not dating Wyatt," I mutter.

Mom tightens her jaw. "I know that. But someone like Wyatt."

She puts a hand over mine. "I'm just looking out for my baby's happiness. You know that, don't you? You want that, don't you? A steady career, a husband, children?"

"A couple of cousins for the illegitimate children Noam will have too early with some sorority girl?" Dad jokes.

Noam groans as our food arrives. I'm suddenly not hungry, but I pour the syrup and butter my waffle anyway.

Yes, of course I want a family. I want to raise children, and I never want to imply that they have to marry someone of the opposite sex and have kids of their own to be happy. I want to let my boys wear dresses and my girls build Hot Wheels tracks. Maybe I want to raise them with no gender at all. I want them to grow up in a home where being queer is as normal as being straight and cis.

More than anything, I want my kids to have a home. To have stable parents like mine. But if I can't even find basic sexual satisfaction in a relationship with a man, is my only chance at giving my future family a stable life to marry a non-man? My heart tugs at the thought. The image of a woman—my wife—cooing over our children has my heart fluttering.

But my parents would have to accept that dream. I take a bite of waffle without acknowledging what my mother has said.

Mom sighs. "Just think about what your father said about rent."

Noam rubs his chin, eyeing me. "What's on your neck?"

Noam just couldn't hold it together, could he?

Mom and Dad snap their attention to me.

"How do you get a bruise on your neck karaoke-ing?" Dad asks.

Mom leans forward, running her finger along it. It makes my skin crawl.

"Luna." Mom looks right at me. "Is this a hickey?"

No. No, no, no, no.

"It was just one date. He"—God, that word makes my whole body ache—"and I didn't click at all. We're not seeing each other again."

Mom and Dad drop the subject. But I hear the sighs of parents who want grandchildren, who have had their hopes raised and dashed in one fell swoop.

But Noam holds his gaze on me a little longer, like he just might suspect.

He drops it before I can really wonder, though.

chapter nineteen

"It's just like, it's actually different," I say from my spot on the floor. "I don't know if it's just luck of the draw, but I've never been with someone who's so . . . sensual? Like she was just kissing up my leg and found this point behind my knee, and I didn't even know that was an erogenous zone, but Jesus. Just *that* felt better than how guys used to touch my boobs. It's just like, I'm lying there like, *Holy shit, if she's doing this to my leg, what the hell can she do to my clit*. She made a pass toward doing oral, and I swear I could've orgasmed from the thought—"

I look up, make eye contact with Julia. She's straight-faced, hands folded in her lap, and she's not writing anything down.

"Oh my god, am I being too graphic?" I ask.

Julia breaks out into a wry smile. "You can process it however you like, including being explicit."

I blush hard-core. When did my anecdotes in therapy become *explicit*?

"So overall, you had a positive first 'girl kiss'?" she continues.

My chest fills with warmth. I almost don't even need these

kids' toys. I'm just blissed out, even calmer than I was on the Xanax.

Which is something I'm still not sure if I'll be mentioning.

"Yeah. It was better than I could've imagined."

Julia smiles. "See? It didn't ruin your entire experience with girls."

"I don't know why I didn't do this earlier. I think she's liked me for a while."

"But you might not have been ready before. Even when we want to do things, sometimes it's better to wait, especially when everything is new, like it is for you. You said you had your first kiss at nineteen, right? Did you have opportunities to do that earlier that you didn't take?"

I shrug. "I never went to parties or knew how to flirt, so it just never happened."

I still can't even do it that well. In fact, Romy's the only one I can keep up witty banter with.

"Whether it feels deliberate or not, I think you unconsciously knew you weren't ready and so you weren't seeking out opportunities. It's similar with queer experiences. You mentioned that you'd been thinking about kissing non-men for years before you came out. You said that Romy probably would've even done it. But you never asked. And you might've even been attracted to Romy then like you are to Valeria now."

I think about Romy, just for a moment. I never vocalized it, but when I saw Valeria's haircut, the first thing I'd *truly* thought was that she kinda looked like Romy. And I'd been dying over Valeria's hair when we first kissed . . .

My chest tightens. "I don't like Romy. Not like that."

Something in Julia's face twitches. "I'm just using that as an example. I'm saying that I think it's healthy to take things at your own pace. Societal pressure can be a detriment to everyone's healthy growth, but it's especially difficult for queer teens and twentysomethings."

I go back to playing with the toy blocks. "I think Val and I are gonna have sex, though. Soon. Maybe even after the wrap party on Sunday. I'm ready."

"So you've continued to see her?"

"Yeah. We've been hanging out almost every day. I go to her place, we get dinner, watch movies, fool around. I've"—I blush—"finally orgasmed with someone. I've made her come too."

And it's only built on everything I thought this could be. We haven't even gone down on each other or broken out a strap or used any of the other advanced sex techniques Romy mentioned. Hell, we haven't even taken each other's clothes off, and somehow I've had more orgasms in a week than I've had the entire time I was dating men.

But I'm ready for the next step.

She smiles at me. "I'm glad you're getting the experience you wanted."

I smile back. "It's . . . it's really nice. Better than I thought it would be."

"So is she your girlfriend?"

A bolt of cold runs through me. "We haven't talked about it."

"Does she take you out on dates?"

"No. I haven't asked. But we'll be at the wrap party together. She's very clearly out. She's said *that* to me."

Julia frowns. "I'd have that conversation with her sooner rather than later. Keep it as clear-cut as possible."

Yeah. Totally. Sooner rather than later.

There was one thing that for *some* reason I could never get Wyatt to do even when we were dating: go into Victoria's Secret. It's one of the reasons I thank the world for femme friends, because Saturday afternoon, Romy and I are contentedly walking into the shop at the Grove. Contentedly mostly because it's a relief to get away from how blazing it is outside. But it's also very nice to not hear any male groaning, *But what's Victoria's secret?* It's also great because Romy's festival premiere is over, it went *amazingly*, and I think she can finally breathe. Everything about her seems a little more polished, a little more energetic. Even her dark hair seems to be shining more than usual. I'm still waiting on an answer from Brendan, so I'm living vicariously through her.

"Are you looking for anything?" I ask her.

Romy nods. "I do happen to have needs outside of your celebrity girlfriend antics."

There's a moment of charged silence where Romy's mouth falters between a frown and a smile. It's like she forgot she was supposed to be joking.

I softly push her shoulder anyway. Take it as a joke. "Too real, Fonseca."

Romy navigates her way over to the basic bras, the ones with medium lining that always come in cool patterns. They're her go-to for summer, when she wears extremely short crop tops. *Gotta have something cute to show off if the shirts can't do their job.*

I pull out my phone as she browses. I know Julia's at least sort of right about Defining the Relationship before the party tomorrow. I *know*. But I can't help but get itchy thinking about it. We've been together for only a week. If Val were a guy, I'd look "insane" wanting to D.T.R. this early. I have no idea what it's like with girls, though.

My gaze falls on a lingerie display. The label says it's a teddy, whatever that is, but it looks amazing. It's a lace one-piece with a deep plunging neckline, bands that emphasize the midriff, and a high-cut bottom that shows off the hips.

It's something I could wear under an outfit for the party easily.

I'm, like, 80 percent sure I could make sex happen after this party. Valeria already said I could crash with her afterward. That we could cut out from the chaos and exhaustion of the wrap and just be us together. A calm after the storm.

I look back at my phone. But if we D.T.R.'d—god, that picture would look different. We could spend the whole party together. She could joke around with Brendan with a hand on my back. I'd have every right to feast my eyes on whatever she decides to wear without being self-conscious. She could look at me the same way. We could grab each other drinks and food and introduce each other to friends. Wyatt said he'd be there. Wyatt would be able to see Val and me together, see what he and I were hoping for. It all sounds like a dream.

But yeah, it'd involve D.T.R.'ing.

"Hey, Rom?" I say.

"Leopard print or weird lips?" she asks, holding up two bras.

A hint of the lips would be a more unique pattern. It would look cool popping out from under a crop top when Romy stretches.

"Weird lips for sure."

She puts the leopard back and bends over to find her size.

"Hey, how long do sapphic couples wait to D.T.R.?"

Romy laughs. "Like three days."

My heart pangs. "Wait, what?"

"Sapphics tend to move very fast." She raises an eyebrow. "Why? Did Valeria ask you to D.T.R.?"

"No, but now is it not gonna happen?"

Romy shakes her head. "You're fine. Are you gonna ask? You seem eager."

I run a hand through my hair. "I just want clarity for what we're doing at this party tomorrow."

Romy smiles. "Look at you, evolving into a smart gay! My baby's growing up."

I give a weak smile. "Julia said to."

Romy pauses a moment before narrowing her eyes at me. "*Julia* is becoming a smart gay. A very impressive skill for a married straight woman. You better catch up."

I glance at the lingerie again. "How do I even word it?"

" 'Hey, are we girlfriends, and can we act like girlfriends at this party?' "

Jesus, that sounds strong. "All of that?"

Romy sighs. "Yes. You have to be clear. It's not like with straight couples, where accidentally revealing your relationship might, at worst, just be awkward. You could get into some seriously traumatizing stuff if she's not out with everyone."

"But she kissed me in a karaoke room. In public. She wasn't weird about that."

"So did you, and you're not out with your parents or anyone in your family." Romy looks at a different bra display. "Or your friends from high school, I want to say."

I have no interest in doing one of those *hi, I'm bi* posts on social media.

"That's different."

"For the love of god, Luna, if you're ready for a relationship with Valeria, you have to be ready for all of it. Including this. Just do it."

I ignore the sting at Romy's little snap. I hope she didn't get any bad news about the play.

I type out the text.

> Hey Val, you're out, right? Like Steven knows?

She responds right away. So much better than the guys I dated.

> Yeah, my team and family know. Anyone
> who's spoken to me in person.

And the only people at this party are people she knows.

I look to Romy. "Yeah, she's out."

Romy raises her eyebrows. "And the party?"

I sigh.

> And the party? Are we going together?

> Lol it's low-key but yeah, meet me at my
> house. It's a professional space, though, so
> hard limit PDA. Let's see how it goes.

"No P.D.A., but we're going together," I say.

"Was that so difficult?"

Why is she acting so patronizing? Or is this how she's been acting the whole time?

"No." I rub my arm. "Thanks."

She shakes her head. "Sorry. I'm not using the right tone. You're doing good. I just don't want you to accidentally evolve into an asshole." She rubs her neck. "So you remember that recent alumna who told me to write the invitations?" I nod. "She didn't tell me, but her agent saw the play and said she loved it. It doesn't mean anything, but something might happen . . ."

I grin. "So great! I'm keeping my fingers crossed hard for you."

She smiles back. "Thanks. Guess now we wait again."

I put a hand on her back. "It'll happen." I turn to the lingerie display. "Do you think I'd look hot in that? I'm thinking the red-pink one."

Romy wheels around to the lingerie display and her eyes pop. "The teddy?"

"Yeah."

She turns back to me. "How are you feeling about all this? I know we always talked about a hook-up with Valeria, but it really seems like she's connected with your cinematography. The D.T.R.'ing is a pretty huge, complicated step, and it could affect your career too."

Despite the blasting A/C, heat crawls up my neck. "I mean, I feel fine. Why?"

We move to the lingerie display. I flip through for my size.

Romy leans into me. "Just—I'm just musing and thinking that you could become anyone's girlfriend, technically." She tucks a piece of hair behind her ear. "But this is Valeria Sullivan. I'd just be, y'know, gentle with any relationship stuff. If I were you, I'd hold on to what she can do for you. For your art."

The conversation feels hauntingly like what my parents were saying. *Take your professional opportunities while you have them.* My stomach turns. My time with Valeria isn't running out, is it? "I'm focused on the relationship right now. Valeria's not going away. Having sex won't change the way she feels about my art."

"But it can—" Romy chomps down on her lip, cutting off her

own words. But I can fill them in; that honey-soaked *complicate things* rings in my ear. Complicate things romantically and—god, I can see it so clearly, like an image from an old nightmare: Valeria dropping me, Brendan fading with her, me back to scraping for rent, back to groveling at nowhere-bound assistant jobs to get chewed up and spat out by someone worse than Alice. Forced to spend nights awake knowing I crushed my own dream right when it was in my grasp. Romy and I wouldn't be able to live together and—

"Look, I'm feeling really good about everything," I say, slapping myself out of the thought loop. I dig a nail into the flesh of my palm, grounding myself with the sting. "About the sex." I seek out Romy's gaze, but it feels like I'm grasping at straws for some shred of assurance I know I'm not gonna get. But I keep talking, keep fumbling. "Besides, aren't you the one who told me to go for the relationship in the first place?"

There's a moment of silence. "Yeah. Okay." Romy tilts her head like she's studying me. "What is going on with you and this sex thing? I thought you were already having sex. You know, that thing where you exchange orgasms?"

The conversation about what dating Valeria could do for my career hangs in the air like dust in the store, but I'm relieved—ecstatic, really—to change the subject. Finally, I find the teddy in my size.

"Well, yeah, we've done . . . you know, hand stuff. But not, like, real sex." I say the words sheepishly as I display the teddy to her.

"Okay. Ignoring that you still don't think fingering is sex for *one moment.*" Romy grabs another teddy off the display to feel the fabric, as if I've already bought the one in my hands and it'd be a violation of my space if she were to touch it. "Have you mentioned you haven't eaten pussy before?"

My stomach tightens. "I've been reading stuff online." Romy's hands move slowly up and down the fabric. I can't help but wonder what it would feel like to be wearing the teddy and have her touching it. Heat slithers up my neck.

"You *also* need to tell her that." Thank god, she folds the lingerie and puts it back. "Assuming you feel ready for that. You've clearly established that you two exchange favors. Plus, you know, open communication."

I drape the teddy over my arm. "I was hoping we could just use a strap."

Romy raises her eyebrows a moment. "Very . . . bold and pillow princess of you."

"Is it?"

Romy's expression softens. She pinches the bridge of her nose. "No, no, I was kidding! It's not bad. It's just . . . it's a thing that you're still so nervous to perform oral sex. You gave B.J.s to some of those guys you dated, right?"

"Yeah."

"So you're not diametrically opposed to genitals. So it's just telling me you're still, I don't know"—she glances at me, her jaw flexing—"not ready for more than hand stuff. Oral should never be something you're scared of, even if you decide it's something you're not into."

"I'm not *scared* of oral." I pause. "And I'm trying this on."

We walk to the dressing room.

"And it's okay to be," Romy says. "It's the one thing you've never had to do in any way. A first solid foray outside of sexual cis hetero normativity, shall we say."

"But I'm not scared of it! I just . . ." I close the curtain on the dressing room. Remove my clothing and slip into the teddy. "I like the idea of the strap. That's it. It's still valid sex, right?"

"It is, just—"

I step out of the dressing room and Romy goes silent. She's having a startled, bug-eyed, *Jesus Christ* sort of reaction. I'm taken aback. Since when does Romy react to me in underwear like this?

"Wow, you look incredible," Romy says.

My whole body goes warm at the compliment—a heart-beating-a-little-faster, tingly kind of warm.

"Thanks, Rom."

She shakes her head. "I'm not done talking about the sex thing. You haven't been out for that long and—"

I return to the dressing room before she can finish her sentence. Strip out of the teddy, get back into my clothes, and head out with it in my arms. A definite buy.

"I'm an adult," I say as we head to the cashier. "I get that you're looking out for me, but I'm making this decision. Please, can we stop with the lectures?"

"But are you *listening* to me? Please, just tell me that you're hearing me. I don't want you to make the mistakes I did, especially this early in the game."

I sigh. "Look, I get it. You're more experienced. I figured this out really late. But you know what? Valeria's experienced too. If she agrees to have sex with me, then clearly she thinks I'm ready."

Romy snorts. "Are you serious? Luna, she *wants to have sex with you.* Of course she'll trust you when you say you're ready. I'm your unbiased *friend.*"

I pay for the teddy, pulling my gaze from her. Wyatt said something about Romy being weird lately. Maybe it wasn't just a onetime thing. And now that I think about it, there was also the whole mousse thing when she was drunk and trying to crawl over me and Valeria . . . Yeah, she was drunk, and she always acts a little off when she's drunk, but I can't shake it. Not that I think Romy would *do* anything outrageous, but she has been *acting* weird. Jealous, perhaps. It's probably unconscious, but I'm tired of it interfering with my life and I'm tired of the advice she's been giving me.

Maybe it's a sign that I need to get more queer opinions. I shouldn't have overwhelmed Romy with all this anyway.

I should be more compassionate. Ask what's been going on with her.

But instead I say, "Sometimes it feels like you're the most biased one," and I stride out of the store.

chapter twenty

It's definitely a casual-formal wrap party, just a private room in a fancy restaurant in Beverly Hills, but I'm shivering uncontrollably parking in front of Valeria's house in Hollywood Hills. I'm familiar with the sight of her not-mansion-but-still-decorated-like-a-mansion house, but everything feels almost uncanny valley. Like I've entered an entirely new time line and haven't quite processed it yet.

"Look at you!" Valeria says as she answers the door. She kisses me on the lips. My body goes hot at her touch, no matter how routine it's become. "You look gorgeous."

It's nothing compared with her look: a shirtless suit with a patterned bra visible underneath and perfect clean black leather slip-ons. It's the chicest, gayest look I've seen from her yet.

I unzip the side of my dress, revealing the teddy underneath. "Well, more gorgeous on the inside."

Valeria's eyes widen, and she bites her lip. A spark ignites in my stomach. And when she runs a finger over the lace, I feel it knock through my whole body. For the briefest second, I taste the words in the back of my throat: *What happens if we go to the party late?* What would parties feel like if I were no longer a virgin?

Instead I ask, "Ready to go?"

She interlaces her fingers with mine. "Ready for about half of it, but that's all I can ask for."

We step into her car. Valeria is driving. Romy mentioned that being a "top thing," and it's weird to think about how we fell into our roles immediately without even talking about it. For now, anyway. I'm perfectly happy to drive if she wants me to. I'm sure she wouldn't care that my car is shitty.

"Who's gonna be there that you're not cool with?" I ask.

She adjusts her grip on the steering wheel. "Just my whole team. I always have to do a little more fake schmoozing when they're around, and I owe them a lot for giving this pipe dream their approval." A grin spreads across her face. "I can't wait for you to meet them. I've gushed about you."

I can't believe this is real. "I'd love to."

Find Brendan, say hi to Valeria's team. This feels so *adult*.

She kisses my hand at a stop sign and then puts hers back on the wheel.

My fingers are already itching to text Romy. Call Romy. Run back to the **apart**ment and tell her, our little fight yesterday be damned. We're best friends. We tell each other when good things happen. It's just like how she'd tell me if the agent offered to represent her.

The restaurant is pretty nondescript. It has the dark walls, thick wooden tables, and pristine tablecloths like any fancy Beverly Hills restaurant. A host leads Valeria and me upstairs, where the decor changes. In this space there are coffee tables nestled among velvet couches. A bar and a buffet are placed off to one side.

Unlike what happens in my dreams, the room doesn't fall

silent the moment Valeria and I show up. The only thing that changes is that Valeria puts a foot more distance between us. Not lover distance, not even friend distance. Acquaintance distance.

And right away, Wyatt and Steven come walking up to us. Wyatt's looking sharp but still very barnacle-like with his former boss. Former, right? I can't remember where in the process he is with the move.

"Looking good," Wyatt says, giving me a hug.

Valeria and Steven exchange a quick hug and a cheek kiss before Steven turns to me.

"Linda, right?" he says.

Valeria and Wyatt exchange a look. Valeria rolls her eyes.

"Yeah," I say, the smallness of my years as an assistant returning with a vengeance. I'm just another hermit crab again, but now I don't remember where I left my shell.

Steven shakes his head. "We've been missing you over in talent," Steven says. "Alice has gone through something like five assistants since you left."

Well, good for her, quite honestly. My stomach twists, remembering where we are. "Is Alice here?"

Steven laughs. "Oh, god no. Just Val's people."

Wyatt turns to Steven. "Hey, Steven, we're gonna grab drinks. Anyone want anything?"

Steven smiles. "You know what I want."

Valeria looks to us. "Gin and tonic, please."

Wyatt and I walk off, and he puts an arm on my upper back.

"Holy shit, Lune, you *showed up with her*?" he says.

I smile, despite myself. "Yeah. Isn't it amazing?"

He shakes his head. "I can*not* believe we actually made this happen." He glances toward Steven. "Are you two together?"

I look over at Valeria, who's been moved over to a new group of people by Steven. "I don't know. She went from hot to cold the moment she stepped in here."

He pats my back. "I'm sure it's just the atmosphere. No worries."

I know she said no obvious P.D.A., but does that mean full-on pretending I'm nothing more than someone to mingle with who needs a ride home?

"Sure."

I can see how the night progresses.

Wyatt and I grab the drinks and nudge our way back into the circle to hand them to Valeria and Steven. Brendan's here now too. He grins and gives me a hug when he sees me, which is at least nice.

"Aw, shit, my favorite camera lackey. Hey, I emailed you," he says. He turns to Valeria. "By the way, didn't you promise we were gonna rent out Universal Studios for the wrap party?"

Valeria takes a sip of her drink. "Did I? See, I talked to them, and they said I was a hundred dollars too short to rent the *Jurassic World* ride where they took out the broken animatronics and replaced it with subpar digital."

Everyone laughs, including me.

"Shit, I think they might've also wanted more enthusiasm," Brendan comments. "Come on, you fucking actress, sell how much you love *Jurassic World*."

Valeria gives a dismissive wave. "Too much effort. There is a crew that's going to break into the ride after this party, though. So let me know if you want to join."

I check my email, my heart soaring.

Dear Luna,

Hey, sorry about the delay. So I'm so sorry, but I talked to my superiors at the next feature, and they already filled the

camera crew positions. But I want you to know your name
is getting featured in the right place on Val's picture and I'm
keeping you in mind for future stuff. It's been a pleasure
working with you.

Best,
    Brendan

"Don't you dare," Steven says. "You know everyone sneaks
cameras into these parties to get something to sell to the press."

I didn't get the job.

Valeria grabs Steven's shoulder. "A little paranoid, don't you
think? Do people even sell to the press anymore? I think they'd
post it on Twitter first."

I didn't get the job. The job that was meant to be the next logical
move upward, the job that I was banking on to make leaving my
job with Alice—a job I sacrificed two years of my life to—worth it.

I don't have a job.

Just then, three additional people enter the group: one woman
and two men. Valeria smiles as they approach, and each of them
gets the hug-and-kiss thing. They take the space between Valeria
and me, and Brendan straight up leaves.

Valeria turns to me and Wyatt. "Luna, this is the rest of my
team. My agent, Bass." She motions to an exceptionally tall white
man with a crew cut and an expensive suit. "My publicist, Tori."
Tori is blond, thin, also designer decked. A wedding ring sits on
her finger. "And my lawyer, Derek." He's short, extremely tan—
like to the point that it seems like he's trying to seem ambigu-
ously P.O.C.—and also wearing an expensive suit. They're all
as nondescript as Steven. I'm almost surprised she'd have such
an . . . older Hollywood team.

"Did you adopt a child, Val?" Bass the Agent asks.

It's a blow to the stomach.

Valeria scowls while I recover. "She's the camera prodigy I told you about."

Bass looks at me without a blink of remorse. "Of course. Quite the prodigy indeed." He finally shakes my hand.

Not prodigy enough to get a fucking A.C. position.

"Hope you're not doing anything to make her uncomfortable," Derek the Lawyer says. Derek leans into me. "She's a flirt."

Wyatt stiffens. I'm sure I do too, but I can't feel my limbs anymore.

"No, she's been . . ." *Dating me? Making me come every night for a week?*

I look at Valeria. She's got her arms crossed, and she isn't even hiding how pissed she is. "Can you guys stop?" she says. "*You're* the ones scaring her."

She doesn't mention the truth about what's going on with us. But I thought she said she was out with everyone at this party? Her words sit in me like ice. Am I just a secret to her? Or is this just not the right time to say anything?

"Oh, Val," Steven says. "Please don't tell me someone's trying to #MeToo you?"

What?

Valeria's face twists in disgust. "What does *that* have to do with this? Do you think I had an affair with her while she was my P.A. and that's why I passed her short along? I'm not a fucking animal. I can control my urges." She looks at me. "Luna, come over here."

"Jesus Christ, Val," Bass says. "I was making a *joke*. You're pulling her up the ladder, and it's only natural that people will be suspicious."

"Yeah, Val," Tori says. "We all know you're not dating anyone. We might as well announce to the press you're asexual or whatever."

I move over so I'm next to Valeria now. She's seething. I swear heat is radiating off her.

"Don't tell people I'm ace," she says, her voice almost a bark. She looks at me and her eyes soften. "And as for Luna, she's amazing. You should give her a little respect."

All these people—Brendan, who didn't believe in me enough to get me a bitch camera position, even after I gave him that shot; Valeria's team, who thinks I'm a child she's grooming or some weird shit like that; my parents, who don't believe in my dream; Romy, who thinks I'm being ridiculous—they're all right. I couldn't spin this. I lost my footing on the third rung of the ladder.

But I still have Valeria. She believes in me.

She brushes her fingers against my hand.

I take it and say, "We started dating after the shoot. No weird boss stuff."

Valeria goes ghost pale. Wyatt too.

And suddenly, everyone's face is white.

Because just beyond the group, someone's holding up a camera. A good camera.

There's one moment of silence, one moment of peace, like someone has hit the pause button.

Then Tori and Derek break out of the group and run after the photographer.

The photographer.

That person has a photo of me holding hands with Valeria Sullivan. If the camera had audio, that person could also have me, on film, admitting we're dating.

Which could go public.

Which means *my family* could see it.

I drop my hand a millisecond faster than Valeria does.

"You *fucked a former assistant*?" Steven screams at Valeria. "This? This is your way of keeping it on the D.L.? Do you even know if she's over twenty-one?"

Valeria stands ramrod straight, pissed off. But tears reflect off her eyes in the light. "Of course I know she's over twenty-one! How fucking stupid do you think I am? And I don't remember there being anything in my contract or in any of our talks about you all having any control over who I date." She looks at me, and it's clear her rage has not melted away. "We're at a party where everyone knows I'm gay. Bad timing is bad timing, but—"

Steven throws his hands in the air. "I can't fucking believe you! You've known her *since* she was an assistant! How long has this been going on? How many favors have you done for her in exchange for sex?"

"None! I've done *no* favors in exchange for sex! She's *talented*!"

"She's been keeping it super on the D.L., Steven," Wyatt adds. "It's okay. I doubt that photographer even has anything."

Steven turns to Wyatt. Slowly. He seems even angrier now than he was with Valeria.

"You *knew about this*?"

Wyatt goes full deer in headlights. "I mean, we knew she was gay. I don't—"

Steven gets right in Wyatt's face. "I have *one rule* with Valeria! One fucking rule, and you don't *keep me updated*? And your *friend* too?"

Another moment passes. Steven turns to me. His eyes dart between me, Wyatt, and Valeria.

"Did you set my fucking client up with your underage friend?"

"I'm not underage!" I exclaim. "And nothing bad happened! No one has ever seen us!"

"And you want to get your *sugar baby* a festival tour?" Bass says, grabbing on to Valeria's shoulder. "What do you think people will think of that? I *told you*. If you think—"

"I'm so fucking done with this!" Valeria yells. "Fuck my career. Fuck all of you. I need some air."

And she just walks away.

And with tears burning in my eyes, my insides melting, I follow her like a lost puppy. I don't know what else to do.

Valeria weaves in and out of the thick crowds like she's been doing it for years.

I just get locked in between the buffet table and some mingling P.A.s. I don't know what happened with the photographer. I don't know whether Steven is literally going to beat the shit out of Wyatt. I don't know where Valeria went. I don't know how I'm supposed to tell Romy I can't pay rent.

Then my phone lights up.

It's a text from Romy.

> HOLY SHIT LUNA HOLY SHIT HOLY
> FUCKING SHIT THE AGENT SAW MY
> SHOW AND WANTS A MEETING. FUCK
> FUCK FUCK FUCK FUCK.

If my insides were melting before, now I can feel them gushing through me, making puddles in my shoes.

An agent wants to work with Romy on her plays. Romy

worked a non-stress-inducing job, focused on her art, worked hard, and it happened. I nearly killed myself and connived my way into getting the most incredible connection of my life, and I just blew it because I was upset Valeria wasn't admitting we were dating. How can I be doing everything so goddamn wrong?

I'm such a fucking idiot.

My phone lights up with one more notification.

From Valeria. A Venmo payment.

A hundred bucks. The caption: *For the Uber back. I'm so sorry, but I need a moment to collect my thoughts. I'm so sorry this happened.*

I can't ruin Romy's celebration right now. And Valeria just ditched me.

I look out at the party, and I see Wyatt. Sweet, kind-of-douchey Wyatt. Wyatt, who supported me through all of this. He isn't standing with Steven anymore.

I practically run up to him. Pull him into a hug.

And he untangles, pushing me back.

"What are you doing?" he demands.

"What . . . ?" I study him. He's . . . His eyes are puffy, like he's been crying. "Wyatt, what happened?"

He takes a deep breath. "What happened? You exposed your secret relationship and Steven knows I knew! He said I'm fired and I can forget the promotion!"

As if I thought this couldn't get any worse. "Wyatt . . ."

"I gotta go."

And he just leaves, no other explanation.

I pull out my phone, pull up Noam's number. I just can't bring myself to return to my apartment tonight.

Are you at Wes's house?

Noam, by some miracle, answers right away.

Yeah, why?

Can I crash with you for a few hours?

Ugh sure.

I type Valeria's address into Uber. Send one more text to Romy.

OMG OMG OMG OMG ROM HOLY
FUCKING SHIT IS RIGHT!!!

It's so easy to fake enthusiasm over text.

chapter twenty-one

I Uber to Val's, pick up my car, and drive over to Noam's friend's house in Santa Monica without talking to anyone. I don't answer a single text, not even to elaborate on the celebratory message I sent Romy. And Jesus, it's ridiculous that I'm not celebrating. It's so incredibly awesome what's happening to her. I am so happy for her.

I text Noam to tell him I'm here, but I get no reply and I have to knock. Noam answers the door, thoroughly disturbed, PS4 controller still in his grubby hand.

"You know we won't stop playing for you," he says. He looks me up and down. "Why do you look so nice?"

Thanks for the compliment, I guess. "I just came from the *Oakley in Flames* wrap party."

Noam leads me to the living room/kitchen, dumping his body onto the couch next to Wes, one of his college friends. Wes glances up at me.

"Hey, Luna," he says.

"Hey, Wes."

We likely won't say much more than that to each other.

I glance at my phone. Nothing from Wyatt or Valeria. I google *Valeria Sullivan, party,* and *gay.* Nothing comes up. Yet. But dread has already soured my stomach. I glance at the bathroom door, mentally calculating how long it would take me to get there if I have to puke.

I refresh my search. Still nothing. I check my social media accounts, on the off chance a notification didn't come through.

Nothing.

I toss my phone onto the coffee table and drop my head into my arms.

"Did you fuck something up?" Noam asks.

"Like you care."

Noam exchanges a look with Wes. Wes pauses the game. "This game is getting boring anyway."

I lick my lips. I don't want to tell them. The moment I say all this shit out loud, it's real. It's painfully real.

Oh, and it also involves coming out as bisexual to my brother and his friend.

Baby steps. Not all at once.

"Romy got a meeting with an agent who saw her festival play."

Noam narrows his eyes. "Isn't that good?"

I sigh. "Yes. And I should just be happy for her, but it just—I think I stalled my own career. There's nothing as good as this shoot was on the horizon, and I don't know where to go from here. And if I don't figure it out, I'll have to move back in with Mom and Dad, which is my nightmare right now."

Noam takes a swig of some canned beer he and Wes have clearly procured illegally. "Well, as far as I can tell, you and Romy are in totally different industries. It's not even worth the comparison. Besides, aren't you, like, a huge fan of her work?"

"Yeah."

"Then go find something else to be sad about."

I roll my eyes. "*Super* helpful, Noh."

"It can be something just as stupid. Like, go be sad that Valeria Sullivan isn't texting you all the time anymore."

Wes's jaw goes slack. "You hang out with Valeria Sullivan? I actually know who that is!"

Yeah, she is—was—fuck if I know—my girlfriend.

But saying that would involve telling Noam that I'm bi.

"I'm already sad about that!" I say.

Noam cracks his knuckles. I wince. I want to hit him again. "What about Wyatt? Anything going on with him you can obsess over?" Noam really thinks I have only two friends, doesn't he? "Or are you *already* sad about him too?"

My chest aches. "He's getting fired and it's my fault."

Wes shakes his head. "Wow, sounds pretty fucked. That's, like, three people who are pissed at you."

Noam looks around the room. "Wait. It's not three people. It's *two* people. Romy's not mad, is she?"

If she's telling me about an agent offer, I guess our fight about Valeria is over. I guess Valeria and I are over too, so there's nothing for us to even fight about. "No, she's not."

"Why aren't you over with Romy bitching, then? Like right now. Especially if you're worried about whether or not you can stay in the apartment you two signed a lease for. Look, we resolved your Romy issue. Go talk to her!"

I text her saying I'm coming home early.

But honestly, I don't want to dump all this on her. I really, really don't want to. Noam is useless, but at least telling him everything would mean I wouldn't have to burden Romy.

Noam, I'm bi.

I don't care if Wes knows. And I know Noam won't even care.

Still, I walk out the door before I can muster up the courage. And even though coming out to my brother wasn't an issue before I got here, my chest feels heavier as I drive to Romy's and my apartment.

Romy answers the door with a bowl of peanut M&M'S and a frown on her face. I've just spent thirty seconds fumbling for my key outside, but I'm still confused by her expression. Why would Romy not be beaming at me? I read those texts right, right? But, oh shit, I should've brought something to celebrate with. Because even though Noam suggested I confide in Romy, I came here solely to celebrate. Maybe I can ask her if we can go to the convenience store below the apartment. God, I'm so glad she's in my life. I've been off the rails for no good reason. I've been shitty to her. I don't say it enough, but I'll say it tonight—

I do nothing to deserve it, but she pulls me into a hug.

"Wyatt told me what happened at the party," she says.

I told myself the whole car ride here that I wouldn't cry, but I hear those words and the tears choke me and drip onto Romy's shirt. She just holds me tighter.

She leads me to the couch, and I drop onto my back, my head on her leg.

"I don't understand what went so wrong," I say once the sobs start to clear.

"We have a lot to unpack, but what Valeria did was bullshit. If her team was going to be so sensitive to her dating a former P.A. or assistant or whatever, she should have *told* you to be as tight-lipped as possible." She looks down at me. "Although I guess she did say to keep it on the D.L. It might be worth apologizing for misunderstanding."

I'm too tired to argue at this point. I still have to figure out what the hell to do about Wyatt and his job, *and* I have to sort out my career now that Valeria's royally pissed off at me and her team, but this is a start. I'll just text Val and then I can focus on being a good friend to Romy.

> I know you said you wanted space, and I will respect that, but I just wanted to say how sorry I am about what happened. I wasn't tactful, and I'm sorry for betraying your trust. It was completely immature and I understand if you're mad at me. But . . . if your team was going to get so pissed about us being together, why didn't you tell me point blank that we would have to pretend not to be dating?

I send the text and let Romy stuff my phone in my bag. Out of sight, out of mind.

"Do you think she's ever gonna talk to me again?" I ask.

Romy shrugs, running her hand through my hair. It feels good. "I think she's much more likely to forgive you than her team, that's for sure."

I dig the heels of my hands into my eyes. "I just can't believe it got this far. For god's sake, all I wanted was to lose my fucking virginity."

Romy stirs, lightly pushing me out of her lap. I turn to her. She doesn't look mad; she looks perplexed. "Why do you wanna lose your virginity so badly?"

I wipe my hands on the couch cushions. "I just wanna have sex like every other allosexual human on Earth."

"Yeah, but we weren't constructing elaborate plans for you to lose your virginity when you thought you only liked guys. Why is it so different with girls?"

The clamminess in my hands isn't going away, and it feels like I'm going to dehydrate through my fingertips. Still, the tears are ready to spill again. "I don't wanna be the clueless one again. You know this. I had to be the clueless one all through high school, then I got to college and, sure, dating a little helped, but I couldn't even sleep with Wyatt. I felt bad enough about everything when it was just about guys. Now"—I throw my hands up—"I'm right back where I was, and I'm so tired of being judged for it."

"Who's judging you? Who is telling you that you need to have 'fucked' a girl to be bisexual?"

I take a deep breath. I have to keep it together. "Society! People like Alice and Devon and my parents and—" I squeeze my eyes shut. They sting. "I don't know what this is. Bisexual feels right but—I mean, what do I even know? If I can't even say I slept with a girl, is this real? I need to go all in, Romy. Because otherwise how the fuck do I explain this to my parents one day? 'Oh, yeah, I'm attracted to more than just boys.' You think that'll be enough for them? I say that, and they'll say then I can *choose* to be with a guy. And just—I need this cemented. I need this to be as real as possible. And I *want* this. Why do you think I don't want this?"

Romy puts a hand on the couch cushion next to my leg. Not on it. "I do think you want it. Luna, I *believe* you. I know bisexual is real. I know what you're going through is real. But that's just what being queer involves. You're gonna deal with biphobic people, and sometimes that's gonna be your family. It just makes them shitty, not you. I've personally never gotten a fire-and-brimstone vibe from them, but god knows Gen X loves surprising you in terrible ways. And that's scary. But you don't have to prove anything to any of them. If you do any of this, you have to do it for *you*."

"How can you say that like it's so easy? And I'm not even talking about whether my bisexuality is valid. That isn't what we've been fighting about for weeks. I've been trying to figure this shit out, but sometimes it feels like I'm just trying to follow your advice to a T, and it's just not working. It doesn't feel right for me. If you're just looking out for my best interests, why won't you just let me fuck someone?"

"Come on. I'm not telling you that you can't fuck anyone. I'm not even telling you that you can't fuck Valeria."

"But you *are*! Can't you see that? You haven't been supportive of this relationship ever since she started showing interest in me! What was that shit with the mousse and cuddling up to her at karaoke? What were you trying to accomplish?"

Romy looks away. "It's not easy to explain. It was a mistake. Maybe I was a little jealous, I don't know. I just—I think you're acting reckless. Of course you can do what you want—"

"Do you even remember what you were like in college? You were reckless all the time! Going to clubs with Wyatt, being with people whose names you didn't even remember, flirting with everyone you could. Why are you of all people calling me reckless?"

"Because this is *new for you*. Your recklessness is different from mine. Look at you! You're ranting about how much it sucks to be bisexual, and then you expect me to think that this obsession with fucking Valeria comes from a place of pure passion and curiosity. News flash, Luna: Fucking Valeria won't solidify your queerness, it won't make your parents accept you, and it won't make it easier for you to accept yourself!"

The tears are falling again. Even Romy's eyes are watery. "Then where's the joy in this? What's the point of doing all this if I can't even get my *family* to fully accept me? I swear to god, Romy, sometimes I just wish I'd never even delved into this. I could've just been a stupid straight girl with a stupid husband my parents set me up with and have occasional fantasies about women and think, *Oh, that's what straight girls do*."

Now Romy is genuinely crying. "Luna . . ." She puts a hand on my knee. "Please, don't give up on this. Coming out sucks, but there *is* joy to this. You were so fucking happy when Valeria was a celebrity crush. You rediscovered your art. You left your shitty job. You *had* Valeria, and she was making you so happy and so confident and . . . and I love seeing you so happy. I love seeing you as your true self. I love . . ."

And then she kisses me.

Her lips are on mine. Her lips are so soft, so gentle, like I'm a piece of rice paper she's scared to break. Her lips taste like chocolate and salt from her tears. And as she cradles my face between her palms, her kisses are practically speaking to me. They speak of evenings when the two of us critiqued our shitty classmates' short stories, of walks through campus sharing an umbrella as we cobbled money together for the student store, of starry nights spent under blankets as we learned constellation names, of moving into dorm rooms together and sharing makeup and T-shirts and secrets in the dead of night. When I realize I'm kissing her back, for a second, it feels inevitable.

Then I pull away. My thoughts are racing so fast it feels like time's frozen.

Romy jolts herself back, touching her lips where mine had been. "Oh my god, Luna, I'm so sorry—"

I mirror her motion, touching my mouth. The spot is still tingling.

"I didn't mean to— You're my best friend and I was being irrational. I'm so sorry. It doesn't mean anything—doesn't change— Just forget it happened. Please. I can't lose you. It didn't—"

I know how she was going to end that sentence, though. *It didn't mean I like you like that. I want to maintain the friendship above all else.*

"But what was—?"

"Nothing!" she yelps. "Nothing," she repeats, calmer, slower. "I shouldn't have done that. I—I don't feel that way. You're my friend. My best friend. That's it."

My phone dings.

I dig it out of my bag.

There's a text from Valeria.

Luna, please, don't blame yourself for what happened. It's between my team and me and you were caught in the cross fire. I know I need to explain what's going on and I should've explained it a lot earlier. Could you forgive me? Or at least can you come by my place? I want to explain in person.

I take a deep breath.

Romy can't even own up to a kiss. A kiss I've been daydreaming about since college. I'm realizing now that I'd always intended for Romy to be my first. But now, I can't even find passion and giddiness in the moment. My throat hurts, my stomach's in knots, and Romy and I are actually in tears. There was no joy in that kiss. If there is, it's tangled up and I'm exhausted. God, I'm fucking exhausted, and I just wanted it to be easy. I always thought it'd be easy with Romy, but looking at her has my brain short-circuiting.

I just wanted to have gay sex. Valeria can do that. Valeria says none of this is my fault. Valeria still wants me. Valeria wants my art to go places. Valeria cares about me. Valeria doesn't know this side of me, all my mixed-up feelings, my desperation. I just need to get past this. I just want it over with. I don't want the emotion.

I look up at Romy. Her face is blotchy, and she's leaning forward like she's preparing for me to slap her.

Maybe I am.

"I need to go over to Valeria's," I say.

I don't look back. I can't do anything but nudge this kiss behind closed doors.

Still, I wait for her to protest. To tell me she was wrong, that she does want me. To make everything simple again.

"Be safe," she says.

I tell her I will.

And I leave.

chapter twenty-two

When Valeria opens the door, she's got Eustace the dog in her arms and a gray cloth robe wrapped around what I assume are pajamas, and she's already removed her makeup. She forms an almost comical contrast to me in my party dress, lingerie underneath, makeup tear-smeared but still on. She smiles as she shuts the door behind me, leaning over to wipe a smudge under my eye.

"You still look lovely," she says. "Should we talk?"

She called me "lovely." She asked me to forgive her. That I'm forgivable. She wants me, she likes me, she'll fight for me. She doesn't question me.

I almost don't care anymore. I take my shoes and jacket off.

"Let's talk after we do something . . ." I say.

I take Eustace into my arms, then release him to the ground. We've seen each other enough in the past week for him to trust me. Valeria watches her dog's claws scratch against her wooden floor with a sort of raw awe in her expression, as though no one has taken her dog out of her arms to do what we're about to do.

"Let me put him in another room," she says.

I shed my dress as she moves Eustace. A miracle, really, that I manage to get the dress into a heap on the ground. I eye the living room, this stark black-and-white space centered by a ten-foot shag carpet, which transforms the floor into a white field. Maybe we don't have to move. If this were a shot in a film, I'd pick this over a bedroom in an instant.

When Valeria returns to the room, she stops dead, mouth falling open.

"Jesus, you look amazing," she says. She eyes her own look. "Like I said, you're the star here and I'm the garbage friend."

"We just got different memos."

I cross the room, pulling her into my arms, my mouth on hers with a hunger I can't quite explain. It's a pull that feels as urgent as air. Valeria is perfectly in sync with me too. The kiss is rough, our grip on each other white-knuckled, and our nails dig into each other's skin. We're clutching each other like it's life and death, like we're both on a log in a rushing river. And when she takes my bottom lip between her teeth, for the first time I genuinely crave the hiss of pain with pleasure.

I drag us to the floor, ripping off Valeria's robe as we go. It hits the ground with a soft thud as our bodies sink into the carpet. Valeria grabs me and rolls us over, pinning me down. My stomach rolls like I'm on a roller coaster.

"I want you inside me," I blurt. "I want to have sex. Do you?"

She laughs. "Yes, Luna, I do."

My hands tingle. "I haven't done this before."

I wince, waiting for her to shy away. But I get barely more than a nod. "Okay. I'll keep you informed of what's going on. You tell me at any point if you want it slower, more gentle, or if you want me to stop. There's seriously never a wrong time to say no." She gives me a tender kiss. "Thanks for trusting me."

I cup her cheek and grab another kiss. "It's gonna be fun, though, right?"

She smirks. "Oh, don't worry about that, darling."

She trails kisses down my neck, onto my shoulders, and down the thin lace of my plunging neckline. The sensitive skin on my chest is electrified, and as she slowly peels away the shoulder straps, exposing my breasts, it's like my nerves are coming alive for the first time. She kisses and licks and bites, but it's the feeling of her breath on my body that gets my insides twisting.

"This teddy is so fucking nice," she says, giggling a little. "Not something you just rip off."

"Oh my god." I smile, grab on to her soft T-shirt. "How about you just match me?"

She lifts her arms to let me remove her shirt. It lands on the couch. I push her to the shag carpet, onto her side. And god, she truly is gorgeous. There's an almost artistic beauty to the flow of her curves. Her rising and falling chest holds my gaze, and when I move to touch and kiss her, all I can think about is how my mouth and fingers rise as her muscles move.

Touching her, it all just feels natural. It's the source of calm I so desperately need right now.

Then Valeria slides her hand down to the crotch of my lingerie. She slides her hand down and all my concentration on her selfishly seeps out my brain through my ears. One moment she's art, and the next she's the fucking artist. She's drawing the moon, the sun, the circle of eternal life. Teasing it out with feathery strokes. I buck into her hand, hold myself up on shaking muscles. Whines are suddenly the only language I know.

I buck one more time, and she holds me down with her free hand. Smirks up at me. "You like that, darling?"

Please say "darling" again. She speeds up the strokes, and the muscles in my abdomen grow taut.

I chuckle. "You gonna make me beg?"

"It's an idea."

She stops for a moment, and I spring up, gripping her wrist. It only makes her grin wider.

"Oh?" she asks, her mouth forming the shape around the word. "You want it?"

I'm desperate for her to keep touching my prickling skin.

"I want it," I say.

She quickens the pace again. "How much?"

Faster and faster and faster. My muscles tighten right along with her. I'm a little cup about to overflow. I tighten my abs, my legs, everything around her hand, savoring the sensation.

"Please don't stop" is all I can say as my breath catches in my throat.

She shrugs a little, barely biting back a playful smile. "If you say so . . ."

And she tumbles me over the edge. I grab on to her shoulders, slamming her to the ground with me as I moan into her hot skin. We rock together in the furry carpet. I'm slow to catch my breath.

Valeria groans. "Okay. So, this isn't over. At all." She clicks her tongue. "But you want to do penetration, right?" I nod. "The trick is to just be as relaxed and turned on as possible. Especially if you haven't done this before. I don't want to hurt you."

No man ever checked in like this. "What do you mean?"

She pauses, a hint of pink traveling up her face. "I just want you to talk to me so I know you're still wet. If you're too nervous, you'll get tight." She pauses. "Please stop me if I'm saying shit you already know."

"No." I blink a few times. "No one's ever cared before."

And it's not like guys haven't tried. But no matter how hard I tried, there was no way to even grit through fingers shoved inside me after ten minutes of making out. I can already tell this'll be different.

She nods. "Yeah. It's just . . ." She shrugs. "Just a way to be a good partner. If it's not working, oral is pretty incredible too." She takes my hand. "So I'm going in now. Okay?"

"Okay."

I take a deep breath as she sinks her fingers into my teddy again. It's familiar, and then her hand's crooked, a finger inside me while her thumb brushes against my clit. Jesus, Valeria is *inside me*. Painting soft, fluid strokes.

"By the way, you talk like a gynecologist," I tease.

She shoots me the finger with her free hand.

"Does this feel good?" she asks.

In all honesty, it just feels . . . there. It's more of a distraction from her thumb than anything else. My chest tightens. "It's . . . okay."

"It should feel better than okay. You're also really tight." She pulls her hand out and kisses me. A tender kiss. "I think we can try a couple of other things, right?"

I smile, my heart hammering. "Yeah." I eye the spot between her abs and the waistline of her pajama shorts. "And it's my turn, by the way."

I climb on top of her, dropping my hand inside her shorts to stroke the skin. She's moaning before she even has a chance to protest. And the thing is, I'm comfortable with this. It's a different angle, but nothing I can't handle now that I've had a little practice. Part of me wishes we could just stay here, doing this.

But that part of me isn't big enough.

And when she's coming against my fingertips, I almost feel confident about all this. Maybe I'm kind of *good* at being gay.

I turn to her flushed face. "Hey, wanna get all our clothes off?"

She smiles. "Thought you'd never ask."

The teddy and her shorts land near the base of the couch.

And when we embrace again, kissing and running our fingertips along each other's bare skin, it's easy to fully disappear in the sensation. We're nothing but fingers and mouths and goose bump–covered skin and tangled limbs.

I'm naked with a girl. A girl is naked with me. The girl is Valeria fucking Sullivan.

At some point while we're tumbling around, slicking sweat into the carpet, Valeria goes inside me again. Same nothing sensation. She frowns this time.

"Are you feeling okay?" she asks. "You're still tight."

My heart leaps. "Aren't I supposed to be tight?" I say, running a finger along her jaw.

She smiles. "Not so tight that nothing can happen." She looks down. "Course, if you're down, there's also the fact I've been dying to eat you out since karaoke . . ."

She looks at me, her pupils so big her eyes are practically black. I wonder if mine look like that. "Yeah, let's do it."

My heart doesn't stop seizing. Not as I watch her.

She kisses my lips, then moves down my throat, down my collarbone, delivers one kiss to each breast.

My heartbeat speeds up. In a bad way.

She kisses my stomach.

She's really going to do this.

A kiss to the sensitive spot above my crotch.

She's going to make me feel great, I'm sure. But no amount of reading, no amount of learning from experience—I have her parts clear in my head, they look enough like mine—none of it has prepared me. I still have no idea what to do. It's like I'm staring at a test written in a foreign language, minutes before the teacher says to start.

She kisses my inner thigh.

I can't do it. I can't reciprocate.

A kiss to my groin.

Maybe she won't ask me to return the favor.

Her mouth—Jesus—her mouth gets to where she wants to go, and just the stroke of her tongue down my opening is taking me out of reality. She strokes down my pussy, steady, sliding up to focus on my clit. I don't know what she's doing. It's stressing me out, but it . . . I never even realized *this* is what everyone was raving about.

The only issue is she's good. She's *incredible*. Something I'll never be able to do. And as she sucks on my clit, I dig my hands into her soft hair and I'm a minion under her control. I need this to last forever, I need to stay in this bubble. I can't let my brain pop it.

And when I come under her tongue, pulling a groan out of her as I tug her hair, the first thought I have is that I can *never* replicate that.

As she lays her head on my thigh, sex-soaked lazy gaze on me, I start to panic. I can't make her as blissful as I am. My chest aches, and guilt sweeps the pleasure away. It's my first time, and I'm such a shitty partner.

"Val, could we do something else?" I ask.

There has to be some other way I can satisfy her. I'll just disappoint her with oral. I refuse to be like those boys I dated, unable to give it as good as they got.

The warmth swoops out from between my thighs as she sits up. She rests on my thigh. "Sure. Do you have something in mind?"

Something I'm familiar with. When Romy described the—no, can't think about Romy right now. Straps. Penetration. It's something I've been primed to do my whole life anyway. Certainly in the past six years. I just take it, and Valeria gets pleasure from it. It's intimate, it's . . . it's exactly what I wanted from all those men anyway.

"Let's do something we can both get off on," I say. "Do you like straps?"

Valeria sits up, off my leg. "You've never been penetrated and you want me to use a strap?"

Why does she sound so surprised? Is it harder than I think? "I mean . . . do you have one?"

"Yeah . . ." She studies me. "You sure?"

I rub my arm. "I feel comfortable with you trying it. I want to. Especially if you can get off too."

She forms her lips into a thin line, releasing them slowly. "Okay. I'll go get the supplies." She kisses my cheek. "Try not to run away."

I take a deep breath. I'm making the decisions here. I'm doing this for my own comfort. I'm doing this because I want to.

But as her footsteps grow faint upstairs, my lungs get tight. It's harder to breathe. I put my hand on my bare chest, forcing the breaths out slowly. Seven seconds in, seven out.

Her footsteps grow louder again. My heart kicks up with each step she takes.

A bottle of lube lands a foot from me. I turn around, and

there's Valeria in a black harness and a strap, just like the one I saw in the Pleasure Chest.

"I cleaned this, but do you want a condom on it?" she asks.

Fuck, I don't know.

"Whatever you want," I reply.

"Okay." She slips one on. I don't know if she's paranoid or if this is normal. "So I think the most contact I can give you is if you're on your side. Same as before. I'll go slow, and you tell me if you want to stop."

I roll onto my side. Valeria is working her magic behind me. She reaches ahead of me and grabs the lube. Her arms wrapped around me, I watch as she squirts a liberal amount onto her hands and pulls them behind me. I take a deep breath.

"Okay. Let's do this."

My throat's tightening by the second. My heart is *hammering*. In a painful way.

She presses one soft kiss on the top of my spine.

My dry fucking overused eyes are filling with tears again. I blink furiously. Take a deep breath.

She takes my hand with her free hand, interlacing our fingers. Her fingertips run against my knuckles, spreading a sticky film onto my skin. The hand-holding should calm me down, but it just reminds me of Romy.

But I can feel the strap, and it's not even in yet.

I don't want it to go in.

Jesus, fucking fuck, I don't *want to do this*.

The tears run down my cheeks.

"Wait!" I say, squeezing my eyes shut.

And just like that, the strap is gone. Valeria's warmth is off me. "Is everything—?"

"We have to stop."

I hear the slick of the harness loosening. "Of course. No problem. We can—"

I don't want to do this. I'm not ready for this.

"Everything."

The word hangs heavy in the air, poisoning it. I rub my eyes with the heels of my hands, barely sopping up my tears.

Valeria turns me to face her. My heart breaks as her expression slips from shock to panic to acceptance in a few silent seconds.

She leans over and wipes away the tears I missed. "Nothing else. That's okay."

There's a weird sort of peace that falls over the house as we pick up the pieces of what just happened. We put our clothing back on. Valeria volunteers to sift through my car to find the pajamas I packed in an overnight bag. She lets Eustace out of whatever room she left him in, and she hands me water while Eustace drinks from his bowl. She tosses me a makeup-removal wipe from her bathroom as well.

We end up in her bedroom, between million-thread-count sheets that feel more luxurious than those at a five-star hotel. The first time I've ever spent the night. It could be the most sexually charged thing we've done yet, but the energy's been spent. It's like sharing the bed with Romy.

Although, thinking about that kiss, I'm not so sure what that means anymore.

"Do you wanna talk about it?" Valeria asks as Eustace curls up on her pillow.

I sigh. "I don't know. I just . . . froze, I guess. Like I couldn't picture it happening, and I suddenly couldn't stand the thought that it would. I thought—I don't know, I thought it'd just be easier. I like you. So much. But I guess that didn't matter."

Valeria bites her cheek a moment. "How long have you been out? If you don't mind me asking."

"Two months or so."

Valeria slaps her hand to her mouth. A wide-eyed *oh fuck* surprise face. "I figured it was, like, within a year, but shit . . ." She takes my hand. "Um, you not being ready for a strap is, like, the most normal thing I've heard. Shit, *two months*? You could've told me."

I sink deeper into the covers. "It's . . . not exactly the cutest thing to say."

"Luna, what are you talking about, 'cute'? Don't be ridiculous. And of course I wouldn't have cared. Jesus, you're— How are you feeling? This is—this is a lot. I did— Are you okay with how things went down?"

I take a deep breath. "Did I lose my virginity? When would you say that happened?"

Valeria's body language tightens, still panicked. "What?"

"We had sex, right?"

"Yes."

"What was it?"

Valeria eyes Eustace, then slowly focuses on me. "I mean, I *personally* consider it oral, but I don't think it's so black and white."

"But I didn't perform oral on you."

Valeria takes my hand. "Luna, it's . . . Would you lose your virginity to a man if he penetrated you but didn't make you orgasm?"

"Yeah."

"Then I guess I don't have to orgasm for you to lose your

virginity." She pauses. "But for the record, we both did come. Like seven days in a row. I know virginity is so confusing and the idea that you have to lose it is so prevalent in society, and . . . I mean, if it makes you feel more confident to have been eaten out or to have had my fingers inside you, sure, you lost it."

I huff. "Why don't you or Romy just have a straight answer?"

She runs her fingers through Eustace's fur. "Because virginity is stupid as a concept. Because why should het sex count if women don't orgasm? But you have to define what sex means to you for yourself. If you get down to the bare bones, sex is, what? A performance of intimacy and sexual satisfaction? Then . . ."

Us naked together on that rug. Knowing each other's bodies. Making each other come and holding each other, knowing those intimate details. That sensation of post-orgasm bliss: smelling someone else's scent, feeling someone else's hands on my back, looking into someone's eyes. Being one of a special few who knows what she sounds like when she comes. And she's the only one who knows what I do when I come. That feeling I had in the Uber after karaoke simmers in me, the feeling that I was *getting* something intangible about sexual desire that I never got with the men I dated. It wasn't earth-shattering like the books I read as a teen said it would be, but it *was* something I'd never felt before.

I want sex to be as simple as that.

"I guess I did."

And I guess it can be.

She studies me. "Were you hoping I'd take your virginity when we started flirting?"

I blush, hard. "Yes."

She swallows. "And I wanted an escape from this closet thing. I guess we kind of played each other."

I don't know how to feel about that. It's bitter, and yet it's also intimate on a whole different level. We were both so uncomfortable with aspects of our sexualities, and we were finally able to break past that with each other. We trusted the other enough to try, at least.

"I guess we should have had that talk you wanted to have earlier."

She smiles, joyfully at first, but then it slips into sadness. "I'm out with people I know. I've been out since I was nineteen. But . . ." She takes a deep breath. "I had a fiancée in my Ph.D. program. But when my dissertation was denied and I got the part in that movie, we just—we ended things. Then the premiere for *Stroke* comes along, and my delightful publicist, Tori, says I have two options: a *certified* female family member or a male friend. Attractive, preferably. I ended up going with Charlie. You met him on set, right?" I nod. "Yeah, he's gay as shit too, but the media hasn't really asked him about it since we 'broke up' before *Goodbye, Richard!*"

My eyes sting.

"I spent more than six years living my authentic life, out and proud, and they just kinda snapped their fingers and it all went away." She blinks. "And the worst thing is they make you believe their bullshit. For so long, I was genuinely afraid of coming out accidentally, thinking it'd kill this career I left my whole life for."

"Would they really keep you in the closet forever? No one even cares now."

"They said I was free to marry a woman and have kids. I'd just need to keep them a tight-lipped secret. But they said that was fine, because why would I want to expose my family to fame anyway?" She pauses. "Mostly celebrities who're in the glass closet want to be there. They want their privacy. I was never even given the choice."

The whole argument with her team . . . It wasn't about her dating someone she worked with. It was about her being seen publicly with a *woman*.

She pulls her phone over to me. Heads into her Instagram, then into the archives.

It's filled with pictures of her with another woman: lying together in parks, kissing while climbing boulders (the Yosemite mystery is solved), even one of them holding Eustace as a puppy.

"I'm not still into her," she says. "It's just . . . sometimes I miss being able to show off someone I like, you know? I don't want these secrets. When I'm with you, when I was behind your camera, all I wanted was to capture us together. I wanted to scream it to the world."

Tears slip down her cheeks.

"Why don't you?" I ask. "Why don't you leave them? I'm sure there are plenty of agents and managers who'd let you be who you are."

She pets Eustace. His bug eyes shut in bliss. "I need enough faith and guts to make that plunge. It never gets easier." She looks at me. "Something I'm sure you can relate to."

I join the Eustace petting party. "What happens to us?"

She raises a brow. "What do you want to happen?"

"I . . . I want something easy. I want peace. I want to grow."

Our fingers touch as we pet Eustace. Neither of us flinches.

"I'm not very peaceful or easy. I think we can both agree on that. I'd never forgive myself if the fucking *National Enquirer* runs a story that accidentally outs you to your family before you're ready." She looks me right in the eye. "But I need you to know that nothing between us happened because I wanted sex. I really think you've got so much potential. I guess I do think the best version of our relationship is . . ." She exhales.

"Professional," I finish. I swallow the lump in my throat. "Brendan couldn't get me the job."

Her expression softens. "Luna . . ."

It stings, but not as much as I thought it would.

I can't believe I'm saying this out loud. I can't believe being in a relationship with Val is what I wanted, what I was so sure I'd get, just this morning. "It's okay. I'm not saying that because I want you to do anything. But I also don't want to destroy the opportunity to work with you in the future." I look her in the eye. "I care about you, so much, but filmmaking . . . I could never ask you to help me with that if we were dating. I think it's best for us both to keep a long-term friendship."

Valeria smiles. "If anything, consider me your stupid older queer mentor. You're definitely not shaking me."

I take her hand. "Please don't leave."

"I won't. But fair warning: my advice is always to act on your lizard brain and then leave your frontal lobe to clean up the mess like science intended."

I finally lean over and wipe the tear stains on her face.

"I want to collaborate with you. When you're a cinematographer," she says. "One day." She smiles. Holds out her hand to shake. "Professional collaborators?"

I smile back. Shake her hand. "Professional collaborators."

She pauses. "Tomorrow, could you take a picture of me for a coming-out post?"

My heart leaps. "Really?"

"Really. I have a long track of disaster lesbian to fix."

"Of course." I pause, give her hand a squeeze, and pull away. "Is there a disaster lesbian?" I ask.

She smiles. "There's a disaster everything." She puts Eustace's face to hers. "Aw, you don't think I'm a disaster, do you?"

Eustace, Chihuahua hell mix that he is, proceeds to bite at her face. She yanks her face away like he does this every day. "Fuckin' A, Eustace, homophobic prick!"

chapter twenty-three

I wake up in a plush bed next to Valeria and the mouth-breathing Chihuahua lying on her neck, and it takes a minute for me to remember what happened and snap back to reality. I take a moment to drink Valeria in: her perfect skin, her long eyelashes lying against her cheeks. Her ethereal beauty is set off by the fact that she's wearing her dog like a scarf. I feel a pang in my chest knowing I can't perfectly capture this image, knowing I'll never see her like this again.

I step out of bed and make my way down to the kitchen. No one asked and I know I can't expect a kiss for it, but I still find myself searching through her fridge and cabinets for breakfast supplies. I settle for a scramble with the Whole Foods produce and eggs I uncover. With each crack of the egg against the bowl, more of last night seeps into my memory.

I royally fucked up the wrap party. There might be a picture circulating of Valeria and me together. Wyatt lost his job because he helped set Valeria and me up. He may never forgive me for that. I didn't get my job.

Romy got a meeting. Romy got a meeting, tried to convince

me not to have sex with Valeria, and kissed me. I have no idea how she feels about the kiss, but she didn't go after me. I don't know if she was supposed to come after me or if I was supposed to stay. If I *was* supposed to stay, I royally fucked that one up too.

Valeria and I had sex, even though it wasn't what I expected—what I convinced myself it had to be.

Valeria admitted that her team closets her. That she hates it almost as much as she hates her team.

I look down at the eggs. Four eggs in a bowl. It doesn't mean anything, but it's a shot I would use if someone decided to make a biopic about me. I add the milk and whisk.

God, *Romy*. Should I have seen that kiss coming? Before we pulled away, I remember thinking how right it felt to be with her like that. I felt calm, cared for, understood, exhilarated. Even now, my stomach tugs at the thought of the sweet taste of her lips, the pressure she held my face with, the heat of our legs touching. It felt too easy, somehow. Friends, real platonic friends, shouldn't be able to kiss *like that* that easily.

Where along the path of our friendship did Romy stop seeing us as platonic? When did she decide she even wanted to kiss me? Sure, our friendship has always been so different from any other platonic relationship I've ever had. I never had a friendship as deep, consistent, and tender as ours. I never had friendships where I couldn't go an hour without taking a photo of something or finding a meme I just *knew* I had to send to them. Friendships where I missed them every time they went on a family vacation. Friendships where we'd snuggle up and share a heating pad and watch reality T.V. when our periods synced up. Where we'd have full-on conversations while the other was in the bath and go lingerie shopping together and actively discuss each other's kinks and jokingly try to seduce each other based on those kinks—

My cheeks burn. Our friendship hasn't been platonic for so fucking long.

Yet I was still so shocked by the kiss. I left her.

Valeria comes down the stairs, Eustace in her arms, and raises her brows as she inspects my cooking scene. The eggs are almost ready.

"You cook?" she asks.

I smile. "Yep. Look at what we could've been."

She hangs on to the countertop, her eyes looking around, alighting on everything but me. "I think you're making the right decision, even though my gay lizard brain is kind of mad about it."

I serve her the eggs. She dumps organic dog food and prepre-pared white-meat chicken into a dish for Eustace. We sit around her glass breakfast nook like this is the most normal thing in the world.

"So we're platonic now?" I ask.

Valeria leans back in her chair. "There will certainly be an attempt at that, yes."

I push the food around my plate. "So . . . we weren't, like, official."

"No." She sighs. "But this photo will be, once you're ready."

I smile. "Let's do it."

But an hour later, I'm shaking with nerves.

Valeria agreed to this, I remind myself. Valeria *agreed* to this. We discussed the composition together and everything. Still, sitting at her house, adjusting the lighting in the living room we had sex in, I can't help but feel jittery for her.

"Jesus, Luna, if you're gonna be this stressed out, we can make you a coming-out post too," Valeria jokes as she strokes Eustace, whose body is also shaking.

"Please don't mention my coming out." I take a deep breath. I'll process how having gay sex hasn't *really* improved that situation another time. It's hot in here, but Valeria's not sweating. "Are you ready?"

She smiles. "Completely."

The idea is simple. Valeria isn't just going to remain closeted while she promotes her queer indie film. She wants to be able to be her authentic self. Even if that means posting nonprofessional-grade coming-out posts to her god-knows-how-many fans without anyone's permission. This post is not about me or my future. Valeria's done a lot to help me, and I want to do what I can for her.

If Steven et al. don't freak out, she'll keep them. If not, she'll leave. They are going to have to respect her decisions and accept her for who she is if they want to remain on her team.

Even though Valeria's not shaking or sweating, I know she's nervous. Anyone would be in her position.

She settles onto the couch, slings one leg over the armrest. She's wearing makeup, but only enough to sharpen her features. And she has Eustace on her lap, chilling. Not chilling, really. Quivering and unhappy, a classic Chihuahua. We're utilizing this huge decorative mirror she has in her living room in order to show off the pièce de résistance: a pink baseball cap worn backward—a lesbian must-have look. The mirror picks up the words *In Dog Years I'm Gay* written on the back of the hat.

"Are you sure about Eustace?" I ask as I adjust the lens.

"Once a year, I stop being Eustace's emotional support dog and he becomes mine. This is one of those times."

She kisses his head, leaving a little ring of lipstick behind. I'm tempted to clean it, but it might be cool to pick up the color in post.

I let her choose the pose. I just hope it won't be completely obscene. But even if it is, this is authentic queer person Valeria.

"Give me your best sultry fuck-me face," I say.

"Don't you mean 'fuck-you face'?"

I . . . actually said that wrong. I wave air on my face for a moment, trying to get rid of the flush. "Yeah, that one."

She chuckles. "You're a shitty photographer."

I throw her the bird before proceeding.

Is it weird to say she's even more fun now that I'm no longer concerned about being datable? The five-year age difference felt like decades when I was trying not to seem like a naive idiot, but now that the pressure is off, I see her as someone with whom I'm on equal footing. Now it feels like *only* five years. We spent twenty minutes before this talking about how Eustace was named after the man in *Courage the Cowardly Dog* and what a great show that was.

She puts on a come-hither face. The image is playful, mischievous even, but still powerful.

"Did Eustace cooperate?" Valeria asks after I finish photographing.

If by "cooperate" she means "look really uncomfortable," then yes.

"He's a Chihuahua. His face is funny. It's inherently photogenic."

We do one more round of photos, and this time I hold up a treat to get Eustace to look at the camera. If I wasn't before, I'm now fully convinced that Valeria is a great actress, because she keeps a straight face the whole way through.

About an hour later, Valeria's typing up her caption and I'm still staring wistfully at my phone. Waiting for Romy to text me, to explain herself. Every second my phone stays silent just sends a shiv deeper into my heart. It tells me that the kiss really did mean nothing. That I don't mean to her what I'm growing more and more certain she means to me.

"Do you want to be tagged or no?" Valeria asks.

I'm trying to take my queer stuff slower. I'm trying to work with only what I feel I have some control over. "No thanks."

She pushes a strand of hair out of her face. "Cool." She takes a deep breath. "Okay. We're gonna do it. Hold my hand?"

I take her hand. It's started to feel natural.

She slams our hands on the tabletop, startling the shit out of Eustace. He runs from the room.

"It's done," she says.

I check my Instagram feed. And indeed, it is done. Caption: *Reddit was right, bless.* Along with seven gay flag emojis.

I like it, and my like disappears among hundreds in the first few seconds.

"Jesus, how do you know if it's blowing up?" I ask.

She checks her own phone. "If it gets posted on another account within five minutes."

Eustace drags his tiny body back into the living room, and Valeria gets the first call.

She doesn't answer.

Then her phone explodes.

I let Valeria deal with her storm, and I turn my attention to my own people. Namely Romy. I think about Romy and the long road ahead of us as we try to heal the wounds we inflicted on each other last night. My affair with Valeria is over. And before Val, my best friend was there, leading me through these tumultuous waters. And I left her drowning. If Valeria can come out to the world, I can reach out to my best friend who kissed me last night.

I open up a text to her.

> Hey can we talk about last night? I'm sorry I ran out on you, and I'm sorry for jerking you around the past few months.

She responds immediately.

> Where are you now?

I glance at Valeria as she snuggles with Eustace, her phone still blowing up beside her.

> With Valeria.

The three dots appear right away. A pebble of dread settles inside me. I didn't spend that long on that apology text, thinking we would talk, and now I'm worried I haven't done enough.

Then the dots disappear.

The dread grows.

I give Eustace some scratches, and by the time I'm done the dots are back again.

Then, within a few seconds, they're gone.

I can't help it. I text again.

> Are you okay?

Finally, a text comes through.

I'm gonna need some time.

I sigh and tuck my phone back into my bag to resist throwing it across the room. When it comes down to it, I think Wyatt will forgive me. We've both done hurtful things, but at the end of the day we trust each other to always have the other's best interests at heart. But Romy, god, that hurts. For the past six years, my life has revolved around our friendship. When we met, my whole headspace changed. Everything from that point on involved her. We'd graduate together. We'd likely stay in L.A. together. We'd help each other navigate adult jobs and adult relationships. Be in each other's weddings and hang out with each other's kids and/or animals.

I can't imagine a world where she doesn't forgive me, where she isn't in my life anymore.

I'm panicking, and I don't know what to do, who to turn to. I have to give Romy space. I know that. I can't go to Julia until our next session. And even if Valeria and I are buddies now and she won't ditch me, I'm still far from her first priority at the moment. And then it comes to me. I have one other coping mechanism.

Filming.

The pathway to the Devil's Gate, a part man-made, part naturally occurring, dilapidated iron gate and rock in the shape of Satan under the 210 freeway, starts at a rather innocuous cul-de-sac at the end of La Canada Verdugo Road in Pasadena. The freeway crosses one of L.A.'s old dams, now abandoned, a desolate shell of infrastructure that can be seen in its functional prime only in movies made in Jack Nicholson's youth. Seemingly half the cities in America claim to have some maw-looking tunnel or hole that supposedly leads to Hell, and this is L.A.'s. At night, even a seasoned Jew like myself might shiver at Romy's descriptions of demons pulling trespassers through the tunnel as the Satan rock watches. But it's daytime now, and the view of Devil's Gate is far from spooky. Right now it's just one of the coolest places Romy ever showed me.

I squint down at the dried-up river and stone arches below me. Given how many off-color comments Valeria's made about Pasadena in the brief time I've known her, I can't help but wonder if she would find this hidden gem interesting or if she'd dismiss it as another unimpressive part of the area. But the thought doesn't last long.

After all, this is Romy's and my spot.

I pass by a bit of graffiti and head through the narrow tunnel that leads under the 210, then I emerge onto the unkempt wooded path that eventually winds around to the Devil's Gate itself.

I more or less manage not to stumble the entire way down the path. Bushes and dead tree limbs scratch my ankles and knock into my face with each step I take. There are NO TRESPASSING signs, but the real deterrent is just how inconvenient it is to get down here. Romy's *absolutely* convinced that this place is haunted. There's enough to make me uneasy between the criminal activity and the drug use, so I've never been as into the ghost stories. But now that I'm scrounging around the area by myself, I sense a certain heaviness to the air. It feels like I'm not truly alone. I can only hope that if there are ghosts, they'll leave me and my memories be.

It only takes being smacked with about fifty branches to reach the actual Gate to Hell and Satan Rock. The structure is perhaps less impressive than myth would suggest. The gate is just that—a literal twelve-or-so-foot-tall metal gate leading into the tunnel. There's a fair amount of graffiti on the rocks around the structure, and that continues into the mouth of the tunnel, becoming a combination of cryptic warnings and more artistic painting.

I look at the rock formation that supposedly resembles Satan. I can see it maybe half the time, but I do see it today.

I turn to the tunnel. Take a few steps inside. And even though the whole place screams *murder cave*, right now I just feel peace. I feel as though nature has cleared the area out just for me. It's serene here.

This was one of the first places Romy took me to, back when we were freshmen. I told her I was scared, going to the old L.A. Zoo, and she told me that Devil's Gate was a step up in creepiness and it involved less hiking. Of course, she lied about the hiking. But she wasn't wrong about the fear factor. The first time we came was during the day, and heading through the Devil's Gate was a welcome relief from the blaring sun of a late-October L.A. heat wave. Romy told me the entire myth surrounding this place as we ventured inside, admiring bits and pieces of the urban art.

I step into the tunnel, flicking the flashlight on my phone on. I should be filming right now, but I just want to see it with my naked eye first.

It's the natural location for a horror short, but all I can envision is a romance.

The first time we came here, Romy and I had stood on either side of the tunnel, leaning up against the wall to avoid sitting on the floor. The cave is narrow, though, so our legs spread into each other's space, although we still kept a few feet of distance between us. But now, I can see the shot I'd want to showcase so clearly: the two people physically separated as they each lean against opposite walls, but as the camera looks into the tunnel, their shadows become one.

Romy had never explicitly come out to me and Wyatt. She just casually dropped that she liked girls and it was cool. But when the two of us were in that tunnel together, she came out to me as nonbinary. She'd floundered over her words, tears brimming in her eyes, desperation hanging off her every syllable. And just like that first day in class, my reaction came naturally. I listened, I comforted her, I assured her that not only was this something I'd never reject but that it was a piece of her I'd fight for every step of the way. She trusted this tunnel not to judge. She'd shared a vulnerable piece of herself, and after she did, I'd admitted that I didn't think the majority of the population was straight. That sometimes I thought about kissing people other than boys.

She didn't question it, though. She just nodded along and gave her own theories about which percentage of the population fell where on the Kinsey scale. We were intertwined shadows sharing secrets that vanished in the air as they were spoken. And yeah, that night, I had wondered what would've happened if I'd asked her to kiss me.

I wish Romy were here to re-create the image that's in my head. I hate that it's *only* in my head.

I wish I could show Romy that I managed to find this place on my own and not get killed.

I wish she could know how much her little trips around L.A. have influenced how I approach my work behind the camera.

I wish . . .

I wish I could have the chance to kiss her back. To satisfy that curiosity I've been sitting with for years. To see if I could feel peace with her lips on mine, her hands cupping my face the way they did last night. To be in the same room as her and just recognize how she makes me feel.

I don't regret what Valeria and I did together. I can't dismiss what she did to help me on my sexuality journey. But I do regret that we kissed only in locked rooms, in houses, in cars. It feels like a tiny piece of what we were was taken from each of us.

I don't want to regret anything with Romy. But it's been less than twelve hours and I feel lost. Like there's a lifetime's worth of stuff to tell her and a lifetime's worth of her life to hear about. Yes, we've been flirting with each other for years, but it feels so much bigger than that.

I don't know what else this could possibly mean.

I mean, how do you *know* you've been ignoring a crush for years?

I run my fingers along a white eye someone has painted in the tunnel.

Thinking about the person in a murder cave seems like a good indicator.

Jesus. I know I love Romy as a friend. That couldn't be more obvious. But this—I don't know, this tug, this anticipation for a future I can't quite picture . . . it's exhilarating and it makes me dizzy, but not in the same terrifying way everything with Valeria did. This is less roller coaster and more running down a hill. The thrill's still there, but I trust that I have enough control not to crash and burn when I hit the bottom. *Romy.* My best friend, Romy, the coolest person I know. Romy, my rock and superhero and favorite writer ever. Romy.

God, I love Romy Fonseca.

And I left her last night for Valeria.

chapter twenty-four

By Tuesday, it's been two days since Romy and I kissed, and still no word from her. I'm back at home, sitting on my bed, tempted to make lists of things to do to get Romy to talk to me, but I'm not quite sure what should be on those lists.

It's been almost twenty-four hours since I came to the conclusion that I like Romy as more than a friend, and I think it's rendered me even more useless. She asked me to give her space. So should I give her space? Or is her asking for space really her way of asking me to swoop in and sweep her off her feet?

I grab my phone off my nightstand. I apologized to Wyatt last night for what happened, and lo and behold, his anger was gone. It lasted less than a day. My fingers ache to text him and ask his opinion on the Romy situation. I'm sure he won't be thrilled to know Valeria and I "broke up."

Then again, I don't know if I want his advice. It tends to be very . . . simplistic.

But he also told me Romy was acting weird and he'd deal with it back before karaoke.

I pull up our text conversation. Fuck it. I need him, and

besides, I want to hear how he's doing after everything that happened with Steven. Wyatt loves to come across as blasé, but I know he must be hurting right now. I know I've been a shit friend to Romy, but I've hardly been any better to Wyatt. He deserves a better me too.

He says he'll meet me in Culver City at one p.m. I type out how will you get off work, but then I remember and delete it. I guess two out of three of us are unemployed. Ironic, considering Romy's the one who thinks Slater is stupid. But at least it means we avoid traffic.

Wyatt's rocking his usual T-shirt-and-board-shorts look, ever resistant to the lessons I imparted that time I practically performed an entire *Queer Eye* episode on him in junior year of college. We get our overpriced coffees and settle at an outdoor table in the shade. Other twentysomethings decked out in sunglasses are sipping coffees at the other tables. Romy and I used to joke that everyone who came to Culver City was a YouTuber, and we'd make up what kind of content they'd put up.

"Did you bring your laptop?" Wyatt asks.

I nod. "Are we gonna multitask?"

"Yeah."

Wyatt mentioned over text that he's applying to every junior creative executive and junior manager job that pops up. His time with Steven makes him more than qualified. His lovable yet sleazy personality makes him perfect.

But when I pull up the entertainment careers website, I don't even know which category to click on. Do I go back to a desk job? Back into P.A. jobs? Something else?

"So how're you and Valeria?" Wyatt asks.

"We . . . don't think we should try to combine romantic feelings with our professional relationship."

Wyatt shuts his computer. "What?!"

I exhale. "I'd prefer to not go into detail. It's still good."

"Wait. Wait. You and Valeria *broke up*?"

"Yeah."

"Did you have sex?"

I click on crew jobs. Not P.A.s. Crew. "Yes. But it . . . wasn't straightforward."

"Okay." Another pause. "Are you okay?"

I shut my laptop. "Wyatt, when you said Romy was acting weird, were you talking about her liking me?"

Wyatt stares at me, goggle-eyed.

"Can I take that as a yes?" I say.

He grabs my wrist. "You didn't hear it from me! Rom's been swearing me to secrecy for, like, three months or whatever. Hell, I—" He leans in closer. "She talked to me about it after you and I broke up. She didn't want things to get weird if she ever chose to tell you. But she never did. Not even after you came out."

Was that trip to the AMC when we watched Valeria's movie supposed to have been a date? "Why didn't she?"

"I dunno. She was scared. I know she acts all smooth and cool or whatever, but we talked about it and this is all new to her. I've been in love more times than Romy, and that's saying something. And with you, obviously, you're kind of her dream girl."

Me? Romy Fonseca's dream girl? I can't even picture it, me in a line along with all the cool, tatted people Romy's mentioned in the past. I can't see her ever picking me.

My cheeks go hot at the thought. "Well . . . what's her deal now? She won't talk to me and she kissed me."

Wyatt slams his hands onto the table. A few possible YouTubers glance over. "What do you mean she *kissed* you?"

I sip my coffee; the heat on my lips reminds me of Romy's

mouth. "She— We were arguing about whether I should try to sleep with Valeria and she kissed me. She said she didn't mean to and I left."

Wyatt gives me a look. "And you're wondering why she's not talking to you? That's, like, a sizzling rejection."

Oh my god. "And I told her I'd slept over. I stayed at her house after . . . She didn't want me driving back home at whatever horrible hour it was."

Wyatt rubs his temples. "Oh my god, Roth, she thinks you're still fucking Valeria. Yeah, no wonder she's not talking to you!"

My stomach sinks. "What do I do? It's so much more than this Valeria thing. I've been *so* shitty to her the past few months. And what if I tell her how I feel and she thinks it's just me rebounding after Valeria?"

"Well . . . is it?"

I squeeze my eyes shut. "I don't know! I just—I always thought I was so far from Romy's type that it wasn't even worth pursuing. Of course I thought about just asking her to kiss me so I could get my first gay kiss over with. Valeria was . . . It was thrilling and addicting and out there, but it was *low risk* on some level. Like we were never friends. So if I fucked things up with Valeria, who cares? But if I do this wrong with Romy, there goes my best friend on Earth."

Wyatt breaks into the tiniest of smiles. "I think you really do like her. Ain't that cute?"

I exhale. "This doesn't explain what I should do to get her to forgive me."

"Lune, come on. You know what to do," Wyatt says.

And that's all he says on the subject. We go right back to discussing job prospects.

There are actual first A.C. and even D.P. roles on low-budget films. It's not good money, but it's practical experience. And it would mean I would get to do what I love to do. It will be consistent work. It'll pay rent. Romy's just been doing what she loves, and look at where it's gotten her. If Romy kicks me out and I have to move back in with my parents, I won't need the money that urgently any—

No. I'm going to fix this with Romy. I'm going to need rent money.

I start by applying to five of them. I tell myself I'll do five more tomorrow. Five, ten, however many until I'm back behind a camera, telling stories.

It's the first time in a long time that I feel good about the future.

I pull out my phone. Scroll to my text chain with Valeria.

There's just one more piece of the future I have to deal with.

I know most of this doesn't make sense and that it may even be cruel to bring these specific problems to Valeria given everything we've been through. But I can't help it. I don't know any other queer people. She may call herself dumb, but she's been out for nearly ten years as an adult—a home-owning, had-a-fiancée, retirement-secure, health-insurance-having, independent adult. She's been dealing with gay love and heartbreak for years.

So here I am, sitting in her home office. It's spacious and gorgeous. Her bookshelves are lined with tomes on philosophy, pop culture analysis, and history as well as novels. Her awards have been turned into a custom chandelier. The silhouettes of an Oscar, a Golden Globe, a BAFTA, a Critics' Choice, and a SAG flicker across the walls.

"Yeah," she says, noticing me staring, "I hooked up with the best supporting actress that year at the Oscars, and we drunkenly decided to make a satanic circle out of awards. But then I realized I was missing an MTV, a Teen Choice, and a Kids' Choice Award, so in the interest of not driving myself completely insane trying to get *those*, we made this instead."

I chuckle. "It's cool. Weird. Very you."

She leans back in her office chair, throwing a leg over the armrest. A true gay icon. The true gay icon she can now be, I think, and my heart swells.

"Can I ask your advice about someone?" I ask. I wince. "Romantic?"

The corners of her lips quirk up. "What's a disaster gay mentor for?"

So I just dump it all. How Romy and I met, how our relationship grew more intimate over the years, how I came out to her, the kiss, her silence.

"And I—" I run my hands down my face. "Now I fucked everything up. She thinks I chose you over her, and I practically confirmed it with my text the next morning and your coming-out photo. She's ignoring me at home and . . . I just don't know how to get her to understand what I'm thinking."

"Have you just texted her clarifying what happened between us?"

"It's bigger than that, though! I fucked up. I've put her through absolute hell over the past few months, using her for advice on how to get with you. How bad does it look if I just turn around after you and I *happen* to not work out and am like, 'I love you'?"

"Well, I think it'd imply things didn't work out between us because you *were* in love with Romy. Which, as much as it hurts *my* ego, is grand and ridiculous and very romantic. She won't turn you away."

God, my chest aches. "I'm such a shitty friend."

"Painfully oblivious. There's a difference."

"What do I do? I just—" I squeeze my eyes shut. "I swear she's never going to forgive me. I'm not the extraordinary girl she thinks she's loved all these years. I'm not even creative enough to figure out a way to show her how much I care about her."

Valeria shifts in her seat. "Well, when I proposed to my ex-fiancée, all it really took was knowing what connected us. We were both these huge Beatles nerds, so I proposed on Abbey Road. She ignored the fact that I almost got run over, and she said yes. It's just about knowing what you love about her and what makes your connection special and showing her that."

"And that works?"

Valeria shrugs. "Usually. Do you two have something like that?"

We do. And I've been neglecting it.

But that ends now.

chapter twenty-five

I honestly never thought I'd be back in Slater Management. Even when I first started the job and was miserable and I spent my days imagining what it would be like to leave, my daydreams never involved visiting again. At my most petty, I even considered never accepting representation from a manager here in order to guarantee I would never have to return. But here I am in the Slater underground parking garage, slightly dressed up in order to blend in, yet completely unable to blend in because of the amount of stuff I'm carrying. Valeria is by my side. She smiles at me.

"You're not nervous, are you?" I ask.

She rolls her neck, and I hear a couple of soft cracks. "A little."

"It'll work out for both of us." I pause. "At least, I'm hoping it works out for you."

She gives me a look. "We're hoping this works out for *you*."

Kiki greets us at reception, and her whole face lights up when she sees, well, *me*. She hugs me over the desk.

"Where the hell have *you* been?" she says, glancing at Valeria.

I shrug. "Got myself a guardian angel."

"So you're not her personal assistant?"

I look at Valeria again. It's a weirdly grounding moment. Yeah, I guess that must be what people would think. Being back here, seeing all the same faces, I know the fairy-tale aspect of this affair with Valeria (God, I love calling it an affair even if it barely was) is gone. I'm at peace with that, though.

"No," I say. I put a hand on her biceps. "Just her hype lady."

Valeria smiles and looks at Kiki. "Unpaid hype lady. We're very opportunistic here."

"Nate will be down to get you soon, Ms. Sullivan," Kiki says.

Valeria and I move to the couches in the lobby. Two sweaty, suit-clad interviewees are reading over their résumés. I really don't miss it here. I look over at the café and my palms start sweating. There's no discreet way to wipe them on my shorts.

"You don't have to wait for me," Valeria says.

I take a deep breath. "It's okay. I'm here to support."

"Lune, you can't even come into the room with me."

I shiver a little hearing her call me Lune. She's become as close as family. "Really. I can wait."

She puts a hand over mine. "It's going to be fine. You two are best friends. That's not so easy to throw away." She presses her hand against my upper back. "Go. Before your brownie cake melts."

I need to learn how to make Romy happy in some way that doesn't involve making two trays of these brownies in less than three months.

I smile, but it comes out more like a wince. "Brownies don't *melt.*"

"But I will if you don't leave and win your person."

She squeezes my hand before I walk off. The café is maybe twenty feet away, and in order to get there I have to pass by the other Laura Owens painting. That has to be a good sign. One more breath and I'm in.

Romy is the only one in there. She's wearing her barista uniform and wiping down the counter. She's in the uniform I'm only now fully acknowledging makes her look so cute. We're alone. I have no excuses. No excuses and—

Romy looks up, her eyes going watery. She blinks a few extra times.

Nowhere to hide.

I force a smile. "Hi."

Her green eyes fall to the bags in my hands. "Did Valeria end up making you her personal assistant?" She doesn't sound mad, just confused. It's good. It's a good sign.

I approach the counter and set my bags down. "These are actually for you."

"Me?" Romy frowns, leaning away from me.

"Yeah." I exhale. "For you. But that's not the important part."

The only noise in the room is the crinkling of my bags.

"Can I pitch a movie for us to make together?" I ask. "Just one more, for old times' sake?"

Romy glances around the room. "As long as no one comes in here. I'm at work. We can't do this at home?"

"Nope."

Romy faces me, but she still won't meet me at the end of the counter. It's as if there's an invisible line she won't cross. "Hit me, Roth."

I take a deep breath. My gaze is steady on her. Even though my whole body is shaking, she's an anchor in the chaos. She makes every second of this possible. "The color palette is pastels against gray—yellow, a soft pink, lavender, light blue. A California sunrise to set the scene after two college roommates have been up all night studying for a goddamn media theory scholar-based film test. Neither of them wanted to take the class, but there they were."

Romy's brow furrows, which it always does when she's trying to remember something.

"They end up in Devil's Gate, which the cooler roommate says is a spooky historical landmark, a good distraction from what they've been doing. The nerd roommate is less into it, but she looks up to the cooler one, and she would even feel safe venturing into the jungle with her. So it's fine. Then there will be a few shots of graffiti and decay, but all within the same palette. When they arrive at the Devil's Gate and venture into the tunnel, the silence is peaceful, not scary. This surprises the nerd roommate. The two roommates lean against the walls of the tunnel, one on each side: the cooler roommate's feet land to the nerd roommate's right, the nerd roommate's feet land to the cooler roommate's right."

I adjust my footing. I still can't decide if I'm doing this in the right order. "The cool roommate tells the nerd roommate that she has a secret, something she trusts only the nerd roommate to know. She tells her that she rejects gender but loves her body, but that she doubts anyone would ever bother to understand, how she thinks they'd question her decision, ask if she was nonbinary enough. The nerd roommate takes her hand and says that of course she's nonbinary enough, that she loves her no matter what."

Romy's eyes are growing watery again. I still don't think she's completely processed this, though.

"The nerd roommate admits that she's wondered for a while if she's bi, that she thinks about gay kissing sometimes." I exhale, my heart hammering. "But instead of changing the subject, talking about bisexuality broadly, the nerd roommate does what she's wanted to do since she met the cool roommate. She asks the cool roommate if she would create a safe environment for her to satisfy her curiosity, even though she knows full well that she'll like it."

"Luna . . ." Romy says, her voice wavering.

"And the two of them kiss, and the nerd roommate understands, finally, that the cool roommate wanted her all along. That one of them had to be brave, and the cool roommate is relieved that she didn't have to but puts every ounce of passion and caring and love into that kiss in Devil's Gate at sunrise. The sunlight spills back in, casting their shadows against the walls for a few precious minutes."

Romy's hands rise over her mouth. "Luna, I don't—"

I pull out the first item from the bag: a single framed image of us at Devil's Gate, our shadows intertwined in the exact way I'd imagined shooting when I was there the other day. Turns out I had the same great idea back in college. I found it among hundreds of artsy photos I've taken of Romy over the years.

"I had this shot all along," I say. "And I never want either of us to forget it."

"I can't believe you captured that . . ."

I smile. "I keep track of everything."

My chest flutters as Romy inspects the photograph, but this isn't just about impressing her. It's about making it up to her. About proving that I know her whole value. "I have to tell you something. Valeria and I slept together, but I wasn't ready. We broke up. We're friends now. I guess she's looking for serious relationships only—she wants to get married, and I'm not ready to marry anyone. And she's not the one I'd even want to marry if I were."

Romy sighs, and her hands fall back down. "I did jump to conclusions—"

"I get it. That makes sense. I left abruptly, and we never had a chance to talk about what was happening. And anyway, you were right. I'm sorry for the way I've treated you over the past few months. I was an oblivious, insensitive friend." I pull out my plate of slutty brownies, which have *I'm Such a Dumbass* written in frosting across the tops. "Now this part was my first idea, before I found the picture, but it still kinda gets the point across."

She laughs as she inspects the brownie tray. "Oh my god, Luna, why are you doing all this?" She blinks back tears as she smiles.

"Because I love you," I say.

The words feel so light on my tongue. Like I've been meaning to say them for years. And I guess I have. But my heart's in the clouds now that I'm finally saying them this way. And man, Romy doesn't even get it yet. I can't believe I'm not the oblivious one this time. I better savor this, because damn, I know it won't happen again.

"I love you too," she says.

I beam, finally removing item three.

A bouquet of red roses.

And when she holds them, it still takes her a bit. She turns the bouquet around in her hands, registering the color, thinking through the reasons I could possibly be doing this. I know it'll hit. I'm ready for it to hit, but I can't help myself.

I lean across the countertop and press my lips to hers. My hand is on her cheek, the other wobbling on the counter to keep me balanced. The kiss is soft, tender. But firm. I don't want there to be any room for interpretation in the way our lips mold together. I feel a buzzing from my chest to my fingertips, those happy hormones shooting off like mad. But in my head, for once—for once in my fucking life—it's silent. This is peace. This is soft, gentle love. It feels inevitable. There's no uncertainty, no performance, no words we can't say to each other.

And when she kisses me back, it's like getting that Hanukkah present I was dying for, it's being told we're going to Disneyland, it's getting into U.S.C.'s production program, it's hearing Valeria say I have talent. It's a sizzling win, and I can't believe it's happening to me.

No, actually, I *can* believe it. That's the point.

We pull away slowly, which gives me enough time to get off the countertop without looking like an idiot. Her cheeks are stained pink, and there's a goofy smile plastered on her face.

"I . . . I never thought that'd actually happen," she says.

I smile. "Me neither, but here we are."

For the first time in what feels like an eternity, I look around the café. There are people in here now, and some are annoyed, looking at their watches. But I recognize Jared from talent. He's beaming, giving me a thumbs-up.

"It's about fucking time!" he says, louder than he needs to.

I still wince, but the embarrassment doesn't last long. Because shit, it *is* about fucking time.

"I'm gonna spit in your drink if you yell any louder!" Romy replies.

Jared laughs. "Don't think I won't get you fired, Fonseca."

"Please do! I don't get good tips here. I'd rather work the deli counter at Erewhon in Calabasas."

"Either way," Jared says. "I love it."

He holds his fingers up and forms a heart. I squint at him a moment before the warmth washes over me.

He's framing us.

I move closer to her, take her hand. Her soft hand, covered in rings. I rub my thumb over her knuckles. A perfect fit.

She takes a deep breath and smiles. "This is so wild."

I kiss her cheek, just to try it out. I can't wait to try all the different kinds of kisses on her. "It's a cinematic moment. And you attract it."

As Valeria and I return to her car, there's serenity in the air. We've both accomplished something. Something big. Something that I never thought I'd be able to do. Julia sometimes talks about how humans can adjust to a new normal, even a life-changing new normal, quickly. It's a survival mechanism, but it can ultimately prevent people from ever stepping back and appreciating things. And up close, the toll going back in the closet has taken on Valeria is clear as day. Her appearance is immaculate . . . save the red and puffy eyes. There's no way to hide the fact that she's been crying.

"How'd it go?" I ask.

She smiles. "He's been fired."

I beam. "Val, that's—"

She holds up her hands, forming a heart. "I'm guessing your thing went well?"

"It went amazing."

And right now, I'm enjoying it.

"What happens next for you?" I ask her.

Valeria rubs her hands together. "Next I take meetings with my hopefully new manager, and we work on culling everyone who didn't want me out. After that, I guess I hope I'm not unemployed and can make my house payments."

"In all seriousness, Steven Wells is an idiot. He never deserved you."

She cracks a smile. "For the record, Alice didn't deserve you either. How's the job hunt going?"

"A lot of applying for little productions. I'm trying to get proper experience for a real first A.C. job in case a bigger gig comes along. I'm also simultaneously applying to jobs in movie theaters in order to keep the rent money flowing."

"I swear you'll make it. Pushing you and Brendan through the system is like telling an eight-year-old to watch an infant, and it's still going pretty well, all things considered."

"Just invite me to the premiere."

"Okay, but you'll have to bring Romy so no one starts rumors about us dating and uncovers that we actually do have history." She pauses. "Although we could get good money for all the footage we have together, if you really need to stay out of your parents' house."

Bringing Romy to a premiere. It's a strange, far-off dream, but I'm one step closer to it being my reality. It gets my heart fluttering.

I laugh. "Are you serious?"

She goes stone-faced. "No. Don't you dare sell footage." But a smile breaks through.

Her phone goes off. She glances at the text. Her bottom lip is shaking a little, but there's no other reaction.

"How's the coming-out post been going?" I ask. "I know your family knew, but have any old friends emerged or anything?"

She puts her phone away and nods her head. "I've been inundated with private Facebook messages from high school friends who either are 'so surprised' or are 'so happy' I finally came out." She rolls her eyes. "But my immediate family has been more or less happy to adjust now that I'm out publicly. The most I've gotten have been a couple of generic *we're so proud* texts, but what're you gonna do?"

I choke up as I think about my own family. "Did things get easier after you told them? The first time?"

She shrugs as she hands the valet her ticket. "It's nice to clear the air, but it's . . . I don't know, not easier or harder. Or it switches between easier and harder a lot. But it makes you appreciate your friends a lot more too."

I shake my head. "That one still . . . It's not like I think they'll reject me, but . . ."

"Waiting is fine. It's your time line. You could date Romy for years and never tell them. Just make sure you discuss it with her." She puts her hand on my shoulder. "And hey, you're young. You won't do all of this perfectly. One day I'll tell you about all the mistakes I've made, and I'm only five years older than you. But it's still *fine*. You just kinda make do with the life you create and improve what you can."

I eye her. "Like Pasadena?"

She huffs. "Oh my god, Pasadena is objectively the most boring part of L.A. while simultaneously being, like, a terrible *Jurassic Park* movie for Eustace because of all the coyotes roaming into backyards. My aversion to Pasadena is not *just* because of my family. I have a little niece and nephew I don't venture out enough to see."

"Then go see them."

The valet comes around with her car. "You say that like it's so *easy*."

"It is," I say. "Just offer to temporarily adopt them when they're teenagers and hate their parents in exchange for the occasional weekend visits to your house. Then you turn them into gay radical communists later on."

Valeria full-body laughs as she gets into the car. "Oh my god.

The sad thing is I could send that word for word and I bet my sister would agree to it."

I don't think Valeria meant to, but something in what she says inspires me.

As Valeria starts the car, I send a single text to Noam. He replies with a barrage of them.

> Oh cool!!!!
>
> Don't worry, your secret is safe with me.
> Thank you for telling me. I've got your back
> when you wanna tell Mom and Dad. 👍

I exhale slowly, realizing just how tight my chest was seconds prior. Noam reacted as I expected—didn't care. But no, it wasn't just what I expected. It's better. Noam, the kid who only talks to me in a deadpan voice and regularly throws me under the bus so he doesn't have to endure an annoying lecture from Mom and Dad—that Noam has my back. It's the closest he's ever come, maybe ever will come, to saying he loves me. He loves me, and I have an ally against my parents if it becomes an *against* and not a *with*.

I can't believe I feel lighter with Noam knowing. One more text comes through from him.

> WAIT. DID VALERIA SULLIVAN GIVE YOU
> THAT HICKEY WTF WTF WTF

I guess sometimes coming out can feel good.

chapter twenty-six

There's an ease with Romy, I guess, that I'm surprised is still around now that our relationship has changed. By the time she's back from her shift after our making up, I've almost forgotten the implications of what we did in the Slater café. I'm facedown on the couch after applying to half a dozen jobs, cycling through the cheapest Postmates restaurants where I can buy a vegetable, since I've had none all day.

But when I lift my head to the keys jingling, when I first see Romy's face again—her perfect eyeliner smudged from rubbing her eyes at work, her summer-pool-blue nails, her half-untucked uniform and scuffed combat boots—it all comes crashing back down on me.

Romy's standing ten feet from me, tossing her keys with the Hot Donna's key chain onto the kitchen counter, scooting her boots over to rest next to the flats I wore today.

Because we live together.

I live with the person I love.

When she smiles at me, I swear there's no way to describe it other than a shimmering across my skin, like waking up in the sun after a rare good night's sleep. I'm still flushed under her gaze, but Romy practically jumps onto the couch, leading me by my chin to meet her lips. It's a quick peck that holds the weight of my world.

She lingers there, our foreheads touching, her eyelashes brushing against my cheek.

"What're you thinking about?" she asks.

She pulls away, a smirk playing on her lips. Her signature look. The same way Romy looks at me when she's horsing around, playing off inside jokes and teasing me. It sends the strangest shiver down my spine. I feel like I've pulled myself back from the edge of a cliff—one I was willing to jump down, sure. I thought everything would have to be different. That me being Romy's girlfriend meant the *girl* devouring the *friend*. But maybe not.

I shrug, a grin on my lips. "Which pizza spot are we ordering from?"

Romy laughs, pulling back to a friendly distance. She claps loudly and laughs even harder when I flinch more than the move deserves. "Hell yeah."

And, honestly, we get through the ordering, the flipping through streaming services as we wait, and the actual dinner the way we always get through our nights together. Work bitching, unemployment bitching, eagerly anticipating movies or activities we could do that weekend. I recount what she missed with me and Valeria. It's one of the most peaceful dinners we've ever had, but I can't help the knot forming in my stomach.

But by the time Romy's breaking down the pizza box and I'm stuffing leftovers in bags destined for the fridge, I don't hold back. I guess that's what's different now—I'm trying not to hold these feelings in.

"Is there a point when everything's changed?" I ask. I manage to keep the question airy, conversational.

Romy stiffens from her space by the garbage. Then her expression becomes downright unreadable, like her brain is a computer running a million programs at once. But I catch her gaze and it all melts. It's like I've walked to the edge of a volcano, and there's nothing left but the smoldering of her eyes as she looks at me. That heat shocks my system.

Romy slides over to me, her soap-wrinkled fingers falling right to my waist. And I'm the one jolted from the fever of her touch, the deliberateness of where she puts her hands. She's never touched me there before. She lingers, sliding along my hips, which are covered in two too many layers of clothing. Then, like she's somehow able to sense it, she leans into me just as my heartbeat starts to thrum.

"What's changed?" she asks, teasing. Her breath is hot against the shell of my ear. "Should something be different?"

She leans her whole body into me, collarbone against collarbone. Her own heart slams back against mine. It's . . . comforting in a way I didn't anticipate. It tells me that maybe she's as nervous as she is excited. That she's unraveling this yarn ball of emotion the same way I am.

But *I'm* the one whose breath hitches when her fingers find the skin between my blouse and the top of my pants. "We could . . . touch each other differently," she says.

I can't help but giggle as color stains my cheeks. I love the way I sound, laughing with her. "Well, you know, as long as it's nothing that couldn't be misinterpreted as BFF roommates just being extra-special friends."

Romy pulls back, and I can see the tiny sprinkling of freckles across the bridge of her nose. She sways against me, gaze on my lips. But she keeps her distance. "Sweetheart, we could fuck each other all night and someone would still say we're just being gal pals."

Sweetheart. The word sends crackles of light through the tension growing below my stomach, from my chest to my fingertips. I already want to bottle up the way she says it, the way she says my name, the way she says everything.

I cock my head a little, playing along, even though I'm quivering from the anticipation. "Is that what we're gonna do?" My voice dips lower, scratches the words.

I love the way Romy looks at me, like she's starving and only having me will sate her. I'm trying to linger on this, pull the anticipation almost to its breaking point, but I don't have the strength to resist anymore. I grab her by the hand and head to her bedroom, already imagining what her skin tastes like. I flop onto her bed so she gets another chance to drink me in before joining.

And god, does she drink me in. "You're so gorgeous," she says, almost under her breath.

"You are too."

She climbs into her bed, her cleavage on full display as she crawls over to me.

"No pressure," she says. She brushes a hair out of my face. "If you don't want to."

I pull her down to meet my lips. "I do." I pause, though, as I take in the hair now falling into Romy's face, my fingers running along the short part in the back. "I told you my limits, but I don't know yours. Is there anything I should know? What you like, don't like, language?"

She breaks eye contact for just a moment, gaze on her fingertip as it traces the sensitive skin on my wrist. "Activity-wise, no. You can touch me anywhere. Language-wise, I've made peace with the word *tits*. But I prefer to use more general terms about down below. *Junk* or *bits* is fine." Her lashes flicker, gaze back on me. "But if you need"—she smiles—"*specific* anatomy lessons, you can say the names of body parts."

But once the limits are set, I'm downright surprised when Romy jumps out of bed.

"Wait, did I—?" I say.

Romy rummages through a side table. "No, just setting the mood."

She pulls out an Apple TV remote first. Clicks on the twenty-four-incher mounted on the wall and opens Spotify. "Name a musician that you hear in your sleep."

It's such an odd question, but I have an instant answer. "Halsey?"

Romy grins. "Ah, yes, the quintessential gay fucking soundtrack." She clicks *Badlands*. "I'm going retro, but let me know if you want to change."

Halsey's haunting croon fills the room, lowering the volume on the thoughts in my head.

I find myself smiling. "No one's ever asked me about music."

Romy shrugs. "It's something that can calm you down, ground you in the moment if you need it." Her hand dips into the drawer again. This time she pulls up a flash of silver that she promptly slips into her mouth. My stomach somersaults as I realize it's her fucking *tongue piercing*. She sticks out her tongue to show it off, grinning. "And something to launch you into space anyway."

Fuck. Every word goes right between my legs.

"Halsey's so hot, isn't she?" Romy says as she climbs on top of me, simultaneously softening into me and growing more violent in her movements.

I chuckle. "Yeah, they are."

"God." Romy's grin spreads, and now it's sparkling in her eyes. "We're so *gay*."

And then she yanks us together, stealing the breath from me, catching the laugh in my throat. One hand cups the back of my neck and the other slides to my waist as our lips come together once more. This kiss is so massively different from the first two. There's no salty taste to this one, no struggling to breathe through hiccuping sobs. No eyes on us, no modesty, no hesitation. But there is this beautiful hunger, this urgency for closeness, this desire to lap up every sensation we can pull out of each other.

I don't know where to put my hands; I'm so eager to run my fingertips along every inch of her, to learn the way the ridges of my fingerprints sink into her. Every part of her is better than the last—her collarbones, her shoulder blades, her chest. I'm drowning in feeling, in molten desire, as my fingers paw her back muscles, as I run my thumbs over the cloth covering her nipples, as Romy opens my mouth and I plunge my tongue to meet hers. Romy sighs and hitches her breath as I tug at her hair, buck my hips against hers, entwine our legs. The pressure builds like stacked bricks—solid, steady, and heavy.

Her lips peel from mine, press to the thinnest part of my throat. "Still good?" she asks, her voice vibrating against me.

I sigh, the sounds escaping more freely from me as each second passes. "Yes."

As she kisses down the middle of my body, I slide my hands lower, past her waistline to her ass. The pressure only continues to build, and now desire is outpacing the snail-like speed with which Romy's kissing me. As she continues to try to play it slow, I grab her ass, press her hips into mine as I grind in circles. The movements are starting to go from excited to frantic. I'm *frantic*.

One particularly deep buck gets Romy to *moan* into me, her fingers dropping off my half-unbuttoned blouse.

"Don't you dare," she growls.

She lifts her hips just out of my reach and finishes unbuttoning my shirt. I pull it off, my gaze falling to Romy. It feels like I've had sexual encounters that involved hands digging between sweaty layers of clothing. With the way my heartbeat is pulsing between my legs, I know I could make that work again. But I'm suddenly overwhelmed with the urge to undress Romy; as goose bumps form on my exposed skin, I want her to be that way too.

"I don't have time to do a whole show like you just did," I say, shooting Romy a grin.

Apparently, neither does Rom. I manage to get three buttons undone before Romy rips her shirt over her head so hard, I hear the fabric stretch. Beneath the shirt, Romy's perfect skin is flushed, the black-and-white tattoos along her ribs on easy display. Her chest and stomach rise, and it's overwhelming. She's somehow even made that lips-patterned bra splay out like a paint-by-number for my lips and tongue.

And I'm wearing some bra from five years ago. I'm suddenly nervous, and the hand I want on Romy is rubbing the back of my neck: "I should've worn something sexier."

All Romy does is snort. "Lune, I'm not here for what's holding your tits."

The way she's looking at my shitty bra says more than her words. But she doesn't rip it off. No, her hands shake, and she looks the way I used to when I played Operation as a kid. I want to beg, but instead I hold the sensation in with my trapped breath as she unhooks my bra. As she tosses it off the bed. As she sighs deeply and touches the soft skin of my breasts like they're holy.

I sink into it. With the warmth of a familiar song hugging me, I let her pull every sigh, every twitch, every desperate breath from me. I let her move her beautiful kisses down my stomach, toward the unbearable feeling between my legs.

"You don't want me to do anything?" I ask, although I'm desperate for her to say no.

"Let me have my moment," she says, flashing me a smile before unbuttoning my pants.

I help her yank the pants off, but Romy leaves my panties on a moment longer. They're Valentine's Day red hipsters with a gray elastic band, and they show a helluva lot of cheek. Romy drinks me in like I'm a syrupy cocktail. Particularly the sweet little stain at the crotch of my red panties that's beaming out how wet she's made me. Her eyes are practically black, she's so deep in her own desire. Romy. My Romy, the coolest person I know, with her honey-eyed voice and her badass haircut and *her lips inches from my clit.* The mounting pressure all but hurts as I wait.

"Excited to see me?" she asks as she *finally* kisses down my groin, hovering over the wet spot. My head spins; I'm not sure if I'm feeling her tongue flick the spot or if I'm just willing it into existence.

"Fuck" is all I say back.

She plants a long kiss on the crotch of my panties, yanks them off, and licks the spot so her tongue flows *right* over my clit. That *fucking tongue piercing.* I gasp, pushing into her. I swear I feel her smile as she digs deeper, trailing that magic piece of metal along with her. The way she eats out, what's going on between us—it's beautiful, it's wonderful, it's smoking hot. I can't believe I could potentially do this with her again tomorrow. I can't believe we could fall asleep in the same bed tonight and do it again first thing in the morning.

But right now, I am soaked through. Her mouth is on my skin, which is steaming hot and slick underneath. When she licks down the length of my pussy, it's as if she's telling me that she's here and she's with me. I wonder if she can feel my heartbeat. It's downright monumental for no other reason than that I'm *with Romy*.

"Now," I gasp. "Can you do it now?"

And, *finally*, Romy listens to me. She rests her head against my body and works circles as I demand harder, faster. By the time my fingers are twisted into Romy's hair, pulling at her as I feel my own muscles tightening, I'm ready to swear that all this was worth it. All the grief we put each other through, it was all leading up to this moment.

When I come, the sound I make is gasping, desperate, but I trail it off with this perfect, low, sexy little sigh that I think I do more for her than for me. But I don't even have time to bask in the orgasm before Romy, the little shit, snakes *her own hand* under her waistband. Sweat beads on her hairline, I notice. A crack in her facade, giving away her desire.

I grab her hand, pulling it back.

"No way," I say. "We're having sex. Let me do some work."

I pull her pants off and run my thumb roughly over her soaked underwear, right where her sweet spot is. She moans the way I did. Maybe a little more dramatically. I wonder if she's ever thought about this before, if she's ever brought about the same sensation with her own hands, her own plastic, thinking about this. My heart flips thinking through how our conversations about sex will change now, how excited I am to know her in a way I never thought I would.

I try not to overthink it; I try to fall into the music every time my mind starts asking questions. I do what I would do to myself,

I do the kind of things that wound Valeria up. And, thank god, Romy *is* winding up. Hell, my own stomach tightens as I feel Romy's muscles go taut under me.

"Baby, no underwear," Romy says, the words barely more than a breath. "I want your fingers on my skin. Please."

But suddenly I don't want to use my fingers. Her soaked panties suddenly look—*god*—delicious. I don't want to learn what I already know. I want to know how every part of Romy feels against every part of me. I kiss the wet spot like she did. I pull her panties off like she did mine.

And I kiss her blazing-hot slick skin like she did. Like Valeria did to me. Like legions of people have done to each other before me. I take a deep breath, relaxing into the scent of her skin, the muted saltiness. I lick her up and down, I circle around her junk, I relish her moan as I suck her most sensitive spot into my mouth and out again.

For a beautiful stretch of time, I fall into the endless void of Halsey's voice and Romy's squirming and moans and *fuck*s, and I don't think. I don't think, I don't think, I *don't think*. I just am. I'm having sex with my partner. I'm making the person I love feel good. I'm making the person I love feel *amazing*. And I enjoy it. I enjoy her reactions, I enjoy the heat and the tightness building back into the lingering throbbing in my clit.

Then Romy speaks again.

"Go inside me, Lune," she says. "I want you to feel all of me."

The command jolts me seconds before I remember that, shit, she said there weren't any limits. I look down at the work I've already done chasing Romy's pleasure. I slide a finger inside her the way I licked between her legs.

I know this texture, but my heart jolts feeling it here, in Romy. When she asks for another finger, I'm downright eager to feel more of her on more of me. She hums as I put my face back between her legs, my fingers thrusting. My hips, by instinct or wanton, selfish desire, thrust against her leg to the rhythm. The humming sizzles to Romy singing along to one of Halsey's sexiest lines, crooning it at me.

And there's a moment when I'm in euphoria. When I can't believe I get to experience the velvet inside someone I love, when I get to live in a world where something that terrified me makes the person I love flush and shake, when I get to feel her muscles clamp and pulse around me. When Romy moans and pulls me up to bury her face into my shoulder after she comes, peace washes over me. I'm so glad I get to do this. Everything is right. This is where I was meant to be.

She pulls her lips back to mine and we taste each other once more. And then we just hold each other, lips pressed together, waiting for our heartbeats to stop sounding in our ears.

When we pull away, when I see those big pupils staring back at me, I break into a grin.

"I love you, Romy."

"I love you, Luna."

There are no sweeter words in the English language.

chapter twenty-seven

It's October in L.A., which means we're experiencing a random heat wave. The city is full of sagging pumpkins and angry adults who are praying that the heat breaks before Halloween. But I don't mind. It's easy enough to cool down.

"Spaceship, Aunt Val!" Valeria's two-year-old twin niece and nephew shout from the shallow end of the pool, where they're floating in their little striped swimsuits and water wings.

Valeria pulls them both into her arms. She's absolutely radiant, shining with pure joy as she interacts with those kids.

"Spaceship, huh?" Valeria says. "Like this?"

She jumps into the air and splashes back into the water as the kids shriek.

Water sprays over to where Romy and I are lounging near the edge of the pool, but honestly, it feels good. It all feels *so good*: the sun on our exposed skin, the warmth of the concrete below us, Romy's hand lazily intertwined with mine as she reads a YA fantasy novel that's likely much too dark for this setting.

I lean over to her. "Those kids are so cute."

She glances at Valeria and the kids. "Yeah, cute." She raises a brow. "Very blond too."

"Who knows? Maybe you'll have a couple one day."

She watches as Eustace, who's wearing a bright blue life jacket with a shark fin on top, barks around the perimeter of the pool.

"Maybe," she says, "but right now I just want, like, thirty Eustaces. In all different colors, though. A Eustace variety pack."

Her gaze runs up and down the length of my body. I still shiver when she does it, like I'm a lovestruck teenager. The past several months have kinda felt like that. All those bubblegum pop songs make sense now. "Besides, our kids wouldn't be blond," she says. "Not with our genes."

I know she's joking. For now, we're taking it pretty slow and not thinking too far into the future. Our physical encounters have been tender and slow and filled with communication, preparation, and boundaries. I feel safe with Romy, in every form that takes: cuddling with her while we watch the '90s movies she loves, stealing each other's fries at gastropub dates, wiping each other's tears on hard work and family days, arching against each other's hot-as-hell touch. If the future is anything like the present, there's nothing to fret about.

"How're the negotiations going?" I ask Valeria.

"Well," she says, running a hand through her hair, a move as slick as ever, "I'm in a pool trying to cast my mind back to when I was two so that I can both relate to these guys and forget that I exist, so great."

She's got plans to submit *Oakley in Flames* to a ton of great festivals. It's looking good; she's got the star power and the topic is timely, but we'll see what happens. This business is fickle. When Valeria switched managers, her agent straight up dropped her.

She replaced him within a week. I think her whole team is different now. Everyone whom I've met seems less sleazy than those on her last team, but I'm sure there's a bit of that classic Hollywood flavor to them. She hasn't booked anything big yet—the only things she has lined up are the projects Steven got her.

But she seems happy.

"It'll happen," I say.

"Feel free to say that as much as you want. It's music to my ears."

Romy nudges me. "Well, your prayers worked for this one."

I smile as the heat rushes to my face. "I got the gig."

"Yes!" Valeria says, jumping and giving the kids another ride. They scream their congratulations as well. I'll take it even though they have no idea what's going on.

The whole thing started when I saw a confidential listing on an entertainment career site. It just said they needed a second A.C., which meant it was a bigger production. I applied on a whim, and then when I interviewed I learned it was for a position working on the first season of a network TV show. It's a little one, one that will struggle to get a second season, but it's steady work for six plus months. It's all I can ask for: six months touching the camera on a production that will be seen by an actual audience. Funny enough, it's exactly how my mom envisioned it months ago.

I glance over at Valeria, deep in her bliss with those kids. I don't know if I'll ever be able to thank her for what she's done for me or what she will do in the coming months. Her new agent just officially confirmed that she's going to be in one of my shorts.

My gaze falls on Romy. I rub my thumb over her fingers. Romy's nails are now orange for Halloween, her favorite holiday. She declined my offer to write a script for the short Valeria and I are doing, saying she's bogged down doing revisions with *her* agent before trying to sell her play on a bigger circuit. But she promises she'll doctor whatever I write and be my arm candy at festivals. As if it'll end up at festivals. I promised the same for her.

"Did Wyatt text you?" Romy asks me.

I fish my phone off the side table and look at it. "Not yet."

We invited him here, but he was at some other pool party this weekend. Typical Wyatt.

Romy pulls me into her arms. "Well, he's missing out."

She kisses me. I shut my eyes as she does it, savoring the now-familiar touch of her lips on mine.

Romy and I are moving into our first apartment as a couple next month. We found a really cheap two-bedroom in Encino, close to the studios I'll likely be working out of and semi-close to her job at fucking Erewhon, which she *actually* got. She claims what she might've lost in terms of prestige she's gained back in "pure ridiculousness." Plus it's given her loads of ideas for her writing. The apartment is tiny and old, and I feel bad that we needed to get a two-bedroom. My parents still think we're platonic, but I'm feeling more confident about telling them soon enough. Romy says after I tell them we'll turn the extra bedroom into that arcade we always wanted . . . either that or something a little adultier.

"Hey!"

Water suddenly cascades over us in a wave. We pull away, and I go red remembering where we are.

"These children get enough of that exposure at home," Valeria says. "Age-appropriate gay kissing only!" She pushes a hair out of her niece's eyes. "Are you two ever going to get in, by the way?"

I grin at Romy. I don't even give her a chance to protest before I roll us both into the pool.

Yeah, this is it.

This is queer joy.

acknowledgments

Like people who practice their Oscar speeches far ahead of any Hollywood success, I've been keeping myself hopeful and practicing my acknowledgments for my first published novel since I was thirteen. Yet, being here, I'm overwhelmed by the wonderful people who've loved and supported me and my writing over the years.

I wouldn't be where I am without my whip-smart, hilarious powerhouse of an agent, Janine Kamouh. It's so hard to believe we came together less than five years ago, yet I can't imagine my career without you. Thank you for taking this leap of faith with me when I dropped *Sizzle Reel* into your inbox.

Thank you to all the tireless and incredibly talented assistants who supported me along this journey, including Gwen Beal, Oma Naraine, and Gaby Caballero.

I never conceptualized a dream editor, but it's truly been a dream to work with my incredible (and equally as hilarious) editor, Caitlin Landuyt. Thank you for seeing my characters as the disastrous, complex people I do and for championing a vision that really has brought this book closer to its heart. The hugest thank-you to my dream cover artist, Maria Nguyen, and the entire Vintage Books team: Suzanne Herz, Edward Kastenmeier, Ellie Pritchett, Maddie Partner, Kayla Overbey, Steven Walker, Nancy B. Tan, Annie Locke, Julie Ertl, Lauren Taglienti, Lyn Rosen, and Andrea Monagle. Thank you for the playlist, for the Valeria face claim–betting, and for being so generous and open and enthusiastic. It's been a dream debut experience.

I wouldn't be where I am as a writer without beloved mentors over the past decade and a half. Thank you to Rachel Lynn Solomon, Kit Frick, Rebecca Barrow, Andrea Davis Pinkney, and Sue Shapiro, among others.

Drafting, revising, and rerevising *Sizzle Reel* truly was a team effort, and I couldn't have done it without the notes, love, and enthusiasm from readers and friends Kelsey Rodkey, Marisa Kanter, Auriane Desombre, Courtney Kae, Meryn Lobb, Page Powars, Lindsay Grossman, Lisa Ryan, Robin Wasley, Carolina Flórez-Cerchiaro, and Emily Miner.

Shout-out to my New School W.F.C.Y.A. cohort. I love y'all. A special shout-out to my lifelines and beloved forever critique partners Kade Dishmon, Taylor Heady, and Kate Koenig and honorary cohort member Will Miller.

The story of *Sizzle Reel* started out in Courier in Final Draft, and it wouldn't have ever come close to becoming a book without my screenwriting group and their sharp story instincts and hilarious joke suggestions. Thank you, Sophia Lopez, Sabrina Batchler, Jacob Arbittier, and Yoni Hirshberg.

Writing goes so far beyond written feedback, so thank you to my dear friends who've supported me mind, body, and soul through this journey: Eva Molina, Charlotte Arangua, Kiavanne Williams, and Nisha Malhotra. I love you all so much.

To my family, immediate and extended. Mom, Dad, Izzy,

Brandon, I wouldn't have the creativity, drive, passion, or love without you. Thank you so much for supporting my dreams even when they didn't entirely make sense to you.

Finally, to my actual A Team: my therapist, Ellen, and all the celebrities I loved before.